Simply Psychic

By: Carolyn Anne Yunek
&
Raymond Alan Yunek

I want to thank all my friends and family who helped and inspired this story, especially my mentor Shari, my loving and handsome husband Ray, and my baby boy, Alan Eugene. Thank you all; this book could never have happened without all of you.

-Carolyn Yunek.

<u>Part 1</u>

Prologue

Great Escape

Agent Huey Driscol sat perched on the branch staring at the guard intently while his partner Alice Coupe watched anxiously at his palm. One could hardly blame her for feeling more than a bit uneasy; their little plan's success depended entirely upon *his* success. She watched keenly and smiled in relief as a red mist appeared in the palm of Huey's outstretched hand, leaving a silver-plated keycard in its place, an embossed insignia glinting in the low light.

"Come on," he whispered near-silently to his companion, jumping out of the tree and running as fast as his feet could carry him. As he silently moved forward, he heard a twig snap a couple of steps behind him, causing him to stop dead. "Oh for Alice," he thought annoyed, "We're trying *not* to be caught here."

Alice ran by embarrassed, making Huey follow behind with a grumble under his breath, the cohorts finally stopping at a security door embedded in an electric fence. He swiped the keycard he'd pilfered from the guard, which stopped the electric current and opened the gate as an excited Alice ran through. Still annoyed, Huey shook his head and ran through locking the door and sending the key back from whence it came.

"Come on, hurry up already!" Alice whispered from the bush nearby. Huey ran up smiling mischievously. "Black Opal, here we come," he thought, smiling as the twosome made their way down the darkened road.

Chapter 1

October 1st, 2162

Ally sat on the bench staring at the almond trees around her. She watched the cool breeze gently blow the falling leaves as it so often does in autumn. She felt the wind blow through her hair, lightly caressing her body it seemed.

"Alette," her aunt called out, "Your father wants you." Ally smiled back at her Aunt Erica. "Ok," she said getting up, turning to the curled-up fox lounging next to her feet. "Come on Femi. Dad's expecting us."

Her red fox yapped happily and got up, quickly following her. Erica followed the duo, dusting off her tan suit while Ally removed her black trench coat and fingerless gloves as she entered the mansion. She walked down the hallway reaching a mahogany door. Knocking on the door nervously, she heard a familiar deep stern voice.

"Come in," The voice tiredly said. Ally carefully opened the door so as not to accidentally break anything, as she'd done in the past. "Hey Dad," she said her crystal blue eyes full of concern.

A middle-aged man who sat behind the antique desk looked up, his stern face easing into a halfhearted smile and his dark brown eyes brightening by several degrees. "Hey Ally," he said getting up and hugging her. "Happy birthday, sweetheart. Please, why don't you sit down?" he pulled out the chair and sat down a ways from his desk, overflowing with papers. Ally sat across from him, Femi by her side.

"Our usual guest will be arriving soon," he said seriously, checking a handcrafted wristwatch for the time, "In an hour actually; I want you to greet him. I trust you will be a courteous hostess?" Ally grinned excited. "Don't you worry Dad; I will be," she answered calmly.

"Alexander!" Erica called, running in, her sea green eyes full of apprehension, "He's early and he's brought Nico with him."

"Oh, well go greet them, sweetheart," he said turning to a surprised Ally, "I'll be downstairs in a minute- paperwork, you see." Ally noticed the apprehension in his strained smile, but put on a smile as she got up. "Ok Dad," she said as she left the room with Femi. "He's earlier than usual," Erica pointed out once she was sure Ally had gone, sighing. "Thanks, you don't need to remind me," Alexander said, annoyed. Erica didn't bother repressing her need to huff.

Nico looked around the room worried as he studied his surroundings. The crème colored walls complimented the black carpet and white leather furniture, all of it clearly antique and quite expensive. He stared at the glass table in front of him, his amethyst eyes filled to the brim with anxiety.

"What're you worrying for? It will be fine, Nico," Sam said trying to calm him down. "How do you know? She doesn't even know about it," he sounded agitated. "She must know, Alex wouldn't be *that* stupid..," Sam pointed out. "Wait, actually, he could be." "I saw her earlier and she still acted the same, Sam, like I'm somehow just an acquaintance of hers. It was- annoying," Nico answered, "I might as well have been-"

Ally entered the room, stopping the conservation midsentence.

"Hey Sam," Ally said walking in, now suspicious. Nico blushed as she sat across from him fixing her tan blouse and black slacks, trying not to look too closely at her. "Happy eighteenth birthday, kiddo," Sam said smiling mischievously, like he was hiding something. "Uh, thank you Sam," she said politely.

She turned to Nico smiling politely. "Hello, Nico" she said perplexed at his reaction, "Long time no see; how are you doing these days? Wait a second, weren't you looking for the bathroom earlier?" "Yes," he said awkwardly, coughing to clear his throat. Sam raised an eyebrow befuddled. "Ally, you do remember Nico, don't you?" Sam asked trying to evaluate the situation.

Ally looked Nico over. His medium length crimson hair was in a controlled mess, contrasting Sam's blonde hair and his amethyst eyes glowed in comparison to Sam's smoke colored grey eyes. Nico played with his hoodie nervously. She suddenly stopped for a second thinking. "Of course I do. You come over every summer; we're practically family," she pointed out.

Sam and Nico stared in shock. "Wait, what?" Sam stammered. "I – I thought you knew, Ally."

"Uh, knew about what? Hey Nico, you okay?" Ally asked turning to Nico concerned. "Fine; I'm fine," he answered morosely, shrugging his shoulders. Sam dusted off his long sleeved grey shirt and blue jeans. "That's enough of that," he said, as Nico looked up. Ally raised an eyebrow still confused.

"Hello Sam," Alexander said, entering the room. Nico looked between the elder Bellerose and his daughter. Ally's long wavy blonde hair, crystal blue eyes and fair skin contrasted with Alexander's brown hair, chestnut eyes, and lightly tan skin. He wondered if they were even really related; the only thing they seemed to have in common was they were both dressed professionally, like they usually were. Nico sighed as he tried to cheer himself up.

"Hello, Nico," Alexander glared refusing to sit down. "Be nice Alex," Sam said, angry now, "He comes every summer." Alexander turned to Sam. "Can we speak for a moment- in private?" he asked. "Sure," Sam gladly got up, "We'll be back in a second, kids."

As the door closed behind them, Ally and Nico heard a muffled slap through the wall. "Ow! You son of-!" his shout was suddenly cut off by loud music. Nico turned to Ally nervously. "Ok," Ally said befuddled. "So.. heard any good jokes recently?"

Nico just stared blankly at her.

"Look, She doesn't know; I never got around to telling her," Alexander said, leaning against his desk with an ice pack on his head. "She doesn't know?" Sam glared at him as he mocked him, "How and why? I mean he came over to your home for several weeks every summer for over a decade and you never thought at any point to explain to her why?"

"It wasn't important at the time," Alexander answered, annoyed. "It wasn't important to tell her she was engaged?!" Sam growled, "You let her spend time with her **fiancé**, alone with no context for why it was happening? What- did you make up some crap about her needing a friend for the summer or something? I always thought you were a bit thick before, Alex, but this is ridiculous! Forgive me for thinking that your common sense hadn't been completely roasted to Oblivion by your body slowly cooking itself to death!"

"Sam, Ally was only five at the time," Alexander pointed out, "Would she have even understood if I had told her?" "Who knows? Maybe she'd have thought she was a princess!" Sam's eyes turned ice blue as he spoke, "I told Nico when he was eight- practically immediately. I told him not to tell her though, cause that's your job as her father. You had over a decade to tell her about this; what in all that's holy was stopping you?!"

Alexander whimpered and hid behind his desk, scared. "Besides," Sam continued mocking, "You left him alone with her- **again.** A handsome boy with an attractive young woman alone in a fancy room complete with comfortable sofa; Why, who *knows* what they could be doing in there?" Alexander's eyes widened as he ran for the door. Sam laughed out loud as he followed

"Say do you remember that time when I was thirteen, you were ten and I decided to glue the bathroom door shut with epoxy resin? " Nico asked. "I don't know what you're talking about, Nico," Ally sipped her white tea trying to avoid the subject. "Yeah right, you were stuck in there for four hours until Alexander got home," Nico was holding back his laughter, but not very well.

The blond set down her teacup and stared angrily at him. "Oh yes, I remember now," she answered scaring the laughter out of him as her eyes began to glow gold. "I remember Dad rushing to send you home before I got my revenge on you." The boy in front of her shook, more than a little scared. "Yeah well, I'm sorry about that, okay?" he asked almost begging. Her temper drained away as quickly as it had come. "It's alright Nico; I forgave you a while ago anyway."

Their conversation was halted by the sound of the office door opening, followed swiftly with the arrival of the two older men and a somewhat worried Erica. "Hey kids, we're back," Sam said, walking in and acting all nice again. Both of them stared at him, not buying the act (it didn't help that anyone with eyes could read the anger scrawled all over Sam's face).

"So how are you two getting along today? Are you having *fun*?" he asked, blatantly implying something. Nico blushed like a tomato as he nervously got up and sat next to Ally. "Are you okay? Why do you look so embarrassed?" she asked him trying to figure things out. Alexander glared as he entered the room sitting across from them. "Okay; What's going on?" She asked starting to get the picture, "Is somebody gonna tell me why Nico's here? I mean, not that I mind seeing him or anything, but I'd like some explanation please."

Sam sat down, still visibly annoyed. "Tell her, Alex," he growled at the elder Bellerose, "Or I will." Alexander gulped, scared. "Ally, Nico isn't just here today because it's your birthday. He's really here because.." he searched for the right words, then settled for, "because he's actually your fiancé," he said regretfully and more than a little ashamed at himself.

The room was suddenly filled with an oppressive unrelenting silence. Ally turned to Nico, then Sam, then Alexander. It surprised everyone when she burst out into a sudden fit of laughter. "You're kidding," she said grinning, "I didn't even know you *had* a sense of humor Dad!" "..I have a sense of humor?" Alexander asked, surprised. Sam held back his laughter, hating that he had to burst Ally's bubble. "I've known your father since you were a child Ally; He has the same sense of humor that your grandmother had," he pointed out, "that is to say zero." Ally suddenly realized the situation as the silence grew, mocking her. "Sorry kid," Sam said, still angry at Alexander but feeling terrible all the same.

Ally let out a harsh laugh. "You're really not kidding, are you? This guy who's been visiting me every summer is actually my fiancé, and nobody bothered to tell me? Neither of you saw a flaw in that plan?" she exclaimed, her volume increasing with every word. She turned her attention to Nico, seeing the guilt written on his face. "You knew!" she practically yelled. "You knew and you never said a word?!" The crimson-haired boy was almost incoherent as he sputtered out, "I- I couldn't tell you- Sam t-told me it was your dad's responsibility to tell you.."

She spun around, stood up and glared at her father, who was quickly growing paler by the second. "Now Ally..-" "Don't you 'Ally' me! You've been planning this all this time and you didn't say a word; not even a hint my entire life? Is this why you never gave me the option of dating, so I could stay 'pure' and 'innocent' for- for **_him_**?!" she shouted, pointing back at Nico who was trying his best to pretend he didn't exist.

Sam (who up to this point was mostly a bystander in this argument) was left staring at the young woman in front of him hanging on to her last point of reality by a thread and could only sigh as Ally's eyes dulled with rage. "Anything else I need to know about?" she demanded, insulted to a degree she'd never felt before. "You're actually going to be moving in with us.. today," Sam said, trying to break it gently (not that it was ever really possible, but points for effort).

Her eyes glowing a white-hot gold, Ally glowered at Alexander as she turned her attention to him once more. "You're giving me away to your best friend's son like I'm just some trophy to be passed on to whoever you feel deserves it?" Out of the corner of the room Erica ran over and pulled her back, grabbing her by the shoulders. "Ally, stop! It'll be fine. Let's just stop and go pack up your things, *please*" she pleaded, trying to calm her down. A still-raging Ally considered for several very long seconds thinking of the choices at hand. On one hand she could do some serious damage to her father. On the other, she could take the high road, but still make her position crystal clear.

Ally turned to Sam for help. "I'm sorry, Ally, but my hands are legally tied," he answered. She then turned to Nico, but the boy she'd known for so long could only dejectedly say, "I- I can't do anything either, Ally." Ally took a deep breath to steady herself. "Fine; I'll do what you want and go," she said reluctantly to her father, "but note that I'm doing it under protest- and because I don't want what I could do to you on my conscience." The three men watched in shocked silence as Ally stormed out of the room, her aunt following close behind. After a moment, Nico got up looking as if in mourning. "Where are you going?" Sam asked concerned. "Just.. just checking on the van," Nico listlessly answered trying and failing to act chipper.

Sam turned to Alexander with rage in his eyes. "You utter moron; I can't even begin to explain just how many ways you screwed up today! Frankly it's a miracle she didn't physically destroy you." he forcefully pointed out as Alexander held on tight to the couch.

"Oh dear Jesus; she's just like my father-in-law," he said scared.

Alice stared intently at her black low heeled boots waiting for her brother to return. Finally after what seemed like an hour, he did. "I'm back. So, good news first?" Huey asked, sitting on the bench next to her. "Good first," Alice said fidgeting with a random stick. "He lives out of town and I have his address," he said, annoyed.

"So what's the bad news?" Alice demanded. "I tried calling and he's isn't home," he glared at the sidewalk. Alice got up from the bench, walking down the street. "Where are you going?!" Huey asked unsure of his sister's actions. "Where do you think? Home," she answered simply.

"Don't you remember? We were told not to return till we found dad," Huey pointed out. Alice stopped in her tracks. "Dad's place is the other way, by the way," Huey said pointing. Alice turned around reluctantly. "Good girl," Huey thought following her.

"How could he do this to me?!" Ally yelled, putting a black waist coat in a black and white fleur-de-lis suitcase. "He couldn't have told me?" "To be fair to your dad, you were five at the time," Erica carefully said while packing a crimson suitcase, "Yes, he might have made some mistakes, but his intentions were good." "For who- the Favres? Nico? You remember how he was when we were kids." Ally said her eyes flashing gold with rage. "He *has* grown up you know. He's not the same bratty kid who used to pester you all the time," Erica said trying to help. "He's grown up, quite handsomely too, might I add, and so have you Ally."

"Aunt Erica, he chased me up a tree, and left me up there for an hour!" Ally exclaimed, shaking uncontrollably. Erica slapped her suitcase shut ready to smack her. Calming herself down, she tried to talk some sense into her niece. "Your father was going through a very rough time and wanted to ensure you'd be safe," she answered,

"Besides, Nico dared you to run up that tree." She picked up a nearby box, deep in thought. "Hey, your grandfather went through the same thing at just about your age. He wasn't exactly happy about it either," she said, not mentioning the fact that he'd gotten divorced as quickly as he legally could soon afterwards. "So, with the knowledge that today was coming, I prepared for it. Here's your suitcase," she said handing her the now-packed suitcase. Ally put it next to her other suitcase, crying.

"She wouldn't have wanted this," she said stuffing a framed photo in her purse. Erica took it out wiping a tear away when she saw a three year old Ally smiling back while being held by her mother, a woman with long dirty blonde hair and sapphire blue eyes standing next to a much younger-looking Alexander. "No, she wouldn't," she agreed, looking at it. She gently placed the photo back.

"I did get you something, well I picked it up anyway." Erica handed her the box she picked up. Ally opened it up to a black fedora with a white ribbon. "Thank you," she said, holding it carefully.

"It was your grandfather's when he was a young man," Erica said, hugging her. "Dad and Stefan thought it would look fantastic on you; I'm inclined to agree."

Nico stood outside her door, brimming with hurt over her reaction. "You okay?" Sam asked, walking up. "I'm fine," Nico dully answered, wandering away in a daze. "Really Alex," Sam thought angrily.

It wasn't much later that afternoon as Ally watched Nico and Sam put her stuff in the trunk while she sat on the steps. "Don't worry. Femi will be there by tomorrow; travel permits should go through for her pretty quickly," Alexander said, turning to Ally. Ally suddenly felt anxious as she watched Sam get in the driver's seat.

"You'll be fine," Alexander said, trying to help her. Ally ignored him altogether while steeling her nerve. "You know, most people get a job or car on their eighteenth birthday. I get a fiancé who, even if we do know each other, I certainly didn't know about the engagement," she thought scared. Ally turned away walking to the van. As hurt as she was, she was going to miss her father- not that she was going to say it out loud, though.

Alexander watched as Nico held the door open for her. As she got in, her feet felt heavy. "That was a bit harsh," Sam said, starting the car, "But I suppose it's understandable, under the circumstances." Nico got into the car closing the door behind him. Sam drove away from the mansion, heading for the exit gate.

Ally watched her dad enter the house in a slump, watching as the mansion disappeared behind them. "So, how have you been?" Nico asked trying to start a conversation. "Outstanding," Ally said as curtly as politeness allowed, staring out the window. 'What do I do?' she wondered to herself. 'I had things I wanted to do, places I wanted to go see; now it's all been taken away from me.' It was taking every bit of self-control she had to stave off the inevitable breakdown she knew was coming.

Meanwhile, Nico turned to his own window, trying to give her some space- as much as could be allowed when sharing the same row of seats. "Is there any way I can help?" He asked. "Not really, unless you can bend reality," she answered. 'I don't blame her, after today she needs her space,' he thought staring out his window. With his dreams about the day shattered and crumbled, he felt sorry for her the most. After all, her dreams (whatever they had been until an hour ago) were shattered as well, it would seem beyond repair.

Nico stayed that way, deep in thought until some soft sniffling broke his concentration. "Hey, You okay?" he asked, turning to Ally. She glared as she looked back sighing. "I'm fine," she lied terribly, a few tears falling down her cheeks. He rolled his eyes and handed her a box of tissues. "Thank you," she said, blowing her nose.

Nico turned back to the window. "Why didn't he tell her?" he thought, "What in God's name was he thinking?" "So you think Alex will be able to take you being gone?" Sam asked trying to break the silence. "Don't really know," Ally answered indifferently, "He hasn't been this alone since Mom's funeral." Nico gave Sam a confused look. "How could he be so stupid?" he thought worried.

"I think he'll have issues with it- especially with that cold goodbye earlier," Sam pointed out, "After all, he's not exactly the loner type." "Time will help, right?" Nico added, "I mean it helped me." "Probably," Sam said. Ally turned to Nico glaring. He turned to the window disheartened as Sam sighed.

'Well, it was worth a shot,' he thought keeping his eyes on the road.

Alice stared at the dugout skeptically. "You're sure he lives here?" she asked, "I mean it's an old decommissioned fallout shelter, how are we even supposed to get in there? The concrete's got to be ten feet thick at least- even *you* can't force your way through that much material." "I'm sure," Huey said, playing on his O-Pal, "And we sneak in later tonight. There's got to be a window or something for ventilation, and that's what will give us a way in." "How do we do that and Why?" she asked glaring at him, "And having fun on that dumb computer of yours?"

Huey looked up annoyed. "I can't currently answer the first question and as for the second, yes I am, because it's fun," he answered. Alice glared at the thin rectangular tablet in his hands. "Oh, and it's *my* O-Pal," he said defensively. "I can do what I want with it, my oh so sweet sister."

Alice huffed and turned back to the dugout. "It seems weird," she said sadly, "You think he'll even recognize us? We were still babies when he left, and he's only ever talked to us through occasional video calls our whole lives." "Most likely," Huey answered, "We do look a lot like him, at least according to Mom anyway." "Really?," She looked at him questionably. "*Really*," Huey said genuinely. "I mean if nothing else, he'll ask us who our mother is and we'll tell him that way; I suppose we'll find out soon just how *that* goes." Alice sighed. "Whatever you say," she said, leaning against the tree trunk.

Ally stared at the sunset amazed by its beauty. "Beautiful," Nico said before quickly giving her a weak smile, "Uh, the sunset I mean." He blushed a bright red as Ally rolled her eyes and turned her attention back to the window. "We're almost there," Sam said, hitting a gravel road, "Just a couple more minutes."

She stared at the woods watching them carefully. "What the…?" she said, watching a hooded figure jump into the woods. She only caught the faintest glimpse of the figure, but it certainly was enough to catch her off-guard.

"Something wrong?" Nico asked, worried. Ally turned to him smiling faintly. "I'm fine," she lied. Nico turned to Sam nervous. "Bullshit," he thought.

"We're here," Sam said, pulling into the paved driveway. Nico opened the door for Ally bowing like a gentleman. "Aren't you laying this on a little thick?" she thought embarrassed trying to ignore him. She thought she heard someone sneeze nearby. "Ladies first," he said trying to be a gentleman. Ally left the van confused. She looked at him apprehensively. "An old fallout shelter? I actually didn't expect this," she thought, suddenly feeling a bit nervous.

"How about you two get her stuff," Sam suggested. "Okay," Nico said grabbing the crimson suitcase. Ally grabbed the black and white one as Sam unlocked the front door holding it for Ally. "Thank you," she said, walking in. Nico walked in following her like a shadow. She stared at the interior surprised. The hallway floor was made out of marble while the walls were a light brown wood with family photos and paintings on them.

"How about the two of you go unpack while I make us something for dinner," Sam suggested turning to Ally and Nico. They walked down the hallway as he entered the kitchen. Following Nico carefully, they stopped at the end of the hall where a black mahogany door stood.

"This is our room," he said opening the door.

"Wait...*our* room?" she asked startled, "Don't I have my own?" Nico felt his shoulders crumple just that little bit more, but shook himself and replied, "Well, we do have four more bedrooms. Want one of those?" "Yes, that's why I asked," she answered. "Alright; there's a room this way," he said leading the way. She followed him to a door made of intricately carved oak.

She entered cautiously carrying both suitcases timidly staring around the room. The walls were a purple color covered in paintings, an armoire sat across from a full size bed with a rose colored comforter and white pillows, two side tables sat beside the bed and one dresser sat against the wall on the other side of the room. She turned to see a woodstove in the corner. "So why this room, and what's with the stove? It doesn't have a flue pipe," she asked. "It's not meant to be used for heating; it just happens to look nice," Nico answered putting her stuff on the bed, "And this bedroom happens to be next door to Sam's." He looked down at the floor, trying not to feel any worse than he already did. "Felt like you'd feel more comfortable in here with him nearby." There seemed to be an added tension in the atmosphere.

"So.. You think you'll like it here?" he asked trying to change the subject. "Not sure; I haven't exactly been given a time limit for how long this engagement is supposed to last," she said, darkly chuckling while putting her stuff away. "One year, actually," Nico said hanging up a sweater. Ally stopped what she was doing. "What?" he asked confused. "A whole **year**? Why that long?" she asked curiously, "You already know me." "So what, you want to elope instead?" Nico asked sarcastically. "Hardly," she answered derisively, thinking *I didn't exactly ask for this after all.* "Didn't think so," he retorted, "Your dad wanted you to get to really know me, and to get used to this whole arrangement."

"He couldn't just *tell* me? I might've eventually gotten used to the idea; you know, had I been told about this at any point," she asked insulted. "Look, I don't know if it escaped your notice, but your dad is more than a little unusual," Nico pointed out, "Can we get done with the complaining soon?"

Ally spun around, facing him down with an angry glare. "I don't know if it escaped **your** notice Nico, but I already had some ideas for what I wanted to do with my life, and it didn't involve getting married off before the age of 20 to my dad's best friend's kid like this was some business arrangement in the 18th century!"

"Don't you think I know that?! Look, I'm sorry nobody told you before today, but there's not much I can do about it now! If you happen to have some ideas of your own for solving this, to be frank I'd be all ears to hear them at this point. Until then, just.." Nico forced himself to stop before he ended up yelling at Ally. "Just leave it be for now. Today's already been a hell of a day, and I just want to see it end, like you probably do."

She stared at him for a moment, a bit shocked at him actually firing back, then shook her head and turned away, concentrating on the clothes. "Good," he thought putting the last piece away. Ally turned around and noticed him putting clothes in the wrong places. "Um, T-shirts and long sleeved shirts go in the dresser," she said taking them out of the closet.

“..Right, sorry,” Nico quietly muttered taking out a sweater. “It- it’s fine, Nico. You didn’t know,” she said trying to be friendly. Nico put up a small smile in surprise. “What?” Ally asked defensively. “You don’t hate me.. **completely**, do you?” Nico asked putting the final pair of jeans in the closet. Ally stared at him wondering what he was thinking. “No.. of course not, we are friends after all. It’s just this whole forsaken situation we’re in,” she looked down about to cry. “Like you said, we are friends,” he pointed out awkwardly, “Maybe I should give you some time to cool down.” Ally slumped onto the bed, finally allowing the tears to fall. “Oh dear..” the redhead thought feeling terrible; then, surprising even himself a bit, Nico walked over to Ally and sat down next to her, holding her hand. “Is this.. okay?”

Ally just nodded, holding his hand tighter.

Chapter 2

Ally stared at the wood stove, deep in thought thinking of better days. She removed the picture from her purse, smiling faintly as a fond memory hit her. *"Ally," her mother said as she bandaged her burnt hand, "You've got to be more careful, sweetheart." A four year old Ally smiled back. "Yes mommy," she said grinning and seemingly unbothered by the pain.*

A sudden knock snapped her out of her little trance, making her look up and noticing the 21-year-old standing in the doorway. "You sure look happy looking at that photo," Nico remarked, walking into the room. Ally looked at him, smiling slightly as she put the picture back in her purse. "How long did he know?" she thought tilting her head at him. Nico blushed lightly trying to ignore her (unnoticed) cuteness. "At least I got one smile out of you," he said, sitting next to her; feeling a bit uncomfortable, Ally scooted away from him, leaving a noticeable gap. "Guess I really should've seen this coming," Nico thought disappointed. Ally stood up, working on folding the t-shirts, trying to avoid looking at him. "This is just like when I caught her crying in the bathroom earlier. She looked so miserable," he thought.

"Do you need any help?" he asked. "Not really," she answered finishing up, "I'm already done anyway. "Wow; she works fast," he thought.

A cleared throat caught both of their attention, and they saw Sam leaning on the door. "Dinner's ready, you two," Sam said. Ally turned to him, smiling weakly. "You know Ally, I have to admit I was surprised to hear you were in this room," he pointed out, "But we can talk about that at dinner; anyway let's eat." He noticed a sad Nico. "It's your favorite, Niccolo," Sam said turning to him. Nico stood up, seemingly feeling better. "Thanks, Papi," he said grateful. Sam closed the door behind them, trying his best to hide his building annoyance.

"No problem, bud," he said, following them into the kitchen. Ally stared at the design in the kitchen. The floor was a dark marble while the cabinets were a dark mahogany. The appliances were black, adding to the room's creepy ambiance. She sat down at the round table, careful not to stand out.

"So.. What do you think?" Sam asked curious. Ally stared at the meal in front of her. The steak kabobs in front of her looked great. "Looks great, Sam," she said, complimenting the meal. Nico smiled in response to her smile. "Sam is a great cook," he said. She tried her meal, loving every bite. "I agree," she sounded happy. Ally stared at the tea in her glass, recognizing the type of tea immediately.

"The white tea looks good too," she sounded curious. "Thanks," Sam answered acting polite. Ally sipped her tea loving its taste. "Thank you. It's good," she said. "Thanks," Sam said looking outside, "It's nighttime, y'all." Ally stared out amazed by the stars in the sky while Nico picked up his plate and got more.

"Say Ally, do you cook?" Sam asked, turning to Ally. He then burst out laughing at himself. "I'm sorry that was rude," Sam apologized, "Nico and I usually alternate cooking days, but we could use some variety." "I took a cooking class in school, so I know some stuff- the basics at least; mostly to keep up with my diet," Ally replied. "That's.. good," Nico quietly said, still ruminating on how everything went down.

"I can teach you; Nico says I'm a fantastic teacher," Sam offered. "Really? Sounds great," Ally agreed. "Awesome, we'll start tomorrow," Sam said, his voice sounding agitated despite what he was saying. Their conversation was interrupted by Nico groaning and standing up from the table. "Look.. it's been a long day; I'm just gonna go to bed," He pushed in his chair and slid his plate into the sink, "See you both tomorrow." He then walked down the hall, shoulders slumped.

Sam watched and waited until he heard Nico's door close shut before catching Ally's attention, his eyes not quite glaring at her, but it was close. "Look, I know it's been a crappy day for you, Ally. I get it- you're mad at your dad for leaving you in the dark all this time and then dumping it on you all at once today. Honestly I'm pretty angry at him myself about how stupid he was about all this, but why are you taking your anger out on Niccolo? It's not his fault your dad's some *idiota* with more money than sense."

Ally slowly nodded. "I know this is all on Dad and that Nico didn't have any hand in this mess, but.." she shook her head, "I just feel so.. so betrayed, you know? I had plans, ideas for what I wanted to do with my life. But getting married at 18 years old? Who gets married that young unless they have a reason to, especially nowadays?"

"I did." At the blonde's shocked stare, he cleared his throat and continued, "It's complicated; happened before I moved here to Greece. I was young and stupid and she was.." Sam paused, sadly reminiscing for a moment before coming back to the present, "gorgeous- rough around the edges, yes, but gorgeous and wonderful and.. perfect. But that was a lifetime ago now; no doubt she's moved on and forgotten all about me and my dumb ass.

"But we're not here to talk about my past regrets; right now my main focus is making this current situation resolve itself without any more undue hardship either on you, my soon-to-be daughter-in-law, or my adoptive son who I cherish like he were my own flesh and blood. Besides, at least your dad chose a good kid to put you with. No denying he was an absolute moron for not at least telling you sometime in the last few years so you could adjust to the arrangement, but with his health going the way it is, he wanted you to be safe above all else.

"I'm not asking you to forgive Alex for this yet; frankly I think he needs to come to you and ask you himself for that forgiveness. But

I would like for you to stop taking your- admittedly justified anger- out on Nico. He's a good boy, with a good heart and he has done nothing to deserve being manhandled like you've been doing all day. You two were friends before today, and it's not like he's some stranger you've never had any contact with. I'm not telling you to fall head over heels in love with him tomorrow, but at least try to rebuild that friendship you guys had. I always thought you two kids could be something special- that's why I let your father talk me into the whole setup. Well, that and I knew his heart was in the right place. Just give my boy a chance, that's all I ask, Ally."

The blonde sat still, considering it all. Her currently broiling feelings about her dad aside, Ally could see that she really was taking it all out on the one person who could honestly be called blameless in all this. And like Sam said, it's not like Nico was some tall dark stranger whisking her away in the night to lock her away in a dungeon somewhere. If nothing else, she could take the tension out of the air between her and Nico.

"Alright, Sammy. I can try. I mean it's like you said, it's not like we don't know each other," she got up putting her plate in the sink. "I'l do what I can.. for both Nico's sake and mine."

"Thanks, Ally," he sighed, relieved. "I appreciate it."

Nico laid on the couch, staring at the ceiling wondering, it seemed, about Ally and her life before him. "Why wouldn't he tell her?" he asked himself in his head. Images of her happy ran through his mind until he realized things were not going to be the way he wants. He remembered his visits to her as a child smiling as he fell asleep on the couch. "We'll be fine," he thought falling asleep.

Ally entered her room feeling slightly guilty for the way she was treating Nico. "He hasn't always been nice to me, but that doesn't matter," she thought as she laid in bed. She heard snoring nearby as she tried to sleep. Looking around she saw no one. "Great,

Sam snores," she said annoyed. "Actually that's Nico. I'm reading a book," Sam yelled from his room. "Great," she thought as she laid down. Looking at her family photo she was about to cry. "Good night," she whispered to herself.

A four year old Ally sat by a pond watching the koi fish swim in a perfect circle. "Beautiful," her mother said sitting by her, her sapphire eyes were full of excitement. "Yeah," Ally said, smiling. "Catherine," Alexander said, sitting next to her mother. He turned to Ally. "Hey Ally," he said, messing up her hair. "What is it?" Catherine asked confused. "Nothing," he said, walking away. Catherine picked up Ally. "You know I love you, right?" Catherine asked a hint of sadness in her voice. "Yes," Ally answered confused. "Then why do you doubt it," her voice faded away as the garden turned into a graveyard. An eighteen year old Ally screamed at the grave marked "Catherine Bellerose".

Ally sat up screaming in shock. "You ok?" She turned to see Nico holding her close. "I'm fine," she said, catching her breath and calming down. Suddenly a vase broke in the hallway causing a slight commotion. "Idiot!" An angry guy whispered nearby. "Someone screamed," a girl whispered now annoyed with him.

"Let's forget about it and find Sam," the guy said as Ally and Nico heard the clicking of high heels go farther away. Nico opened the drawer of one of the side tables pulling out an O-Pal. Ally watched as he pressed an icon making two dots move on the screen.

"This is the kitchen," the girl hissed. Nico pressed a button on the O-Pal's screen causing the duo to scream. She ran out of the room following Nico as he ran into the kitchen. A boy and girl were caught under a net, both looking annoyed in their own way. The girl looked eighteen with long straight strawberry blonde hair with piercing smoke colored eyes, which looked angry, dressed professionally, except for her black high heeled boots. The guy looked twenty-one with short dark red hair and cat eyes. He was dressed in a long black sleeved shirt and blue jeans with grey tennis shoes contrasting the girl.

"Who are you?" Nico asked confused. "Alice Coupe," The girl introduced herself annoyed. "Huey Driscol," the boy smiled mischievously at Ally. Ally looked at them, especially the boy, befuddled.

"What happened?" Sam asked, as he entered yawning. He looked at the net in shock. "Let them go," he demanded glaring at Nico. "Why? They broke in," Nico explained as he pressed a button releasing the net as Alice glared at Huey.

"I'll explain tomorrow," Sam answered, "It's too late and I'm tired." Huey got stood up putting his hand out for Alice. She glared as she grabbed his hand. "What?" Huey asked confused. "There were traps?" Alice answered with her question. "You didn't ask," he answered.

"You can sleep in the guestroom," Sam said embarrassed. Ally sighed annoyed herself. "They get one on the spot," she thought as Nico stepped two steps away. Huey and Alice walked out annoyed puzzled. "You two should get some sleep too," Sam said, turning to Ally and Nico, "Tonight was a surprise."

Nico yawned tired. "After she relaxes," he answered. "As long as it's in your separate rooms," Sam said leaving. "Come on," Nico said taking Ally's hand. Ally pulled her hand away walking down the hallway. Alice gave Nico a nervous look, and then turned to Ally. "Don't ask," he said following her. "Ok," Alice said, entering her guest room.

Sunlight poured into the room illuminating the dark. Ally opened her eyes disappointed by her surroundings. "It wasn't a dream," she thought sadly. She looked around the room spying a calendar of the next year with a circled date. She walked over to see what date was circled: October 1st, 2170. "My birthday," the thought hit her hard; it made her whimper sadly. Suddenly the door opened making her jump.

"Good morning! How did you sleep?" Nico said walking into the room, dressed and ready for the day, "I just wanted to check on you after yesterday." "Fine enough I suppose," Ally grumbled, jumping back on the bed in a huff. "I want out of this," she said, admittedly more than a bit childishly. Nico sighed thinking of what to tell her. "I'm afraid that's impossible," he said sadly. Ally stared at him confused and more than a bit angry. "What do you mean, impossible?" she demanded.

"Okay, here's how I understand it. After what happened to your great-great-grandmother Angeline, it was decided that there needed to be legislation in place to avoid another tragedy like it happening again. So the law was written that certain categories of 'specially gifted individuals' would be encouraged to have arranged marriages with those who they would have a high degree of compatibility. Among other requirements, the concerned parties- us in this case- need to have regular contact before such an arrangement comes into effect to ensure viability of the relationship. The initial arrangements are typically made between the legal guardians of the concerned parties, but the final decision must ultimately be made by the couple themselves within a year of the scheduled date of the wedding, thus allowing their free will to be exercised."

Ally blinked, trying to wrap her head around all the legalese he'd just spouted out. "Wow; I feel like a law book just came to life and threw words at me. Did you memorize all of that yourself?"

The redhead seemed to blush. "Yeah, actually I did. On the off-chance that I had to explain why we weren't dating in the traditional sense; I just never thought you'd be one of the people who'd need the explanation."

"Right well.. I still don't like it. It was never in my future plans to end up as a housewife, no matter who I ended up marrying."

"No need to worry. You were never going to be a housewife, Ally; I couldn't stop you if I wanted to." Nico said playing with the string of his black hoodie. "Besides you know how persistent your father is."

"Yeah, you have a point." Ally got up revealing normal pajamas, grabbing a black waist coat and white t-shirt from the dresser. "Are you wearing a bra?" he asked surprised. "None of your business," she answered. He blushed as he slumped. She then walked over to the closet grabbing a pair of blue jeans going behind the divider, remembering Sam's words. "Sorry, it's the morning," she pointed out. Nico grabbed an O-Pal putting on music.

"It's too early," Ally complained. He turned off the music starting to get annoyed. "It's eight o'clock. Breakfast will be ready soon," He said as she kicked him out. Sam walked by seeing Nico outside the door and Ally closing it. "Do I need to ask?" he asked. "No," he answered. "Isn't love grand," Sam pointed out. Ally put on a pair of black flats and black fingerless gloves finishing her outfit.

"You look nice," Nico said trying to start a conversation and hide how annoyed he was as she left her room. Ally glared at him lightly. "Thank you," she felt a little weird. "Breakfast is ready," Sam yelled down the hall. Nico and Ally walked down the hallway together making it awkward. "So how did you sleep?" he asked curious. Ally looked at him surprised. "You know how I slept," she pointed out. "Afterwards," he said. "Better," she answered.

"I heard someone scream," Alice said, her voice being heard from the kitchen unnerving both of them. "I get the point," Huey said giving in. Ally entered puzzled about the duo staring at her. Nico followed shortly with the same reaction. "That would have been Ally," he pointed out. "Ha!" Alice said as Huey put his head down.

"Ally, Nico. These are my twins," Sam said, taking a seat. Ally stared at Alice and Huey confused and nervous. "What's your name?" Huey asked as Ally sat next to him. "Great, the pheromones are kicking in," she thought annoyed, "Prepare for a dog fight." "Her name is Alette and she is taken," Nico said sitting next to Alice annoyed. Alice glared at Huey.

"Sorry. My brother is an idiot sometimes," She said turning to Nico. "Okay...a cat just entered the fight," Ally thought to herself. Alice gave Nico a light glare making Nico glare back defensively.

"Get along," Sam said taking a bite of his toast. Ally sipped her juice ignoring the situation. Nico looked at her nervously. "Are you two dating?" Huey asked curious. "We're technically engaged," Nico answered. Huey turned to Ally who was ignoring Nico.

"Really?" he asked scared. "It's arranged," Sam pointed out. "So," Huey answered back. Sam sighed. "Respect that," Alice demanded annoyed still. Huey took a bite out of his toast. "And the cat wins," Ally thought, "Yay! And she hates me, even better."

Night sat against the pillar smiling mischievously at the starry sky. She played with her bangs carefully avoiding her black eye patch. "Night", came a familiar voice. She turned to a teenage girl standing in front of Athena's statue. "Yes?" she asked curious.

"When do we meet her?" the girl asked inquisitive. "We see her tomorrow. Sam wouldn't like us being early," Night answered in her calming voice. The girl looked down sad.

"Don't worry. She will like you Carmen," Night said trying to comfort her. Carmen smiled at Night with excitement in her eyes. "You think?" she asked enthusiastically. "I know," Night said standing up, "Now let's head home." Carmen followed Night thinking of the day to come.

Ally sat on the couch staring at the blank television screen. She suddenly heard a truck pull up and a knock on the door. "I'll get it," Sam said running to opening it. She heard indistinctive talking.

"Okay, let her out in the yard. Ally, Femi is here," Sam said loud enough Ally could hear. He walked into the living room a concerned look on his face. "I would leave her alone for five minutes," he suggested. "Okay," Ally said excited.

Chapter 3

The man entered the abandoned apartment building anxious. Who wouldn't, what with the crumbling drywall and peeling paint everywhere? And that wasn't even the worst part of this trip.

"Hello," said a creepy voice. He jumped and turned around to see a young man leaning against the wall. He had blood red eyes and messy jet black hair with pale skin and wore a black leather trench coat with black jeans and leather shoes. The word sinister could have been created just for the job of describing the dark figure.

"Here's the information," the man said handing him a flash drive.

"Good job, Joshua," the young man said taking it, "Now run on back to Alexandria." Josh ran away terrified of his employer.

The man entered a room to an O-Pal that sat on a bed. He pressed a button causing a young woman to appear on the screen. The woman smiled slyly at him, her black hair was cut short covering her blue eyes slightly. Her pale skin glowed in the dark room with her black suit, giving her an unearthly aura teeming with malevolence.

"Hello Reaper," she said, suddenly acting pleasant.

"Hello Mother," Reaper said bowing, "I got the file."

The woman's smile turned mischievous all of a sudden. "Send it," she ordered abruptly.

Reaper pulled out the flash drive putting it in the O-Pal. Minimizing the call window, he pulled up a file marked E.M. Carefully he hit send going back to the call window. The woman smiled excitedly as she went through the file ignoring him completely. She turned back to Reaper still excited. "Nice! We'll wait a little longer. It will be suspicious if she disappears now," she pointed out. "Yes mother," Reaper said grabbing his sword. "Call me later with more observations," she said hanging up almost immediately. Reaper left the room grinning to himself.

"Josh," he called. Josh ran up almost immediately. "Keep an eye her," he commanded. Josh shook his head running away. "This is going to get good," Reaper thought to himself, "Now she has the Coupe-Driscol twins."

Ally left the living room Femi by her side following her like a shadow. "Hello Miss Bellerose," the voice came off as snide and rude. She turned to see Alice behind her, a defensive look in her eyes.

"Hey," Ally said confused by her challenger. "You look nice. How much did you spend on that outfit? I hope it wasn't too much," Alice's challenge became deadly. Ally glared at her, insulted by her words. "It wasn't at all," she said sneering. Her eyes glowed gold with rage making Alice give her a piercing glare in response. "You don't say," she said calmly.

"Something wrong, girls?" Nico asked walking up with Huey.

"Nothing, I was saying, I mean telling your fiancée she looked nice," Alice said walking away. Ally sighed ignoring her ignorant comment.

"I'm going outside. Anyone want to come with me?" Nico turned to Ally hoping she would say yes. Ally looked at him thinking.

"No thank you," she said trying to be polite.

"How about you?" he turned to Huey now sad.

"Sure," Huey answered sighing. "Come on," Nico said entering the kitchen. Huey followed ignoring Alice who sat at the table reading a magazine. Ally smiled slightly as she walked down the hallway toward the living room.

"Finally, some alone time," she thought, "That's good."

Nico leaned against a tree staring at the clear blue sky. "How long has it been? She seems so closed off," he said out loud by accident making Huey think.

"You're talking about Ally I'm guessing?" Huey asked not surprised as he figured it out.

"Of course," Nico answered not realizing what he was saying. Huey turned to the clouds. "What's so special about her?" he asked confused. Nico blushed a bright red making him look like a chili pepper. "A lot, She is sweet, kind, down to earth...," Nico pointed out starting to look a tomato.

"And you can tell this by one meeting?" Huey thought sighing, "You do know she is a Healer?" Nico stared into space before he answered. "I suspected that. Why else would her eyes glow gold," Nico laughed lightly most likely in denial of Ally's rejection, "And besides we've been meeting every summer ever since she was five." "How old were you?" he asked. "I was eight," Nico explained. Huey gave him a surprised look getting the picture.

"He's used to the pheromones I guess," he thought, picking up a leaf. "Lucky girl," he pointed out. "You really think so?" Nico asked. "Yeah," Huey turned to a tree where a flash of red disappeared. "You see something," Nico asked curious. "Not at all," Huey ignored it as if it never happened.

Alice walked down the hallway, Huey and Nico's conversation still ran in her head. "Hey," she said passing by the kitchen, where Ally sat at the table eating a sandwich.

"Hey," she said smiling still suspicious of Alice's insults. Alice sat across from her staring out the door. She turned to Ally giving her a bewildered look. "We don't eat lunch together?" she asked. "Guess not. Sam said to help ourselves," Ally said, sipping her white tea while staring at Nico as he entered. Nico walked in heating up a piece of pizza in the microwave. "Hello," Alice said grinning slyly.

"Hey," Nico said pulling out the plate, "Hey Ally." He sat next to Ally almost immediately, making her upset. Ally stared as she put her sandwich down, making Nico gave her a confused look. "She looks lovely," he thought hurt, "I wonder why she so distant." "So where's Huey?" Alice asked mischievously. "Grocery shopping with Sam," Nico answered. Ally got up putting her dishes in the sink. "I'm taking a nap," she said apprehensively.

"She is wary of you and I don't see why," Alice got up making a sandwich herself. "Really," Nico raised an eyebrow. "Yeah, you're nice to us. Treating Huey and me like family," she said taking a bite. Nico got up putting his plate in the sink.

"You are family," he said leaving. Alice looked at him confused. "That's right...Sam adopted you," she pointed out nervous. "No, I just live here," Nico retorted. "Sorry," Alice left the room embarrassed.

Ally laid in bed whimpering in her sleep as Nico walked into the bedroom checking on her. "You okay?" Nico asked instinctively. Her whimpering got worse it seemed. He sat next to her putting a blanket over her in an attempt to make her comfortable. Ally suddenly became silent cuddling her pillow. He moved her bangs out of her eyes revealing a content look.

"Nico!" Sam yelled from the kitchen. "Coming," Nico ran out the room as fast as he could. "What?" Ally asked sitting up. She stared at the blanket with one raised eyebrow. "Nico must've come in," she said stretching. She got up grabbing her gloves. "How sweet," she thought.

Night stared at the stars, her pitch black hair blending in with the dark room. "Night," Carmen said peeking into the room shyly. Night turned to her, her eye patch now white adding to her creepy and mysterious aura.

"Yes Carmen," Night's calming tone made Carmen smile. "Good night," she said leaving as the door silently closed. "Good night," Night said turning back to the moon. "To be as changing as the moon," she said as she laid down, her skin as pale as the full moon, "One should never wish such a thing."

Ally stared at the moon smiling to herself. "Beautiful," she said pulling her legs close. She sat in the living room admiring the stars. "What is?" Nico asked curious.

"The moon...It's smiling," she acted slightly childlike, in a positive way. Nico smiled faintly back as he went to his room. "I'll head to bed," he said. Ally got up too heading to her room. "I think I will too," she pointed out. "You don't want to stay up with the twins?" Nico asked. "Not really," she answered. "You can't build a wall forever," he pointed out. "Why?" she thought trying to sleep, "It's only thing I know."

Ally stood in her home garden surprised she was there. "It's beautiful," Catherine said staring at a cherry blossom in bloom. Ally turned to her slightly nervous. "Mom," she said surprised. "You act like it's been forever," she said walking over, "I said I would never leave." Ally stepped back worried about the situation. "But then again...you believe I'm gone," Catherine sounded disappointed. She suddenly disappeared causing the scenery to change. The garden was dead while the mansion was in ruins.

Ally screamed as she woke up freaking out. Nico ran to her aide holding her close as fast as he could.

"It's alright," he said trying to calm her down. She pushed him away still terrified. Nico looked at her disappointed in himself.

"Something tells me you're going to keep me up," he pointed out trying to calm her down some more.

"Are you alright?" he asked concerned as Ally sat there shaking. "Yeah," she said avoiding his gaze. "Why is he trying so hard?" she thought.

"As long as you're okay," he sighed in relief. He got up returning to his room. "You should try to sleep," he said closing the door.

Ally laid down looking at her family photo. "Mom," she thought sadly. She buried her face in the pillow covering up her tears. She pulled up her blanket attempting to go back to sleep. "Goodnight," she thought.

"I guess she has night terrors," he said, lying down. He thought about it for a second. "I'll have to wait till she trusts me," he thought surprised.

Night stood in the kitchen making breakfast, singing while Carmen sat at the table staring at the empty nest outside. She thought about the baby birds she used to watch in the spring.

"Here you go," Night said putting a plate in front of her. Carmen smiled excited as she looked away from the window. "Thank you," she said taking a bite. Night sat across from her turning to the empty nest.

"What do you think she'll be like?" Carmen asked curious. "One of the nicest people to meet," Night answered honestly. Carmen took another bite getting even more excited. "That's good," she said, sipping her milk.

"What do you think she'll be like?" Night asked curious. "I don't know," Carmen answered, "but I hope she's what you said she'll be." "Me too," Night said, about to take a bite.

Carmen turned her attention back to the birds nest. "They were pretty," she said sadly. "How is school?" Night asked curious. "Great," Carmen lied. "Is it...?" Night was cut off by Carmen. "NO! I'm doing fine," she answered, hoping to get Night off her back. "Remember you said it," Night thought to herself.

Ally stared at herself in the bathroom mirror thinking about her father. "He's lost without me," she thought about his pain. Shaking her head she returned to her appearance. The purple long sleeved shirt and faded jeans complimented each other. She grabbed a pair of black boots and a black and a white glove off the counter.

"Hello," Alice said poking her head in. "Hey," Ally said putting the white glove on first. Alice watched as she put on the black one in an attempt to ignore her. "Well Nico wanted me to get you," she said trying to be nice, "He said it was important." Ally looked at her suspiciously.

"What?" Alice asked befuddled. "Nothing," Ally grabbed her fedora. Following Alice out both girls ran into Huey. "Hey Alette," Huey said smiling. "Just call me Ally," she said politely. "Okay," he said, embarrassed, "Sorry." He seemed very hyped up for the morning.

"Did you have caffeine or sugar?" Alice asked Huey worried. "No...I'm just happy," he answered contently. Alice whistled as she walked away unsure if he was lying. Ally looked in the living room as she walked by.

Nico was asleep on the couch talking in his sleep. "No, I want the white chocolate," he said unknowingly. "Are you sure?" she asked raising an eyebrow. "Yes," Nico answered.

"Yeah," Alice answered from the bathroom. Ally entered the room sitting across from him as he got up yawning. "Hey Ally," he said surprised. Ally smiled back weakly. "Alice said you wanted to see me," she said unsure of herself. "I did?" Nico sounded confused.

"Did you?" Ally asked. His look went from surprise to shock. "I did," he said sitting next to her. Ally looked away as if by instinct. Nico raised an eyebrow. "I was just going to warn you that Night was coming today," he said sighing.

"Night comes all the time," Alice pointed out making Sam laugh. "Night Fiore," Nico said annoyed. Alice glared at Sam as he calmed down. When Ally got a scared look on her face she got suspicious.

"What's wrong?" Alice asked sitting down. "Does she have a creepy eye patch and usually dressed in dark clothing?" Ally's question peaked Alice's curiosity. "Yeah...Why?" Nico asked. "She remembers her from the funeral," Sam said putting a cup of hot chocolate in front of Ally. "Funeral...That's right," Nico said embarrassed. "What funeral did he go to?" she thought. Ally eyed him, suspicious.

"Yeah. Catherine Bellerose died during the Durand war," Alice pointed out insulted. Ally looked at her surprised. "He was at my mother's funeral?" she thought. "What?" Alice asked. "How did you know that?" she asked even more suspicious. "It was all over the news," Alice suddenly got jumpy. "Okay," Ally spoke concerned. "I won't prod any deeper," she thought to herself.

Night drove down the gravel road whistling a happy tune. "This is cool," Carmen said fixing her baseball cap. Night smiled slyly trying to keep her eye on the road. "I hope you're talking about nature," she said. "No, I'm finally going to meet Alette," Carmen said excited. Night pulled into the driveway as the sun went down making a beautiful sunset.

"How about you get the door," Night suggested. They got out as Sam exited the van next to a covered car. "Hey. You're early," he said holding a grocery bag. "How early?" Night asked curious. "Five minutes," Sam said laughing. He opened the door for them. "Ladies first," he said holding it open. Night walked in gracefully while Carmen followed. "The kids are in the living room," Sam said walking into the kitchen, "Except Nico, He's getting the wood for the bonfire." Night's eye glimmered giving her an air of mystery. "Okay," she said walking down the hall.

She walked into the living room surprising everyone, especially Ally. Ally looked at her scared as though she seen the grim reaper. Night's long black wavy hair was in a messy bun leaving bangs covering her black eye patch, her violet hyacinth eye was full of wisdom, and her skin was pale. She took off her black trench coat revealing a black sleeveless blouse and slacks with high heeled boots that matched her shirt. She removed her black gloves revealing black nail polish matching her outfit. "Long time no see," she said mischievously turning to Ally. "Yeah," Ally said hiding behind her fedora.

Carmen entered shy, but curious. Ally looked up at her trying to figure her out. Carmen's medium length brown hair and brown eyes matched, she wore a blue sweatshirt and faded blue jeans with white tennis shoes. "This is my daughter, Carmen," Night said introducing her. Carmen grinned in response. Alice rolled her eyes. "Who are you?" Night asked turning to Huey and Alice.

"Alice Coupe," Alice said, with a piercing glare. "Huey Driscol," Huey said, mischievously. Night smiled to herself. "So these are Sam's twins," she thought. "Nice to meet you," She said, sitting next to Ally. Ally pulled her fedora lower. "Don't worry, I don't bite," Night said joking.

"It's ready. Hot chocolate will be served shortly," Nico said walking into the living room. Night grabbed her trench coat and gloves disappointed in the short meeting and reunion. "Let's go," she said putting them on. Carmen stood up following her. Ally walked out putting on her trench coat as fast as she could. Nico walked over as Alice and Huey followed.

Ally turned to him then Night. "What?" Nico asked. "Nothing," she said walking out. He sighed as she ignored him. "They have the same smile," she thought.

Night laughed as Carmen smiled not sure if she should laugh too. "I'm serious," Sam said, sipping his hot chocolate. Nico looked at him scared and confused as Ally laughed.

"That makes it better," she said calming down. "I didn't want to know that," Alice thought annoyed. The night turned to Ally and Nico, a kind look in her eye.

"How's the engagement?" she asked curious. "Not so good," Sam answered rubbing his forehead, "Alex never told her." Night turned to Ally worried, but not surprised. "I'm very sorry. That must've been a great shock on your birthday," she said shaking her head, "Especially knowing his condition." Carmen shook her head in agreement. Ally smiled sadly at her words.

"What condition?" Nico asked out loud. "My dad is a flame," Ally answered trying to avoid Nico's stare, "Plus he is in his forties. At this point the heat is killing him slowly. How do you not know this? He takes meds!" "Really? How much time does he have left?" Nico asked realizing why she came and why he visited. "Not much," She answered, "With the way he's been deteriorating recently, if he even knows my name this time next year I'll be surprised." Night turned to Carmen who gave her a sad look as Ally stared at the fire, deep in thought.

"Well how about a dating period," Night suggested, attempting to change the subject, "You already know each other, why not strengthen your relationship. You don't want end up like Seth." "How?" Ally asked. "He found a loophole in his arranged marriage. And before you ask, that loophole was your mother," Night pointed out. Everyone stayed silent. "I can see that," Ally thought.

"Great idea," Sam said in agreement, "The dating period." Both turned to Nico and Ally. Ally turned to Nico smiling slightly. "Why not?" she said shrugging. Nico smiled excited. "I'm in," he said turning to Ally. Ally turned away freaked out. "Idiot," Sam thought.

Carmen whimpered feeling left out of the conversation. "It's alright, we all know you're here," Night's words made her smile. Ally looked at Carmen still trying to figure her out.

She removed her glove preparing for a surprise. "Want to see something cool?" she asked turning to Carmen. Carmen shook her head yes. Ally's eyes glowed gold as her hands gained a gold shield making Nico stared amazed. She put her hand closer to the fire taking a flame. Ally stared at the flame in her hand turning it into a butterfly. Carmen stared in amazement as the butterfly flew back into the fire, disappearing.

"That's good," Sam said slightly impressed. "How did she train?" Night kept the thought to herself, "I thought it was only speed she trained with." Nico put his hand over her now gloved hand. She pulled away suspicious of his intentions. "Well we better get going," Night said picking up her empty mug, "After all you guys need your sleep as much as we do." Carmen followed yawning.

"We are tired," Alice said yawning. Huey stood up following his sister. Sam picked the glasses up carrying as many as he could. "How about you two?" He asked. Nico poured dirt on the fire smothering it. "We'll get some sleep as well," he said picking up his and Ally 's glasses. Ally got up ignoring Nico's stare. "Well, good night," Sam said closing the door to the dugout. Ally tried to open the door only to see it was locked.

"This is a dirty trick you...," music played as she spoke. "What, Do I bite?" Nico asked. "No...do you?" she asked suspicious.

"Maybe," Nico answered acting innocent. "Why you...?" music played as she finished her sentence. Her eyes turned bright gold with fury. "Crap," Nico said running through the front door. Ally followed running to her room. Nico tried opening his door, but it was in vain.

"Where do I sleep?" he asked. "Go away," Sam demanded, "I'm doing your laundry." Nico hid behind Huey scared. "What's going on?" Huey questioned. "I want my mommy," he said terrified. "Bye Nico," Night said leaving.

Ally laid on her bed deep in thought. She turned to the window remembering her first memory of Nico. *A five year old Ally sat across from an eight year old Nico who stared at her smiling nervously. Sam sat next to him looking twenty-two and still mischievous. A twenty-five year old Alexander stared at Nico and Ally nervously as he started to introduce the two. "Ally, this is Nico," he sounded scared, "Nico this is Ally." Sam rolled his eyes almost annoyed looking. "He'll be visiting you for two weeks every summer," Sam explained.* The memory faded back as she attempted to fall asleep. A knock on the door woke her up. "Hello," Nico said opening the door, still terrified. "Hey," she said turning to him.

"I'm so sorry," Nico apologized. "How much of this was planned?" she asked. "Tonight was completely planned with slight improvising," he answered looking down. He sat on the edge of her bed going into his own reminiscing. *Sam sat at the table with Night staring down a nervous Nico. "Should I have helped her?" he asked shaking. "No you didn't do anything wrong at all. In fact she's now your fiancée," Sam winked trying to make Nico laugh. Nico looked at him confused. "You're engaged to her. She is your future wife," Night attempted to put in his terms. "Ohh, does that mean I get to kiss her?" he asked them. "No, let her get to know you," Sam pointed out. "Okay, Sam," Nico answered.* The memory faded as he turned to Ally. "I just came to say goodnight," he left the room grinning. "At least she's getting to know me," he thought. Ally pulled up her cover. "Good night," she said surprising him.

Chapter 4

The alarm went off making Ally jump out of bed almost hurting herself.

She turned it off annoyed at the music it was playing. Sitting on the bed she stared at the room around her. The quaint bedroom made her feel uncomfortable. "Why did I choose this?" she thought, "What time is it?"

Ally turned to the alarm clock, trying to ignore the sleeping fox in the corner. "Eight o'clock? No thanks," she thought going back to bed. The door opened making her cringe.

"Good morning," Alice said opening the door. Ally flinched feeling uncomfortable that someone was watching her sleep. "I don't want to get up," she complained.

"I'm only here to tell you breakfast is ready," she said staring at Ally confused, "That's all." Nico stood behind her insulted, "You took my line." He sounded annoyed.

Alice stared at him puzzled. "That was your line?" she pointed out as he laughed, "That's not funny." "My alarm woke her up," he answered annoyed. Alice followed, closing the door behind her. "Your alarm?" she asked raising an eyebrow. "Yeah, that was my teenage room," Nico broke off entering a smaller hallway as they walked down it. "Why is she in there?" Alice followed surprised by the direction he took. "Cause it's the closest room to Sam," he answered. She noticed him heading to the last room of the hallway.

"Where are you going?" she asked curious. "Work," he answered bluntly. He entered a room marked 'Workshop' leaving Alice in the hallway. "You okay?" Huey asked finding her. "I'm fine," She said attempting to hide her confusion.

"Where did Nico go?" he asked curious. " 'Work'," she quoted. "I wonder what he does," Huey thought. "Come on, I'm hungry," Alice ran into the kitchen excited. "She is like a big kid," Huey thought to himself, "But she is my sister."

Sam put foil over a plate putting it in the microwave. "Not saving any for Ally?" Huey asked surprised. "That is Ally's, Nico's plate is in his workshop," he said sitting down. "Are you sure she will wake in time?" Alice asked. Huey took a bite staring at Femi. "She already ate," Sam said, "I don't know.. by the way, what do you want to do today?"

Huey looked at him raising an eyebrow. "Nico is planning on surprising Ally with a date when he gets off work," Sam said, grinning. "Already?" Alice laughed out loud as the thought hit her. She calmed down trying to act professional. "I already made plans," she said stopping. Sam turned to Huey. "How about card games?" Huey suggested. "Sounds like fun," Sam said.

Alice glared at Sam as she put her plate in the sink. "What's wrong with her?" Sam asked worried, "Does she hate me?" "She's just being Alice. She'll get over it," Huey pointed out. "Over what...?" Sam wondered, "Breakfast?"

A fifteen year old Ally stared at the school in front of her, her anxiety rising. "This is so unfair," she said grabbing her suitcase. Erica held the door open for her. "It's your first year at career level," she said trying to comfort her, "You should be happy." Ally whimpered worrying Erica. She walked down the hallway resenting every minute.

"Here's your dorm," Erica said stepping aside. Ally unlocked the door unwillingly. "Have a good school year," Erica said kissing her forehead, "Your roommate promised to help, we love you." Ally entered to clothes sprawled everywhere on one of the beds making half the room a mess.

"Bonjour," a Cajun accent came from the closet. A young woman who was Ally's age stepped out smiling. Her long black hair was straight as a pin, her black eyes had a velvet quality and her skin was fair. Her outfit suggested she was a tomboy. She kind of resembled a porcelain doll. "I'm Sybil Jackson. You must be Alette Bellerose," the girl said welcoming her. "Yes," Ally said gulping nervously. "Don't be so worried. We're only rooming together," Sybil laughed as she patted Ally on the back. "This will be fun," Ally thought, attempting to smile.

Ally opened her eyes disappointed at her scenery. "Great; I'm still here," she thought with a grimace. She stared at the woodstove and armoire like they were bombs about to explode. "Great," she thought aggravated. She turned to the clock to see the time was now 11:30 am. Ally sighed as she got up attempting to wake up. She walked over to the armoire grabbing a pair of black slacks and a white blouse. "I'm adaptable, right?" she thought while getting dressed. She put the bra on carefully. Suddenly the bonfire came back to her in a memory. She quickly put it out of her mind. "I remember when he picked on me. Now he's acting like a gentleman," she talked to herself out loud. The thought bothered her. She sat on the bed deep in thought as she glared at the door. "What do I do?" she asked herself.

Putting on her shoes she went deep in thought as Sybil's words returned to her: "Don't worry. We're only rooming together." "It's not the same," she thought frightened, "I only saw him during the summer and...and I should've seen this coming." "What's the difference?" The thought left her slightly annoyed. She thought for a second. "It's a guy," she thought.

"So?" her mind retorted. She got up grabbing her fedora ignoring the thought. "Good morning," Alice said standing outside her door. "Hey," Ally said giving her a surprised look. "Your hair looks crazy," Alice pointed out. Ally glared as she made her hair back to its wavy appearance using her static electricity. "How about now?" she asked, putting her fedora on.

"Looks good," Alice said embarrassed. Nico walked out into the hallway bumping into Ally. "Sorry," he said picking up her fedora. "May I please have it back?" she asked, a serious look in her eyes. Nico handed back her fedora disappointed. She took it back putting it on her head as she walked away.

"She's in a bad mood today," Alice pointed out. "Really, I couldn't tell," Nico said sarcastically. Alice followed him. "Well I get off at one o'clock. I just came to grab lunch," he said walking into the kitchen. Alice sat at the table. "Really," she said pretending to be surprised. Nico grabbed a pre-made meal microwaving it. Ally sat at the table eating a salad.

"See you later," Nico said taking the meal with him. "He's probably planning something," Alice said trying to cheer her up. "Probably," Ally's mind thought of the bonfire. She got up putting her plate in the sink. "I'll be outside," she said sternly leaving the kitchen. Alice watched as she grabbed her trench coat. "Mind if I join you?" she asked. "Why not," Ally answered. Alice smiled mischievously as she grabbed a brown jacket following her.

Nico sighed as he stared at the O-Pal in front of him planning its electronics assembly- or at least that was the *plan*, the problem with that was a certain blonde on his mind. "She still has problems with me," the thought cut like a knife. "Knock, knock," Sam said knocking at the door. "Don't come in," Nico answered still annoyed, "I'm assembling an O-Pal, and they're delicate at this stage." "Well what if I had something to drink?" Sam shook the bottle. Nico opened the door carefully to check. "Alright, come on in," he said taking the soda and going back to his desk. Sam raised an eyebrow confused. "What's wrong, bud?" he asked sitting down. Nico shook his head and picked up a computer chip from the tray where he kept them using a pair of tweezers.

"Ally is the problem. I don't know what to do about today," he said putting the chip in the incomplete O-Pal. "Really," Sam stared at him shocked, "You've known her how long? How about a walk through the park. She loves nature." Nico gave him a surprised look. "May I ask why?" he asked. "Try it," Sam said. "Ok," Nico said in agreement, "And I only visited two weeks out of the summer." "That is true," Sam thought leaving the workshop.

Ally sat there watching Femi play with the leaves. "She hates me," Alice said watching Femi closely, "She's really getting on my nerves." "She's my bodyguard," Ally pointed out annoyed. "I know we just met, but most people say you're pretty optimistic," Alice raised an eyebrow. "Blame Nico," Ally looked at the cloudy sky, "It is his fault." "Do you hate him that much?" she asked causing Femi to stop. "No, I know him slightly," she answered as she picked up a leaf. Alice watched as she crushed the leaf in her hand. "He was a jerk as a kid. He only started being nice at fifteen," she pointed out.

"Of course," she said worried. Ally turned to the woods where a shadowy figure disappeared. "Who is that?" she thought worried. Alice turned to the woods. "What do you see?" she asked curious. "Nothing," Ally got up checking the time. "One o'clock," she thought entering the dugout.

Nico sat at the table reading a book. "Hey," he said looking up. "Hey," she said trying to pass by.

"Wait," Nico said putting his book down. He lightly grabbed her hand. "I thought we could go out," he said sweating nervously. Ally looked at him as he radiated anxiety. "Sure," she said remembering the night before. Nico's face lit up almost immediately. "Great! The car is this way," Nico said opening the front door.

Ally followed confused about what he was talking about. "You mean the van?" she asked turning to him. He walked over uncovering the small car next to van. Ally stared at the small blue car underneath it in shock. "You have a Reaper?" she asked surprised. "Yeah, you like it?" he got in the front seat as he asked.

"It does match my eyes," Ally entered cautiously not knowing what to do. She stared at the blanket in the back seat which was in a weird shape. "For the cold," Nico said starting the car. Ally played with her trench coat nervous as Nico looked at her concerned. "I'm fine," she said shaking. "You don't look it," Nico said worried. She gave him a faint smile. "Alright," he said driving slowly.

Sam walked inside going through the mail. "Looks like Alex sent her something," he said holding a box not surprised, "Knew he would miss her." Huey looked at him now amazed. "Alexander Bellerose," he said sitting next to Huey. Huey gave him a thumb up. "Isn't he a famous weapons designer?" he asked. "Yeah, he's also Ally's dad," Sam pointed out. "His wife died during the Durand war," Huey bit his lip.

"Guess that's big news still," Sam said going through the mail still. "Plus Ally was ignored," Huey said angrily. "That's a vicious rumor. Now, how about a game of cards?" Sam asked trying to change the subject. "Sure," Huey said now embarrassed. Sam put down the mail. "Okay. You pick first game," he said mischievously. "Five cards draw," Huey answered. Sam shuffled the deck.

"So did you know Catherine Bellerose?" he asked. "Yeah," Sam's voice sounded sad. "What was she like?" he asked curious. "She was and is still a kind soul to the world and the only thing that kept Alexander on his feet," Sam pointed out, "You do know why Ally is engaged to Nico?" Huey shook his head no. "Alexander is a flame," Sam's answer made Huey's eyes grow, "He is dying fast thanks to his high body temperature. This wasn't originally planned." Huey understood Alexander's life and intentions finally. "He just wants her happy," he thought.

Ally watched the scenery pass by in wonder at the beautiful city. The classic buildings shined in the sunlight adding to its beauty. "Do you like it?" Nico asked curious. Ally turned to him as her excitement was suddenly subdued. "Yeah," she said trying not to smile. Nico turned into a park's parking lot surprising Ally. She stared at the trees in front of her amazed. The trees themselves added on to the landscape.

"Beautiful," she said. "Come on," Nico got out of the car still smiling. "He's a little too happy," Ally thought. Ally stared at him as he opened her door walking out completely in shock. Both started walking on the trail.

"What school did you go to?" he asked trying to start a conversation. "Miss Blanchet's Girls Academy," Ally answered reluctantly. Nico snickered. "What?" Ally asked glaring. "Nothing, just sounds silly," he said sitting on the bench, "No wonder you hid where you went to school as a kid." Night watched from close by not surprised they were there. She turned to a tree, her eye glimmered. "How about you?" Ally asked curious. "Olympus high school. I majored in technology," he answered, smiling. Ally sighed. "Must be nice," she said staring at the tree in front of her. Nico turned to squirrel running by.

"Any more questions for me," he asked curious. Ally smiled slyly. "Yes," she answered, "How long have you known?" Nico raised an eyebrow. "Thirteen years," he answered. Ally's eye twitched. "What's your birthday?" she demanded. "February 14th, 2141," Nico answered. Ally looked at him surprised. "You're twenty-one and your birthday is on Valentine 's Day?" she asked confused. "I don't look it, right?" he asked smiling, "I was born romantic after all." Ally slapped him lightly. "No. You look eighteen," she said as twig a snapped. Nico turned to the tree in front of him. "Probably a squirrel," Ally said getting up, "Let's continue." Nico followed as Night watched from the nearby tree, her hand over Alice's mouth. "Hello Miss Coupe," she said as Alice glared at her.

Huey glared at Sam intensely. "What?" Sam asked innocently. "That's weird," Huey said turning to his small pile of poker chips. "Don't be a sore loser," Sam said smiling mischievously. "I'm not. It's just strange," Huey pointed out annoyed. "Just put your hand down," Sam said confident. Huey put down a losing hand about ready to yell as Sam put down a winning hand grinning. "He calls me a sore loser," Huey thought as Sam sorted the chips, "He's a sore winner and cheater."

Ally walked toward the car blushing and confused. "Hey ,Nico," Somebody yelled getting their attention. Both turned around to see Night, cheerful as always. "Hey Night," he said excited. Ally stared at her ready to run. "Hello Ally," Night said smiling mischievously. "Hey," She said watching Night's eye glimmer. "I'd be careful. Who knows who's watching," she said as she walked away.

"She's always acting creepy. Then again you met her before," Nico said getting into the driver's side. Ally got in deep into thought trying to decipher Night's riddle. "What did she mean?" she thought. "Something wrong?" Nico asked confused. Ally looked up around stopping at a giggling girl with fan. "Nothing," she said nervous.

Nico looked out as he changed shift. The girl entered the trail talking on an O-Pal. "Why would that bother her?" he thought. He drove into town preparing his words. "Did you know her?" he asked concerned. "Not really," Ally lied. "Good or bad?" he asked. "Bad, she was part of the group that bullied me," she said smiling weakly. He immediately tried to drive back to the park. "What the name of Haven are you doing?" she demanded. "They picked on you," he whined as he stopped in the middle of the street. "Just go where you were going," she ordered.

Nico smiled back as he drove off down the street. He pulled into another parking lot. "Well, it is my job to cheer you up," he pointed out. Ally stared at the restaurant in front of her. "Gemini," she said confused. Nico opened the door holding it for her. "Here you go," he said exited. Ally blushed as she got out of the car.

"Welcome to Gemini, Table for two?" A waitress asked glaring at Ally for what appeared to be no reason. Her chocolate eyes were green with envy. "Yes actually," Nico said glaring back. "Follow me," the waitress led them away. Ally looked at her nametag, planning. "Justine Smith," she thought smiling. "Here you go," Justine said stopping at a table in the back.

"I'm sorry," Ally said politely, "I was for a table by the window." Justine's glare worsened. "They're all taken," she said with a fake smile. Ally turned to see one empty. "I'll take that one," she said. "It's reserved," Justine lied.

"Is something wrong?" A man asked walking over. Ally read his name tag: Sean Redwood, manager. "We were asking for that table over there," she said politely. "Certainly and your name?" Sean asked. "Alette Bellerose," she answered. Sean turned to Justine annoyed. "Miss Smith, my office," he said. Justine walked away grumbling.

"Follow me," he said leading the way, "Sorry for Justine's behavior." He handed them menus happily, "I'll send a waiter right away." Nico looked at Ally surprised by her actions. "What?" she asked. "What just happened?" He sounded befuddled. She took off her trench coat putting it on the chair.

"Nothing important," she answered. "We just got the best seat in the house," he pointed out. She stared at him silent. "Hello and welcome to Gemini," A waiter came up casually, "What can I get you?" "How about a white tea, Jeff," Nico said snapping out of it. "And you," Jeff turned to Ally. "White tea, too," she answered turning to him. Jeff walked away putting his notebook in his pocket.

"You know him?" she asked. "We went to high school together," he answered looking at the menu nervously. Ally looked up from her menu in shock. "This is going to happen a lot," she thought.

Sam stared at Huey waiting for him to move. "Make your move," he said slightly annoyed. "I'm thinking," Huey picked up a pawn putting it down in the same spot. Sam gripped the table. "It's chess, not...," Huey cut Sam off.

"Where's your patience? Now I see why Alice is the 'instant gratification' type," he said moving a knight, "Checkmate." Sam looked the board over. "And I'm a sore loser," he said sarcastically. Sam glared turning to Huey. "Like father, like son," he thought. "Let's play another game," he demanded. "And Now I see where Alice gets her temper. Here I was thinking it was Mom," Huey thought scared, "Dad's is worse."

Ally tapped her empty plate bored. "Was it good?" Jeff asked returning. "Yes. Thank you," she answered politely. "Great," he turned to Nico picking up his plate. He turned back to Ally. "Nice to finally meet you," he said picking up hers. He put the bill down leaving for the computer. Nico took out twenty soleils putting them in the folder. "I talked about you a lot. No names mentioned though," he said casually.

"Don't worry, I talked about you too. Just not as much," she spoke regretfully. "Is she starting to trust me?" he thought. Suddenly he felt like they were being watched. Nico looked around stopping at a nearby table. Alice covered her face with a dessert menu. "Really," he thought annoyed, "Not even one moment alone."

"Thank you," Jeff took the folder back to the computer. Nico turned back to Ally. "We should get going," he said. "Here you go," Jeff said leaving the receipt. "Thank you," Nico said standing up. Ally followed suit grabbing her trench coat. "Let's go," Ally sighed at the thought.

"Nice girl," a guy said pushing up his glasses. "The redhead?" a woman asked in a sarcastic tone. She stared at Alice as she walked by. "Not her...Alette," the guy smiled mischievously as he spoke. "You don't say," she said playing with her long pink hair. "I do, Alora," he said watching them leave, "She seems attached to him." "Damon, it's a miracle you could tell," she said. "Alora...we're not bird watching," Damon pointed out. "But she's cute!... Fine," Alora sounded disappointed, "I don't get to have any fun."

Alice left the restaurant surprised to see Nico standing outside next to his car. "Hello Alice," he said politely, "Need a ride?" "No," she lied. "Ok, I'll just go then," Nico said getting into the car. "Wait!" Alice yelled stopping him, "I'll take the ride." Nico turned to Ally. "Come in," he said opening the door.

Alice entered giving him a piercing glare. Ally looked at her confused. "Do you drive too?" she asked. "Yes," Alice answered insulted, "I don't have a car though plus I don't chauffeur." "Not what I meant," Ally complained. "Then how did you get here?" Nico asked pretending to be curious. Alice stayed silent gripping the blanket. "Of course," he said acting surprised.

Ally glared at Nico as he started the car. "Let's head home," he said turning to Alice.

Chapter 5

Huey put the last chess piece away ignoring Sam. "You lost, so what?" he asked. Sam got up putting the game away. The door quickly opened startling them. "She followed us," Nico yelled entering the front door. "I know," Ally said annoyed. "Anyway you look tired," he pointed out. Ally whimpered in response. "I'll go take a nap," she said running down the hall.

Nico sighed as he walked pass the living room listening to Ally slam her bedroom door. "It's gonna take more than one date," Sam pointed out. "Where's Alice?" he asked. The front door slammed closed. "Huey!" Alice yelled annoyed. "Coming," he said getting up.

Alice glared at him as he entered the hallway. "Bedroom now," she demanded, "We need to talk." "What's wrong?" Huey asked confused. "She's a retro teacher," Alice explained closing the door in shock. "Who? Ally?" Huey asked surprised. "No! Night Fiore," she pointed out.

Huey looked at her even more surprised. "I thought she was weird, but a retro cognitive," he said deep in thought. Alice sighed. "It's hard to believe," she said angry. The memory came back to her tormenting her.

"Really Miss Coupe, You should be more careful," Night held Alice's hands behind her back, "I'm quite sure Khepri would hate to see you injured." She removed her hand. "What are you?" Alice retorted. "A retro teacher," she answered tauntingly. " I'm not going to hurt them," Alice said frightened, "I'm here to protect them." Night smiled in response. "Good to hear," she said jumping out of the tree. "See that you don't fail; I will be watching."

"Alice," Huey said bringing her back. "Sorry," she said shaking. "Did she threaten you?" he asked worried.

"She thought I was a threat," she answered finally calming down. Huey looked at her concerned. "It will be fine," she said comforting him, "She was just a...really scary woman." "What did she do?" Huey demanded. "Just being overprotective of Ally and Nico," Alice answered. "So, she did threaten you," Huey said. Alice shook scared it seemed. "She is twisted," she pointed out. "We'll have to keep an eye on her," Huey spoke while in deep thought. "Agreed," Alice said.

Everyone sat at the dinner table finishing their meal. "So, who wants to go out?" Sam asked bluntly. "Why not?" Nico answered, "You want to come along?" He turned to Ally. "Not really, drinking is not my thing," she pointed out. Sam gave a worse death glare then Alice. "I'll be happy to," she spoke cheerfully. "We'll stay here," Alice sounded scared, as if Sam actually cursed.

"I'll meet you in the car, after all we'll take the reaper," Sam got up, heading out followed by Nico. "Oh no, not the screaming metal death trap," she said worried. "Actually it's safer than you think...not as safe, but safer," Huey pointed out. "Not helping," Ally said as she left the table scared.

"Where are we going?" she asked weirded out. "Haven's best; the Drunken Shillelagh," Sam answered. "Sounds more like Haven's cheapest," Ally grumbled quietly. Sam's death glare returned. "I mean...Sounds great," she sounded too cheery. "By the way, you're the designated driver," Sam pointed out turning to Ally, "After all, you don't drink."

Ally sighed disappointed in herself. "So I don't," she thought. They pulled up to a nicer looking establishment then she imagined. "Come on," Nico got out, slightly excited. All three of them entered to a basic bar. She sat in a nearby chair only to have Nico motion to have her sit next to him. "What's the worst that could happen?" she thought sitting next to him. Night was the bartender.

"You might want to be careful, we do get some undesirables," Night said washing out the glass in her hand. "This is your bar?" she asked. "No, I'm a part time bartender," she answered handing two drinks to Sam and Nico. "That explains it," Ally thought not surprised. She watched Nico down his drink in one big gulp. Raising an eyebrow she attempted to sneak away. "He's a light weight," Night pointed out stopping her. "Great," Ally thought attempting to form an escape plan.

Alice sat on the couch reading her book. "So, how is your night going?" Huey asked. "Good," she answered, now suspicious of his intentions. "I have an idea...why don't you spend time with Ally?" he suggested. "Alright, I will," Alice answered trying to get him off her back. "Great," Huey thought relaxing, "At least you will have a friend."

Ally sipped her water staring at Nico who was now silent. "Is he okay?" she wondered out loud accidently. "He's fine, physically. Though I can't say the same about his heart," Night pointed out. "What do you mean?" she asked curious. "You scared him Ally and you're lucky he's a gentleman and gets affectionate when he's drunk," Night pointed out. Ally gulped scared.

"I'm sure everything will be fine," Alora said nearby. "Thank you, miss," Night said returning to Ally, "You should head home." "Okay, Can you help?" she asked. "With what?" Night asked. Ally motioned to Sam and Nico. "I will," Alora said. "Thank you again," Night answered.

The car pulled up as Ally parked the Reaper. Getting out, she noticed Sam opening the door and slamming it. "Is it something I did?" she thought. She entered followed by Nico heading for his bedroom. As she entered the living room, she sat on the couch. Nico entered sitting right next to her. Staring at him, scared in anticipation, she didn't know what he was going to say. "Do you like me?" he asked randomly. He turned to her a loving look in his eyes.

"Of course I do," Ally's eye twitched as she realized she was telling the truth.

He leaned against her staring at the television. "Thanks, that's all I wanted to know," he said getting up and pulling her in. "Easier," he thought. Ally blushed confused by her feelings. "We should head to bed," she suggested. "Fine," he sounded disappointed as he got up. She watched as he laid on the couch. "Poor guy," she thought heading for her bedroom, "This really shouldn't have been different."

Ally turned to Femi after she had trouble sleeping. "Do you think he likes me?" she asked her. Femi laid in the corner yawning asleep. "Great," Ally thought annoyed, "My fox likes him." A knocking on the door caught her attention. Ally opened the door to Alice standing there annoyed. "Hello," she said trying to be polite. "Hi," Ally stared at her surprised as she walked out of the room. "I came to apologize. I felt we started off on the wrong foot," she said. "I forgive you," Ally spoke honestly.

Alice smiled back. "Great. Then how about we hang out while Nico works tomorrow," she said giving her a hopeful look. "Sure," Ally answered unsure. "Great," Alice said hugging her, "See yea then." She ran into her bed room confusing Ally as she closed the door. Ally closed her door as she reentered her room unsure. "Tomorrow should be fun," she thought.

Huey turned on his O-Pal, bored. "Typing your report?" Alice asked curious. "Yeah," Huey said hitting send. Alice took the O-Pal and started to type. "You could ask," Huey pointed out. "We share it," Alice glared at her brother as Huey ignored her comment. Huey covered up tired. "Good night," he said going to sleep. Alice turned to the O-Pal and continued typing. She pulled up a file marked "Alette Bellerose". "She's nothing like I expected," she thought. She put the file back pressing send. "That's a good thing," she said smiling, "Good night."

Alice stared at her reflection in the bathroom mirror. "Look at these clothes; how plain can a girl look?" she asked herself. She buttoned up the last button on her sleeveless tan blouse and put on her high heel boots. "Hey Sis," Huey greeted her as she walked out. "Hey," she greeted him sarcastically, "Where is Ally?" Ally walked up in a white t-shirt with a flower design and blue jeans. "What do you want to do?" she asked turning to Alice. "How about we go outside?" Alice suggested grabbing her brown coat, "Come on." Ally followed leaning against a tree as Alice leaned against a tree trunk.

"I thought you didn't like me," she said confused. "I don't," Alice pointed out, "Huey keeps telling me to talk to you." "You mean spend time?" Ally asked. "Yeah, spend time," Alice growled. Ally sighed turning towards the woods. "Thought so," she said watching a figure run deeper into the woods, "Did you see that?" "See what?" Alice asked confused. "Nothing," Ally said sadly. Alice stared at her starting to feel sympathetic.

"So...do you have hobbies?" she asked trying to get Ally's mind off the woods. "I draw and train," Ally answered. "Train for what?" Alice asked curious. "I'm a Healer. I have to train," Ally answered sighing. "How do you train? I mean there are different methods in which to train energy," Alice pointed out. "Speed and agility," she answered. "How do you do that?" she asked curious. "I did three sports in school, in order: gymnastics, track and football. Each one helped me gained control over three basic needs: Mind, body and strength," Ally spoke almost fluently as she explained. Alice yawned as she attempted to be interested. "So you're like Huey," she said smiling slyly, "Only his training is different."

Ally raised an eyebrow curious. "How?" she asked. "If I told you, he would kill me," Alice smiled mischievously. Ally stared at her extremely confused. "I'm kidding, but still he would be mad," she said sighing. Ally turned her gaze to the woods. "Well he was trained in speed and agility too," Alice looked around scared. "Who is that?" Ally thought. "So, since you grew up in the high life," Alice was trying to NOT sound insulting, "Has everything been handed to you on a silver platter?" Ally glared at her intensely. "No," she answered honestly. Alice stared at her in shock.

"Really are you sure? You've never left home aside from school." Alice pointed out. "Because my father is a flame!" Ally said calmly, "You have yet to watch your father slowly degenerate and not even know you're there sometimes. At the rate he's deteriorating, I'll be shocked if he's still alive this time next year!" Alice looked at her sadly. "I'm sorry, I didn't know," her voice full of regret. "Let's forget the conversation," Ally's eyes turned gold for a second. "Okay," Alice said sadly.

Nico left his workshop excited. "Why so happy?" Huey asked inquisitive. "Nothing," Nico answered nonchalantly, "My project is almost done." "Project?" Huey asked. "Yeah," Nico walked into the kitchen turning to the clock, "Where's Ally?" he asked. "Outside with Alice," He answered. Nico walked out to Ally petting Femi. "Ally," he said walking over slowly. She looked up not scared, but befuddled.

"You want to go for a walk?" he asked politely. Ally smiled faintly. "Sure," she said getting up, "You don't mind if Femi comes along?" Nico looked at the fox. "Not at all," he said petting her. Femi purred in approval. "Will you be alright alone?" Ally turned to Alice. "I'll be fine," Alice answered still sad. "What happened to her?" Nico thought. Ally followed Nico into the woods smiling pleasantly. Nico took her hand making Ally stare at the gesture puzzled. "You okay?" Nico asked moving his hand away.

"No," she answered taking his hand, "I'm fine." Nico looked at her surprised. "You're not pulling away," he pointed out puzzled. Ally looked at him with the puppy dog eyes making Nico smile as he looked ahead. "She's acting weird," he thought, "Even weirder than when she hit puberty." "Femi is quiet," he said trying to start a conversation. "She's a fox," Ally said blushing. "His hand is warm," Ally thought weirded out, "I wonder why?" Nico sighed lightly as

Femi barked at the trees. Ally let go of Nico's hand, her eyes glowing gold. Suddenly a hooded figure jumped out throwing a dagger at Femi.

Nico dived grabbing the blade with his left hand as the figure ran into the woods leaving them in the dust. "Nico," Ally said as he dropped the blade not making a sound. She stared at the gash in his hand. "You idiot!" Alice said walking out from behind a tree. She removed her scarf about to wrap it around his hand. "You okay?" Came a random voice. The trio turned to see a young man with short brown hair and chocolate colored eyes hidden behind glasses walking over concerned.

Ally stared at him confused. He wore dark blue jeans, blue tennis shoes, and a grey jacket. The stranger stared at Nico's hand not surprised. Alice stared at him in shock and suspicion. He put his hand in his pocket pulling out a roll of gauze covering Nico's wound in it carefully. "I'm Damon by the way," he said politely, "Does it hurt?" "No," Nico answered sarcastically. "Probably an adrenaline rush," he pointed out. "I'm Alette," Ally said suspicious. Damon taped it up putting the rest in his pocket. "Nice to meet you," He said pushing up his glasses. "Alice," She glared at the intruder. "What are you doing here?" she thought.

"I'm Nico, Thank you," Nico said carefully. "Well you should take him to a hospital," Damon suggested. "Thanks," Ally said following the group. "Oh and Alette may I ask a favor?" Damon asked. Ally turned to Femi smiling as the group headed on forward. "Go with Nico," she ordered, "I'll be fine." Femi obeyed her master's request. "What's the favor?" Ally asked still suspicious. "Come with me for a second," Damon said walking down the trail, "And be careful of the traps." Ally followed reluctantly.

Nico stared at his cast nervously. "Luckily you're right handed," Sam said trying to cheer him up, "And was a goalie." Nico glared at him. "It was going good," he said worried. "Yeah, she never lets you hold her hand," Alice said staring at the window, "Wait you played football?" "Yeah, Ally played so I played," he explained. "You really have no life," Alice pointed out. "Of course he does," Sam said protecting him. Sam looked at Nico surprised. "Great, she took after her mother," he thought.

"Were you following us?" Nico asked ignoring her words. "I have my reasons," she answered annoyed. "What about Ally?" Nico asked. "Huey and Night are looking for her," Sam said trying to calm him down, "At least Femi came back." "Huey won't let her disappear," Alice said reassuringly. Nico smiled faintly back. "Night won't either," Sam thought.

Ally followed Damon still suspicious. They came upon an abandoned prison that looked at least fifty years old. "After you Miss Bellerose," Damon said holding the door open. Ally walked in staring at the decaying building she just entered. "Is this Sam's prison?" she asked curious. "Technically, Now this way," Damon said heading up the stairs. Ally followed looking at the empty cells wondering about the history. "Here we are," Damon said opening the door to the Warden's office.

The door creaked a little as Ally entered. She saw two women sitting in the chairs. One looked eighteen and had long bubblegum pink hair in a braid with grey eyes wearing a black leather jacket and black jeans with black stilettos. The other looked fifteen with long jet black wavy hair, cat green eyes and fair skin wearing a black hoodie, blue jeans and black tennis shoes.

"Well if it isn't the great Alette Bellerose," The one with pink hair said, "I'm Alora Jones. Damon's fiancée and personal body guard." Ally turned to the other girl. "I'm Amunet. Nice to meet you," she said solemnly. Ally looked her over carefully. "You attacked Femi and Nico," she said calmly. "Who's Femi?" Amunet asked. "My pet fox," Ally answered angrily. She walked over ready to strike.

"No fighting," Damon said annoyed. "You're lucky," Ally said gritting her teeth. Amunet glared as her cat eyes shimmered with anger. "I didn't know," she pointed out. Damon and Alora sat there watching them throw insults at each other. "This is funny," Alora said laughing, "Let them get their aggression out." "Fine," Damon sounded annoyed.

Nico laid on the bed deep in thought. "At least you're home," Sam said sitting down next to him. Nico managed a weak smile as he looked down at his cast. "At least in football, I didn't get this badly hurt," Nico pointed out. "Agreed, Huey and Night called. They found something, but Night said she would be home soon," Alice said giving them an update. Nico gave her a scared look.

"They're still looking. They're just following a trail," she added. Nico turned to the window. "She'll be fine. She's tough," Alice said leaving. Nico sighed worried about Ally's safety. "She right," Sam said, "Ally may be able to tap into 10% of her power, but she tough." Nico sighed relieved. "Wait, only 10%?" he asked. "That's right. Remember: Happy wife, happy life," Sam closed the door leaving as a shoe was thrown.

Ally sat in the chair staring at the desk in front of her as Damon sat across from her tapping a pencil. "Now...are you angry?" he asked raising an eyebrow. She turned to Amunet who glared back. "No," she answered. "Good," he said excited, "Now it's my turn." Ally looked at him surprised. "He's like a child," she thought. "Allow me to introduce myself fully. I am Damon Bellamy," he said bowing, "And I know you very well." "You do?" Ally asked confused and concerned.

"Of course, you're the Healer Alette Bellerose- not exactly a lot of Healers running around," he said sitting. "Please...call me Ally," she said confused still. Suddenly she looked at him surprised figuring out who he was. "You're the former prince of Psyche," she was shocked. "That's right, I was first in line until I stepped aside. And now I am here to ask for your help," He said bluntly, "My younger brother is a 'vampire' and the Emperor of Psyche. Not very popular with the public. You see there's a plot to kill him."

Ally thought about this for a second. "How do I know you're not the one doing this and this is a trick?" she was suspicious now. "You jerk!" Amunet yelled insulted. "Easy, Amunet. It's a pretty legitimate concern given the circumstances. How about this for an offer, I'll give you time to think about this and I'll send Amunet to get you in nine days at the mouth of the woods at noon," he said. "Deal," Ally said in agreement. "I'll show you to the exit," Damon said getting up. Ally followed unsure of what was going to happen.

Nico leaned against the tree, his eyes fixated on the woods. "They're going to be home soon," Alice said sitting next to him. Nico stared at her as he sighed. "I know, but I didn't expect her to run away," he said bluntly. "She has a crush, she's not going to run away," Alice pointed out. "She does...how can you tell?" he asked. "She let you hold her hand," she answered, "She was exploring 'feelings'."

"Really," Nico smiled as he spoke. "Not like that, you pervert! You've known her for years," Alice pointed out. A rustling noise broke the fight as Ally walked out of the woods with Night and Huey. "She's fine," Night said reassuringly. He ran up hugging Ally and making her blush embarrassed. "He missed you," Huey said laughing. Femi ran up licking Ally's face. "So did Femi," Night said laughing as well. "I missed you too," she said turning to Nico. He let go as he kissed her cheek. Ally backed up not knowing how to take this. "Quit scaring her," Sam said stressed, "Now I have to call Erica." Ally glared at him. "I wouldn't lie to her," Sam pointed out. "Of course you wouldn't," Ally thought.

Night stared at Ally her eye glimmering. "You're not actually telling us what happened?" Alice asked concerned. "I don't want to at this time," Ally said putting her plate in the sink making Nico get up and follow her. "You can tell me," he said charmingly as Ally walked down the hallway. "Not right now," she said going to her bedroom. Nico gave her a confused look hurt. "You didn't mind earlier," he said sitting on the couch. "I was in a better mood," she said honestly. "Maybe you should be happier more often," he pointed out.

She looked up as her eyes turned cold. "That's hard," she said. Nico walked over sitting next to her. "I've known you for years. Don't you have a crush," he said surprised. Ally blushed realizing he was right. "Only a little," she pointed out. "Well I'm going to bed," he said leaving. Ally watched him head to the door. "Please don't," she said surprising Nico.

"Alright," he said sitting next to her. Ally blushed even more realizing what she said. "Do you want to talk more?" he asked. "Ask him," she thought. "No," she lied. "Idiot," she thought, "you should've asked him about himself." Nico sighed. "I'm going to bed," he said. "I'm taking a shower," Ally said getting up.

Chapter 6

Sunlight poured into the room landing on Alice. "What the…? That burns," she said shielding her eyes. "Good morning," Huey said doing pushups. "Good morning," she said yawning. Huey stood up showing off his muscles. "How did you sleep?" he asked mischievously. "Good, I didn't wake up once," she answered, "And get a shirt on. Ally is taken." It hit her hard. "I slept well for four days," she said in shock. "Yeah, in fact it's been awhile since Ally got lost in the woods," he said putting on a shirt that still showed of his muscles.

Alice ran out of the room forcefully opening the door to Ally's room to Ally cuddling a pillow in her sleep smiling. "Is something wrong?" Nico asked standing behind her. Alice glared at him realizing Huey didn't listen. "Nice pajamas," he said sarcastically. Alice sighed. "Shut up," she said turning to Ally, "She looks peaceful." "She's been cuddling that pillow every night," Nico said moving hair out of her eyes, "Well for the last four nights." Alice looked at him surprised.

"Mail for Ally," Sam called from the kitchen. Ally sat up yawning. "It's on your O-Pal," Sam said nervously. Ally typed on the virtual keyboard. A video message popped up making Ally click on it. "Hello Ally. Surely you remember me," a pale young woman with short dirty blonde hair and aquamarine eyes appeared on screen, "Well, if you don't my name is Cassandra Favre and your invited to the Seasons in honor of your engagement. October 9th, 2162 at 7 pm. The dress code is formal." The message ended making Nico scared. Ally turned to him worried.

"It's fine," he said as his stare went away. Ally gave him a relieved look. He looked at the clock. "It's ten," he said deep in thought. Ally walked over grabbing her clothes for the day. "We still have till tonight," she said picking up a pair of flats, "Plus I'm kind of related to her." "How?" he asked as his eyes widened. "My grandmother was a Favre," she answered, "Technically, She is a second cousin. No more questions." "So he has to go?" Alice turned to Nico. "Yes I do," he said annoyed. Alice walked out holding back her laughter.

Cassandra looked at her reflection disappointed by her status. "Bixenta," she said turning to her friend. Bixenta's black curly hair complimented her sky blue eyes which was full of mischief. "Yes," she said in a sickly sweet voice. "What did you say he was like?" Cassandra asked. "Well, he was nice and caring but it looked she rejected him," Bixenta sipped her soda. "You're sure they're engaged?" she asked a brunette with grass green eyes. "Yep. Apparently he couldn't stop talking about it," he said walking over. She smiled slyly at the thought. "Tonight should be fun," Cassandra said leaving the room, "A secret engagement. She has always been so perfect, and now she's getting married. How sweet...I guess." Bixenta sighed as she realized the situation. "Alette always is...sane," the guy said grinning. "Agreed, that guy might shake up her world, Remy," Bixenta pointed out, "After all she's only mad she's not a noble."

Ally stared at herself in the mirror. Her black dress and high heels complimented her hair in its bun. "I don't like this," Nico said buttoning up his shirt. Ally walked over. "Why?" she asked confused. "I just don't," he said as his eye twitched. Ally fixed his shirt pulling it out of his pants. "You look better like this," she said staring at his casual look. Nico blushed as he put on his shoes. "We should get going," he said putting on his coat. Ally grabbed her trench coat following. "Something wrong?" she asked. "No," he answered in high pitched voice.

Sam sat in the living room watching television with Alice and Huey. "Are you going through puberty again?" Sam asked. "No," Nico coughed making his voice go back to normal. "What happened to you?" Huey asked. Nico whimpered nervously as Ally dragged him. Sam noticed his shirt. "Did you do that or Ally?" he asked. Huey laughed out loud. "I can guess," he said as Nico buttoned the last button on his coat.

"Come on," Ally said opening the front door, wind blew chilling her slightly. Nico held the door open allowing Ally to leave first. The wind blew hard helping Nico close the door. He opened the car door for Ally letting her enter first. "Thanks," she said noticing his anxiety. Nico smiled back faintly. "You okay?" she asked worried as he entered the driver's side. Nico shook his head yes as he drove off. "It will be fine," she said trying to calm him down. "I'm going to regret this," she thought. Nico gave her a faint smile.

"I'll be fine," he said in a high pitched voice. Ally stared at the darkened city. The street lights illuminated the busy night owls as the car drove by. Nico pulled into the parking lot almost hitting the sidewalk. She watched as the car was parked. Opening the door, she stared at the other cars. "We're a little late," Nico said shaking, his voice back to normal. Ally took his hand attempting to calm him down. Nico blushed as he let go running into the room embarrassed. "Nico, wait for me," Ally said running up. She stared at her former class mates embarrassed.

"Ally," a woman Ally's age walked out of the crowd. Her medium length straight black hair was in a bob, her skin was fair and black eyes had a velvety texture. She wore a sweet Lolita style. "Hey Sybil," Ally said as her eyes brightened. Nico stared at Sybil. "You forgot this," A guy Nico's age walked up holding a drink. Sybil took the drink happily. "You're not going to introduce me," she said acting sad. "Nico, this is Sybil Jackson," Ally said excited, "And this is her husband Justin Klein." Justin glared at Nico.

"The bathroom is to the right," he told Nico. "Thanks," Nico said taking off. "Hello," Justin said turning to Ally. "Be nice," Sybil admonished. "If you wish," he said taking her hand. Sybil giggled childishly as Nico returned to Ally looking better. "Let's find a table," she said sighing. "You can sit with us," Sybil said walking to a nearby table. They sat at a table marked Alette Bellerose and Sybil Jackson. "Your name is on it," she said sitting.

Alice stared at the woods trying to see what Ally saw. "Are you tired?" Huey asked noticing. "Not really," she answered. A shadowy figure suddenly disappeared into the woods surprising her. "Did you see that?" she asked amazed. "See what?" he asked confused. She turned back to the woods frightened. "That's not good," she thought, "Are we in danger?"

The music played as Nico and Ally danced slowly. He held her closer giving her a soft look. Ally looked at the bar trying to ignore him, she wasn't surprised by the bartender. "Nico turn around," she informed. He turned around to see Night Fiore as the bar tender. "Night," he said running to her excited. Night looked up smiling slyly. "Hey Nico," she greeted him. Ally walked over following Nico. "You look like a mess," Night pointed out looking at Nico. Ally smiled at him hoping to cheer him up. "There you are," Sybil said walking over, "You alright?" Nico gave two thumbs up staying silent.

"He's probably nervous," Night said getting out a glass of water, "Ally did make him nervous." Nico sipped his water nervously. "Told ya," she said. Sybil sat next to him waiting for him to calm down. "I came to warn you about Cassandra," she pointed out. Ally glared at the thought. "She's looking for you two especially," Justin said sternly. "This is because I'm engaged?" she whispered to herself. "Yeah, I knew it from the start," Sybil pointed out. "Wait a minute, you knew we were in an arranged marriage?" she asked.

Justin just smiled awkwardly as Ally turned to Nico. "I was told a week ago," she said regretfully. "Why? Is Alexander an idiot?" Sybil gave her a surprised look. "Yeah," she answered sipping her glass of water. Sybil turned to Nico still in shock. "Hey Ally," Cassandra showed up sounding rude to everyone, "Long time, no see." Bixenta stood next to her with a mischievous, regretful grin. "You must be Nico," She said faking a glare. Nico glared back at

Cassandra. "You don't talk," Bixenta spoke trying to act tough, "Especially to your hostess." Nico stayed silent. Remy walked up staring at him. "You should control your fiancée'," Night said annoyed, "She's immature." Remy glared back as Bixenta walked away with him. "You're creepy," Sybil retorted to them as they followed Cassandra. She turned to Night grinning. "I like your style," she pointed out.

Sam laid in bed trying to close his eyes not fully asleep. The front door opened and closed waking him up. "Interesting friends," Nico said trying to stay calm. "You were nervous, she was trying to calm you down," Ally said passing Sam's room. "She did it in an odd way," Nico said running up to catch up with her. Nico ran in his room grabbing his pajamas. "I'll take a shower tomorrow. How about you?" he asked turning to Ally. She stared at the clock as she before she went behind the divider. He threw her a pair of her pajamas. "It's too late to take a shower," she said getting dressed behind the divider. Nico perked up it seemed as he put on his sweatpants. "Anyway we should get some sleep. Is it okay if I sleep on the couch?" she asked walking out from behind the divider. "Sure," he answered. Leaving the divider early, she stared at Nico blushing as he put on his white t-shirt and quickly ran behind the divider.

"You ok?" he asked concerned. "I'm fine," she said embarrassed and pink as a flamingo. Nico raised an eyebrow confused at her actions. Ally left the divider, her face was still pink. "You sure?" he asked feeling her forehead. Ally walked over to the bed cuddling a pillow for comfort. "Alright," Nico said setting up his bed on the couch. "Didn't know he was hiding that," she thought trying to get the image out of her head. She laid down trying to sleep. "Good night," Nico said smirking. "Good night," Ally said not noticing.

Alice banged on the Ally's door a she attempted to wake her up. "Come on, I thought we could hang out today," she explained. "I'm not in there," Ally walked up opening her bedroom door.

"Where did you sleep?" Alice asked curious. "With Nico, and no it's not what you think. He slept on the couch," she explained. "Oh," Alice stared in shock, "He sounds like a gentleman." Ally grabbed her clothes for the day slightly annoyed and well rested as Alice walked away and Nico replaced her. "So how did you like my bedroom?" he asked. "It was comfortable," she answered. "Would you switch?" he asked. "Sure," she answered. "Great, your stuff will be in my room by the end of the day," he explained before he left. "It won't hurt," she thought, "At least he's s safe."

Alice stared at Femi annoyed as Ally watched from a tree nearby ready to laugh. "You won't win. She can stare forever," she yelled. Alice's glare worsened. "Blink," she said. Femi growled lightly. "Your little shape shifter is annoying," she told Ally. Ally turned to the woods. "It's been two weeks and two days since I turned eighteen," she said sighing. Alice gave her a surprised look losing the staring contest. "You've kept count?" she asked surprised. "Yeah. Pretty easy when the calendar is across from the bed," Ally answered. She suddenly saw a shadowy figure in the woods. "I'll talk to you later," she said getting up. Femi followed her in as Ally entered to Amunet staring at her.

"Follow me," she said going onto the trail. Ally followed not knowing what was going on. "Your lessons...Since you showed up, you're saying yes," Amunet pointed out. "Of course," Ally said embarrassed. Amunet rolled her eyes knowing she forgot. "My boss sent me to get you," she pointed out, "Don't forget that." Ally sighed in defeat. "Where is he?" she asked reluctantly. Amunet stepped over a bush as Ally followed her entering a clearing. She stared at the crystal clear pond and tall trees with their orange and brown leaves. Damon sat under a tree with Alora holding her close.

"Hey Ally," he said as Alora and Him stood up. Ally sighed to herself as Alora noticed her confusion. "Doesn't Nico hold you?" she asked. "Why would he?" Ally asked surprising everyone. "So...ready for your first lesson?" he asked diverting from the question. "Yeah,"

Ally answered. "Good, let's see what your best move is," he said pushing up his glasses. Ally smiled slyly as her eyes turned gold. "Prepare for an Ally original," she said. She got into running position making the bottom of her shoes glow gold as well. Next thing any normal person could tell, she seemingly disappeared, reappearing next to Alora.

"Nice," he said yawning, "So we're starting at square one?" Ally glared at him. "There's so much more you are capable of, ever thought of that?" he asked, "So let's begin. You seem to have control down slightly. So let's try something that takes a small amount." "Slightly...don't you mean a little?" Alora asked. "What do you mean square one?" Ally asked. "Every Healer as a level they start out, this is their original move. Now this defines their skill set. Yours happens to be speed and agility. Seth's is strength and intelligence...and weaponry. Your great-great grandmother Angeline's was defense. To put it bluntly no Healer has fulfilled their true potential," Damon explained.

"So you're going to teach me?" Ally asked. "Yes," Damon answered. He walked over to a tree. "Try and save a leaf," he said bluntly. Ally stared at him not thinking. "Just use your energy to save one leaf," he explained. Ally turned to the bush her eyes turned gold as she picked one leaf. She watched in amazement as it bloomed in her hand only to die. "What the...?" she said disappointed. "A little too much. Try less," he suggested. Alora leaned against a tree watching the show. Ally picked up a different leaf this time being more attentive. She watched as it stopped halfway.

"Not enough," he said. Alora walked over holding her leather coat tight. "Try finishing," she said in her naturally sarcastic voice. "Control is basic," Amunet said with a dark look in her eye as she picked up a leaf, "Too much or too little can be deadly." She crumpled it in her hand. Ally gave her a scared look. "Quit it," Alora said glaring at Amunet. Amunet's smile turned mischievous. "Ignore her," Damon said annoyed. She stared at the leaf.

"I've taught myself for years," she thought sad. "Maybe you should head home. This could be homework," Alora suggested. "Fine by me," Amunet sounded bored. "How about you escort her back?" Damon asked Alora. "Fine by me," she said entering the trail. Ally and Femi followed. "Don't worry. Amunet is nice when she gets to know you," Alora pointed out. "Good to know," Ally said, worried

Nico watched the woods bored it seemed. "I'm getting cold," he said out of nowhere. Sam stood nearby raking the leaves. "You just noticed," he said relaxing. Ally left the woods followed by Femi surprising both of them. "What were you doing in there?" Nico asked concerned. "Nothing," she answered turning to his left arm which was in a cast. "It's better," he said sitting down. She sat next to him unknowingly putting her hand on his cast. He put his good hand over hers blushing a bright red.

"Nice to see the two of you are getting close," Sam said laughing. Ally looked down moving her hand back immediately. "Nice walk?" Alice was trying to figure out Ally's trip. "Yeah," Ally answered. Nico sighed as the cat fight started. "What?" Ally asked tilting her head cutely. He blushed as Femi barked in a way that sounded like a laugh. "We should get inside," Ally said standing up. Nico stood up following her in.

"I'll be in soon," Sam said putting the leaves in a pile, "That's good enough." He looked around at the blanket of leaves on his property. "That's enough leaves to me," he said grabbing a trash bag, "Now let's bag."

Nico cuddled a pillow on the couch obviously lonely. "What are you doing?" Ally asked confused. "I'm tired," He answered yawning. Ally sat on the bed holding back laughter. "So you're holding a pillow?" she asked trying to calm down. "I've done this a million times," he said sitting up. Ally laughed lightly. "What?" Nico asked insulted. "I'm just wondering why you're cuddling a pillow," she said stopping. "No reason," he said trying to think. Ally gave him a sympathetic look. "Is it because of me?" she asked.

"Not at all," he lied. She suddenly felt bad. "You want to sleep in the bed?" she asked staring at his cast. Nico gave her a surprised look. "We can start tonight," she said regretfully. "What changed your mind?" he asked curious. Ally looked at his cast. "No," she said remembering how he got injured. "You don't have to," he said noticing her guilt. Ally smiled back. "I want to," she said surprising him. Femi rolled her eyes leaving the room.

Chapter 7

"Good morning," Huey said entering Nico's room. He stared in surprise at Nico as he caressed Ally. "What?" he asked getting up. "Breakfast is ready," Huey said as Ally woke up. "What happened?" she asked looking at Nico. "Nothing," Nico answered. Huey held back his laughter. "He was cuddling you," he said laughing loudly. "Get out," Nico said annoyed. Huey walked out attempting to calm down. Nico grabbed a grey shirt and black hoodie. "Are my jeans clean?" he asked turning to Ally.

She blushed as she shook her head yes. Nico grabbed a pair. "You agreed to sleep in here and I'm not letting you sleep on the couch," he said walking behind the divider. "I know," she said grabbing a red t-shirt and pair of blue jeans. She sat on the bed as Nico walked out grabbing a pair of socks and tennis shoes. Ally grabbed a pair of socks walking behind the divider.

Huey walked back in again. "It's getting cold," he said as Nico tied his shoes. Nico threw an O-Pal nearly hitting Huey. "We'll be out in a minute," he said deep in thought. Huey began to walk out. "Wait, My breakfast is in my workshop," Nico pointed out. Ally walked from behind the divider walking over to the calendar. "It is Friday," she said. Nico got up from the bed. "I'll see you later," he said leaving the room.

Ally blushed as he closed the door. "How long have you two known each other?" Huey asked. "Fifteen days," Ally said sighing. She sat on the bed annoyed. "I shouldn't have said that last night," she thought embarrassed. "Are you coming?" Huey asked sarcastically. Ally zipped up her last low heel boot. "Yes," she said running. "Sleep well?" Huey asked smiling mischievously. "Yeah," Ally answered, "What was so funny this morning?" "The way you looked when you woke up," Huey said entering the kitchen.

Ally stared at her plate then to Huey. "Take a seat," Alice said confused, "Unless Huey's being an idiot." "No he isn't, I'll explain later," Ally said taking a seat. Sam turned to Ally for answers. "Don't ask," she retorted. Femi looked at her master puzzled. "You offered," she thought weirded out.

Night drove into the driveway of the school stopping at the front door. "Have a good day," she said giving Carmen her lunchbox. "Okay," Carmen said grinning. Night watched as she entered the school. She drove away watching the people pass by finally pulling into the parking lot of a building marked 'Midnight's Nursery'. "Hello Miss Fiore," A short woman said excited. "Hey Samantha," Night said walking in. The teachers ran around taking care of the kids. One smiled mischievously as a block disappeared nearby reappearing in green smoke in front of him. "No Brendon," Night said, walking into the classroom, "Give it back." The boy glared making the brick disappear and reappear next to its original owner. She walked out entering the teacher's lounge. Two teachers stared at her.

"What?" she asked. One walked up. "We just heard that Alette Bellerose moved in with Sam. Was it for Nico?" he asked curious. "They're engaged," Night said calmly. "They just met," A young woman said nearby, "Didn't they?" "It was arranged thirteen years ago," she pointed out, "And they visited during the summer." The two employees stared in shock unaware of this information. She walked out walking into the same room. A little girl gave Night the puppy dog eyes. "What is it?" Night asked. The girl turned to Brendon.

"If only she could speak," Night thought annoyed. She turned to a teacher nearby. "Could you take care of Brendon please?" She asked. "Sure," he answered.

Nico stared at his completed work, the completed O-Pal that begged to be designed. A knocking on the door caught his attention. "Hello," he said as his eyes narrowed. "It's me, Sam sent you something," Ally said dryly. Nico opened the door surprised as she gave him a weird look. "I'm getting used to living here and being around you," she said handing him a coffee. Nico took the cup gladly. "Thank you. Want to come in?" he asked stepping aside. Ally raised an eyebrow. She pointed to a sign that said 'Leave me alone'. "That's contradictory to your sign," she said.

"Well the sign doesn't include you," he blushed. "Perhaps another time," she said trying to get away. Nico gave her a sad look. "I mean...I'd love to," she said walking in. He covered the O-Pal. "What do you think?" he asked turning to her.

Ally looked around the room. The walls were covered with pictures and models of O-Pals, the workbench was full of tools and parts and a picture sat on the nearby table. She walked over removing the dust off the old photo. "I didn't know you had a picture of me from three years ago," she said staring at the picture in shock. The fifteen year old girl in the pink school uniform smiled back. Her wavy blonde hair and crystal blue eyes showing what her smile hid. "I guess it makes sense," she pointed out.

"Yeah I was a brat until that picture showed up," Nico pointed out concerned. Ally turned to him empathetic. "Is that why you changed?" she asked putting the picture back. "Yeah, you looked like you needed a friend," he explained, "Of course we didn't know Alexander didn't tell you." "He has memory lapses. Good thing sometimes cause he had a bad childhood. My mother was the best thing that happened to him," she explained. "Sounds a lot like me," Nico thought concerned. "Well Alice is waiting for me," she headed for the door. "Thanks," he sounded happy, "I'm glad you swung by."

Josh listened to the conversation in the closed room nervous. "What's wrong?" A girl asked walking up. Her long straight grey and white hair made her stand out of a crowd, while her ice blue eyes glimmered. She wore a black and red tank top and black jeans with low heeled grey boots making her slender figure obvious. "He's talking to her," he said nervous. "Really," the girl smiled excited as she listened in. "He found her, Alexandria," Josh gave her a terrified look. Alexandria laughed. "What's funny?" A tall man asked curious. Alexandria gave him a death glare. "Damon found Alette," She said smiling big revealing her fangs.

"He has what?" Alice gave Ally a surprised look. "It wasn't that creepy," Ally pet Femi who purred. "It isn't, it sounds like it," Alice pointed out. Ally stared at the ground. "He's three years older and completely obsessed," she said nervous. "From what I heard Alexander is pretty clever. He would not have set this up if he thought Nico was dangerous," Alice pointed out. Ally stared at the clouds. "But he was eight," she said anxious, "But still..." "That's my point, you grew up with him. You know him," Alice pointed out.

"Hello," Night said popping out of nowhere. She looked at Ally, her eye glimmering. "You should take that as a compliment. It means he's trying," she said sitting in the grass. "How is he trying?" Ally asked. "He has a few friends, you are one of them. Plus you had your own room for a little awhile," Night pointed out. "I guess you're right," Ally thought out loud. "You're just like Alex," she said her eye glimmering again. The scene around Night changed to Alexander at age sixteen fighting with his dad. She returned to the present. "He was a rebel too," she said smiling slyly.

Alice laughed. Suddenly she stopped. "You're serious," she said scared. "Of course I am," Night said turning to the Ally, "Nico's looking for you. He just wants to explain." Ally got up heading towards the dugout. "Where are you going?" Alice asked. "To find Nico," Ally entered the dugout followed by Femi. Nico sat on the couch writing in his journal, Ally's reaction running through his head.

"Hey," Ally said still keeping her distance. He ran up hugging her. "Hey, so you're not freaked out by the picture are you?" he said looking her straight in the eye, "It was just a small keepsake." Ally's body became somewhat rigid. "So what is it you do?" she asked curious. "O-Pal designer," he answered honestly. He held her close. "I'm not quite comfortable yet with…intimacy," she spoke honestly. He thought for second as he let go, attempting to let go.

"That makes sense," he said grinning. Ally looked at him puzzle. "Dinners ready," Huey said poking his head in. She got up curious about Nico. "We made such progress," he said positively. "That's good, at least she likes you a little," Huey agreed. "You think?" Nico asked. "Yeah," Huey said plainly, "That's great you've made progress. Just don't lose sight of what you're doing. Now how about we eat before Sam gets mad." "Yeah," Nico followed him out.

Night glared at the television screen as Ally's face sat in a box next to the reporter. "That's right people. Alette Bellerose is now engaged. But people have to ask why and how?" the reporter said trying to engage the audience. She turned off the television trying to ignore her anger.

"Night," Carmen said running downstairs, "Why didn't you take me?" "You had homework," Night said getting up. Carmen sighed. "Can I go tomorrow? It is a weekend," she said giving her the puppy dog eyes. Night smiled in response. "Sure," she said, "But your homework has to be done." Carmen smiled and ran upstairs as Night fell on the couch tired.

Alice poked at her steak. "Looks good," she said gulping nervously. Sam glared at her. "You like everything else I cook," he said insulted. Ally stood up putting her plate in the sink. Nico followed suit, leaving the room. "Does he do that on purpose?" Huey asked. Sam gave him a weird look. "Finish when she does," Huey pointed out. "Probably," Sam answered. Alice took a bite of her steak. "He does most of the time," she said. "I've noticed. Now how about we stop talking about him?" Sam's eye twitched. "Fine," Huey and Alice said in union. Sam sipped his drink. "Good," Sam spoke calmly.

Nico closed the door behind him. He turned to the divider where clothes hung as he walked over to the dresser grabbing pajamas. "Did you take a shower already?" he asked curious. "Yeah," Ally said still in shock. Nico opened the door. "I'll be back," he said closing the door. Ally walked out from behind the divider blushing. She sat on the bed shivering from anxiety.

"Knock, knock," Alice said knocking on the door. Ally opened the door carefully. "I come in peace," Alice said grinning. Ally stepped to the side as Alice entered laughing. "I take you don't hate me anymore," Ally said raising an eyebrow. "More like I can tolerate you...and you're the only other girl here," Alice pointed out sitting on the couch. Ally sat on the couch too.

"So this is how you get girl talk?" Ally asked confused. Alice laughed. "Yeah," she said staring at the stars. "The moon is beautiful," Ally said feeling the coffee table. She opened the drawer revealing the notebooks. "What do you think they're used for?" Alice asked curious. "They're probably private," Ally closed the drawer.

The door opened scaring both girls. "Hey, Nico," Alice said turning to him as he closed the door behind him. "Hey Alice," Nico said surprised. Alice stood up heading toward the door. "See ya later," she said turning to Ally. She smiled weakly back.

"You two seem close," Nico said sitting next to her. "She only comes to me for girl talk," Ally said embarrassed. "Of course," Nico said not surprised. "We should get some sleep," he said standing up. Ally stood up getting into bed.

Nico's sneezed surprising Ally. "Must be allergies," he said holding her close. "Not tonight," she said pushing him away. "Okay," Nico gave her a confused look grabbing a pillow.

Night drove into Sam's driveway. "Be polite," she said turning to Carmen. Carmen gripped her backpack tightly.

Night knocked on the door. "Coming," Sam said answering the door. Carmen stared at him nervously. "You're early," he said surprised. Nico sneezed in the hallway. "His allergies are acting up," Sam sighed.

Night entered removing her glove. She pressed it against his forehead. "He has a fever," she said worried. Sam walked over doing the same thing. "It's a cold," Sam said embarrassed he didn't catch it.

Ally stared at Nico horrified. "Cold," the word slithered out as she ran to the bathroom. "You should laid down," Night said concerned. She turned to Carmen. "You sure you want to stay here?" she asked. Carmen watched as Sam escorted Nico to his room. She turned to Night shaking her head yes. "Fine," Night sounded worried.

Ally left the bathroom. "He's in your room," Night said closing the front the door behind her. Ally looked at the bedroom door warily as Sam left the room.

"Hey Ally. Kind of surprised you're scared of colds," he said pulling her fedora down. "Not scared. Hate! My roommate had horrible remedies," Ally said shaking. "I doubt you're going to get sick," Sam said shrugging.

He turned to Carmen. "How about you put your stuff in the guest room," he said showing her the way. Carmen followed. Ally stared at them as they walked away. "So I'm scared of being sick," she thought, "It's not a phobia."

Nico cuddled the pillow sick as a dog. "Knock, knock," Alice said knocking on the door. She entered holding a bowl of soup. "From Sam," she said putting the bowl down on the table. Nico gave her a worried look as he sat up. "Well I better go," she said leaving.

"What about Ally?" he asked. "We're trying to get her in here," Alice closed the door.

"Ally," she said going to the living room, "Could you check on your fiancé?" Ally looked up from the television. "Why?" she asked defensively. "He's sick," Alice pointed out, "And he looks lonely." Ally glared at her. "Just saying," Alice said walking away.

Carmen gave Ally a weird look. Ally got up grabbing her trench coat. "Want to come?" she turned to Carmen. She shook her head yes. "Let's head outside," she said happily.

Huey entered the bedroom cautiously. Nico gave him a worried look. "She's outside with Carmen," he said trying to cheer him up. Nico sneezed as he sat up. "She seemed pretty scared of me earlier," he said blowing his nose.

"She doesn't want to catch a cold apparently," Huey said. Nico laid down grabbing the nearest pillow. "Can't sleep?" Huey asked concerned. Nico glared at him. "Fine. I only came to talk to you," Huey said leaving.

Carmen stared at the storm clouds. "That's not good," Ally said sitting next to her. Carmen shook her head yes as Ally gave her a weird look. "Do you talk?" She asked trying to be polite. Carmen shook her head yes. "Is there a reason you don't?" Ally asked curious. She shook her head yes. "Can you tell me?" Ally asked. Carmen shook her head no. She took out a small notebook and pen out of her sweatshirt pocket. She opened it writing it something down handing it to Ally.

"Do you hate Nico?" Ally read surprised, "I'll make a deal. You talk and I'll answer your question. Plus I'll stay with Nico the whole time he is sick." Carmen gave her an excited look as she prepared to speak.

"So she's actually going to talk," Alice said walking over. Carmen stopped embarrassed. "Scared," Alice said concerned. Ally glared at her. "What?" she asked confused. "Ignore her," Ally said turning to Carmen. Carmen got up going back to the dugout. "Alice," Ally thought angrily.

Alora stared at Amunet intensely. "Give it up. It's futile," Amunet said apathetically. "No way," Alora said slightly annoyed. Amunet's eyes narrowed. "Hey guys what are you doing?" Damon asked walking up.

"Staring contest," Alora answered. "You know she wins every time," Damon said sitting next to her. He kissed her cheek. "I forfeit," she said leaning against Damon as she blinked. Amunet walked down the hall. "She does that every time," Alora pointed out. "She's smart," Damon said.

Alice stared at Huey. "You said you needed air," He said sitting outside. "I did," Alice reluctantly agreed. Huey watched the woods as a shadowy figure came into view. "Stay here," he said turning Alice. "Yes sir," Alice said playing on her O-Pal.

Huey ran into the woods looking around carefully. The figure ran by going off the trail. Huey followed fast as the figure ran into a clearing disappeared. Huey stood there confused.

"Hello," he said as the red mist formed a dagger. "Drop the dagger," a cold apathetic voice said from behind him. Huey dropped the dagger making it disappear. "Who are you?" The voice demanded. He felt a hunting knife against his neck. "Huey Driscol," he squeaked.

"Why did you follow me?" She demanded again. "It's my job," he half screamed. The woman lowered the knife slightly. "Give me one reason I shouldn't kill you," she said. "It's my job to deliver and protect Ally and company," Huey answered. The woman lowered her knife completely. "Thank you," he said catching his breath.

He turned around to a teenager standing behind him. "That's my job too. I'm Amunet," She said, "Nice to meet you." Huey held his throat for safety. "Nice eye color," he said attempting to compliment her, "Are you here alone?" "I'm here with friends," Amunet eyed Huey suspiciously.

Huey let go of his neck noticing the look in her eyes. "Where are your friends?" he asked. "Home," she answered. "She looks dead," he thought sadly. Amunet headed for the woods.

"Wait, may I escort you?" he asked. "No, I can get there myself," she answered. "You sure," he said. She disappeared as an answer. "Great," Huey thought worried, "She's gone."

Carmen sat on the couch staring intensely at Ally. "The deal is still in effect," Ally said mischievously. Carmen smiled excited. "Really," she said in a musical voice. Ally eyed her suspiciously. "Yeah," she said. Carmen laughed.

"I don't hate him. I'm confused at the moment," she answered staring at the rain outside. Carmen gave her a confused look as Ally stood up. "Now to fulfill the second part of the deal," she said putting on a white mask. Carmen followed.

"You're going to join me?" Ally asked confused. "Yeah," she said shaking her head yes. She cautiously opened the door to Nico asleep. She walked over sitting on the couch. Carmen sat next to her.

"Ally," Nico said sitting up. She turned to him nervous. His face lit up making Ally smile under the mask. He turned to Carmen. "Night won't be happy if you're sick," he pointed out. Carmen hugged Ally before she left.

"She likes you," Nico said. "You think," Ally retorted surprised. "Yeah," he said smiling. He blew his nose making Ally scoot away. "You don't have to stay," he said turning to her. "I made a deal with

Carmen. She talks, I stay," She said tying her mask, "Besides it's just a cold."

Nico smiled weakly. "That's you," he said laying down, "Thanks." Ally gave him a puzzled look. "You okay?" he asked yawning. Ally looked at the table. "Yeah," she said tired.

"Knock, knock," Sam said opening the door. "Hello," he looked at Ally surprised, "Are you his nurse?" "Yes, can't you tell by my mask," she answered sarcastically. Sam laughed. "Okay Nurse Bellerose," he said putting medicine on the side table. Nico sat up taking the medicine. "Take good care of him," Sam said leaving the room.

She laid down staring at the ceiling. "What have I gotten myself into," she thought.

Chapter 8

Alice stared at the night sky curious. "What are you looking for?" Huey asked as he laid in bed. "Nothing," Alice lied. "You should get some sleep," Huey pointed out. Alice laid down sleepy. "Good night," she said yawning. "Good night," Huey repeated. "I wonder how Amunet is sleeping," he thought sadly.

Amunet laid in the bed confused by the day's events. She wondered how Huey was and why he was so nice. "Not many people are nice to me," she thought, "It's because of the eyes I think." "Are you alright?" Alora asked worried. "Did something happen?" Damon sounded concerned, "You never have trouble sleeping." "I ran into someone," she answered. "A crush perhaps?" Alora thought. "Who was it?" Damon asked. "Huey Driscol," she answered. "You mean Huey Stephen Driscol?" Damon asked surprised. "Yes," Amunet answered, "Though he didn't say his middle name. Why is he important?" "No reason," Alora answered nonchalantly, "Let's just go to bed." Amunet went back to bed even more confused.

Ally laid on the couch attempting to sleep as Nico watched from the bed. "We can switch places," he suggested. Ally looked up her, mask gone. "No thank you," she said laying down. Nico sighed. He closed his eyes attempting to sleep. Ally whimpered at she fell asleep making Nico look at her nervous. "That's not good," he thought.

Ally stood in her parent's mansion watching the clock on the wall. The room was empty except for two chairs. "Take a seat," Catherine said sitting down. Ally sat down confused. "You know I love you," her mother said sounding hurt. "Of course I do," Ally answered getting drowned out by the clock's ticking. "Then why do you doubt my words," a closet door opened at her mother's words revealing complete darkness. Ally screamed as a light illuminated a tombstone marked 'Catherine Bellerose'

Nico held Ally close trying to comfort her. Ally looked up screaming. Nico's white mask scared her half to death. "Sorry," he said sniffling, "I didn't want to get you sick." Ally cuddled back as he let go. "I should go back," he said laying down in bed. Ally laid down attempting to sleep. "She finally gets comfortable enough to cuddle and I can't," he thought.

Sam felt Nico's forehead the next day. "You're fine," he said relieved. Nico smiled happy. He then turned to Ally who was still wearing a mask. "You can take it off," Sam pointed out. Nico watched Ally carefully as she remove her mask.

He got up sitting next to her. "Don't worry it's gone," he pointed out. Ally sighed. "At least you're better," Alice said optimistically. "He's better," Sam pointed out.

Carmen walked in sitting on the bed. Nico stood up looking outside as Ally stared at him confused. "Night's going to be here at noon. You might as well relax," Sam turned to Carmen who shook her head yes. "It still looks like rain," Nico said watching the storm clouds.

Ally played with her fingerless gloves as Alice sat next to her. "How about a game of checkers?" she asked. Ally turned to Carmen. "How about something Carmen can join in," she suggested. "Yeah, bring out the playing cards," Alice said dryly. Carmen looked at Ally smiling.

"How about we watch a movie?" Ally turned to Alice. "What movie?" Alice eyed Carmen suspiciously. "The story of Echo," Ally suggested. "Fine," Alice said begrudgingly, "Let's watch a movie about a nymph." "It is a drama and horror movie in one," Alice thought. Carmen gave Ally two thumbs up. "Let's go," Ally said getting up.

Nico stared at his reflection. His hair was no longer in a controlled mess. He grabbed a brush nearby. "Knock, knock," Huey said entering the room. "What's up?" Nico asked. "She's watching a movie with Alice and Carmen," he said sitting on the couch. "I heard," Nico answered. "Is something wrong?" Huey asked concerned.

"It feels she's still getting used to me," Nico answered. "That's all," Huey gave him a surprised look. "I can't get used this," he pointed out, "I mean we grew up together." He walked over sitting next to Huey. "She probably views you as a friend," Huey suggested trying to cheer him up. Nico glared at the floor. "Doubt that," he said turning to the picture on the side table.

Ally grinned back. "What are you thinking?" Huey asked worried. "If only," Nico answered. Huey looked at him confused. "If only her mother didn't pass away," he pointed out. Huey went deep into thought. "You can't change that, but you can continue to do what you are doing. Just don't come on strong," he suggested. Nico stared at him with a blank stare. "Just saying," Huey said leaving the room. "Such a drama king," He thought.

Alice glared at Carmen. "What did she do?" Ally asked annoyed. "She was talking," she answered. Huey walked by. "What happened?" he asked watching her wipe off the disc and putting it back in. "It was dusty," she said sitting down.

Ally stared at his coat. "Going outside?" She asked, her curiosity now peaked. "Yeah," Huey answered. They watched him leave, hearing the back door slam. "Weird," Alice thought turning to Carmen who just reentered the room, "She's not talking and Huey is acting out of sorts. Why isn't she talking though?"

Huey entered the woods looking around carefully. He looked around to see any footprints. He found none making him nervous. As he walked along the trail he listened carefully for any sign of life.

A breaking branch caught his attention. He turned around to see a thin branch fall from the tree.

"I know it's you," he yelled. Amunet jumped down glaring. "Hello Mr. Driscol," she said in her usual apathetic tone. "Just came to check on you," he looked at her sympathetically. She looked at him annoyed. "How nice," she sneered. "It's that how you treat someone who is worried about you?" he asked insulted.

Amunet walked over standing at his shoulder. "You don't look worried," she pointed out. "I try not to worry," he said sighing. Her eyes narrowed as Huey looked at her straight in the eye.

"Where are you staying?" he asked starting to get nervous. "Somewhere safe," her answer made him think, "You should hurry. It will rain soon." She pulled over her hoodie entering the woods. Huey turned around worried. "I know, I just thought about your safety," he pointed out. A hunting knife flew past his head. "You don't Have to worry about me, Mr. Driscol," she grabbed the knife walking away from a shocked Huey.

Ally walked down the hallway putting the movie back on the shelf. She turned around to Alice. "How do you do it?" she asked. "Do what?" Ally asked in response. "Get Carmen to talk to you," Alice sounded desperate. "I was polite," she answered honestly. "Really?" Alice said, surprised. "Yeah," Ally answered. "Is that why she doesn't like me?" Alice asked. "You're not the most 'personable' person," Ally said, trying to be careful. "I'm not, huh. I'll prove to you I am," Alice said, taking on the challenge.

She walked into the living room sitting next to Carmen. "Hello, how is your day?" she asked. Carmen just stared. "Do you have any hobbies?" Alice asked. "Can you talk?" she asked curious. Carmen glared. "Yes jerk. Now leave me alone," Carmen's voice suddenly got a mystical quality to it that almost otherworldly. "Yes of course I will," Alice said too willingly.

Ally stared at Alice suspicious. "You're psychic aren't you?" she asked turning to Carmen. Carmen shook her head yes. "You should reverse it," Ally suggested. "You can bother me," Carmen said.

Alice shook her head puzzled. "What happened?" she asked. "Nothing," Ally said. Alice looked at her confused. A knock on the door caught her attention. Sam answered to Night as Carmen ran up excited.

Alice walked up. "What happened?" she asked turning to Ally. "She's a siren. It's a type of psychic that controls you with their voice," Night explained closing the door. "She can't be serious," Alice said in shock, "I thought they lived in Scotland." Ally sighed. "That explains it," she thought, "She must have Scottish heritage and pretty strong heritage at that."

Ally sat on the couch watching the news. "And it will snow tonight," The reporter announced happily. It's been three days since Carmen's secret came out and Alice had the biggest problem with it. She said the word 'registered' so much that Ally usually had to leave the room. Plus it's been twenty days since Ally moved in. Nico didn't help by crossing out the days on the calendar. Alice walked by the living room silent. "We were getting along so well," she thought sadly.

Huey walked in sitting across from Ally. "Alice ignoring you too?" he asked. "Yeah. She has been for three days," she answered hurt. "I seriously thought she liked you," he turned to the television, "Snow? Cool." Alice walked by again disappearing with a door slam. "At least she leaves the door unlocked," Huey said sighing.

Nico walked by stretching his newly freed hand. "What's wrong?" he asked sitting next to Ally. "Alice is ignoring everyone," Huey said annoyed. "You're telling me," Nico said, frustrated. "We've noticed," Ally said cuddling up to him. Nico held her close. "I'm in here," Huey pointed out. Ally pushed away. "Come on," Nico said annoyed, "This is unfair." Huey sighed as Nico kissed Ally on the cheek. She got up blushing. Nico watched as she left the room. "I blame you," he told Nico. He heard the door close. Huey got up entering his room.

"Weird," Nico thought, "You would think she would lock the door." He entered his room locking the door. Ally stared at the stars through the window. "We should get some sleep," Nico grabbed his pajamas, "Did you take a shower?" Ally shook her head yes.

Nico walked behind the divider while Ally grabbed her pajamas. "Could you stay behind there?" she asked remembering the night of Cassandra's party. "Sure," Nico answered confused. Ally got dressed quickly. "You're safe," she said.

He walked out from the divider smiling mischievously. "I guess we're even," he pointed out. Ally glared at him. "I accidentally tripped," he said blushing embarrassed. "You knew I saw you," Her voice was full of rage. "What's the big deal?" He asked nonchalantly. "I was embarrassed," Ally said. Nico listened as she ranted for a couple of minutes. "And you're not shutting me up," she said surprised. "You're venting. Why would I?" he asked.

Ally blushed. "Now how about you go to bed," he suggested. Ally laid down in bed embarrassed by her actions. Nico moved her bangs trying to calm her down. "That looks better on you," he said moving to the couch and grabbing a notebook. "Good night," Ally said lying in bed and closing her eyes.

Alice took a bite of her cereal ignoring everyone. "Who is she angry at?" Ally wondered. Huey put his plate in the sink smiling at the snow. "Looks like fun," he said turning to Alice. Alice ignored him. "You should at least watch," Sam pointed out annoyed. He picked up everyone's dishes, "How about you? It is snow."

Ally grabbed her trench coat. "Come on," She said turning to Alice and Huey. Huey followed acting childlike and trying to get ahead of her. Alice followed sitting against a tree as Ally made a snowball throwing it at Huey. Huey dodged it, throwing one back. Alice glared at them intensely as she watched. Sam watched from the kitchen. "At least she's having fun," he thought.

Nico stared at the snow from his workshop. He put the final touches on his latest design. "Everyone's having fun," he thought turning to his electronic. He turned to the clock to see it saying 12:00pm. "I could get off early," he said, "That's a great plan." He grinned at his plan. "I think I will," he said excited.

Ally threw a snowball at Huey hitting his arm. "Two out of three," he said mischievously. "Fine," she said turning to Alice. "Want to join?" she asked inviting her. "Do I want to join?" she echoed insulted, "You two are hiding something. Why would I?" "You've disappeared four times this month," she said to Ally unusually calm. "And you won't tell me what's going on," she pointed out her voice raised talking to Huey. "Calm down," Sam said trying to calm her down. "You're one to talk. You did the greatest act of all: disappearing for seventeen years," she said angrily. "Just calm down," Ally said concerned. "You would want that. You would want me to be happy. I don't even like you," she said. Ally glared as a tear fell down her cheek.

"I'm going for a walk," she said entering the woods. Femi followed growling at Alice. "That was uncalled for," Nico said surprising everyone. Everyone turned around to see Nico looking actually mad. "She's been nothing but nice to you," he pointed out, "Plus she's overemotional. Why would you tell her that?" Huey and Sam walked away avoiding the situation. "Well look how you've been treated," she said protecting him.

Nico glared at her with a glare worse than Alice's. "Apologize," he demanded. Alice glared back. "You heard me," he said pointing to the woods. Alice entered the woods reluctantly.

""Ally! Ally!" Alice yelled annoyed, "Ally!" A familiar growl caught her attention. She turned to see Femi sitting behind her. "Where is she?" she demanded. Femi ran away leaving her paw prints in the snow. Alice followed unsure of Femi's intentions. She stopped to Femi being petted by Alora.

"Who are you?" she asked. "Ally's friend. Who are you?" Alora asked. "Alice Coupe," Alice's tone turned dignified. Alora smiled slyly. "Nice to meet you," she said. "What's your name?" Alice demanded. "Alora," She answered sweetly but slyly .

Alice raised an eyebrow. "She's that way. She seems hurt," Alora said pointing the way, "That wouldn't be your fault?" Alice walked by ignoring Alora and Femi.

She walked around confused finally stopping at a tree. Ally sat underneath it crying. "What do you want?" she asked hurt. "Just to talk," Alice said trying to hold back her anger. Ally glared at her. "I'm sorry," Alice said crossing her arms and sitting down. "You don't mean it," Ally's eyes turned gold out of anger. "I did," Alice retorted.

Ally pulled her knees in close in while wiping her tears. "Stop crying," Alice said. Ally glared at her. "Fine," she said, "Let's talk." A sudden whipping wind suddenly got their attention. Alice noticed the wind stopped after a few seconds. Looking up she saw what looked like a golden a barrier. Ally glared. "I'm listening," she said.

Nico looked around nervous. "Ally," he said. "This is harder than it looks," Night said looking around. Nico sighed. "Will we find them?" He asked. "Of course. I haven't lost anyone yet," Night said proudly. "Note she said yet," Huey thought.

"Hey, guys. Looks like Femi is looking for her as well," Huey yelled nearby. Everyone walked up to see fox tracks. "She's leading us to her," Night pointed out. "How are we sure those are Femi's tracks?" Sam asked. "I am a retro-teacher," Night pointed out. Nico ran following them. "Wait for us," Night yelled.

Ally put the barrier down slowly. She picked up the snow making it into a ball. "Cool," Alice said trying to start a conversation. Ally threw the snowball at her. "I deserved that," Alice said. Ally stayed silent. "You're going to have to talk sometime," Alice grinned. Ally sat there quietly. "Fine, Just listen," Alice sighed,

"I was suspicious of you and...everyone else," She looked deep in thought, "The truth is you're my first friend outside my family." Ally gave her a sympathetic look. "Say something," Alice demanded. "You're my friend too," she said surprising Alice. "Is that good," Alice thought. "Wait what about everyone else?" Alice asked. "Yeah," she said, "They are all my friends." Alora came to mind only to be pushed out. Ally looked down sad.

"What's wrong?" Alice asked concerned. "Nothing, "She looked up putting on a fake smile. "She's sad about Nico. He knows what he wants. She doesn't know what she wants," Alice thought.

"Have you ever flirted?" She asked curious. "No," Ally answered, "I went to an all-girls' school. I did flirt with him over the summer." "I didn't know that actually stopped flirting," Alice thought, "it's not like that kind of human urge magically goes away- especially with teenage girls." "Well Nico cares," she said, "Try remembering that." Ally shook her head in agreement. "I know, everything seems different now that we're engaged," she pointed out. "Marriage makes everything...," Alice stopped for a second thinking, "Better!" Ally raised an eyebrow. "You mean 'friendships', right?" she asked. "Yeah," Alice agreed. "Good, you were scaring me," Ally pointed out.

Femi ran up jumping on Ally. "Femi," Ally said surprised. "Ally! Alice!" Nico said running out of the woods. Night walked out calmly. "Nice that you're safe," she said. Nico helped Ally up. "Really sis," Huey said helping Alice up. Ally was shivering cold as Nico held her close, picking her up bridal style, warming her up. "Let's hurry home," he said feeling her forehead, "Looks you might be sick." Ally's eyes widened as Night led the way out. "Watch out for Nico's traps," she said.

Alice looked at Huey scared. "We're smarter than that," Alice said. She was suddenly caught by a net. "Warned you," Night pointed out. Huey untied the rope. "Thank you," Alice said embarrassed.

Chapter 9

Ally laid on the couch taking a nap. "She's tired," Sam said worried. "I haven't seen her sleep this much since last week," Nico said holding a screwdriver. "How did she sleep last night?" Sam asked curious. "Well except for the nightmares fine," he answered.

Ally yawned as she opened her eyes. She looked at Nico smiling slightly. He sat next to her. "Good morning," he said. He moved her hair out of her eyes. "Your hair is getting longer," he pointed out. "I know; that's why I have a hair appointment today," she said feeling her hair which was now down half her back. "Would you mind terribly if I come along?" Nico asked curious. Sam laughed making Nico stare. "You're serious," he said stopping, "Of course you're serious." He left the room quietly.

He left the room whistling. "So.. can I?" Nico looked innocent. "Sure," Ally answered. He hugged her happily,surprising her with how strongly he squeezed . "Uh, I thought you just jogged a bunch?" she asked. "No, I work out too," Nico pointed out. letting her go to set his arms in a pose, which only made her good-naturedly roll her eyes at him.

Ally walked over grabbing her trench coat as Nico followed. "So where's the appointment?" he asked. "Salon Flame," Ally answered, "You the place I assume." "Well in that caser, we should hurry," Nico said starting the car. Ally stared out the window as he pulled out the driveway. "I have an acquaintance who works there," he said driving carefully. Ally gave him a befuddled look as they entered the main road. "Nice guy- well, once you get to know him anyway," he explained. "Is that good?" Ally asked. "Not really," Nico said driving to town.

Nico drove into the parking lot taking the closest spot. "Come on," he said opening her door for her. Ally gave him a confused look. "Please don't give me that look. You've known me for most of our lives. You should actually trust me by now... a little bit," he said unknowingly taking her hand. Ally blushed as he led her away.

They entered to two giggling girls at the cash register. Both stopped as they entered with one looking at Nico annoyed. "May I help you?" The other said typing. "Alette Bellerose," Ally said letting go of Nico's hand. The annoyed girl looked Ally over carefully as if inspecting her. "You're not Cassandra Favre," the other girl pointed out. Ally looked at her nametag. "Lizzie, that's my cousin," Ally glared at the girl insulted. "Lizzie, don't insult her. Artemis would shoot us," Stephanie warned, "Now, who's her stylist?" "Steven," Lizzie answered. "Did you say Artemis as in Artemis Favre?" Nico asked. "Yes," Lizzie answered. Nico stared at Ally in shock. "The family matriarch is her grandmother," Nico thought.

A guy with brown hair and green eyes walked up glaring at Nico. "She's your one o'clock," Stephanie said giggling. Steven turned to Ally surprised. "Follow me," he said. Ally followed turning to Nico. "Please follow me," Steven continued. Ally turned around following. "Here you go," he said stopping at chair across the room. Ally sat down puzzled. "Don't worry. He's being smart," he said as she sat, "He talked about you nonstop." Ally blushed.

"So what do you want?" he asked curious. "Anything as long as it's this long," she answered, "With bangs." Steven looked at her carefully. "Okay," he said mischievously. Nico watched from far away scared. "So who Artemis Favre to Ally?" he asked. The girls looked mortified. "Who are you to ask?" Lizzie demanded. "Ally's fiancé, Nico Katsaros. What, did you think I was just some random groupie of hers?" he asked. "Maybe," Lizzie answered. "Artemis is her grandmother," Stephanie said freely, "But I would talk to Adrian about that." "Adrian?" Nico asked. "Her ex-husband," Lizzie answered, "Here is his address." Nico took it realizing it was just

down the street. "Tell Ally I'll be right back," he said. "Good luck,"
Stephanie sounded sarcastic, "Guy's a total loon far as I can tell."
"Always helping," Lizzie thought.

Nico knocked on the studio apartment door surprised by the
abode. "I'm coming," Adrian yelled coming to the door. He opened
the door to a man in his mid-fifties with straight, short salt and
pepper hair and chestnut eyes wearing a polo shirt, blue jeans and
Velcro tennis shoes. "Hello, I'm Nico Katsaros and I know your son,
Alexander," he said. "Xander? How is he? How is Kitty and Ally?
Please come in," Adrian stood aside as Nico entered worried. "He's
doing fine, Mr. Bellerose," he entered unsure. The door closed
changing the room. "So Nico, you're the guy who's been visiting my
granddaughter," Adrian changed almost completely.

"I thought...," Nico stuttered unsure of how to answer. "Chill,
young man; I'm not Seth and I'm not going to kill you," Adrian
pointed out, "I honestly wanted to know how my Xander and Ally are
doing." Nico stared in shock. "What's wrong?" he asked. "Most
flames, don't get to this point, especially sane," Nico pointed out,
"You're actually...healthy." "Only to a point. Ally's energy wave isn't
going to last too much longer," he explained. "Ally's energy wave?"
Nico asked. "I almost Burned when she was a toddler, when I started
to change. Her body reacted by sending a wave of energy to block
and slow down the process," he explained, "The doctors don't how
long I have. I personally think it's five years on the outside if I'm
lucky; though it seems like a cruel irony that my son might Burn out
before I do." Adrian grimaced at that. "Don't tell Ally I said that; last
thing I want is to not sound grateful for what she did."

"So you're not what I expected," Steven said surprised. "What
did you expect?" she asked not knowing the answer. "Someone rude,
like Cassandra Favre," he said turning the chair around, "Long
enough?" She looked at her hair which was now one third past her
shoulder.

"Yeah," she said. "Personally Nico got really annoying with the description. Never a name," he said moving onto the bangs.

Ally closed her eyes. "Take a look," he turned her to the mirror. Ally looked it over carefully. "Looks good," she said, "Thank you." She got up walking to the register paying her bill only to see Nico gone from the waiting area. "Where is Nico?" she asked. "Went down to the street to see Adrian Bellerose," Lizzie said bluntly as she paid, "Here's the address." "Do you always drop numbers," Ally asked. "Only your relatives," she answered. Ally left shocked.

A knock on the door interrupted them. "Nico!" Ally almost yelled. "I'll get it," Nico was stopped by Adrian. "I'll get it, how about you hide," he suggested. Nico ran into a closet closing the door while Adrian answered his door. "Who are you?" Ally asked staring at Adrian. "Kitty, please come in," he stood aside. Ally entered as the door closed making a change in the room again. "Okay Grandpa, what's going on?" she asked. "You never call and end up on my doorstep," Adrian pointed out. "I'm sorry grandfather, you're the one who just vanished after mom died," she pointed out. "Xander needed to take care of you and he didn't full excess to the money. The only way he would get it, and not Artemis, is if I gave it to him," he explained. "Then why disappear?" Ally demanded. "Quit acting spoiled! Have you met your grandmother. She was pissed when she found out," he exclaimed. "Found out what?" Ally asked. "You're a Healer," Adrian answered. Ally sighed. "Nico, out of the closet," He said. Nico walked out sad. "Did they send Kitty off to war?" he asked. "No," he answered. "Let's go," Ally left angry with Nico. "She had to find out sometime," Adrian thought.

Huey laid on the couch taking a nap. A loud noise bothered him waking him up to Sam watching TV. "Good morning," Sam said mischievously. Alice sat across from him reading a book as Ally entered the room. "Nice," Alice said noticing her hair. "At least it's lighter," Huey pointed out yawning. Nico entered smiling mischievously as he tried to lighten the mood. "What?" Ally asked curious attempting to ignore him. "Nothing," he answered going to the bedroom.

Ally entered carefully. Nico sat on the couch deep in thought. He got up pushing the hair out of her eyes. "I like that look," he said. She watched as he sat down. "So what did you two talk about?" he asked trying to keep preoccupy her mind. "Nothing important," Ally answered sitting next to him. Nico gave her a look.

"Ok, but I heard my name," he pointed out. "Why didn't he like you?" she asked. "Talked about you too much," he answered. Ally shivered at the thought. "You okay?" he asked concerned. She shook her yes her mind no longer distracted. Nico bit his lip realizing his mistake. "It's my fault, I went to see him," he thought, "She didn't have to learn the truth." "I wonder what's going on in your head?" he inquired worried. Ally looked at the clock. "We were there for one hour," she said surprised. "No wonder Sam was laughing," he thought.

Alora walked through the woods, acupuncture needle ready. "You're sure they went this way?" Amunet whispered, unsure. "Yeah," Alora answered serious, "I'm sure." She heard a crackle in the leaves nearby causing her to throw her needle. She listened closely as it hit a tree. Amunet watched as she ran to the tree like a fox removing if from the trunk. "You missed," Amunet spoke blandly. "I never miss," Alora smiled slyly as she washed a drop of blood off her weapon.

Alice typed on her O-Pal bringing up a file. A woman with red hair and familiar grey eyes popped up. "Alora Jones," she thought worried. "Why bring her up?" Huey asked concerned. "No reason," Alice said remembering Alora from the woods. She read her file getting more nervous by the minute. "She's a Class A assassin," she thought worried. The memory came back to her of Alora talking to her about Ally. "Why and How?" she thought. "Well come on," Huey said turning off the O-Pal. Alice followed reluctantly.

Ally sat at the kitchen table talking to Night and Nico. "I'm fine," she said nervous and scared. "What's going on?" Alice asked worried. "She's been having nightmares," Nico said biting his lip. "They look pretty serious for you to act like that," Night said worried, "There more like 'night terrors'." "I'm fine. It's nothing," she said trying reassure everyone. Alice sat next to Ally. "I'm sure she's fine," she said defending her.

Nico glared at Alice intensely. "She pushes me away every night. I can't comfort her," he said angrily. "She let you cuddle her some nights," Night pointed out attempting to comfort him. "Still," Nico got up leaving the kitchen table. Ally gave him a confused and anxious look. "He just wants to know what's wrong," Night sighed, "How about you think about telling him." Ally got up leaving the room unsure.

"She's got used to him," Huey said trying to stay optimistic. "She still doesn't trust him," Alice's voice sounded rational. "Everything changes with time," Night said nostalgically, "After all no one can stop the day turning to night." Alice stared at her, scared. "What happened to you?" she thought worried.

Ally sat in the living room depressed. "You okay?" Sam asked worried. "He took the day off for me," she answered hurt. Sam raised an eyebrow. "Nico worries about you all the time. He doesn't understand you sometimes," he pointed out.

Ally thought about her mistake sadly. "And you turned him down," Sam gave her a disappointed look. "He surprised me," she explained. "I thought you liked surprises," Nico stood in the doorway concerned. Sam walked away whistling as Nico entered the room sitting next Ally. She blushed lightly.

"You know I won't hurt you," he said looking down. "I know," she said honestly, "My dad wouldn't have picked you out if he thought you would." Nico glared. "Remember the time I put static electricity in your hair?" she asked trying to start conversation. "My hair is still that way," he pointed out. "I know, you were eighteen when I did that," she pointed out, "Before that your hair was, slicked back you called it?" Both laughed at the memory. "What was I thinking," he said calming down, "Besides your hair was short at fifteen." "I know," she sighed satisfied at the thought, "You always laughed." Ally gave him a sympathetic look. "You okay?" she asked. "Yeah," he said getting up. He gave her a weak smile.

Alice sat against the tree staring at the clear blue sky. "He's been depressed today," she said talking to her O-Pal. A woman with black hair in a bun and cat eyes wearing a black suit talked back. "You don't say?" her voice was forceful yet kind. "Yes mom. Ally is also getting depressed easier too," Alice said her normally rational voice shaky.

Her mother picked up a nameplate marked 'Khepri Coupe' playing with it lightly. "She's getting used to him," she said smiling. Alice smiled comforted by her mother being on the other end. "So how about your father?" Khepri asked almost demanding now. "He's…full of surprises," Alice answered. "He's always has been," she thought, "Short tempered too, but that's another matter. Is Nico as good as explained?" "Of course," Alice answered, "He reminds me of Dad." Khepri glared at something off screen. "I'll have to call you back," she said hanging up.

Alice sighed. "I haven't spoken to her in how long?" she thought insulted, "Someone probably took an unauthorized break." Huey sat next to her. "Talk to mom?" he asked. "Yeah, she's busy," Alice said disappointed, "Sorry you missed it." "She runs the Crimson Knights. Doesn't surprise me," Huey pointed out. "She doesn't seem to worry much…. at least on the outside," she said deep in thought. "She's probably worried to death," Huey said sighing. Alice sighed as well. "Yeah you're right," Alice answered.

Alora looked out the window annoyed. The shadowy figure disappeared into the woods. "I don't like this," she said turning to Damon," They're waiting." Damon sat down deep in thought. "On who though?" Amunet asked slightly confused. "Isn't it obvious," Alora said turning to Damon and Amunet, "Ally's their target." Damon sighed. "You pick her up next time," he said turning to Alora, "I'm not stopping the lessons just yet. We've only had four." "As you wish," she said bowing.

Chapter 10

Ally felt people stare at her as she walked through the grocery store. "Did we have to go grocery shopping today?" She asked nervously. "Nico usually comes along and he wouldn't this time unless you did," Sam answered. "It was Sam's idea," Nico lied. Sam glared at him. "Let's go check out the candy aisle," Nico said dragging Ally along. Ally stared at the aisle full of sweets. "What do you want?" Nico asked curious. She gave him a slight smile. "How about those?" she said pointing to a bag of chocolate bars. Nico picked them up. "Sure," he said grabbing them and a box of cookies.

"Find what you need?" Sam laughed as he pushed the cart over. Nico put the treats on top of the pile. "Yeah," he answered. Ally followed as Sam got into line. Nico put the food on as the girl gave Ally a strange look. "Is there something in my teeth?" Ally asked getting her mirror out. "You must be the girl Nico talked about," the girl said swiping the food, "I'm Rocket." "Nice to meet you," Ally said embarrassed. "Hey Rocket, this is…," Nico was cut off by Rocket typing on a virtual keyboard. "Alette. It was in the paper," She said fixing her blonde dyed hair. Sam paid while Nico took the cart with Ally who was curious.

"How many people do know you?" she asked turning to Nico. "I had a lot of acquaintances," he said unloading the cart, "And only a few friends." "Of course," Ally said not surprised.

Alice sat against the tree staring at the driveway. "They should be home soon," Huey said sitting next to her. She looked up to the rain clouds. "It doesn't look good," she said ominously. Huey raised an eyebrow as Sam drove in.

"Here to help?" Sam asked exiting the van. "Yeah," Huey said standing up. Alice followed suit. Nico opened the trunk handing Ally two bags. Alice grabbed three of them handing them to Huey. "It went well?" she asked grabbing three of them for herself. Sam grabbed some as Nico grabbed the rest closing the trunk. "It did," Nico said opening the door. Huey and Ally were putting food away. Alice was putting refrigerated stuff away. Ally stopped for a second staring outside. Nico gave her a concerned look as Ally quickly put a jar of peanut butter away. "I'm taking a walk," she said going out the glass doors. Alice stared at her worried.

Alora stood there holding a kunai. "Hello," she said smiling nervously. "Hello," Ally gave her a puzzled look. "Amunet is with Damon, so I'll be guiding you today," Alora said in her usual sarcastic tone. Ally followed her closely.

"You look happier," Alora pointed out. "Of course I am," she said grinning. Alora looked at her surprised. "Could it be you like him?" she asked. Ally blushed. "Just saying," Alora pointed out. Ally looked around.

"You could tell too," Alora took out an acupuncture needle. She threw it causing Nico to fall out of a tree his arm paralyzed. She took the needle out putting it somewhere else releasing his arm. Ally glared at him. "I was worried," he said walking over. He took her hand making her blush. Alora stared wide eyed. "How cute...let's keep moving," she said taking the lead.

Nico held Ally's hand tight. "So what's the deal? Are you two dating?" she asked smiling mischievously. "We're engaged," Nico pointed out. "I'll have to tell Amunet. I'm sure she didn't mean to injure your hand," Alora pointed out. Nico turned to Ally. "I'm ignoring that line," she said annoyed. Nico sighed. "Here we are," Alora said entering a clearing revealing the abandoned prison, "He figured he would teach you here today."

Ally gave her a suspicious look. "Don't worry...What's your name by the way?" Alora turned to Nico. "Nico," he answered. "We're not going to hurt you," Alora's sarcastic voice didn't help, "Well Amunet might but she's not exactly a people person."

She grabbed an airborne dagger by the handle. "Amunet! He's with Ally," she yelled annoyed. Amunet jumped out of the tree annoyed and angry. "Avoid her at all cost," Alora said in a serious tone. Damon walked out as Ally walked into the prison. "Ally," he said excited. Nico stared at him surprised. "Who are you?" Damon turned to Nico surprised. "Nico Katsaros, her fiancé," He answered defensively. "Nice to meet you," Damon said, "Well follow me." Both Ally and Nico followed him.

Ally stared at the light bulb on the table confused. "What is that for?" she asked. "Your lesson," Damon explained. "What am I supposed to do?" she asked. "Light it," Alora said about to laugh. Ally glared at the thought.

"You can't be serious? This is your bright idea?" she asked. "Yeah," Damon answered. "Fine," she picked the light bulb. "Now just transfer your energy to it," Damon explained. Ally sighed as she easily lit the light bulb. "Really," Alora said surprised, "Looks like lessons one paid off."

"Yeah," Damon said, "Now onto lesson two." Ally gave him a confused look. "Amunet said you could manipulate fire a little...How good is that skill?" he asked. "About half way," Ally answered. "Great. Now let's see where we can start," Damon said excited at the thought.

Nico sat outside with Amunet. "Why did you follow her?" she asked. "To make sure she's safe," he answered. Amunet sighed. "Whatever?" she said. Nico looked around the prison staring at the barren contents. "Can't you live somewhere else?" he asked. "Not without the press knowing," she pointed out. "Because of Damon?" he asked curious. "Yeah," she answered, "It's not easy being him. Fake IDs don't help either." "What can I do to help," he thought.

Alice sat in the tree watching the abandoned prison carefully. She yawned as she stared at the windows as if watching TV. "I thought she caught me," she said relieved. Alora's stare came to mind. "I'm just lucky Nico was around," she said smiling, "That dagger looked sharp." A breaking twig caught her attention. She looked around suspicious. Another twig nearby snapped it seemed. "Idiot," she thought jumping into action. She ran swiftly chasing the culprit. All of a sudden she ran into a clearing with nobody to be found. "What the...?" She said entering cautiously. Alice looked down scared. A picture of her chasing the culprit, from the culprit's perspective, stared back.

Ally smiled as she controlled the candle in front of her perfectly. "How's the lesson going?" Nico asked walking in. Ally stopped keeping calm. "I'll escort both of you out," Amunet said opening the door. Ally and Nico followed.

He held her hand for support scared of Amunet slightly. His gloved hand felt weird against Ally's fingerless gloves. "You shouldn't worry. There are worse people than me," Amunet said opening the exit for him. The door shut behind them. "Friends of yours?" he asked. Ally stayed silent for a second. "Yeah," she said. "Why haven't you bought me with you? Especially with all the traps," he pointed out, "Some are majorly dangerous." Ally stopped in her tracks. "Can't I explore the land a little," she said.

Nico gave her a hurt look. "At least you're honest," he said. Ally looked shocked. "I am?" she asked confused. "Yeah, you're one of the rare people I allowed in," he said leading the way. Ally followed. "How sweet?" she thought feeling guilty. Rays of sunlight shined through the branches lighting the way to their path. "This will be fun," Alexandria watched Ally and Nico surprised by their guide. "Project Feline," she whispered angrily, "That traitor. Well let's give them a show."

Suddenly an explosion went off releasing colorful poisonous smoke surprising the trio. Ally coughed covering her mouth as Nico grabbed her pulling her out of the multicolored cloud. "Damn," Alexandria said angrily. She glared at the couple as they ran away.

She concentrated on them as water in her hand formed a cherry bomb. "Dodge this," she thought throwing it on the ground. Vibrant pink smoke engulfed Ally and Nico suddenly making them sleepy. They were pulled out by a forceful hand.

"Be careful and run for it," Amunet said as Ally and Nico woke up. "Will you be okay?" he asked. "I was built for this," She answered. Nico ran into the woods carrying Ally. Amunet ran into the pink smoke making Alexandria smile. The smoke disappeared revealing no Amunet.

"What!" Alexandria jumped down to investigate. Suddenly a dagger flew out of nowhere hitting Alexandria's leg. "Knew it was you, Project Feline," she said sadistically. "It's Amunet Argyis ,Project Canine," she said throwing another hunting knife hitting her forehead. Alexandria fell landing on the ground as the Amunet watched sorrowfully. "I'll see you later," she walked away.

Josh held his crossbow, aiming it at Ally and Nico, ready to strike. "Not today," Alice kicked it out of his hand. He jumped out of the tree missing Ally and Nico by a mile. "Where do you think you're going?" Alice jumped down scaring him. He ran taking out a hunting knife. "Idiot," Huey yelled as the knife disappeared, "You're up sis." "What is the brat going to do?" Josh laughed, "That Reaper won't do to me for failing." Alice kicked him hard killing him on the spot. "That's what I'll do," she exclaimed.

Ally looked around confused as she finally woke up. She suddenly glared at Nico as he held her. "Down," she yelled as Nico put her down. Nico put her down as bullet hit a nearby tree. Cameron glared as he prepared his sniper rifle.

Ally and Nico ran just before the second shot was fired hiding behind a tree. Cameron jumped down looking around confused and grabbing a hand gun enraged. Suddenly he felt a pain through his arm. He looked to see an acupuncture needle.

"Want to try that again?" A sarcastic voice asked tauntingly. He looked around scared. He yelled in pain as another needle hit him. "I'm not going to miss again," Alora said from nowhere. Cameron ran away frightened. She jumped out of the tree walking over to where Nico and Ally hid. "He's gone," she said smiling. Nico sighed in relief.

Alice sat next to Huey embarrassed. "What were you doing out there?" Ally asked curious. Alora stood nearby holding close by Damon. "You should've told us you were out there," Alice glared at Damon.

"I had Alora and Amunet," he protested. Alice turned to Ally as her tone changed. "We are part of 'the Crimson Knights'," she said professionally. She turned to the fire in the living room seeking warmth. "It is an organization bent on protecting international law and the royal family at all cost," Huey continued the conversation in a serious tone. Ally raised an eyebrow.

"They followed in their mother's footsteps," Sam said disappointed. "Anyway," Alice turned to Ally, "We are here to safely deliver you to Psyche." "She's not even fully trained," Damon pointed out annoyed. "True, but we have teachers for her," Alice retorted.

"I want Damon to teach me," Ally said. "Fine, but they can't stay in the woods," Alice said attempting to cooperate. Damon shook his head in agreement. "Where are we supposed to stay?" he asked concerned.

"With me," Night said walking into the room, "I'm a teacher myself so it's a safe environment." "Fine but she comes every Tuesday and Thursday," Damon turned to Night annoyed. "Agreed, so long as you follow my rules," She said shaking hands with Damon. Ally sighed in relief. "We'll get your stuff tomorrow," Alice up turning to the night sky.

Ally laid on the bed tired. "Don't worry," Nico said holding her close. "She's basically my bodyguard," she said cuddling up. "At least you're safe," he pointed out.

"What do I need to be guarded from?" she asked nervous. "Those assassins tonight were pretty bent on taking care of you," he said trying to make a point. Ally gave him a wide eyed stare. "I mean I can see where they are coming from," he changed his answer. Ally sighed as she cuddled up to him. "At least Alice is protecting her," he thought trying to sleep.

"It came out of nowhere, I had to run," Cameron sounded frightened as he spoke. Reaper stood in front of him, his blood red eyes narrowed. He pulled the needle out of Cameron's arm looking it over carefully. He put it on the table next to him suddenly pulling out his sword.

Cameron's eyes widened. "Please don't," he said terrified. Reaper took the sword finishing the job. "Should've finished," he said annoyed. He picked up the needle walking into a nearby room.

His 'mother' waited on the screen impatiently. "We found her, mother," he said holding up the needle, "And she is still alive." Her expression changed to excited. "I take it the attack failed," she said. "Yes, your theory was right," Reaper said washing his sword, "Alora has joined Damon." "And Amunet?" she asked crudely. "She is still missing," he answered.

"Watch them for a while. I want a full report," she said hanging up, "Especially on Project Feline and the Healer." Reaper stood up putting his sword in its sheath. Quickly he picked up the O-Pal leaving the room. "Done and done," he thought.

Yvonne stared at the three bodies in front of her as the girls head wound caused her lunch to return. She turned to the blonde. There was no visible wounds on the outside, but he was found on Sam Driscol's property dead just like the girl. The final one was a man who's throat was slit. He was found in an abandoned apartment complex, but evidence suggested he knew the other two victims. "Did we get names?" she asked fixing her medium length brown hair with its blood red bangs. "Yes," the officer next to her said. She glared at him with her teal eyes despising her youthful appearance.

To look eighteen at twenty-three was a crime to Yvonne, especially since the other officers looked down on her. She reached out her slender arm pulling the covers over the victims. "What are they?" Her question was direct and forceful. "The girl was Alexandria Lapis. The blonde was Josh Brookes. The black haired one is Cameron Green," he said solemnly, "All of which had criminal records." Yvonne turned around her pixie like face full of surprise making her fair skin light up. "What crimes?" she asked tilting her head cutely. The officer glared at her. "Please stop that," he said opening a file. "Murder," he said closing it, "They were official Black Lotus assassins." Yvonne sighed bored. "There was no trace of a fourth person?" she asked, her big teal eyes were full of curiosity. "No. No one saw anyone leave," the officer stared at the bodies. Yvonne tilted her head curious. "This will be an interesting case," she said sighing.

Chapter 11

Amunet stared at her new surroundings. The wall around was painted a dull red while the furniture was a rustic brown, and the tables had some sort of strange items on them. Plus the windows were covered allowing just enough light in to dully light the house. "I like it," Alora said sitting on the couch, "Reminds me of home." "Which home?" Amunet thought. It was a week since the attack. The calendar now said November 6, 2162 on a Saturday. "Feet off the table," she said scaring Damon. "She always says that," Carmen said sitting down. "It's polite to not put your feet on the table," Night pointed out. Damon rolled his eyes. "I saw that," she exclaimed entering the table. "Is she always so motherly?" Amunet asked. "Yes," Carmen bluntly answered.

Alora walked into the kitchen. The dark purple walls complimented the black equipment and gray counters. The wooden cabinets glowed matching the table. "Dinner will be ready soon," Night said stirring the spaghetti noodles. "Okay," Alora smiled mischievously as she left. "Wanted to see what she was cooking?" Damon asked curious. Alora sat next to him. "A little," she answered. "Want to go upstairs?" Amunet asked Carmen. "Sure," Carmen answered excited.

Amunet entered the bedroom staring at the cot she slept on. "They do that often?" Carmen asked curious. "Yeah. They are the odd couple. It's alright though; they are the only family I have," Amunet stared out into space. Carmen sat on her bed worried. "What school did you go to?" she asked. "I've never been to school," Amunet looked down regretfully. "Have you seen any good movies?" Carmen asked. "Never had the chance to," Amunet stared down as she sat on the cot. "Do you have any hobbies?" Carmen asked picking up her guitar. Amunet shook her head no. "How did you meet Alora and Damon? Is Alora your cousin?" Carmen asked closing her mouth immediately.

　　"They found me and no," Amunet wiped a tear from her cheek. "They sound nice," Carmen's voice cracked a little. "She is in the dark," she thought, "But why?" Amunet stood up feeling her hair. "Can I borrow a brush?" She asked Carmen politely. Carmen handed her a small brush. "Thank you," Amunet said brushing her hair lightly. "I like your hair color. It's natural, right?" Carmen asked. "It is," Amunet looked at her suspiciously. "School starts tomorrow," Carmen pointed out. "I know, I go with you," she sounded sarcastic. "Great!" Carmen squealed with joy as Amunet laid on her cot bored. "How does Night put up with her?" she thought annoyed.

　　Ally leaned against the tree thinking. "Is something wrong?" Huey asked. "I'm fine," Ally answered watching the sun go down. "Hey Ally can you come here for a second?" Nico asked walking up. Ally followed him back to the dugout where two local police sat at the table. Nico glared at them intensely. "Hello Miss Bellerose," The man said politely, "I'm officer Maxwell and this officer Archer." Yvonne glared at Ally as if she knew her. "Nice to meet you," Ally said sitting down. "We have some pictures with us. Can you please look through them?" he asked. "Sure," she answered. Maxwell got some photos out laying them out on the table. "Does anyone look familiar?" he asked. Ally stared at the photos of Alexandria and Josh. She looked at Cameron's surprised. "Naturally, They attacked me three days ago," she said as Nico sat down.

　　"So how did this happen?" Yvonne asked pointing to the pictures. "I can't remember," Ally lied. Yvonne glared at her knowing her lie. "If you remember please call us, Thank you for your time," Maxwell stood up motioning for Yvonne to do the same. "I'm coming," she said in a musical tone. "Who are they?" Ally asked as the door closed. "No one in particular," Sam said annoyed, "Yvonne Archer is new." Ally left the kitchen muddled and concerned. "You should follow," Huey said walking in surprising everyone.

Nico followed troubled by her circumstance. "She didn't believe her, did she?" Huey asked confused. "Yeah. Yvonne Archer. Nice Name," Sam said putting steaks on the skillet. Huey laughed. "She always comes off as creepy," he said stopping. "Agreed," Sam pointed out.

Night drove up to Olympus High school parking in the parking lot. "Carmen head to class. I'll take Amunet to the main office," she said closing her door. She noticed a raindrop landing on the windshield. Both entered the school as Amunet wore a blue uniform with a yellow blouse. She entered as everyone stared at her making her feel uneasy. "The school nurse is by the main office which we are almost at," Night pointed out. Amunet checked out the school. The walls were painted blue with yellow doors. "They've changed their color scheme since Nico left," Night continued stopping in front of the double door, "Here's the main office." She opened the door revealing an almost organized office. "I'm checking in an Amunet Argyis," Night spoke professionally for five minutes. "Thank you Miss Fiore, We'll take it from here," a young woman said behind the desk. A younger man walked out from the nearby office. "Hello Miss Argyis, I am Principal Wielder," he said orderly, "I'll be showing you around the school." Amunet looked around to Night gone. "She did say good luck," the receptionist pointed out as she followed.

"Now over there is the cafeteria," he opened the door revealing a clean dining hall, "And right down the hallway is your class." She followed him to a classroom stopping at the door. "Now stay here, I'll introduce you," he said walking in giving the teacher a piece of paper. She watched him walk out as she talked to the class. "After you," he opened the door. Amunet entered apathetically. "Please tell everyone who you are," the teacher said. "Amunet Argyis, My name is Amunet Argyis," she spoke fearlessly. "Welcome, please take a seat next to Oscar," she looked at the teacher's desk. Mrs. Ricci was written on her bag as she went to sit down. "Now let's move on to the roman empire," Mrs. Ricci sounded ambitious. Amunet sped through the book reading every word as she attempted to catch up to class. "Miss Argyis," Mrs. Ricci's words made one student stare, Oscar, "Please tell up about Rome's downfall." "It happened 476 AD, and The last Emperor, Romulus Augustus was sixteen years old. Theoderic the Great was the one who did it and started Italy," she explained making the class stare at her silent as she stood there rigid. The teacher clapped surprised by her intelligence and speed. "Please take a seat," she said nervous. Amunet sat down befuddled.

Ally laid there asleep as Nico sat on the couch reading a book. Suddenly the door opened scaring both of them. Sam stood there embarrassed. "The twins and I are going to work on the traps outside for a while. Get our minds off of the police visit two days ago," he said calmly. "Alright,"" Nico said closing his book. Ally got up yawning as Nico smiled slyly. "How about we go out," he suggested. "Sure," she answered. "Great," he blushed lightly, "You have anywhere you want to go?" Ally went behind the divider with her outfit. "You have any idea where you want to go?" she asked. "I have an idea," he said grabbing his outfit for the day. Ally left the divider annoyed as Nico ran behind it in a hurry. "Where's the fire?" she asked jokingly. "Very funny," he sounded not amused.

"Can I have a hint of your plan?" she asked hopefully. "It's a surprise," Nico answered. He walked from the divider excited. Ally raised an eyebrow as she stared. "I was told you like surprises," he said. Ally sat down with him sitting next to her. "True," she said. "It is Monday. What do you want to do before tonight?" he asked. She turned to the rain outside. "Something inside," she said standing up. Nico looked deep into thought. "Want to play poker?" he asked. "Sure," her eyes lit up. Nico smiled slyly. "Let's begin," he said shuffling the deck of playing cards. "What's he planning?" she wondered and worried.

Alice tied the snare in front of her. "That's the tenth one," she said annoyed. The rain slid down her raincoat as it poured. "Well I just got done fixing a giant hole," Huey said. "Quit complaining," Sam said in an annoyed tone making them fall silent. Alice walked over to a snare staring at the cut rope. She remembered Ally's attack. "Who do you think fell for it?" Huey asked walking over. She picked up a long strand of black hair suddenly remembering Alexandria. Huey's eyes narrowed confused. "Of course," he said staring at the snare. "Alexandria Lapis falling into a trap? Only at Sam Driscol's," she pointed out jokingly. "I agree," Huey laughed to himself. "That's right," Sam sounded full of himself. Alice rolled her eyes as she walked away.

Ally stared at Nico's pile of poker chips in shock. "Just like Night," she said optimistically. Nico gave her a puzzled look. "You're out," he said putting the deck away. Ally put the poker chips in the desk away turning the lock. "It's lunch time," she said fixing her purple sweater. "What do you want?" He asked putting the cards in the closet. "How about spaghetti, There some leftover from one night ago," She pointed out while putting her hair in a ponytail. Nico walked over pushing the hair out of her eyes. "Sounds good," he said kissing her cheek. She sat there surprising him. "I'll get lunch," he said leaving. Nico watched as she put her black flats on. "I'll be there in a second," she said annoyed. Nico left the room. He stared as the rain stopped slowly becoming a sprinkle. Ally left the bedroom following Nico from a distance to the kitchen. He stared at the rain for the glass doors.

"Looks like we're stuck inside. The road is flooded," he turned to Ally. "So that's what he was planning. To get me alone with him," she thought worried. A knock on the door made her jump. "I'll get it," Nico said walking to the door, "Wait, who knocks on the door in the hard rain?" "People who need help?" Ally answered. He opened to Yvonne holding a guitar case as the rain sped up again. She tilted her head giving her an innocent appearance. "Hello, Can we stay and wait this rain out?" she asked politely. "Sure," Nico answered reluctantly. "We can stay," she yelled as Maxwell put an umbrella over her head. "Thank you," he said politely. "You didn't tell…," he was cut off by Yvonne who entered smiling. "Yes, thank you," she said. Nico slammed the door. "There goes my plan," he thought annoyed.

"I hate this," Alice screamed while leaning against the prison wall. "The roads probably flooded," Sam sighed. Huey picked up an acupuncture needle thinking of Amunet. "It had to be cold staying here," he thinking out loud anxiously. "Shut up! You're making it worse," Alice said shivering. "Why did we do this anyway?" Huey asked suspicious. "To fix the traps," Sam answered. "You wanted them to have alone time," Alice said annoyed, "And us to get a cold." "Did not," Sam answered childishly. "Then why are we here?" Huey demanded. "For the traps," he answered sitting on the floor stubbornly. Huey turned to Alice glaring. "What?" she asked confused. "You haven't been forgiving," he pointed out. Alice turned to Sam. "Yes, I have," she said walking away. Sam watched her walk away sadly. "She'll come around," Huey said sitting next to him. "I know I have been gone, but I tried to keep in contact," he pointed out. "I talked to you," Huey retorted. "The first time I saw her was when I saw both of you under that net," Sam sighed disappointed. "She will be fine," Huey noticed his father's melancholy, "She will be fine."

Yvonne sat on the couch tuning her electric guitar ignoring her host. "Where are the speakers?" Ally asked confused. "Built in," She smiled slyly. "Cool," Nico sounded impressed. "Surprised me too," Maxwell said sipping his drink. Ally stared at him then Yvonne trying to them out. His Auburn hair complimented his green eyes which showed kindness while Yvonne's eyes showed discontent. His uniform was slightly ruffled indicating he's been in the rain. She turned to Yvonne. She looked pixie like with her big teal eyes and her medium length brown hair with its blood red bangs, and her fair skin. Her short height didn't help. Though the thing that got Ally was her uniform and coat's perfect appearance. "What?" Yvonne gave Ally a death glare. "Nothing," she said startled.

"So where are you from?" Nico asked curious. "Cat's Eye City," Yvonne answered mischievously. "The capital?" Ally asked surprised. "Yep," she put her guitar back in its case. "She's nicer then she looks despite being new," Maxwell pointed out. "I'm twenty-three," Yvonne glared at her partner. "It's hard to remember," he said embarrassed. Yvonne's glare worsened. "How about I get us something to eat," Ally offered. She stood up going to the kitchen. "A salad please," Yvonne's voice became polite. "Nothing, thank you," Maxwell said. Ally turned to Nico. "Nothing, Thank you," he said politely. Ally left smiling charmingly. "She's nice," Yvonne's musical tone turned mischievous as she turned to Nico, "So is it true she found out about your engagement one month ago." Nico glared at her. "If it is?" he asked defensively. "I'm just saying. She's probably still getting used to you...might even be frightened," Yvonne touched the latch on her guitar case. "We've known each other since we were kids, why would she be frightened?" he asked. "Don't know?" she asked.

"Here," Ally put a salad in front of Yvonne and a tray of Brownies on the table, "Just in case." Yvonne took a bite of her salad. "Thank you," Nico said smiling charmingly himself. Ally blushed as Yvonne laughed silently. "What's funny?" Ally asked turning to Nico confused. "Nothing," he glared at Yvonne as Ally left the room. "See," she continued to laugh silently. "So sorry," Maxwell said sighing. Nico looked down nervous.

Alice stared at the warden's office angrily. "You could treat dad better," Huey nagged. She glared at him. "You act like you've known him for years," she said hurt. "Mom told us stories plus I've talked to him beforehand," Huey's voice became calm. "He left when we were one," she clenched her teeth. "To find Ally," Huey pointed out, "He just wants you to like him." Alice turned around walking down the hallway. "You can't always be optimistic," she said annoyed. Huey sighed. "I can try," he yelled as she walked away.

Nico rinsed the bowl deep in thought. "Might even be frightened", the words were stuck in his head. "Need help?" Maxwell asked trying to help. "Sure," he put the bowl in the dishwasher. Maxwell walked over cleaning a plate.

"She's only helping, even it's an odd fashion," he said handing him the plate. Nico laughed as he put it in the dishwasher. "Ally trusts me, I know it," he said hopefully. "Yvonne probably knows that," Maxwell sighed. A bolt of lightning suddenly struck nearby causing the lights to go out. "Great," Nico glared at the dishwasher, "You're still helping right?" "Yeah," His voice was full of concern. Nico opened the dishwasher to a full load. "Great," Maxwell thought scared, "They wait to do dishes."

Ally lit the candle grabbing a flashlight. "You're resourceful," Yvonne mocked. "Very funny," Ally laughed lightly. Femi walked by sniffing Yvonne. "It means she likes you," Ally said sitting on the bed. Yvonne took the couch as thunder boomed. "It's cool you have a pet fox. I don't think they're allowed to walk around free," she pointed out. "She's still a canine," Ally retorted. "True, but dangerous," Yvonne almost sounded human. "What's Cat's Eye City like?" Ally asked changing the subject.

"Beautiful. There's the Roman Coliseum and all the newly designed buildings of course. The cuisine is to die for and they recently rebuilt Vatican City which is right in the middle of the city," Yvonne spoke enthusiastically. "How long did that take?" Ally inquired. "Fifty years, which considering the damage from both the war and years of abandonment is amazing it only took that long" she answered, "At least the catacombs survived."

Ally stared at her in amazement. "What's the best part?" Ally's voice became childlike. "The Empress's palace. It's snow white and built to look like it's from ancient Rome," Yvonne's eyes suddenly lit up as she spoke. "Sounds lovely," Ally's voice cracked a little, "Wait...why?" "No one knows," Yvonne answered. She noticed the look in Ally's eyes.

"What's wrong?" Yvonne became nice. "Nothing," She crossed her legs terrified. "It's Nico, right?" Yvonne's question sent a chill down Ally's spine. "He's nice but...No one told me we were engaged," Ally said deep in thought. Yvonne raised an eyebrow curious. "We're friends that's it," she gripped her jeans confused. "I think I know what you need," Yvonne went deep into thought. "What do you mean?" Ally sighed. She left the room smiling. "She is flaky," she thought to herself.

Nico put the plate in the cabinet taking a deep breath. "That was too many dishes," he said annoyed. "Didn't bother me," Maxwell said laughing. Nico glared. "Hello," Yvonne entered the kitchen holding the flashlight, "What smells like apple?" "The sink. We had to do dishes by hand," Maxwell said jokingly. Yvonne gave him a weird look. "Have you thought about telling her how you feel?" she asked turning to Nico. "Yeah. Why?" he gave her a hopeful look. "No, she's trying to figure out how you feel," she pointed out. Nico looked down disappointed. "Maybe you should try telling her," Yvonne grabbed two cans of soda as she left the room. Nico looked deep in thought as Maxwell gave him a weird look. "Just try it," he said following Yvonne, "Hey did you ask for those?" "No," she answered. "Can we have two sodas?" he asked. "Sure," Nico answered. "Thanks," he answered. "I'll try," Nico thought nervous.

Alice walked down the hallway. The rain down poured on her head through the cracks in the ceiling. "Hello," Sam said greeting her. "Hello," her eyes narrowed. "So any ideas how to keep busy," he laughed anxiously. Alice stared at him, her eyes narrowed more. Sam sighed attempting to speak. "I know you don't like me, but at least I'm trying," Sam glared at her lightly. "I'm supposed to be impressed," she yelled annoyed. "First off I'm sorry, but it was your grandfather's idea to look for Ally. And I found her soon as I came," he pointed out.

"Why not come back earlier then?" she gave him a confused and angry look. "The legal system," Sam sighed, "I couldn't kidnap her. Especially with her father being Alexander Bellerose." Alice laughed lightly. "And Seth Alkeav's granddaughter," she pointed out. "True," Sam agreed, "He is pretty influential. Plus I think he would kill me." Alice laughed a little in response.

"That's good," Sam thought happily. She stopped glaring at him. "Well it was going good," he thought sadly. "Why not tell us about Nico?" she asked. "I told your mother and Huey," Sam's voice cracked a little. "Huey and her didn't tell me until this mission and she put him under our protection," Her eyes narrowed again. "Well that's a good thing," Sam's voice cracked with anxiety as he tried to stay calm. Alice walked over.

"What's wrong?" she asked concerned. "Nothing," Sam answered nervously. "You honestly want me to like you?" she asked sighing. "I'm trying," he tried to calm down. "Fine, One chance," she said letting go. He smiled relieved.

Yvonne stared at the flickering candle. "So where are you from?" she asked curious. "Village Pourpre," Ally stared at a photograph in her hand. "Who's that?" she asked curious. "My mom," she answered as her crystal blue eyes turned dull.

"Hello, there" Came a familiar voice. Both women turned around to Nico standing at the door. "Maxwell is looking for you," he said cheerfully.

"Thank you," she stood up leaving the room. Nico sat next to Ally staring at the candles. "If we had firewood we could light the fireplace," he pointed out jokingly. He walked over putting firewood in the fire place. Ally watched as he lit it putting out the candle. "Better?" he asked sitting next to her. Ally shook her head yes.

"Can I tell you a story?" he asked. She shook her head yes. "There was once a girl who seemed to have everything," Nico watched as Ally raised an eyebrow, "Well one day she lost someone dear and the funeral was held at her house. Her father wasn't much help seeing as he got lost in his own world. Well she finally couldn't take the pain and left quietly." Her eyes widened in confusion. "Well there was a boy at the funeral. He noticed her, but no one else did."

"He followed her finally finding her in a coat closet. When he tried to comfort her she pushed him away since they never met before." Ally pulled her legs closer. "She finally broke down on his shoulder. Her father must've heard cause he stared in surprised by his daughter's trust in the boy. So he led the girl and boy back to the funeral, the girl staying by the boy's side. He couldn't help wondering why she didn't go to her dad for support. She stayed by the boy's side the whole time," he turned to Ally who just gave him a scared look.

"I remember that, I didn't really think you did," she stopped halfway stuttering. "It's okay," Nico said as he held her close. "I was five, of course I acted that way," She said anxiously as a tear ran down her cheek. "Your dad took it the wrong way," he said. Ally gave him the big eyes nervous. "You haven't changed much," he said charmingly. She pushed away confused. Suddenly the lights turned on. "Found the wires," Yvonne said walking in.

Ally scooted away from Nico. She suddenly turned her head to the window. "The rain stopped," she said surprised. Yvonne smiled mischievously. "Thank you for letting us stay," she said grabbing her coat. Maxwell grabbed his coat following her out. She closed the front door behind him. Nico stared at the glass door as Sam opened it drenched while Huey and Alice followed. "You look good," Nico said joking. Sam glared at him slightly. "I'll send you in the rain next time," he joked back. Nico gave him a scared look.

        “We are friends after all,” Ally thought as Nico laughed, “Why did I lose my trust?” Nico turned to her grinning. “Tired?” he asked concerned. “No,” she answered smiling back. Nico gave her a surprised look. Alice chuckled softly. “Well then, let’s get back to the fire,” he said. Alice looked at them surprised watching them as they left. “Did we miss something?” Huey asked confused. “Of course we did,” Alice said concerned, “We missed something big for this to happen.”

Chapter 12

Ally stared at the koi pond surrounded by the lovely garden. "They're beautiful," Catherine said her sapphire eyes glowed. "Yeah," she watched them swim in a circle continuously. "Do you trust me?" Catherine asked smiling. "Yeah," Ally's crystal blue eyes lit up. "Then why doubt my trust?" she faded away as the mansion quickly decayed around her killing the garden. Ally turned around to see a grave marked 'Alette Bellerose October 1, 2163' screaming in fear.

"No!" Ally screamed as she woke up. Nico held her close trying to calm her down. "Stay away murderer," she pushed him away shaking. "What happened?" Alice ran in holding a bat. "Who's in here?" Huey ran in holding a butcher knife. They turned to Nico who looked hurt. "I tried to calm her down," He said sitting on the couch, looking disappointed in himself.

Sam walked over to Ally cautiously. "Ally," he said sitting next to her. A shield went between them as Ally attempted to protect herself. "It's just me, Sam," he said trying to calm her down. Ally's eyes turned back to normal as the shield went down. "Good, you want to talk about it?" he asked concerned.

"She hates me," Ally stuttered scared. "Who?" Sam asked confused. "Mom," Ally started cried. Nico gave her a sympathetic look. "She doesn't hate you," Sam gave her a compassionate in response. "She hates me," she said looking down.

Nico bit his lip anxiously. "So that's what's wrong?" he thought. "Nico will stay with you," he said getting up. Ally shook a little. Nico held her close calming her down. Sam left the room followed by Alice and Huey. "It's alright," Nico said. Ally sighed as she calmed down.

Alice stared at Femi as she played in the snow. "You scared us, we're still watching you," she turned to Ally. "That was the seventh...It's the eleventh," Ally threw a ball at the snow which the snow which Femi grabbed. Alice sighed. "Are you scared of him still?" she asked curious. "I used to be. He's more like a friend now," Ally smiled at the clear sky.

"It's beautiful," Alice said staring at the snow, "Like a Christmas card." "Yeah," Ally smiled at the thought. "You smile more than you used to," Alice smiled back. Ally took the ball from Femi as she ran up. "I guess I am happier," she grinned. "You really are nice. Why not that way at the beginning?" Alice asked confused.

"I was told I was engaged. I basically got a fiancé as a birthday present," she answered regretfully. "If only it was natural," Alice sighed. "I haven't spoken to my dad in two weeks," Ally's words surprised Alice. She turned to Femi thinking. "I've never seen a red fox play fetch," she thought. "I'm sure he's fine," Alice stood up stretching.

"Yeah," Ally answered worried. "Why don't you call him?" Alice asked curious. "I tried," Ally answered. Ally looked at her watch. "It's one," she said walking into the dugout. "Of course, time to meet Nico," Alice thought laughing to herself.

Nico sat at the table. "Hey Ally," he said excited. "Hey," she answered grinning sheepishly back. "So how about we eat out?" he asked curious. She turned to Alice then back to Nico. "Sure," she answered. "Great," Nico said grabbing a winter coat, "Let's go." Ally followed him out. Alice stared at them grinning. "You're not going," Huey said walking into the kitchen. "Why?" Alice demanded. "Because you have a report to send," he said handing her the O-Pal. Alice glared and growled as she started.

Nico drove carefully. "So I hear you're no longer scared," he said pulling into Gemini's parking lot. "You heard that?" Ally asked surprised. "Yeah, I was going out to talk to you and I saw you were to Alice, so I overheard you two talking," he said opening the door for her.

"Thank you," she said getting out. "Oh, and your dad did try to call you last night while you were asleep," he said walking up with her. She gave him a shocked look. "I told him you would call him today," he opened the door for her.

"Thank you," she said walking in. Nico's eye twitched as he entered as Justine glared at Ally. "May I help you?" she asked with a fake smile. "One by the window, please," Nico requested. "Taken," she said turning to the now empty table. She sighed annoyed at the sight. "Follow me," she said going over. He pulled a chair out for Ally. "Thank you," she blushed as she sat. Justine rolled her eyes as she walked away. She came back with two menus putting them on the table.

"Welcome back," Jeff said grinning closely, "What may I get you?" "White tea," Ally answered. "How about you?" he turned to Nico. "Same," He said nonchalantly. "Coming right up," he walked away putting the notepad his pocket.

Ally stared at the menu. "What looks good this time?" Nico asked curious. "I know what I want," she said, "Why did you start drinking white tea?" Suddenly Jeff walked up with two white teas. Justine gave him a death glare from the podium. "Cause it looked interesting," he answered. "In other words, *I* was drinking it," she thought.

Alice finished her report and pressed send, watching the 'REPORT SENT' notification fade away. "Good," Huey said taking back the O-Pal. She turned around to him glaring. "Don't give me that look," he said glaring back. "I should've followed," Alice's smoke colored eyes radiated with anxiety. "You need to trust them. Nico can protect her," Huey picked up a file marked 'Nico Katsaros'.

"Somethings off about him," he said laying down on the couch. "How?" Alice gave him a confused look, "Plus Ally can protect both of them, she doesn't realize it." "It says O-Pal designer, but he has designs I've never seen before," Huey went deep into thought, "Just saying."

"Maybe he likes to tinker with it," Alice thought, "Or maybe it's more." She picked up the O-Pal from Huey's hands noticing pages missing his file. "Someone tinkered with this," she thought, "Huey didn't want to say anything cause of Night."

Yvonne pranced to her car quickly, flash drive in hand. "I see you got what wanted," Maxwell said staring at the flash drive surprised. She put in her O-Pal pressing the file marked 'A.B.'. Ally's picture popped up as well as a list of topics. She clicked 'psychic types' opening up a bountiful of information.

"She's a Healer at student level, but looks like she used to beginner recently," Yvonne pressed family popping up a family photo. "Mother died when she was five- assassinated during the Durand war ongoing at the time. She was put in an arranged marriage with Nico Katsaros the same night as her mother's funeral," she continued stopping at Alexander's photo, "Father is considered a workaholic and spent most of his time in his workshop sending Alette to Miss Blanchette's Academy for Girls." She closed the file removing the flash drive. Suddenly she put the flash drive back in pressing 'career'.

"Seems that she's a weapons expert specializing in gun design," the three victims came to mind making her smile slyly, "So she would know how to use a dagger." "But would she? She doesn't seem to be the type," Maxwell remembered Ally's calm lady like demeanor. "We will need to dig deeper," Yvonne drank her coffee. "Of course," Maxwell glared at her.

Ally tapped her empty plate with her fork. "That was good," Nico handed Jeff his plate. "Here's the bill," he said taking Ally's plate. Jeff walked away leaving the plate. Nico picked it up putting money inside the folder. "You're happier," he pointed out. "We maybe I am," Ally said blushing. Jeff came back taking the folder.

"Thank you for coming," he said. He came back giving them the receipt. "Come again," he said cheerfully. Ally stood up grabbing her trench coat. Nico lead the way holding the door open. Ally left confused by Justine's attitude as Nico closed the door behind them. Both got into the car. "Let's hurry home," he said starting the car. He pulled out slowly make Ally stare out the back worried. "What?" he asked confused. He freaked as he suddenly hit another vehicle.

Nico ran out of the reaper concerned. He stared at the big black car in front of him. The door opened as a short young woman with her long black hair was in a tight bun, her deep blue eyes was filled with rage, and her black suit complimented her pale skin. "I hope you're paying," she demanded in a naturally angry voice.

"Reggie," a teenage boy walked out of the vehicle, "I'm sorry. My assistant should not have said that." Ally walked out of the confused at the stranger. His dark brown hair was in a messy fashion and his electric blue eyes shined with excitement. His black jacket and dark blue jeans complimented his black tennis shoes. "I'm Adonis Chevalier and I'll be happy to pay for the damages," he said smiling faintly.

"Nice to meet you. I'm Nico and this is Ally," Nico said politely. He checked the damage. "I'm sure I can pay," he said. "Prince Adonis?" Ally gave him a strange look. "Yeah, I'm very sorry. Reggie was in a hurry," he said turning to Ally. "It's Regina," she barked at him. Adonis ignored her words.

"Look, your majesty, let me pay for this," Nico said trying to diffuse the tension. "I couldn't allow that," Adonis said returning to Nico, "And please call me Don." "How about we take it to a mechanic and see the price. Or see if someone else can do it," Ally intervened annoyed.

"Night will do it for a good price," Nico pointed out. "Who's Night?" Adonis asked. "A family friend," Ally answered. He took a minute to think. "Ok," he said in agreement, "We'll follow you."

Alice glared at Yvonne as she sat across from her. "Just tell me what happened?" Yvonne smiled mischievously. Alice's penetrating glare frightened Huey. "There is nothing to say. They were going to kill her," she answered angrily. "How bad cause they murdered others?" Yvonne's musical voice had a childlike yet serious tint to it. "It was life or death. That's all you need to know," Alice pointed out. Yvonne glared at her. "I know you know aikido," she put a picture of Josh in front of her, "He had no external wounds, but he did have some on the inside."

She circled Alice like a hawk, her teal eyes full of rage. "You bought me in for this? What if someone else did it?" Alice sounded insulted. "You were closest. Now tell me what happened?" Yvonne demanded. "International law states anyone trying to kill a member of any monarchy is to be put to death on the spot," Alice said in a professional manner.

"She's not part of any monarchy," Yvonne pointed out insulted as well. "Not according to Damon Bellamy," Alice smiled mischievously making Yvonne nervous. "Escort them out," she said turning to Maxwell.

Ally watched Night assess the damage. "Looks like a full day of work," she said smiling slyly. Adonis gave her a confused look. "I didn't know what type of payment," Nico shrugged his shoulders. "Of course I'm not going to make Prince Adonis work," Night said turning to him. "I'll work," he said calmly. Ally gave him a confused look. Night's eye glimmered as she stared at Regina. "Fine, here's a list of chores," she handed everyone a list.

"I only have three," she turned to Adonis, "How about you work with Ally?" "Sure," he said walking over to her. "Good…Oh and one more thing: my daughter is at an all-night school project, but my guest are allowed to help," she said getting her tools. "Okay," Ally said walking in as Adonis followed. Nico looked at her suspiciously.

"What's first on the list?" Adonis asked turning to Ally. "Dishes," she said walking into the kitchen. They both stared at the pile of dishes in the sink. "She doesn't have a dishwasher," she said as her eye twitched. Adonis stared confused.

"We should get started. This is only the beginning," she said handing him a towel. Adonis took it enthusiastically as he followed. Ally started the water. She turned to Adonis staring. "Sorry," he said nervous. Ally raised an eyebrow. She turned off the water.

"Well let's begin," she said washing a red bowl. She quickly finished handing it to Adonis. He took it drying it immediately. "This is creepy," she thought. She handed him a mug. "What are you doing in Black Opal anyway?" she asked curious. "Sightseeing, " he answered. "As a tourist, huh?" Ally grinned.

"Yeah, I got permission from Terra to go on a trip before she left," he said putting a plastic bowl away. "You mean Terra Hunter," she said surprised. "Yeah, she's my bodyguard to a point. So she only lets me out every so often," he put a fork away. "Where is she now?" Ally asked curious. "Don't know, but my new assistant decided I needed to get out," he said smiling.

"How old are you?" she asked bluntly. "Seventeen," he answered. Ally laughed. "Finally! Someone who looks their age," she said stopping. "That's rare?" Adonis asked confused. "No, it's just my fiancé is twenty-one and he looks eighteen. Yvonne Archer is twenty-three and she looks eighteen," Ally picked up the last dish, "I was starting to feel left out."

Adonis laughed. "Glad I could help," he said. "Here," she put a butcher knife on the counter. He picked up. "Was that the last one?" he asked curious. "No," Ally stared at the last half.

Chapter 13

Nico left the bathroom running out. "Dis-gusting," he said making a puking motion. He heard someone curse down the hall. "Hello," he turned to Regina dusting. "Clean this house inside out," she said imitating Night. "It doesn't hurt," Nico gave her a confused look. "Who's whining?" Damon exited the guestroom, "Hey Nico." Alora followed wearing a hoodie. "Let's go," she said hiding her face. Amunet walked out annoyed and glaring.

"Move it," she said hiding her face. Regina stared at the trio confused. "Don't worry about them," he said trying to take her attention away from them. Regina glared at him turning to the trio again. "I'm stuck with the anger prone assistant and Ally has Adonis," Nico turned green with envy. "Calm down," he looked at his list. Regina walked away annoyed.

Alice left the police department irritated. "She seemed a little rough," Huey spoke rationally. "What a...?" Alice was cut off by Huey. "Be nice," he said getting into the van. Alice followed suit. "We need to stop by Night's house. She has Nico's car," He started the van. "Got that," Alice looked through her text.

"Mom sent us something," she said opening her text. A file popped up. "She sent us Reaper's file," Alice gave him a confused look. She looked through it anxiously. "He's here isn't he?" Huey asked concerned. "Yeah," Alice gulped, "And she wants let's to keep this to ourselves." Huey sighed as he drove away.

Ally mopped the floor turning to Adonis. "Can I ask a question?" he asked curious. "Sure," she answered handing him the mop. He took it mopping the floor. "You're a Healer, right?" Adonis asked. "Yes, why?" Ally asked giving him a weird look.

"I'm trying to figure you out," he answered handing her the mop. "May I ask why?" she put the mop away. "For starters you seem easily agitated," he said concerned. "Well...I've just recently really worked," Ally pointed out insulted. Adonis drew back.

"Sorry," Ally walked over, "You seem jumpy." "I'm usually allowed out only for school and important functions," he said nervous. Ally suddenly remembered Miss Blanchette's Girl's academy and being left at home. "I'm sure your mom can talk to Terra," she said pushing the memories away. "She's too busy," he said sadly. Ally thought of her father. "Then how about we hurry up," She said positive. "Ok," he said getting up.

Regina glared at the picture in front of her. An eighteen year old Night smiled standing next to a beautiful blonde. "Done already?" Night asked curious. "Yes Miss Fiore," Regina snarled. "Good," Night's eye glimmered. "You're a Psychic I'm guessing," Regina's lips twisted into a smile.

"Of course," Night said smiling. "You look good for your age. You're thirty, right?" she laughed lightly. "Thirty-eight and yes I know I take care of myself," Night glared at Regina. "Damn it," the thought filled Regina's head. "Reggie," Adonis ran up excited.

Regina glared at him as she turned around. "Yes, your majesty," she hissed. "I was just checking on you," he turned to Night. "It's fixed," Night pointed out. Nico entered the hallway. "Really?" he asked. "Yeah," Night answered. "That's good," Ally said walking up. "Ally," he ran over hugging her. "Hey Nico," She said. Regina walked away annoyed. "Reggie," Adonis followed her.

Alice pulled into the driveway. "Nice driving sis," Huey joked. "Very funny," Alice glared. She looked at the stone house. "She lives here?" she asked surprised. "Yep," Huey knocked on the door. Night answered her eye glimmered as she smiled. Huey glared knowing what she was doing. "Hello," he said calming down. Alice looked inside. Adonis sat on the couch chatting with Ally. "Not really," she said.

"Do you have any pets?" he asked curious. "They just finished cleaning," Night said as they walked in. She closed the door behind them. Regina noticed Alice and Huey immediately. "We have to go," Regina said leaving the hallway her eyes flashing red. "Fine," Adonis said sadly. Both left.

"Is that his new assistant? His mother would be ashamed," Night said turning to Alice, "His last one was a lot nicer." Alice got an anxious look on her face. "I'll be back to pick you up," she ran outside running to the van. She started it driving off with Huey.

"I said, I 'll be back to pick you up," she pointed out as she followed the black vehicle. "I know," Huey said as they turned to a country road. Alice parked nearby the car hiding it. "What's going on?" Huey whispered concerned. "You'll see," she ran into the woods. Huey followed.

Regina walked out of the vehicle. "Come on," she said smiling. Adonis followed suit confused. "What's going on?" he asked turning to Regina. She pulled out a gun. "I've worked for you for a year and you're annoying," she yelled angrily, "Now I can do this." Adonis looked at her terrified as she prepared to shoot. Suddenly a rock hit her head causing the gun to fall out of her hand. She looked around cautiously.

"International law states anyone trying to or succeeding in killing a member any monarchy is to be put to death," Alice said professionally. Regina snarled as a dagger flew from nowhere. She grabbed it throwing it back. Adonis ran for it. "Where do you think you're going?" she asked him sadistically. Alice jumped out of nowhere pinning Regina to the ground.

"Get off," she kicked her off easily surprising Alice. A red mist started appearing in Huey's hand forming Regina's gun. He pointed it at her shooting her arm. "You suck," Regina smiled evilly as she faded away confusing Huey and Alice. "What just happened?" Alice turned to Huey. "Who knows?" he turned to Adonis, "We'll take you to the police station." Adonis shook his head in agreement. "Who was she?" Alice thought.

Yvonne glared at Adonis. "She just disappeared," Maxwell mimicked confused. "Possibly a Magician," Yvonne said concerned. "Magicians are rare," He gave Yvonne a confused look, "Plus aren't they supposed to suffer from delusions of grandeur?"
"Mr. Chevalier, Please tell us why you didn't check if Regina was a Psychic," Yvonne demanded. Adonis's look turned into a glare. "Terra Hunter was in charge of that. She disappeared a year ago for a job," He pointed out.

"Well she's been known to do that," Maxwell turned to Yvonne. She flushed red with anger. "Well your mother is sending you a ride," she said annoyed. "Of course," Adonis said looking down. He got up leaving the room. He suddenly heard a familiar voice. "Are you okay?" Ally ran over confused. "Yeah," he said calmly.

"That's good," She smiled back relieved. "I didn't like Regina anyway," Nico said annoyed. Ally tilted her cutely. "Don't do that please," Nico said blushing. Adonis held back his laughter. "Sir," A woman in a grey suit walked up, "We're here." Adonis followed. "Bye Ally. Bye Nico," he said sadly.

"Bye," Ally said concerned. "He'll be fine," Nico took Ally's hand gently. "Hello," Yvonne said out of nowhere. "Hello Officer Archer," Ally said pulling her hand away embarrassed. "You should head home. It's almost midnight," Yvonne walked away mumbling. "She's right," Nico said leading the way. "Okay," Ally said following him.

Alexander sighed staring at the blank sheet of paper in front of him. "I've lost it," he thought, "I can't think of any design." "Alexander, sir," Erica said walking in, "They want that new design."

He walked over picking up a design from Ally's folder. "Give them this," he said handing it to Erica. She took the design worried about his health. "You know, you could call her. She tried to call you a couple times. It has been a month anyway," Erica opened the door.

"A month and two weeks," his voice reflected his regret. "How do you know?" Her voice was full of concern. "She left the first of October and it is now Monday the fifteenth of November," his voice sounded unstable. "Maybe you should call her," Erica stood there concerned. "Why? She hates me," he said concerned. "Because you care," Erica pointed out. Alexander ignored her as she left.

Ally stared at the clear sky as the clouds went by slowly. "Ally, you got a call," Sam said standing at the doorway. She entered staring at a familiar scene on her O-Pal. "I'm coming," Alexander said sitting down in front of the O-Pal. He looked at her in shock. "Ally," his voice sounded nervous.

"Dad," Ally said surprised. His usually perfect appearance was as unstable looking as him. "I guess I caught your call," he said smiling. "He thinks I called," she thought turning to Sam. "Play along," he mouthed.

"Um... Yeah. How have you been?" Ally asked concerned. "Great, Erica is taking care of things around here," he answered nervously. "Really that's good," she smiled faintly. "How are you?" Alexander asked concerned. "I'm fine," she answered. "Are they treating you well?" he asked worried.

"Yes," she sighed. "How is Femi?" he asked curious, "Is she being a good bodyguard?" "She's being great," Ally answered. "Well I gotta go. Talk to you soon," he said hanging up. "He's going insane," Sam said sitting down. "Yeah," Ally said sadly. She turned to the glass doors. "Don't worry. He'll be fine," Sam said trying to comfort Ally. She sighed sadly.

Femi ran around excited. "What a beautiful Christmas Eve," Ally thought excited. She stared at Nico as he worked on the engine of his car. "How could it go out?" he yelled angrily. "It is an old car," she said annoyed. "I know that," he said annoyed. Alora laughed nearby as she walked up. "Who fixed it up anyway?" she asked fixing her black and white winter coat. "Me," Nico answered. "Good job," Alora played with her gloves nervously. "Where's Alice and Huey?" Ally asked Alora curious. "Talking to Khepri with Damon," she answered looking at Nico's handy work. "It's your belt," she pointed out. "I know, but there's a second problem," he said pointing to a black puddle. "Ouch," she scooted away scared. Ally walked into the dugout ignoring Alora and Nico. "I'll let them fight," she thought.

Ally walked down the hallway. "I'm sorry. I guess everyone was looking for her," Damon said talking to someone on an O-Pal. Ally peeked in carefully. "She's under our protection just like you are," a woman nagged him from the O-Pal, "You had no right to hoard her." "You tell her that. She is right here," he turned to Ally, "She won't bite." Ally walked in carefully toward the O-Pal. Khepri stared back from the screen. "Hello Miss Bellerose," she spoke in a professional manner similar to Alice's tone, "I'm Khepri Coupe." "Hello Mrs. Coupe," Ally said trying to be polite. "I'm sure by now you know that I've sent Alice and Huey to be your bodyguards," she said with a pleasant smile. "Yes," Ally said.

"Well we didn't see Damon's arrival. He's under our protection as well," she said glaring at Damon, "So he's first priority temporarily." "Not fair! She's my cousin," Damon blurted out. Ally looked at Damon scared. "He's telling the truth, though he left out 'distant'," Khepri's glare worsened. "Explain," Ally demanded. "Daman Chaput and Angeline Drac were lovers," Khepri's voice got a strange tone to it. Ally stared at her in shock.

"You're lying," she exclaimed. "She isn't," Damon pointed out. "That was one century ago," Ally said scared. "It's still true," Khepri's stare wondered off, "Gotta go." Damon and Ally watched as the screen turned black. "Nice woman," he said sarcastically. Ally gave him a shocked look. "Ignore what she said," he said annoyed. He stood up leaving the room. She got up walking out confused still. "Hey Ally," Sam said putting a cake in the oven. "Hey," she said sitting at the table. "You look lost," he sat next to her. Ally sighed realizing he was right. "I am a little," she said trying to be optimistic. "Ally," Nico said walking in covered with oil. "Hey Nico," she smiled back.

"I'll be right back," he said walking down the hallway. She heard the bathroom door close. "That old clunker," Alora said sitting down. Femi ran to Ally's side. "The reaper is in pretty good shape," Sam pointed out insulted. "Say's you," Alora said annoyed. "Say's the three years Nico spent on it," He pointed out. "Why spend three years on a car?" Alora asked. "I don't know," he turned to Ally. She blushed thinking of the effort put into the car. Alora sighed embarrassed. "I'm sorry, didn't know," she said.

Amunet stared at the woods as she leaned against the tree. "You must be freezing," Huey said sitting next to her. "You're a talkative one," She said irritated. "Well I'm curious," he said. "About what?" She smiled mischievously. "For starters...Don't you act a little emotionless for a teenager?" Huey asked concerned. "Not really," she glared a little at the woods. "You know what date it is right?" he asked. "Christmas Eve. Alora and Damon couldn't stop talking about it," Amunet said blandly. "I can see why," he said looking at the clouds. "Huey, we got to call mom," Alice said walking up. "Go ahead," Amunet said sighing. Huey stood up worried. "You honestly care about her," Alice said surprised. "Yes," he answered. Alice lead the way. "She's nice," she said worried. "She needs help," Huey pointed out. "You don't say," Alice said walking into the bedroom. She picked up the O-Pal. She pressed 'Dial' under mom.

"Hello," her mother said smiling. "Merry Christmas," Huey and Alice said in unison. "Merry Christmas," Khepri said back. "Merry Christmas honey," Sam said running in. "Hello Sam," Khepri's eyes lit up. "How about some alone time," Sam said turning to Huey and Alice. "That won't be necessary. I'd rather talk to all of you," Khepri said happy, "Anyways nice to see everyone together. How is everyone doing?" "Ally and Nico are being completely into each other," Sam answered jokingly. She laughed as an ornament broke nearby. Khepri's head turned as someone screamed in joy. "Got to go we're having our Christmas party and Charlie is a little too drunk," she said getting off. "She hasn't changed," he thought smiling. "Hey Sam." The trio turned to see Night. "I thought you were cooking," Sam walked over.

"I was, but I decided to check on you," she said slyly, "Beside the meal will be ready soon." "How soon?" Alice asked. "One hour," Night laughed. "Sounds good," Huey said in agreement as he left the room. "He's returning to Amunet," Alice said annoyed. Night's eye glimmered as the scene changed. Huey sat against the tree talking to Amunet. She focused on Amunet making the scene change again. This time to a young girl with black hair and amber eyes sitting in a white room crying. Night blinked returning to the present. "You okay?" Sam asked walking over. "Yeah," she said concerned.

Nico stared at the little black box in his hand. "Nico," Carmen said as she entered. "It's for Ally," he said opening it. A precious opal engagement ring glimmered inside, "Night gave it to me so I could give to Ally." "It's beautiful," Carmen said excited. "I know she will love it," he said closing the box. "You sure," she said worried. "I'm sure," he said leaving the room. "I hope she does," Carmen thought following.

Chapter 14

2143

Sam stared at the ceiling deep in thought. At age eighteen he was given a hard task. "What's wrong?" Khepri asked concerned. "Nothing," he said smiling. "I can finally rest," she said laying down. Sam listened to the uncomfortable silence. "Well the twins are asleep," she said smiling. "And I'm packing," Sam stared at his half empty suitcase. "You're still doing it," Khepri sounded hurt. "I'll be back soon," he said trying to comfort her. "If you say so," she said annoyed. "She can't be hard to find," he sighed. "Keep telling yourself that," she said. "What does that mean?" he asked. "What if something goes wrong?" she demanded. "Nothing will. You know me, I have the patience of a Saint," he pointed out. Crying broke the silence. "I'll get it," Sam said getting up.

2163

Sam watched Alice as she put gifts under the Christmas tree as Ally put the star on top. "It's clean," she said turning to Nico. He smiled back as Huey sat next to Amunet. "There's gifts for you and company," he said turning to Damon. "Really," Damon said surprised. "Yeah, Ally did the shopping," Sam pointed out, "You will love them." Damon gave him a weird look. "He does that naturally," Night said tuning an acoustic guitar. She handed it to Carmen. "Can I play?" she asked giving Night the big eyes. "Sure," Nights eye glimmered. "You sing," Carmen turned to Ally. "How about Crimson Lullaby," Ally said. Carmen played the guitar starting a sad tune. The soft beat filled the air as Ally began to sing.

Nico sat next to Ally and listened intensely as she sang the old tune; dating back to the dark difficult years just after WW3 when survivors were huddled in the ruins of the old world, just trying to survive the post-apocalyptic quagmire they found themselves. The name was a reference to the phenomenon caused by so much ash and dust in the air post-war that it changed the sky to a red haze, which lasted for the first decade or so after the war. It spoke to both the fears of the author (the identity of which was a matter of stiff debate even after a century and a half) and the scattered hopes that sunlight would shine on the world once more.

Everyone clapped as Carmen stopped playing. "That was beautiful," she said putting the guitar down. Ally smiled embarrassed. "Thank you," she said. Nico looked at her surprised. "Didn't know you could sing," he said blushing. A knock on the door caught everyone's attention. "I'll get that," Ally said embarrassed still. "I think she liked that," Alice chuckled. "She did," Night said smiled to himself.

"Hello," Yvonne stood at the living room doorway. "Merry Christmas," Sam said being polite. "Merry Christmas," Maxwell said cheerfully. "Merry Christmas," Yvonne stared at the tree. "Nice," she smiled mischievously. "Any reason you're here?" Ally asked confused. "I came to check on everyone and wish you a merry Christmas," Yvonne turned to Damon. "Anyway, we should get going," she said heading toward the door. "See you later," Maxwell followed. Nico turned to Sam confused. "I don't know," Night sighed. "She's weird," Ally said deep in thought.

"Agreed," Nico said, "You want to go on a walk with me?" "Sure," Ally answered. Nico stood up grabbing his winter coat and his satchel. "Come on. I got a surprise for you," he said excited. Ally raised an eyebrow as she put on her trench coat. Nico dragged her down the hallway. "You know too," Night turned to Carmen, "What's in the satchel?" Carmen whimpered.

Nico held Ally's hand gently as he guided her through the woods. "Don't worry," he said pulling her to a familiar clearing. Ally stared at the frozen lake and now barren trees. Nico put his satchel down grabbing a box. "Here," he said passing it to her. Ally opened to a pair of skates. "I've never done this," she said freaking out. Nico put on his skates getting on the ice. "Come on," his amethyst eyes shined with enthusiasm. Ally walked over putting on her skates. He carefully took her hand helping her on as Ally hugged him tight.

"You really never skated before," he said putting his arms around her. He took her hands helping her out. "Have you ever seen me ice skate?" she asked. "No," he answered. Ally gave him a worried look, her eyes glowing brighter as he started. "Keep calm," Nico said as he took the lead. Ally stood still breathing in and out. Nico watched as her eyes turned crystal blue. "Sorry," he said sheepishly. "Allow me," he took her hands helping her off the ice. "It was worth a shot," he sighed.

Ally gave him a scared look, her eyes turned a bright gold. Nico watched her eyes return to normal giving her a gentle kiss. He took the little black box out of his pocket. Ally turned from her just tied boot surprised. "It's for you," he said handing it to her. Ally took it surprised. She opened it making her eyes widen. The opal engagement ring stared back at her. "You like it?" Nico asked looking for approval. "I don't know," she said confused. He looked at her confused. He cleared his voice. "I've trying to tell you this," he turned to Ally who was terrified, "I love you." Ally gave him a terrified look shaking. "How long?" She stood up angrily. "Ever since eighteen," he answered. Ally blushed still angry.

Nico watched as he instinctively put the ring in her pocket. "I need to think," she entered the woods nervous. Nico watched hurt not sure what to do. "You're kidding me," he thought in pain. "That could've gone better," Amunet jumped out of a nearby tree confused, "Why didn't she accept?" "She just didn't," he looked down sad. "Try giving her time," she suggested. "I'll try," he entered the woods carrying his satchel. Amunet followed him silently. Nico glared at the path ahead. "Maybe I should tell Alora," Amunet thought annoyed.

Ally laid on her bed confused. "Nico dump you?" Alice joked as she entered. "No," Ally cuddled the pillow next to her. "You're both acting like it," she sat at the edge. "He surprised me," A tear came to Ally's eye. "How?" Alice gave her a concerned look. She pointed to the box on the nightstand. Alice opened it surprised. "Wow," Her smoky eyes widened, "He must care." She turned to Ally who was shivering. Alice put the ring next to her. "Where's Nico?" she turned to Huey. "Talking to Carmen and Alora," he said playing cards with Amunet. "You look strange," Carmen said talking to Alora. "Thank you," Alora said smiling. "That wasn't a compliment," she said. "I know," Alora retorted mischievously.

Nico stared at the pile of presents blankly. "You okay?" Alice said walking over. "No," he answered playing with a pen. "Want to talk about it?" she sat next to him. "No," his eyes glowed dark. "What did she do?" Alice gave him a curious look. Nico glared at him. "Nothing," he said fixing his hoodie. "He's hurt," Amunet gave Alice a concerned look, "She rejected his proposal." "More like needed time to think," Alora sighed. "I told him to give her some alone time," she got out an O-Pal and started typing. Alice gave her a muddled look. "Sam's letting me borrow it," she said blandly. Alice stood up. "She was scared," she thought leaving the room.

Reaper watched the cars below uninterested. "Reaper," his mother's voice came in loud and clear. He turned to see a call from his O-Pal. He walked over answering the call. "Hello mother," he said sitting straight. "What is the report about?" she demanded. "Her allies," Reaper pulled his long sleeved black shirt. "Alice Coupe?" she raised her eyebrow, "How about Terra Hunter?" "She doesn't know it herself," he smiled mischievously. "But she does know about Alice Coupe and Huey Driscol?" she gave him a confused look. "Yes mother," Reaper bowed his head. "I'll look into this," The woman hung up annoyed. "She'll look into it," Reaper stood up picking up the O-Pal. "It came from this way," the musical voice surprised Reaper as he put the O-Pal in his bag. The door opened to Yvonne. "There's no one here," she looked around staring at an empty window. "Looks like they escaped," Maxwell said leaving the room and grabbing his O-Pal. Yvonne followed unsure.

Ally left the bedroom annoyed. "Hey Ally," Alice said running up. "Yes," she said wiping a tear from her eye. "Dinner is ready," she said excited. "Ok," Ally said following her into the dining room. She entered the room in shock. Alice sat across from Nico making Ally sit next to him. She turned to him only to have him turn away. "So how is everyone?" Alice asked trying to start conversation. The table stayed silent. "Come on we're all friends here," she said. "Nice ring," Huey said turning to Ally. She looked down at her engagement ring. "Thank you," her eyes turned gold with embarrassment. Nico looked at her surprised. "What's wrong?" Alice asked Nico. "Nothing," he played attempted to play cool. "How's work?" Huey asked curious. "Good," Nico answered smiling. Alice gave Huey a concerned look. "I'm trying," he mouthed.

Alice stared at her and Huey's plates. Both looked half done. "We're going to grab more," she said dragging out Huey. Nico turned to Ally. "It looks good," he said sheepishly. "Thank you," she smiled slightly. Nico stared at his plate embarrassed. "It is from you," she said embarrassed herself. Nico blushed. "She doesn't hate me," he thought smiling.

Yvonne stared at the file in front of her. Alice's picture flashed next to a crimson coat of arms with a lion and stag in it. "Crimson Knights," she thought confused. Alice's words rang in her head. "International law states anyone trying to kill a member of any monarch is to be put to death on the spot." "I wonder how she knew that law," Yvonne picked her guitar up, "Maybe I should pay her a visit."

Ally stared at the wall. "It really does look good," Nico said sitting next to her. Ally stared at it. "Yeah," she said playing with the ring. "Why did you put it on?" he asked confused. "You're my friend, I don't like it when you're hurt," Ally's eyes glowed gold again, "And I'm sorry for overreacting." Nico kissed her cheek making her blush. "I meant what I said," he said making her blush brighter. "You okay?" he said concerned. "Yes," Ally said. Nico sighed. "I really do forgive you," he pointed out. "Knock, knock," Night said at the door. She walked in fixing her antique black diamond ring. "Just checking on you," she said, "You look tired." She felt Ally's forehead. "At least you're not sick," she said worried, "Nice ring by the way." Her glimmered a she spoke. Ally stared out the window as she left. The crescent moon shined through the window. "We should get some sleep," Nico said grabbing his pajamas. Ally grabbed hers as he left the room. She went behind the divider. She walked out from behind laying down on the bed. Nico walked in laying down. He moved her bangs out of the way. "Better," he said yawning. Ally closed her eyes tired. "Good night," she said.

Carmen smiled excitedly at her new guitar case. "Thanks," she said turning to Nico. Ally played with her ring nervously staring at everyone. Alice smiled mischievously as stared at her new O-Pal glad to have her own. She turned to the lonely present under the tree. "It's from Alex," Sam said handing it to Ally. Alora raised an eyebrow. Ally opened the medium sized box to a choker locket. The initials 'A.D.' was engraved in it. She opened it to find it empty. "It's pretty," she said. "It was Kitty's," Night said surprised, "She told me it was a family heirloom." "Leave it to Alex," Sam said staring at the thorns outlining the initials. Ally put the choker in the box carefully. A knock on the door broke the silence. Night stood up getting the door. "Hello Miss Archer." Ally's eye twitched at the name. "Hello, may I come in?" Yvonne asked. "Sure," Night answered. Yvonne entered the living room. "Hello Miss Coupe," she turned to Alice, "May I speak with you alone?" She glared at Huey. "Sure," Alice followed her out. "What's her plan?" Huey turned to Night. "Don't ask questions you don't want answers to," she answered. Huey turned to the door confused.

"Alice Coupe. Daughter of Sam Driscol and Khepri Coupe. Plus a Crimson Knight specializing in offence," Yvonne smiled cruelly as she spoke. "Terra Hunter. Empress Chevalier's right hand woman and head of the Haven International Police," Alice mocked back. Yvonne glared. "How did you know?" she asked annoyed. "Your guitar. Specially designed by you, right?" Alice asked mischievously, "You specialize in long range and short range attacks." Terra cringed in fear. "You're smart," She said sitting across from Alice, "Now how about you tell about Josh Brooks."

Terra's smile turned mischievous. "We've been hunting down team Epsilon for a while now. It was lucky for me they attacked two months ago," Alice's professional voice became taunting, "He didn't fight back really. I don't know what to say about Alexandria Lapis and Cameron Green. I do know he seemed scared of someone named Reaper." Her tone became professional. Terra's eyes widened. "Reaper?" she asked. "Yes," she answered, "He's here or we wouldn't be here." "No more questions," Terra left the room grabbing her coat. "Thank you," Alice said following, "Have a nice day Yvonne." Terra left annoyed. "What did she want to talk about?" Huey asked curious. "Nothing important," Alice answered.

Ally stared at her reflection as she put on the choker. "Need help?" Nico asked watching her. She opened the latch clicking it shut. "No," she said putting her hair down. "Well we better hurry. It is New Year's," Nico took Ally's hand gently. Ally followed blushing a bright pink. Alice sat in the living room watching the news. "Hey love birds," Huey said jokingly. "Beautiful day," Nico grabbed his coat, "Want to go to the park?" Ally shook her yes. "Great," he said excited. Ally grabbed her coat. She got into the reaper sitting down relaxed. "To think you used to get in cautiously," Nico said grinning. Alice watched as he pulled out. "Come on Huey," she said annoyed. "I'm coming," he said.

Nico pulled into the parking lot. Ally got out staring at the bare trees and evergreens. "Let's go," Nico took her hand gently. Ally looked around at the scenery. Her eyes rested on a nearby bench. A guy stood next to it, his sapphire eyes fixed on her. "Hello," he said in an apathetic tone. "Hi," Ally said smiling. The guy gave her a concerned look. "Is there a problem?" Nico asked. "No," The guy stood up fixing his tan trench coat. He walked away annoyed. "Who was that?" Nico asked concerned. "I don't know," she answered. Nico gave her a confused look. Suddenly a scream broke the silence. Ally ran towards the source. "Ally," Nico followed worried. She ran finally finding a woman stuck under a heavy branch. "Don't worry," Ally pulled the branch off carefully. "Thank you," the woman said gratefully. "You're welcome," Ally begun to walk away.

"Where are you going?" said a deep male voice. Ally turned around terrified. Reaper stood behind her clutching his sword. Ally stepped back slowly. "Reaper!" Alice jumped out of a tree in defensive mode. Huey jumped out making a gun appear in his hand. Ally stared in shock.

"The Coupe-Driscol twins, huh. The crème de la crop," Reaper smiled as he drew his sword, "Nice to meet you." He attacked them head on making both dodge. "Run!" Alice yelled turning to Ally. "Where are you going?" Reaper laughed as she ran. Alice grabbed him by the throat pinning him to a tree. "She's escaping," she said as Huey aimed the gun. "She won't make it," Reaper said pushing her off and knocking out both Huey and her. "Too bad it wasn't fatal," he thought going after Ally.

Amunet jumped into the tree watching a young man walk by. His dirty blonde hair was in a mess, his sapphire eyes full of sorrow, and his fair skin complimented his tan trench coat which hid his outfit. Suddenly he turned around looking at her. "Show yourself," he said in an apathetic tone. She jumped down dagger drawn. "You're with Reaper," she sounded insulted. The guy tilted his head confused. "I'm Dante," he said taking out a revolver, "You are?"

"Amunet," she threw the dagger hitting his arm. "That was mean," Dante said pulling out the dagger. His wound healed in a minute. "Now it's my turn," Amunet grabbed a hunting knife. He shot the gun as she deflected his bullets. "You're good," he said smiling faintly. Suddenly his eyes widened in terror. "Benjamin," he said running away. "Benjamin?" Amunet thought confused.

Ally stopped catching her breath. "Thought you could get away," Reaper taunted. Ally glared. Suddenly a needle flew out of nowhere almost hitting Reaper. "Show yourself," he yelled angrily. Alora attacked from a nearby tree throwing a kunai. "Nice try," Reaper caught the kunai annoyed. He threw it back leaving a small scratch on Alora. Ally ran faster than usual. "I won't allow it," Alora drew a small dagger.

"You won't allow what? Her death? Too late," Reaper attacked head on. "I'm not an idiot," she said as she tried to kick him. She missed him scaring her a little. "Started the party without me," Came a hyper and excited voice. Alora looked up to see Terra jumping out of a tree dressed in a punk rock outfit and holding her guitar.

"How about you leave this to me," she said getting a pick out. "Fine," Alora ran following Ally. "Who are you?" Reaper demanded. "Terra Hunter, Local Police," she smiled mischievously. "You're not local police," he pointed out. "You catch on fast," She strummed her guitar lightly then hard making Reaper cover his ears. She put the pick in her pocket attacking head on slamming the guitar in the ground causing it to cover itself in spikes.

A gun shot out of nowhere made Reaper disappear. "What the...?" Terra thought of Regina. "You can thank me later," Night said walking out from behind a tree. "Yeah I am lucky," Terra's teal eyes were full of enthusiasm. "I see," Night said surprised.

"That's right. He attacked out of nowhere," Alice said trying to explain the attack to Khepri. "Who scared him away?" she asked confused. "Night Fiore," Alice said proudly. "Thank you Miss Fiore," Khepri spoke with gratitude "Gotta go," she said getting off annoyed. "Someone is in trouble," Alice thought putting the o-Pal up. Damon sat next to Nico. "It's only going to get worse," he said concerned. "I know," Nico said concerned as well. "We should prepare," Damon pointed out. "Agreed," Nico said. "I wouldn't let anything happen to Ally. I promise," Damon said worried. Nico looked at him surprised. "Thanks," he said happily.

Amunet sat alone the image of Dante stuck in her mind. "How's that possible?" she asked herself confused. "You alright?' Alora asked as she entered the room. "Fine," Amunet lied. "Of course," she sat next to her. Amunet stood up. "I gotta go," she said annoyed. "Poor kid," Alora thought sadly.

Ally sat down staring at Nico's photo of her. "He does care," she thought sadly, "Why can't I care back?" She looked at the O-Pal in front of her. "If only I was told," she said sadly. "You look confused," Night sat next to her. "I'm just wondering," she answered sighing. "Wondering what?" Night asked. "If I consider Nico a more than a friend," Ally's answer surprised Night. "That's up to you to decide. Not me," she said smiling slyly. Ally stood up.

"I think I'll get something to eat," she said leaving the room. Night's eye glimmered bringing her to a beautiful garden. A four year old Ally stared at the koi pond excitedly. "They're beautiful," Catherine said turning to Alexander. He smiled back. "Not as beautiful as you," he said back. He turned to Ally who continued to stare. "I think she likes them too," he said picking her up. She hugged him. "She's a kid. She's supposed to," Catherine pushed Ally's bangs out of her face. The scene disappeared returning to the present. Night sighed sadly. "One can wish," she thought nostalgically.

<u>Part 2</u>

Chapter 15

2156

Jesse sat under the tree reading a book as he tried to study. A sound made him stop as he suddenly scanned the area with his jade green eyes. Whatever it was, it was whimpering nearby. Slowly he got up carefully staying silent walking over to a tree. A girl popped her head out confused and frightened. "Hello," he said politely. "Hello," she said walking out from behind the tree. He looked her over. Her purple uniform contrasted his red school uniform. At the point she looked twelve as he looked fifteen.

"What's wrong?" he asked curious. She looked at two girls nearby. "I'll take care of this," he walked over to the girls acting cocky. "Hello ladies, May I help you?" he asked. "No," The older one answered. "Okay, I thought you were looking for the little girl crying in the boys' room," he pointed out. The girls bolted off making him laugh on the inside. "Thank you," the girl said surprised. "No problem, I'm Jesse," he said trying to look cool. "I'm Alette," the girl said embarrassed. Jesse gave her a befuddled look. "Nice to meet you," he said putting his hand out. Alette shook his hand. "Nice to meet you too," she said smiling at the teenager.

2162

Ally laid in the dew covered grass staring at the clouds. "Beautiful right?" Nico said sitting next to her. "It is," she sat up. She fixed her trench coat. "Pretty soon it will be spring," she pointed out. Nico nodded his head in agreement. Ally blushed as she stared at her ring. "It's been five months," she thought confused, "The wedding seems to be getting closer by the minute." She turned to the O-Pal next to her, a thoughtful gift from Nico. "February, 5, 2163," she said surprised.

"Valentine's day is coming up," Nico said excited. "Isn't that your birthday?" Ally asked not surprised. "Yeah. I'll be twenty-two," he looked at the sky absent mindedly. "What's wrong with that?" She asked. "Nothing," Nico pointed out, "I'm looking forward to it." She smiled back pushing back her new black ombre style bangs letting them cover her eyes lightly. Nico sighed as he stood up. "I don't get it. Why just dye your bangs?" he looked at her puzzled. "Stephen did it himself. I told him as long as it is black and my hairstyle is the same," she stood up as well. "Well it does look good," he leaned in kissing her cheek, "We should head inside."

He headed for the glass doors as Ally grabbed a sketchbook that was hidden behind her. "I'll stay out here," she said. "Your choice," Nico pointed out. "Time is weird thing," Sam said talking on the phone in his room. Nico stopped curious. "They're getting along?" Khepri asked. "All four," he answered. "He must be happy," Nico thought as he walked from the door. "There's always calm before the storm," Khepri's words stopped Nico in his tracks. "I know," Sam sighed. "She's optimistic isn't she," Nico thought as he walked away.

Femi jumped around landing in a puddle causing water to land on Alice. "Who? What? Where?" she asked jumping into fighting position. Huey sat down wrapping a gift for Nico. "I already have yours wrapped," he said, "and no one is here." "No one has attacked in a month. I'm getting paranoid," she said annoyed. "You're telling me," he opened the front door, "I'm trained for defense, not relaxing."

Alice turned to see Ally holding a pencil and paper. "What are you doing?" she asked sitting next to her. She looked over Ally's shoulder to see a picture of Nico and Ally together. "You're drawing a picture of you two together?" She asked confused. Ally smiled faintly. "It's his birthday gift," she said.

"Didn't know you could draw," Alice said surprised. "I design weaponry...I had to learn," Ally raised an eyebrow. "You design weaponry?" she asked sitting next to her. "Yeah," Ally's voice sounded hollow. "Do you want to?" Alice's smoky eyes narrowed.

"Of course," Ally lied. Alice sighed as Ally stood up. "You don't, right?" Alice asked. "No I don't. I don't know what I want to do, but it isn't designing weapons," Ally confessed. Alice looked at her shocked. "I think I'll head inside," she said closing the sketchbook. "Okay," Alice thought confused, "Did I offend her?"

Nico laid on his bed tired. "Sleepy?" Ally asked curious. "Not really," Nico said sitting up and yawning. "You sure," she said sitting down. "I'm sure," Nico held her close. Ally blushed she pushed him away. "I thought you were over that," Nico said sighing. "I still have moments," Ally said nervous. Nico laid down again. "At least you're smiling more," he said happily. "Of course, everything seems brighter," she answered. She felt her face blush red.

"Anyways, what's the big deal with me smiling more?" she demanded. Nico laughed lightly. "Cause when we first met you wouldn't smile at all," he pointed out. He looked outside at the setting sun. "Dinner should be ready soon," he turned to Ally. "That's good," she said looking at the window. She sighed deep in thought. "I was hurt," she thought, "That's why I wouldn't smile."

Alice took a bite of her meal. "Tastes good," she said. "Ally made it," Sam said turning to Ally. Alice gave her a weird look. "I can cook," she glared back. "No one doubted you," Nico pointed out. "Sorry," Alice turned to her plate embarrassed. Ally stared out the glass doors staring at the full moon. "It's beautiful," she said putting her plate in the sink. Nico put his plate in the sink following her out. "She needs space," Huey said sighing. "He gives her space," Sam pointed out. ""Just saying," Huey said calmly. "He does give her space sixty percent of the time," Sam pointed out. "I see," Alice took a bite. "They really did get close," she thought.

Ally laid in bed trying to relax, nervous. "Tired?" Nico asked. "Yeah," she said yawning. She got under the covers. Nico got in holding her close. "Please stop," she said blushing. "Fine," Nico said disappointed. He held her closer. She blushed redder unsure what to do. Looking up she saw he was asleep. "Good night," she whispered as she fell asleep. "Hope you're really asleep," she thought. "Good night," Nico whispered back. "How are you awake?" she asked tired. "I just laid down," he pointed out. Ally smiled gently back. "Good night," she said finally falling asleep.

Sam stared at the calendar amazed. "It's the fourteenth already," he thought worried. He left his room bumping into Nico. "Happy birthday," he said getting up. "Thank you," Nico stood up carefully, "Happy Valentine's day." Sam sighed. "And I'm spending it alone," he said walking away sad. Nico turned toward the bedroom door. He opened the door to Ally napping on the bed. Staring at the wrapped present next to the bed he wondered what was inside.

He looked at the envelope on top of the box. "To: Nico, From: Ally," He looked at her befuddled. He put the card down as she opened her eyes. "Nico," she yawned sleepily. "Yes," he pushed her bangs out of her eyes. "What are you doing here?" she asked. "What do you mean?" he questioned, "This is our room."

"Nico, come here for a moment," Sam yelled from the living room. Nico looked at Ally confused. "Yes," he said entering the living room. Night sat there in her usual black outfit. "Hello," she said holding a present. "That's great! Everyone's here," Sam said excited. Nico turned to the small pile of presents and then to the small group of people. "This wasn't necessary," he pointed out. "It is," Night handed him her gift. He opened to a new tool kit designed for computers. "Thank you," he said as Ally sat next to him. He opened up Alice and Huey's next to a sketch book. Ally watched the pile dwindle as if it were water.

Finally it was her turn. "Here," she said handing him her gift. He smiled as he opened it. "Nice thank you," he said hugging her. Night stared at the drawing of Nico and Ally together. "That is good," she said surprised. Ally blushed as Nico let go. "It's good," he said holding the framed picture carefully. Ally blushed a bright red.

Nico pulled a card and box from the drawer next to him. "Here," he said handing them her. She opened both very carefully. "Thank you," she said smiling at the Valentine's day card. "Glad you like it," Nico said kissing her cheek. She opened the box next blushing a bright red. She stared at the rose gold bracelet with a fire opal. "Thank you, but how did you...?" she stopped herself from asking. "Your welcome," Nico hugged her. "How did he find a 19th century relic?" she asked.

Sam walked outside getting the mail. He went through the mail carefully looking through bills as entered the dugout. He stopped as he reached a surprising envelope. The royal seal was plain as ever it seemed. Turning it around he saw Ally's name. "Ally," he yelled in shock. Ally ran in enraged. "First question: What's wrong?" he asked annoyed.

She threw a magazine on the table. Sam picked it up cautiously. "Heiress magazine," he gave her a confused look. His widened when he saw the title. "*Alette Bellerose's hidden marriage*," He held back his laughter. "This isn't funny," she demanded. "This magazine is nothing but rumors."

Sam sat down, "Now try this." He held two letters: One with the Empress of Haven's Seal and the President of Durand's seal. Ally stared at them trying to think of why she was being contacted. "They're for you," he said handing them over. She opened the one from the royal family first. Her eyes scanned the letter carefully. "I'm invited to the palace along with Nico," she said scared.

"Why?" Sam asked worried. "She wants to talk to me in person," she said surprised. She opened the Durand letter next. "Same thing," she said worried. "Great," Sam said nervous. "In both letters I'm allowed to bring my body guards," she said excited. "That's good," Sam smiled relieved, "Can I come?" "You're on the list too," she pointed out. "So it's a family affair," she thought not surprised.

Damon stared at the woods anxiously. "Calm down," Alora looked at him concerned. "Who knows what she's doing to him," he said. "Is he okay?" Ally asked worried. "He just misses Blaine," Alora said taking Damon's hand. Damon gripped it tightly. "This happens often. Usually at night," Amunet said sitting next to Ally. Nico stared concerned as well. "So when are you going to Cat's Eye city?" she asked curious.

Damon lit up at the words. "In two days on the seventeenth," Ally answered. "Can we go?" Damon asked hopefully. "I only have enough for me, Nico, Sam and the twins," she answered. "As your teacher I demand you take us with you," Damon said.

"I can pay for the train ride," Nico said grabbing his O-Pal, "And the boat ride." Everyone stared making sure he wasn't lying. "You're sure?" Amunet said confused. "Yeah," he said making the reservations. He turned the O-Pal around. "See you're booked," he said explained. "Thank you," Damon said hugging Ally.

"He's the one who booked your ride," she said. "Yeah, but hugging him would awkward," he turned to Nico who glared. "We should pack," he said grabbing Alora and Amunet. "Smart move," Nico said annoyed. "I don't know about you, but I'd more worried about Alora," Ally pointed out. "Why?" he asked. Ally gave him a look. "I get it," he said, "Still Damon is no better." "You're right, he is only friendly," she pointed out. Nico sighed as he realized he lost.

Night stared at the invitation confused. "Who's it from?" Carmen asked. "Empress Eva Chevalier. She wants to talk to me in person," Her eye glimmered, "I don't why either." Carmen watched as she put the letter down. "Pack up, we leave in two days," she said annoyed. Carmen got up walking upstairs. "This isn't going to end well," Night thought, "After all, Eva Chevalier doesn't invite you on a dime. What does she have up her sleeve?"

Ally walked onto the ferry's walkway carefully. "Don't look scared," Nico said taking her suitcase. Ally turned around surprised. "I'm not the only one who got an invitation," she turned to see Night and Carmen. "How did you guess?" Night asked. Alora passed them slightly green. "I'll keep an eye on her. She gets seasick easily," Damon said carrying two bags. "Have fun," Amunet said smiling mischievously. "Come on, this isn't a pleasure cruise," Alice spoke in a serious tone as she walked by.

"Yeah, well I'm happy to see I'm not the only one invited," Ally walked next to Night. "Inviting two psychics...makes one wonder," Night said deep in thought. Huey walked up smiling slyly. "I'll have to keep an eye on him," Sam said sighing. "How about inadvertently inviting the crazy twins?" Ally suggested. "Agreed," Night didn't think for a second even, "But I thought they were Knights." Ally laughed as the ferry went off.

The boat rocked slowly making Alora turn a dark green. "Come on," Damon said taking her outside. "This is interesting," Night said eating a bag of chips as she sat at one of the tables inside. Ally read a book as Nico sat next to her. "Hello Ally," Sybil said excited. Ally turned around exited to see Sybil Jackson run up and hug her. Her medium length hair was hidden under a white fedora, she wore a white blouse with black slacks, and black high heeled boots. "Long time no see," Ally said happily. She fixed her black t-shirt and blue jeans. "Hello Mrs. Katsaros," Cassandra said tauntingly, "Where are you going?" "Cat's Eye city," Night walked up defensively. Sybil gave Cassandra a glare. "We're visiting Shiori Hasu," she said in her famous Cajun accent.

Nico got a scared look on his face. "Shiori Hasu," he said. His face showed complete shock. "Yeah, you have to stop at Shiori Hasu before Cat's Eye City," Night pointed out. "Great," Nico turned to Ally for support. "You okay," Sybil asked concerned. "Yeah," Nico lied. "That's where the boats stopping," Ally pointed out while sitting next to him. "Of course," Nico felt the anxiety rise in chest. Night stood up. "Come on Carmen," she said leaving the dining area. Carmen followed curious. "We need to use the restroom," Sybil dragged Cassandra out.

Sybil glared at Cassandra. "You can't be nice," she said annoyed. "Of course I can. I choose not to," Cassandra said walking down the hallway on the opposite end. "You know she may not be a noble, but she is a human being," Sybil pointed out, "And she is your cousin." "What does that mean?" Cassandra asked. "It means she has feelings just like you and me. What do you hold against her?" She demanded. "She's a Healer!" Cassandra answered, "And will always be one." Sybil burst out laughing. "You share a grandmother. You can't hate her cause she is a Healer," Sybil left, "No wonder you spend time with me. I think we'll part ways when we reach Shiori Hasu." "You don't know what you're doing," Cassandra pointed out. "I know you are ruining your family's reputation," Sybil smiled as she left, "Along with Artemis." Cassandra glared attempting to ignore her words.

"So what's up with you and Cassandra?" Nico asked curious. "You heard my grandfather, she is Favre. She was born and raised to hate the fact that Artemis Favre was forced to give money to my dad when he got married," she pointed out. "Wait a second, this is all a pity fight over money?" he asked. "Yes," Ally answered, "It was part of my grandparent's divorce papers. To ensure health insurance in case the kid was a flame." "She didn't for see you," Nico pointed out. "Yes," she answered, "The Favre's are ruining themselves." An elderly woman walked out leaving the room. Ally stared at her recognizing her slightly. "So she heard her mistake," Ally thought, "I wondered who funded Cassandra's trip."

Night stared at the birds flying by. "Hello," a man said standing next to her. "Do I know you?" she asked annoyed. "My name is Javier, I'm here with a warning," He said looking at her directly, "Watch the moon's phases. After all they are ever changing." "You're a pre-teacher aren't you," Night said surprised. "Watch the moon's phases," the man said walking away. "I should really try focusing on the stars, not the moon," she said worried.

"Knock, knock," Ally said walking into the girls restroom. Alora sat against the wall green faced with her jacket off. She quickly put it back on. "You saw nothing," she said wobbling up. "I saw nothing?" Ally thought. Suddenly it hit her like a ton of bricks. "of course I saw nothing," she said thinking of her black lotus tattoo. "Good," Alora said running into the stall. "I came to tell you we're almost there," she said scared. Alora gave a thumbs up. "So, I will send Damon down," she closed the door behind her. "What was that?" she thought.

Alice sat in front of the O-Pal. "We still can't find him. But knowing Reaper, he's following you," Khepri said worried. "Got it. We'll keep alert," Alice said professionally. "Yeah," her mother said annoyed. Alice sighed. "Talk to you later," Khepri said hanging up. "We're here," Huey said smiling mischievously. "Great," Alice said excited, "Let's go." She ran out with her O-Pal making Huey follow.

Chapter 16

Ally walked off the ferry's walkway carefully. She looked around amazed. The classic look seemed to stick out. "It hasn't changed," Night said sadly. "You're from here?" Alice asked confused. "Of course. I'm well known here. Usually as the rebel," she said getting off. Nico walked off shaking. "Night?" Came a sickly sweet voice. Night turned around in horror to see a woman with short black hair and amber eyes. Her red t-shirt and blue jeans complimented her fair skin.

"Sol," Night's usually calm voice had a hint of anger. Sol walked over excited. "It's been a long time," she said. "There's a reason for that Sol," Night complained. "Who's your friends?" Sol asked her voice more soothing then Night's sarcasm. "Alette Bellerose and company," Night said angrily.

Sol looked Ally over surprised. "You're Kitty's daughter," she said. She turned to Nico. "Nico," She ran over hugging him. "Hello Sol," Nico said trying to push her off. She let go staring at the luggage. "Need a place to stay?" she asked nicely. "Sure," Sam answered before Night had a chance to speak. "You haven't changed Sam. Is there anyone else in your party?" she asked curious. Alice and Huey raised their hands. Carmen shook her head yes. Damon and Alora raised their hand while Amunet shook her head yes. "I know someone. You can wait at my place till they get you," she said walking towards a minivan. "I might not have enough room," she said thinking.

Ally looked around the enormous living room of the Fiore family home turning to Night. "Don't be so down," Sol said optimistically. Night growled as the doorbell rang and Sol walked over opening the front door. "You called," A man walked in looking around. Ally stared at his short ash blonde hair and champagne colored eyes. He dressed in a white button up shirt and black slacks.

"You must be Alette," he said walking over to her, "I guess all Healers do look alike." Nico glared at him. "How do you know me?" Ally gave him a confused look. "I'm sorry. Alec Alkeav, Erica's younger brother," he said politely. She looked at him even more confused. "She does talk about me?" he looked worried. "Yes, about how strict you are," Ally said anxious.

"So I'm taking you two," he said looking at Nico and Ally, "and who else?" "Sam, Damon and Alora," Sol answered. "Fine by me," he turned to Ally, "Come on. The car is this way." "So how is Grandpa Seth?" Ally asked. "He's doing well," Alec answered. He started the car thinking and realizing. "You haven't seen him since you were five. He will be happy to see you," Alec said all excited. Ally stared at him worried. "It's been a long time," she sounded concerned. "Are you okay?" Sam asked her. Ally shook her head yes. "Okay," he thought.

Sol stood in front of the stove pouring cooking wine into spaghetti sauce. Loud music interrupted her cooking going throughout the house. "Can you watch this?" she asked Alice. "I'll be happy to," Huey said standing up. He walked over stirring the sauce. "Turn that down," Sol told a teenager with long brown hair and Amethyst eyes. "It's Ares Army, So no," the teenager said defiantly. Sol sighed. "Please turn it down," she pleaded. "You heard your mother," Night walked up to the room, her eye glimmering. "Fine," she walked over turning down the music, "Now who are you?" Night smiled in response. "Your worst nightmare," she said calmly. "She's you're Aunt Night," Sol said embarrassed. She turned to Night. "This is my daughter, Jessica Fiore," she said rubbing her forehead. Jessica glared at Night. "The only other Fiore," Night glared back scaring her while Sol walked away embarrassed again.

Alec turned into a long drive way as Nico stared at the horses surprised. "Welcome to the Alkeav Ranch," he said parking his car, "So your train leaves in the morning?" "Afternoon," Nico said grabbing Ally's and his luggage. Alec unlocked the front door revealing a nature based interior. "Beautiful," Alora said in astonishment. "This is the way Uncle Seth likes it. So I keep it this way," Alec said holding a random bag, "Whose is this?" "Mine," Alora said walking up. "Sorry," he said handing it to her. Ally walked over to the family photos. She stared at one of her mother. "Whose with her in this photo?" she asked. "Night," Alec answered staring at it, "I believe she was in her third month. But enough about that, after all that incident has been handled." Sam stared at him surprised.

"She was pregnant," Ally said in shock. "That's enough," he went deep into thought. "Where's the kid?" Damon asked curious. "I don't know. Only Night, Kitty, and the father knew that," Alec looked at them surprised. He calmed down. "It isn't something you would talk about," A calming voice said sighing making Ally excited. She turned around to see a fifty year old man. "Grandpa," she said running up to him and hugging him. "Sunshine," he said hugging her back, "How is everything? No, wait...how is your father?" He sounded displeased. "Dying," she answered. Seth looked down sadly. "Poor guy, he'll be meeting Kitty soon," he pointed out. "I thought you were mad at him?" Sam asked. "I don't wish for him to go young," he pointed out. He saw the fear in Ally's eyes.

"Allow me to show you to your rooms," he said leading the way. He walked up the stairs as everyone followed. "Here's where you'll be staying," he turned to Sam. Sam looked at the spacious bedroom not surprised. "Yours is across the hall. I assume you are a couple," Seth turned to Damon and Alora grinning. "You guessed right," Alora smirked in response. He turned to Ally and Nico smiling. "You'll stay in Kitty's room," he opened the door to a classically designed bedroom. "Cool," Ally said walking in amazed. "Your mom had taste," Nico said putting the luggage down. "One thing Ally got from her mother," Seth pointed out, "Like the hat." He stared at her white fedora. "Thanks," Ally said putting it down.

He walked away deep in thought. "He'll be fine, right?" Nico asked concerned. Ally shrugged her shoulders. "He hasn't been the same since mom died," she pointed out. "He does seem happy to see you," he pointed out, "And in good health, for his age." "Healers do need to exercise, after all we do have a lot more energy to burn through than your average person," she pointed out. "Explains why he is slightly buff," Nico answered. "No, most Healers look like that apparently," she explained.

"By the way I haven't seen a picture of your grandmother," Nico spoke randomly, hoping to change the subject. "He doesn't talk about her...much," Ally answered. "Why?" he asked. "He was put in an arranged marriage with a controlling, manipulative woman," she was cut off by Nico. "By who?" he asked. "Angeline Durand's own son, Blaine," she explained. "His grandmother is Angeline Durand?" Nico asked. "Everyone in town knows it," Ally explained, "So don't bring it up." Nico did the silent symbol.

Jessica snuck into the kitchen quietly. "Hungry?" Night asked. She turned on the lights to see Night sitting at the table. "How long have you been sitting there?" her eyes filled with terror. "Two hours," Night got up and started circling her like a vulture, "Who is he?" "Who is who?" Jessica's sarcasm turned into anxiety. "Your boyfriend," Night said angrily. "I don't have a boyfriend," she said shaking. "Your mother never told you that I'm a retro teacher," she smiled mischievously. Jessica whimpered. "Cairo Jefferson," she said scared. "He's eighteen and you're an idiot," Night pointed out. "What does that mean?" Jessica demanded.

"I fell for an older man at sixteen. But he was never at the birth. Plus your mother took my son away," Night's violet eye turned black, "It's all because your mother sent your grandparents on a vacation. She wanted me to focus on school...not a child. Such a blatant lie. She was eighteen and still living at home. She could've just moved or married. " Jessica gave Night a sympathetic look. "I never got a chance to raise my kid," she said sadly, "But I will let you in on a secret." She handed a copy of the lease. "Call it 'insurance'. You can kick Sol out if she wants to get rid of the kid," she pointed out, "And if you need help, call Seth Alkeav. You didn't hear it from me." "Thank you," she said. "Your welcome," Night walked away smiling.

Ally sipped her tea as everyone talked. Alora turned to the moonlit ranch staring at its beauty. "It's wonderful," she said turning to Damon. "One of the perks of living of here," Alec said happy to have company. Alora grinned. "Must be nice," she said anxiously. Damon gave her a concerned look. "I'm sure we'll settle down," he said comforting her. Seth washed the dishes ignoring everyone. "Grandpa?" Ally's voice made him leave. "You do look a lot you're your mother," Alec pointed out. Nico stared at the stars. A clanging bought him back. "Ally," he watched as she stood at the exit. "Yes," she said surprised. He got up putting his plate in the sink. "Don't forget me," he said. Alec watched them leave surprised. "He does that often," Sam said annoyed. "Really?" Alec asked. "Yeah," Sam sighed.

Carmen laid in bed feeling for a pillow. "Here," Amunet said. She turned to Amunet handing her a pillow. "Thanks," she said taking it. Amunet turned around returning to her cot. "You can take the bed," Carmen said concerned. "I'm fine," Amunet, said closing her eyes. "You don't sleep well, do you?" Carmen asked. "Not with you talking," Amunet answered. "Well, have you tried looking at the bright side?" Carmen asked. "No," Amunet said more annoyed. "Just wondering," Carmen said sleepily. "Night doesn't seem fond of Sol," Carmen pointed out. "I haven't noticed," Amunet said. "She seems controlling, Sol not Night," Carmen continued. "So Night is different than day?" Amunet snickered. "Yeah," Carmen laughed a little. The door opened making them silent. "It's just me," Night said making them sit up, "Now don't get involved into things you don't know." She closed the door worrying them.

Ally twisted and turned as she tried to sleep. She turned to Nico who held her close as he slept. "Alice stop that," he said in his sleep. Ally pulled away putting a pillow in her place. She left the room staring at the engagement ring on her finger listening to the silence. Suddenly the front door opened and closed making Ally jump. She left the house following the faint sound of voices. "She's just like Kitty in appearance," Seth said sadly, "But she has Alexander's attitude." "Night thinks so as well," Sam sighed. "Makes me miss Kitty more," Seth's words surprised Ally causing her to step on a branch. "Who's there?" Seth asked defensively. Ally walked out frightened. Sam smiled. "It's okay. You surprised us," he said trying to calm her down. "You can join in the conversation," Seth said embarrassed.

The woman walked down the hallway, her long sleeved black Goth Lolita dress was covered in blood. She fixed her top hat in her medium length light pink hair and wiped off her tights and heels. Quietly she pressed her earpiece. "Target terminated," she said emotionlessly. "Understood," the male voice on the other end said excited, "Now return to get your next assignment." "Yes sir," she said signing off. "I didn't have to do anything," Came an arrogant voice. The woman turned around to a man to see with medium length brown hair and jade green eyes. His black leather jacket complimented his dark blue jeans and combat boots. "You should keep your voice down Jinx," she said annoyed. "Like you were Lyric?" Jinx laughed amused. Lyric stared at the case on his back. "We need to go. We have another assignment," she said leading the way. Jinx followed curious. "Yes Mam," he said joking. "I wonder what the next assignment is?" he asked. "It's not our job to ask," Lyric answered. "Okay...I guess I hit a button," Jinx thought to himself.

Ally stared at the night sky astounded by the stars. "Why was Nico embarrassed to come here?" she turned to Sam. "He was born here," Seth answered sighing. "Really," Ally gave him a surprised look. "His father raised him up to the Durand war," Seth continued, "Him and his step-mother died in an attack on Shiori Hasu." "After that Sol and her husband took him in. She could handle him, he couldn't leading to a divorce. She never forgave him for that," Sam gave Ally a serious look, "I came after his parents' death. He ran up to me curious, he was only four. Of course, I knew he ran up for safety and shelter. As he left I saw how sad he looked and how mad Sol looked. It was unnatural. Plus, as a psychometric, I knew what was going on by holding his hand." Sam turned to Ally sympathetically.

"Well during my stay I talked to Sol and we decided it would be better if I took him in. He was excited. I finally took him in a couple months later. He loved living with me, especially when he met you. He wasn't very social," Sam pointed out. Ally looked down remembering the funeral. "Anyway, we should get some sleep," Sam opened the front door. "Agreed," Seth said walking in. Ally entered The conversation stuck in her head.

Chapter 17

Ally put her plate in the sink. "What was Night like as a kid?" Alora asked putting her plate in the sink. "Rebellious," Seth laughed, "She cared about Kitty though. Never let her out of her sight. Kitty was hurt when she left." Damon raised an eyebrow as Nico put his plate in the sink. "Makes sense," Alora said yawning. A ringing broke the silence. "Hello," Sam answered his O-Pal. A high-pitched yelling made him cringe. "She's your sister," he said sighing. The yelling continued. "Gotta go," he said hanging up. Alec stared at him confused. "Don't ask," he said embarrassed. "I knew Night would explode eventually," Alec sounded scared. "She hasn't actually, she's about to," Sam answered. "And no one will stop her," Seth pointed out.

Alice bit her toast viciously. "You have issues," Jessica stared at her. Amunet glared at her, her cat eyes glowing darkly. "What?" her eye twitched in fear. "I'm sure it's nothing," Sol said putting down her juice. Night got up putting her dishes in the dishwasher. "I've never seen her act like that," Huey said surprised. Sol stood up putting her dish in the dishwasher following her out. Jessica looked around the dining room scared. "It's too silent," she said frightened.

Sol walked into the backyard concerned. "Night," she said walking over to tree. "Hello Marisol," Night leaned against a tree. "Why walk out?" Sol asked confused. "I don't know," Night said as her eye glimmered, "Ask Dimitri." "Night, Dimitri is dead," Sol said sadly. Night laughed. "You shouldn't be happy. Your son suffered terribly," she leaned against the fence. "At your hand," Night pointed out, "If you let me keep him instead of sending mom off and giving him to Dimitri...maybe he wouldn't have suffered." "He scared Cain away," Sol said glaring back. "Why? Was he scared of a toddler?" Night said nonchalantly. "He took after you, Notte. Only thing he didn't have was your ability," she pointed out.

"So you blame me for a failed marriage," Night smiled, "Why don't you see you cause your own problems?" "You can't hold a grudge forever," Sol walked over annoyed. "Watch me," Night walked away angrily, "After all your time here is limited." "What did you do Night?" Sol asked. "Nothing," Night answered, "Just evening out the playing field." "This is about Jessica and the fact I kept her," Sol said. "Not completely, Yes, you're right that I couldn't keep him, but I still got to raise him and did it with a wonderful man. You lost, Marisol," Night entered the house leaving Sol confused, "I'll call a taxi." The door closed as Sol broke down and cried. Sol turned to the fence where a nosy neighbor watched eating popcorn. "Was it really that entertaining?" she asked. "We knew that was going to happen," she answered.

Jessica stared in the mirror trying to think and remembering the conversation that Night and Sol had. "He's my cousin," she thought smiling, "I have a cousin. She lied to me." A knock on the door caught her attention. "Remember," Night whispered. Jessica shook her head yes. "I look forward to seeing you," Night gave her a hug, "Give me a call." "Thank you," Jessica said as she left. Night walked passed an angry Marisol. "Have a good day," she said entering the taxi and closing the door before she threw something. Sol turned to Jessica. "What did she tell you?" she demanded. "I'm pregnant," Jessica answered holding up the lease in her name, "And moving in with Seth Alkeav."

Ally stared at the bronze train marked 'Eden'. "Wow," Nico said standing next to her. "Yeah," she said excitedly. "It looks safe on the outside," Alice said walking up. Alora sighed relieved. "At least it's not a boat," she laughed. She turned to Ally glaring lightly. Ally looked back scared. Amunet turned to Nico. "Which car?" she asked curious. "Royal car. She wants us to be comfortable I guess," he said joking. Sam walked onto the train. "Come on guys," he said. Nico grabbed his and Ally's luggage. "Come on," he said. Ally boarded last amazed by the golden interior. "Needs to be toned down," Alice complained. "No it doesn't," Amunet said apathetically. Alice ignored her comment. "Come on. Our car is this way," Damon said leading the way. Amunet and Alora followed. "Ours is this way," Sam turned to Alice and Huey. Both followed as he walked the opposite direction. Nico turned to the door on the opposite end. "Come on," he said taking Ally's hand. She blushed as people stared at them. Nico stopped as Ally fixed her waist coat making it look nicer.

"This is it," Nico said opening the lavishly designed door. Ally stared at the tan couch and glass tables. She opened the door in the back to a small bedroom with a bed decorated in gold sheets and a red comforter. "We should be there tomorrow," Nico said closing the door. Ally looked around the car still surprised. "Who's picking us up?" she asked curious. "Terra Hunter," he answered. "You mean 'Yvonne Archer'?" she asked jokingly. "Yeah," he said laughing. Ally sat on the couch as the train started. Nico sat next to her pushing her hair back gently. "What?" she asked curious. He moved her bang from her eyes. "Nothing," he said looking down. She gave him a confused look. "Is it something in my teeth?" she asked. He kissed her gently. "Nope," he answered, "It's the fact we finally have alone time." Ally laughed. "That is true," she pointed out. He gave her a loving look making her blush. "Okay," she thought, "This is getting awkward."

Alice walked down the train scanning with her piercing gaze. "Looking for someone?" a conductor asked concerned. "No," she answered, "Thank you for asking." The conductor walked away suspicious. "Ok," he said. "That was close," Alice thought entering her car. "How was the check?" Huey asked sipping his soda. "Good on my end," she said sitting down. "Mine too," Huey said playing on his O-Pal. "Why check the train in the first place?" Sam asked curious. "We need to make sure everyone is safe," Alice answered. "Okay," Sam said in agreement. "Well I'm going to the dining car," Huey said standing up. His stomach growled loudly. "Okay," Alice laid back. "We both know what he's up to," Sam said slyly.

"No, what's he up to?" Alice asked curious. Sam glared at her annoyed. "To talk to Amunet," he said. Alice sighed. "You're just like your mother," he thought, "Just a little more naive." "Sean asked about you," Alice said randomly. "Who?" Sam asked curious. "Sean and Flora," she answered, "They were worried about you while you were gone. You should check on them when you get back." "My parents worried about me," he explained, "They probably weren't happy with me leaving in the first place." "They weren't, Flora told me to say hi and get your ass home," she smiled genuinely enjoying her time. "When you call her, tell Flora will do," he agreed.

Huey walked down the hallway staring at the scenery as it passed by. The green hills and beautiful country side made the view fantastic. "Bored too?" He turned to see Amunet standing behind him. "Yeah," he answered. "Hungry?" she asked curious. His stomach growled loudly again answering her question. "Yes," he sighed. Amunet smiled back. "Can I join you?" she asked curious. "Sure," he answered. Amunet took the lead. "You're not too happy. I thought you would like my invitation," she clarified confused. "I'm still trying to figure you out," he said. "How much have you figured out?" she asked as her cat eyes filled up with curiosity. "You act older then you should," he answered. Amunet looked down. "So...we're all different," she said smiling weakly. Huey sighed as ran up opening the door to the dining car. "Ladies first," he said.

Amunet entered cautiously. "Thank you," she said politely, "So what else have you figured out?" Huey sat down. "That you're hiding something," his words made her mad as she suddenly got defensive. "So?" she asked angrily. "You don't have to tell me," Huey said calmly. Amunet glared. "He knows something," she thought, "Let's hope it's not what I think." "What else?" she asked. "Are you're not fully human are you?" he asked. "We'll talk about this later," she answered. "He doesn't know, but he suspects," she sighed relieved at the thought. Huey looked at his menu embarrassed. "Sorry," he said. "It's alright," she answered. She saw a familiar face at a nearby table freaking her out, Alexandria Lapis. In the blink of an eye she was gone. "Didn't think it was going to be so soon," she thought.

Ally entered the dining car carefully looking around as she took a nearby seat. "Hello," Alora sat across from her, her sarcastic voice suddenly serious. Ally looked at her scared. "Can we talk in private?" Alora asked calmly. She shook her head yes. Alora stood up motioning her to follow. She followed her down the hallway into an empty room. "Now let's talk," she closed the door behind her, "You saw something you shouldn't have ever seen." She took off her leather jacket revealing her black lotus tattoo. "You don't want me to tell," Ally said as her voice cracked. "Of course, This if from a special gang I'm trying to forget," Alora glared at her intensely, "in fact it's a special brand."

Ally gulped. "Who would do that?" she asked. "Don't ask questions you don't want answers to," Alora answered. Footsteps interrupted their conversation as the door started to open. A conductor walked into see Alora kissing Ally. "What are you doing in the conductor's car?" he asked. "We got lost," Alora answered, "We just wanted some...," the conductor cut her off. "I don't want to know. Just leave please," he said. Both left in a hurry. "I won't tell," Ally whispered. "Of course you won't. We are friends after all," Sarcasm returned to Alora's voice, "I see why Nico likes you." "Can I go now?" Ally asked scared. "Go ahead," Alora put her jacket back on as Ally walked away almost running.

Nico laid on the bed asleep. "Ally?" he said waking up. He looked around the empty room. "She's probably at the dining car still," he thought leaving the room. He stared at Ally as she slept on the couch. "Maybe not," he thought walking over. She yawned as she woke up. "Hey Nico," she said smiling faintly. "Hey," Nico sat next to her as she sat up knocking his wallet out of his pocket. "I'm sorry," she picked it up upside-down causing everything to fall out. Ally stared at the money in the pile suspiciously as he picked it up. "I have a good job," he said embarrassed. She turned to a piece of paper picking it up. "It's a royalty check," she said nervous. She stared at the name on the paper. "You're the creator of the O-Pal," she said surprised. "Yeah," he took the check back defensively, "And you wear lip gloss."

"No I don't," Ally sighed. "Then why are wearing it?" he asked. She felt her lips tasting the lip gloss. "Cherry, oh crap," she thought. "I'm sorry," she said embarrassed. Nico blushed. "It's okay," he said sitting down. A knock on the door ruined the moment causing Ally to jump. "I'll get it," Nico got up opening the door. "Hello," Night smiled mischievously. "Hello," Nico said still red. She turned to Ally grinning. "Hello," Ally said politely. "Just checking on you two?" she smiled mischievously, "Have a good day Ally?" Nico gave a Night a confused look. "Night," Carmen walked up. "And to invite you to dinner," Night said embarrassed. "Sure," Ally said excited. "Great. Meet you in the dining car in one hour," her eye glimmered as she walked away.

Nico twitched as he turned to Ally. "She creeps me out sometimes," he admitted sitting on the couch. She sat next to him still in shock as she wiped off the lip gloss. "I should've told you," he said, "And what's with the lip gloss?" "Alora kissed me," she answered. Nico felt numb. "You were kissed...by Alora?" he asked. "I saw that coming a mile away," he pointed out, "So...why?" "We were having a conversation and the conductor came and she kissed me," she answered. "How?" he asked. "She went all out," she answered. Nico kissed her in a similar fashion. "How was that?" he asked. "Perfect," she answered. "It's okay," she said smiling slightly, "I should've seen it coming. You being rich." Nico looked at her surprised. "Yeah," he said nervously. "You're still the same guy to me," she said. Nico smiled sheepishly. "Thank you," he said. "You're welcome," she said back.

Night laughed as Ally started to calm down. "That's a bad joke," she turned to Alora. "My dad told it a lot," she said laughing. Nico took a bite out his steak staring at Alora then Ally. "It's still bad," he said sipping his white tea. Damon gave him a glare. "What is his problem?" he thought. Amunet stared at Huey confused. "What?" Huey asked staring back. "Nothing," she spoke with slight emotion surprising everyone. Ally stood up heading for the exit. "Where are going?" Sam looked at her concerned. "Back to the royal car. Thanks for the meal," she said turning to Night.

"No problem," Night said. She turned to the clock. "Twelve o'clock midnight," she thought sighing. Nico got up. "How about you stay?" Night suggested. "But...Sure," he returned defeated. Night smiled slyly. "You're not leaving your 'mother' so early," she said joking. "I'm still looking for my mother," he said sadly. Sam glared at Night. "You're looking for your mother?" she asked surprised. "Yeah, I've searched every database, but it's a closed adoption," he smiled faintly. Sam's glare worsened. "Really," Night glared back. "Yeah," he poked what was left of his steak. Night sighed. "Well...good luck," she said with melancholy.

Chapter 18

Lyric entered the abandoned building carefully. She listened as her heals clicked on the pavement. "Where is he?" Jinx asked annoyed. His leather jacket was open revealing a red t-shirt. "Who knows?" came a creepy voice. Jinx turned to a tall woman walking out from the shadows. She played with her long wavy auburn hair staring at Jinx and Lyric with cold unfeeling jade green eyes. Her black blouse and blue jeans hid her hour glass figure. "What do you mean?" Lyric asked. The woman walked over, her heels clicking on the pavement. "I mean 'who knows'?" she said sadistically. Lyric glared at her with her steel grey eyes.

"Hello," Reaper said scaring everyone, but the woman. The trio turned around to see Reaper holding three folders. "Here's your assignments," he said handing them out. Jinx took his surprised by how thin it was. Lyric smiled mischievously. "Here you go Amethyst," he said handing on to the red head. Amethyst smiled as she took it. "They'll be on the 'Victory'. A train heading towards Durand," Reaper said slightly angry. Jinx looked at this profile shocked. "Something wrong?" Reaper demanded. "No," he answered. "Good. Bastet will be informed of your progress," Reaper said smiling slyly as he left the building. Jinx looked at the profile anxiously. The name Alette Nicole Bellerose was written on the paper.

Night stared at the scenery as it passed by. "Good morning," Sam said sitting across from her. "We'll be stopping soon," she said in a serious tone. "Are you like this every morning?" he asked. "On occasion," Carmen answered him. "Good morning," Alice said cheerfully. "Yeah, Good morning," Huey yawned. "We'll be stopping soon," Night said turning to them. "Cool," Alice said excited. Night sighed as Ally stared out the window amazed as Cat's Eye city came into view. The buildings glowed in the sunlight, there modern yet classic designs making them stand out. She watched the scenes as the train came to a stop. Ally left the train, her crystal blue eyes full of wonder. "Pretty cool," Nico said following. "Agreed," Night said sarcastically. Alora laughed as she stared at the ads on the wall. "That one is selling I don't what," she pointed out. "That's a movie, plus it's kid's film," Nico retorted. "I thought it was a website," Damon said randomly. "So let's just wait," Night said ending the conversation. "Sounds good," Nico said in agreement.

Damon sat on the staircase staring at the clock. "She's late," he pointed out. Nico played on his O-Pal. "You okay?" Carmen asked concerned. "Yeah, I'm fine," he said worried. "Hello," Terra said from behind. Everyone turned around surprised to see her. Terra looked at them befuddled as Ally noticed her different look. She wore a punk style outfit, but her hairstyle stayed the same. "Hello," Ally said embarrassed. "She looks like a teenager," Night thought. "Follow me," her musical tone sounded serious. "Strange I always thought you were a teenager," Huey said sarcastically. "Well Mr. Driscol, I always thought you were the younger one," she joked back. Huey felt his eye twitch. "I am," he felt insulted. "Please follow me," She smiled mischievously as she walked. Ally sighed as she left to three minivans.

"We expected you to bring extra guest," Terra said slyly. "Then why not pay for us?" Damon demanded. "I don't know," Terra answered. "She was too busy doing background checks on all of us," Night thought rolling her eyes. Ally watched as Nico gave their bags to a Terra who put them in the trunk. "Come on," he said opening the door for her. Ally played with her choker nervously as she thought of meeting the empress. Looking in the back she saw Night and Carmen as she sat down in the front. "Let's go, shall we," Terra started the van driving fast. "Slow down," Ally turned to Alice in the back. "I'm already late," she glared. Alice stayed quiet reluctantly.

Carmen watched the scenery pass by. The newly designed buildings made her eyes widen while the Roman Coliseum amazed her. "That's been around forever," Ally said surprised. "It's a national landmark," Terra pointed out, "Especially to Eva. That's where she met her husband Alberi."   "Alberi Chevalier," Ally thought, "Makes sense." Alice turned to it watching it pass by. "So you must know the history of this town," She pointed out. "A little. I'm not a Cat's Eye native," Terra answered, "I was born in the Celtic Union." She took a sharp turn. "Celtic Union?" Ally asked. "Yeah, My parents are Scots-Irish," she answered, "Only there my ability is rare. Here it's massively common."

She drove through a huge gate into a circle drive. "We're here," she said smiling. Ally stared at the huge roman palace in shock. Terra stopped the car opening the trunk. She then opened the doors allowing Ally to walk out following Nico as two people grabbed their luggage. "I wonder how long it took to build this," Carmen asked curious. "Twenty years," Night answered, "The original emperor didn't want to be. So they built it." Terra smiled slyly. "That's right. Now follow me," she said. Ally watched others in uniform came to help out.

Everyone followed Terra as they entered the grand palace. "Wonderful...right?" she turned to the empress's guest. "I think so," Alora answered. Ally looked around not impressed. "Now," Terra announced, "We will need to make sure you're not carrying anything that might harm someone." "You're doing a search?" Alice asked, "Sounds good." Huey glared at his sister wondering what was going on in her head. Everyone was checked making Ally nervous. "I'm last aren't I," she thought. Terra walked over concerned. "Okay?" she asked concerned. "Yeah," Ally answered shaking. "I'll search you than," Terra spoke calmly. "She suspects me doesn't she?" Alora thought, "I'll have to be careful."

Terra walked up the stairs entering a long hallway. "Your room is to the right," She turned to Night pointing to a huge brown door, "Carmen yours is next to hers." Carmen grinned excited. Terra continued down the hallway. "Mr. Bellamy, you and your fiancée get the red door," she pointed to a beautiful crimson door. She continued putting everyone in a certain room. She stopped at a black door. "This is your door," she said turning to Ally and Nico. Ally opened the door to a purple and black room. "Nice," Nico said sitting on the couch. "Please enjoy your accommodations," Terra said closing the doors behind her. Ally looked around confused. "Something wrong?" Nico asked concerned. "No," she answered. "Okay," Nico sighed as Ally sat on the bed overwhelmed by all the stress.

Suddenly the door cracked open. "Hello?" Nico asked surprised. Adonis walked in in shock. "Ally," he said excited. "Hey Adonis," Nico said greeting him. "Hi, Nico," He said excited. He turned to Ally then to his clock. "Nice to see you both again," he said taking a seat. Nico sighed. "Nice to see too," Ally greeted back. "How have you been?" he greeted her smiling. "Pretty well," Nico answered before Ally. "Adonis," Someone called out. "Sorry, I got a dance lesson," he left the room. "I would almost call him your shadow," Nico joked.

"Ha-ha, very funny," Ally answered, "So, what's the Celtic Union?" "The Celtic Union is the reconstructed United Kingdom, only they are under Scottish rule," Nico pointed out. "Are there any other places like us?" Ally asked. "Sure, the Netherlands is one," Nico thought for a second, "Let's just say there are lots of them. As far we know, we're the only who changed our name and renamed our cities. The rest of the world thinks that is silly." "I see," Ally spoke not sure what to make of this. "We are not the center of the world," Nico pointed out. "I know, I just didn't expect everyone else to do the same," she said.

Adonis walked down the hallway deep in thought. "I can't believe they're here," he thought excited. Suddenly he bumped into someone. "Sorry," he said getting up. "It's my fault," Carmen said rubbing her head. Adonis looked at her surprised. "What something in my teeth?" she asked. "No, I don't have much of a social life. I usually hide unless needed," he blushed. " "Congratulations...You've talked to people," Amunet said in an apathetic voice. Carmen glared at her. "Don't mind her," Carmen said talking to Adonis. "Ok," he blushed even more.

"I'm Carmen Crimson Bello. What's your name?" "Adonis Chevalier," he said sheepishly. "Amunet," Amunet glared at him. "Nice to meet you," Adonis said. Amunet's eyes narrowed giving her the appearance of a tigress. "Sir," Terra walked over angrily. "What?" Adonis asked annoyed. "Your mother wants you," she said crossing her arms. "Fine," he said following her, "See you later." "Nice guy," Amunet smiled mischievously, "Wouldn't you agree miss Bello?" Carmen walked away nonchalantly. "Not funny," she exclaimed. "I know," Amunet followed her laughing, "That was smooth 'talking'." "Not funny," Carmen pointed out.

"She was nice, but Amunet seemed distant," Adonis said excited. His mother smiled slightly. "Sounds good," she said calmly, "Carmen sounds sweet. This Amunet, what was she like?" "Distant, naive, and apathetic," he answered, "Almost like she doesn't want to know you." "Maybe she doesn't," Eva explained, "After all we all have something to hide." A knock on the door interrupted them. "Come in," his mother said. "Dinner is almost ready," Terra said opening the door. "Get all our guest together then," she spoke gently, "And please get information on Amunet and Alora." "Yes, Your majesty," Terra stayed in the watching. "Do you want to sit next to miss Bello?" she turned to Adonis. "Sure," he answered almost immediately.

"We'll save her a seat," Eva stood up, "We should get ready to greet our guest." He gave his mother a nod in agreement as he left. "Why Alora?" Terra asked curious. "I've seen her picture before.

Please look for both in the Black Lotus Dossier," she ordered. "Yes, Your Majesty," Terra almost left grinning ear to ear knowing what she wanted to know. Suddenly she stopped. "I did hear a rumor that they were putting together Project Canine and Project Feline, But they couldn't get Project Feline to work," she pointed out. "How?" Eva asked. "No one knows. Project Canine and Project Feline's files were destroyed by my predecessor," she pointed out, "I did see two names: Alexandria Lapis and Amunet Argyis." Eva's eyes widened. "Continue your work," she ordered, "And fill me in later." Terra left immediately. "So Lapis's daughter was alive," she thought sadly, "That monster."

Ally took a seat confused by the look of the table. "It will be fine," Nico said sitting next to her. Carmen stared at her seat puzzled. "Take a seat," Night said taking her seat. "So where is our hostess," Alora asked. "Hello," Came a calm voice. Everyone turned around to see a woman with short burgundy hair and emerald eyes. She wore a thin black suit and low heels. "Welcome everyone. I am your hostess Eva Chevalier," she smiled slyly.

Ally looked her over. Like Adonis, she looked her age and had a natural look of excitement while Adonis stood next to her nervous. Night's eye glimmered as she smiled. "So that's why she wants us here," she thought. Eva sat down smiling mischievously at Ally and Night. "Nice to meet you miss Bellerose. Adonis has told me a lot about you," her emerald eye glimmered the same as Night's did as she spoke. Ally turned to Adonis surprised. "Hello," he said talking to Carmen. "Hi," she said back. "This will be interesting," Night thought surprised, "Something seems off about her, and familiar."

Alexander poked at his steak. "You ok?" Erica gave him a concerned look. "Yeah," he lied. "You miss her," she sighed, "I called her, she's fine." Alexander gave her a surprised look. "She is? Did she ask about me?" he asked anxiously. "Yes. I told her you were fine," she said trying to calm him down. He smiled relieved. "I also told her to calm down too," she thought, "She freaked out more than he would have."

Night watched Eva carefully as she ate her meal. She turned to Carmen who was enjoying her time with Adonis. "Really," he sounded surprised. "Yeah, Sadly we sent Femi back to Alexander's," Carmen explained. "Miss Bellerose. Miss Fiore," Eva said smiling. "Yes," Ally responded. "Can you please meet me in my study tomorrow?" she asked politely. "Sure," Night answered, "Ally will be there too." Ally stared at both of them confused. Eva smiled slyly reminding Ally of Femi. "Looking forward to it," she said. Night's eye glimmered. "This will be interesting," she thought.

"So what do you think she wants to talk about?" Ally asked walking with Night down the hallway. "From what I saw, something called the 'Black lotus," Night answered. Ally remembered Alora's tattoo. "Speaking of which, why did Alora kiss you?" she asked. Ally blushed a bright red. "To hide the fact we were in the conductor's car to talk," she answered. "How did Nico take it?" She asked. "He kissed me," Ally answered. Night laughed out loud scaring a maid. "So he marked his territory," she calmed down as she spoke, "You should probably get back to him." Ally stared at her as she left. "What are you looking at?" she asked the maid as she walked away. The maid whistled as she cleaned.

"He likes you," Alora said talking to Carmen. She brushed her hair as the bright pink waves rolled down her back. "You think so?" Carmen said shyly. "He probably requested you sit next to him," Alora pointed out. Carmen glared at her. "You came to me for advice," she stood up her hair falling down her back. "Thank you," Carmen said standing up. Damon walked in just as she left. "Excuse me," she said politely leaving. "What happened?" he asked confused. "Just gave her some advice," she laid on the bed. "Must've been good," he said as he laid next to her. He held her close. "You should really cut your hair when this is all over," he said stroking her hair. "I know," Alora said yawning tired. Damon took of his glasses putting

them on the side table. "Good night," he said kissing her gently.
"Good night," Alora said cuddling closer.

Ally stared at herself in the mirror. Her black t-shirt with its white butterfly design and dark blue jeans complimented her one black flat and one white flat. "You shouldn't worry," Nico said as she put on her white fingerless glove. "I don't know what's going on," she said putting her black fingerless glove on. A knock on the door made Ally jump five feet in the air it seemed. Nico opened the door up to see Terra. She looked up to see Ally on the lights. "She'll see you now," Terra stood at the door in her Crimson Ares Army shirt and black jeans, "And how did you get up there?" "Hyper vigilance," Ally jumped down carefully as she walked over. Night stood there glaring at Terra as she dressed in all black as usual. "

Follow me," Terra said walking ahead. Her combat boots echoed against the marble floor. Night snickered as she turned to Terra. "Something funny?" Terra asked turning around. "You have toilet paper on your boot," she said politely. Terra removed the toilet paper throwing it away. She stopped at a snow white door opening it. "After you," her musical tone sounded sarcastic. Ally entered surprised by the huge library. She stared at the second floor stopping at a ladder which Eva had climbed on. "Hello," she said she said climbing down, "Go keep watch." She turned to Terra. "Yes Your Majesty," she walked out closing the door behind her. Eva walked down the stairs, her heels clicking against the marble floor. "Why call us here?" Night attempted to ask nicely. Eva put a book on the table. "Take a seat," she said sitting down and opening it. Ally and Night sat down unsure. She opened up to a page smiling. "Do you know the history of Angeline Durand, Damon Chaput, and Ares Dolan?" she asked. "Well...not really...what I learned in school and family stories," Ally answered.

"Let's hear your family stories," Eva said with a pensive look. "Well there's one about how they founded Black O-Pal," she said deep in thought. "How did they find it?" Eva asked. "They all ran away from the same camp unknowingly heading for the same location, Athens. They knew they reached it cause they saw the Temple of Athena, so they decided to build there," she said still deep in thought still. "Now how was Gaia formed?" Eva asked. "When Ares decided to create the Crimson Knights. The only way it would work was if all three countries worked together," Night pointed out.

"Very good," Eva said smiling, "See I called you here so history doesn't repeat itself. It seems someone is trying to cause some trouble. And there's more to the history you don't know. For instance the original Reaper. His name was Benjamin Dempsey and he was an 'assassin', but he never killed anyone. He acted as the guardian of the trio cause they were put on his pay load. Then again you know this Notte. Your family is still guardian to the Alkeav family, now the Bellerose family." "So that's why you hung out with my mom?" Ally looked a little shocked. "That's how it started out," Night answered, "We ended up friends just like all our predecessors. Marisol was a disgrace. She always cared for herself. And now she's moving out of my inheritance in one month for her actions." "How?" Ally asked dumbfounded, "I mean no one has told me anything."

"They're trying to recreate Gaia with world war 4. In a word they are trying to expand it," she answered. Night and Ally looked at her surprised. "They're called the Black Lotus and they are bent on taking down the Psyche royal family to do so," Eva said serious, "You've already dealt with team Alexandria and of course the new Reaper." Night's eye widened at the last name. "How do you know about that?" Ally asked worried. "I'm a phantom," she said smiling. "Remote viewing," Night said glaring. "I had to keep an eye on her," she sighed. "Next time ask permission," Night suggested insulted.

Eva glared lightly. "Why do you think I sent Terra a year early? I needed someone to protect Ally," Eva pointed out, "But back to the main topic. Little is known about the Black Lotus except that and a couple names." Night's eye glimmered. "Plus...Our research hasn't yielded much information. So I'll conclude with this: Be careful," Eva said worried. Ally's eye turned gold. "With your powers you could stop their plans," she said closing the book. "No pressure," Ally thought.

Terra watched Ally and Night walk down the hallway. "Terra," Eva demanded. Terra entered concerned. "Yes," she said sitting down. The doors closed ominously. "Did you do the research?" Eva's emerald eyes radiated with anger. "Yes Miss Chevalier. Alora Jones is on the Black Lotus assassin list," her teal eyes shined with fear, "And Amunet is Project Feline." Eva's eyes lit up with shock. "I thought they died," she sputtered. "Apparently they could never find the two year old, alive or dead, in the ashes," Terra pointed out. "I thought they had Copper hair and amber eyes. That was a trademark," Eva pointed out. "It was the Black Lotus who burnt it down," Terra rebutted. "How about our contact?" Eva demanded. "He hasn't contacted me in a month," her voice cracked as she spoke. "How sad?" Eva said calmly, "We'll keep an eye on him. I doubt he joined." "Yes Miss Chevalier," Terra stood up. "Keep an eye on Miss Jones. She might know something we don't," Eva smiled mischievously. "Yes Miss Chevalier," Terra smiled back. She left smiling in relief. "Remind why I took this job again," she thought.

Chapter 19

Alora walked down the grey hallway, her eyes full of fear. "They know me," she thought, "Why else would they send Terra." She stared at the blood trail in front of her. A door opened nearby grabbing her attention. "Hello," she said as the sarcasm in her voice was replaced with dread. She inched closer to the door scared. She fully opened the door making her eyes widen in fear. The silent bodies stared back from where they laid. "No," she said ready to run. Suddenly a cold breath caught her attention. She turned around to see Reaper. "You did good," the words slithered out of his mouth as she fell into the room screaming.

"Calm down," Damon said holding her close. Tears flowed from Alora's eyes. "They all stared at me," she pointed out frightened. Damon held her closer calming her down. "You don't have to worry. That's all in the past," he said gently. A knock on the door interrupted them. "Come in," he said still comforting Alora. Ally walked in playing with her locket. "I heard screams," she said worried. "Everything is fine," he explained. Alora looked at her surprised. "Yeah I'm fine," she said wiping away a tear. "Okay," Ally left concerned.

She walked down the hallway thinking of her friends scream. "What's going on," Ally pondered. She walked down the hallway to her room. Opening the door she saw Nico playing with his O-Pal. "What's up?" he asked curious. "Not much...I think," she answered. "Well you sound fine to me. How about we check out the city. Just the two of us?" he suggested. "Sure," she sounded excited. Outside the bedroom door Terra overheard the couple talking. "Not a bad idea," she thought to herself.

Night stared at the painting in her room. Vincent Van Gogh's "wheatfield with crows" stared back at her as she sat there calmly. A sudden low bump got her attention. Opening the door, she saw

Huey on the ground laughing, while Alice glared at him intensely. "Not funny," she said sternly. "What's going on?" Night asked curious. "You're not going to look?" Alice asked. "It's fun when the facts reveal itself through others," she retorted. "We were looking for the restroom," Huey answered getting up and calming down.

"Anything break or fall?" she asked. "No, though I did hit my head on 'The statue of David'," Alice sounded serious. Night smiled as she used her power to flash back. "Sneaking around are we. Or are you looking for something," she looked confused. "Fine…," Alice said, "We were looking for my O-Pal," she answered. "It's in your suitcase that you never opened," Night explained. Alice sighed in defeat. "Thank you," she said heading to her room. Night went to her room satisfied with her progress.

Nico led the way to the door as Ally followed. The sun shined through the windows making the art on the windows brighter it seemed. "We should hurry," Ally said as she felt stressed. "Why?" Nico raised an eyebrow worried. "Hello miss Bellerose," Terra snuck up on them it seemed. Ally glared at her subtly. "I'm here to show you around Cat's eye city," she sounded excited and fake at the same time. "Sure," she answered warily. "Follow me," Terra led the way to one the SUV they rode up in. "I don't like this," Ally thought.

Alora walked the busy streets of what was formally Rome. "I wonder why they changed the name," She asked out loud. "Because the first person to name it was a child," he answered. "Harsh…who named it then?" Alora was still worried. "A man named Antonio," Damon stopped in front of a boutique for made just for Alora. He turned to Alora knowingly. "Fine, why must we do this?" she asked. "Cause you like it," he answered. "You are not wrong," she said entering the store. "Finally!" he said excited, "A mechanic shop."

Terra drove through the city attempting to explain its history. "What do you think?" she asked curious. "What's that wall over there?" Nico asked. "That's Vatican City," she answered, "It's amazing. Plus... It is its own country." Ally still looked worried. "We better head home." Nico pointed out. "Okay," Terra sounded sad. Suddenly she sped up heading back, making her guest a little worried. "Don't worry, we'll be back soon," Terra said trying to comfort them. "If that's' what you say," Nico thought.

Alora watched the sunlight dim in the sunset. "I should probably head in," she thought trying not to worry. She got up from the palace stairs ready to walk in. Suddenly a black SUV drove up a little too fast. Ally walked out with Nico looking concerned. "Hello Miss Jones," Terra spoke almost coldly as she walked out scaring everyone. Suddenly her voice went back to normal, "It's nice to see you." Alora headed inside freaked out. Ally ignored what just happened guessing what was going on. Nico seemed blissfully unaware of the situation. "Lucky," Ally thought trying to stop the uneasiness she felt. She checked the time. She sighed as Nico opened the door bedroom. Ally walked in remembering the tattoo on Alora's arm...it was in the shape of a black lotus. "Not good," she thought.

Nico put on his black t-shirt as Ally put on her outfit. A knock on the door caught Both of their attention. Another knock made Ally walk up to the door and open it. "Good Morning Miss Bellerose," Terra spoke in a weirdly calm way. "Good morning," Ally said surprised. "Hope you slept well. So I'm going to get to the point. How about a girl's night? You can even bring your friends," she said smiling excitedly. "Sure," Ally gave her a confused look especially since Alora acted weird around her. "Good we'll go at six," Terra said smiling mischievously. "Okay," she smiled unsure. "What is she planning?" she thought to herself. "Sounds like fun," Nico randomly commented. "Are you sure? Alora is terrified of her," she sounded concerned. "I noticed that too. Maybe you shouldn't invite her," Nico suggested. "I have a feeling I have to," Ally retorted.

Carmen stared at the angel statue as the statue stared back at her. "How beautiful," she thought. "Hello," Adonis said sitting next to her. "Hi," Carmen said blushing lightly. "I like your outfit," he said trying to start a conversation. Carmen stared at her white t-shirt and faded blue jeans as she pulled on her baseball cap anxiously. "It suits you," he said blushing. Carmen smiled. "Thank you," she said shyly. "Where are you from?" he asked curious. "Black O-Pal," Carmen answered. "What grade are in?" he asked. "Career level," she answered still shy.

"That's great," Adonis said excited, "I'm graduating next year. How about you?" "I have three years," she said now quiet. "You were louder before. Something wrong?" he asked concerned. She shook her head getting up. "It was nice talking to you," she said walking away. "I wonder what's wrong?" he thought, "Do I offend?" "It's okay, she is careful about her words. She doesn't like talking when she gets to know you. Plus it's rare when she talks to you right off the bat," Amunet walked away after explaining her friend's actions. "So it's good she talked to me right off the bat," she thought. "Yes," he exclaimed, "She likes me."

Alora put a hair tie in to keep her braid in place. "Looks good," she said putting on her black t-shirt on still hiding her tattoo. A knock on the door caught her attention. "Coming," she said in a hurry. She opened the door to Ally. "Hello," Ally spoke with intent. "Come in," Alora gave Ally a confused look. "So...Terra is taking us out tonight," Ally said cautiously. "So," Her eyes narrowed. "I'm just seeing if you are coming," Ally's voice turned weak. "I'd love to," Alora's voice sounded more sarcastic than usual. "Good," Ally said heading for the door, "See you then." "What's Terra planning?" Alora thought worried. "She didn't figure it out did she?" Damon asked worried. "I hope not," Alora sounded serious. "Just be careful, okay Alora," Damon suggested. "I will," she answered.

Alora walked down the hallway annoyed. "Hello Miss Jones," she turned round to see Eva standing behind her. "Hello Your Majesty," she smirked as she spoke. Eva walked up, her black heels clicking against the marble floor. "I guess I'm just curious, why hasn't Damon talked about you?" she asked curious. Alora looked at her worried. "He wants to surprise people with our engagement," she felt angry, "Especially his brother, Blaine."

"When?" Eva's question seemed vague. "It's a surprise," her sarcasm went into overdrive, "After all I don't even have a ring." "Alora," Damon walked up holding her hand. "Nice to see you again Damon," Eva sounded befuddled. She turned to Alora. "Nice to see you again too. Now if you excuse me, I've looked everywhere for her," he walked away pulling Alora gently. "I can't leave you alone for a second," he whispered to her. "I know," she gave him a sweet smile. "Alright," he said, "We will head back to the room." She followed him.

Alora walked slowly towards the exit shaking uncomfortably. Terra stood next to the van waiting impatiently as Alora walked out sheepishly. "Ready?" Terra asked. "Yeah," Alora gripped her arm tightly. "Come on in," she entered the front seat smiling slyly. Alora sat next to Ally shaking as Terra pulled up to the gates driving away as they closed. "Now first step, the 'Black Cat'," Terra said excited. "Sounds great," Alora's voice cracked worrying Ally. "You okay?" she asked. "I'm fine," Alora answered. "Are you sure?" Night asked. "I'm sure," Alora answered. "In that case, let's have fun," Terra attempted to speak honestly. "Something is wrong," Ally thought to herself, "Does she have a grudge against Alora?" Night looked like she was thinking. Suddenly she smiled as if she saw something beautiful. Ally stared at her apprehensively. "Definitely something wrong," she thought.

Adonis sat on the couch staring at the painting in front of him until Nearby laughing made him turn around. "It wasn't that funny," Amunet said confused. "That was a good joke though," Carmen said holding her side. "It wasn't a joke," she sighed. "Hello," Adonis said walking up. "Hello," Carmen's voice became a whisper. "She's shy," Amunet pointed out. "Hey Amunet," Huey said walking up. "Hello," Amunet said giving him a weird look. Huey gave her a confused look. "Just checking on you," he pointed out, "How about we play a video games since Terra's taking out Ally and friends?" Adonis smiled at the suggestion. "Sure," he turned to Carmen. "This should be fun," Alice said joining them. "I'm not going to like this," the thought made Amunet nervous

Night looked her food taking a bite. "You know I love this place. So much history," She exclaimed. Ally finished her gelato in front of her. "What do you mean?" she was curious now. "To look in the past is pleasing," Night answered staring Terra Hunter. "What do you mean?" she retorted. "Life is strange...One minute you're at the bottom. The next you're with the big wigs," Night explained almost triumphantly. Terra stared in shock. "Right! She is a pre-teacher who looks into the past for fun," she thought.

Alora stared at her plate all edgy as Ally stared at her concerned. "Beautiful, right?" Terra said sipping her wine starring at the sunset, "I mean the view is lovely." "Yeah," Ally said looking at the black and white walls complimenting the rustic brown tables. Terra smiled at Alora slyly. "You okay? You haven't relaxed since we arrived," she said. "I'm fine," Alora glared at Terra as she nonchalantly ate her dessert. "I see," She turned to the window to see the setting sun. "Wait till you see the night life," she kept her eye on Alora. "Sounds like fun," her voice cracked again making Ally nervous. Terra smiled back slyly. "Good to hear," she said taking a bite of her chocolate cake. "What's going on?" Ally thought, "Are they fighting or cat fighting?"

"I win," Huey sounded excited as held his game controller playing an elf in the video game. Amunet stared surprised by how childish he was acting. "He's always been this way, fun-loving and kind," Alice pointed out. "Really?" Amunet wasn't shocked to hear this. She turned to Carmen and Adonis who was talking in the background. "School has always been hard, they think it's because I take after dad," Adonis pointed out. "I think you take after your mother. She's highly intelligent in her own way," Carmen spoke honestly. "Thanks," he said smiling. "How sweet," Amunet thought almost smiling, "They make a sweet couple."

Night glared at Terra knowing what she was doing and the she had to play. Terra drove slowly stopping at a park parking the car gently. "Follow me," she said getting out. Ally stared at the night sky amazed. She noticed a man and woman in H.I.P. uniforms stood nearby. "Arrest her," Terra snapped her fingers as they both walked over putting hand cuffs on Alora. "What are you doing?" Alora squirmed attempting to free herself. "Alora Jones, You under arrest for crimes against international law," Terra's voice became serious. "What crimes?" Ally demanded. "Why, murder. She's a former Black Lotus assassin," Terra glared at her as Ally stared at Alora confused. "I've changed, I swear," she said pleading for help. "She might be able to help," Ally glared at Terra. "I know, that's why we are bringing her in," she glared back.

"I won't if I'm handcuffed," Alora yelled as she was being put in the police car. "She really has changed," Night's eye glimmered as she spoke, "Just ask Damon." Terra turned to Alora. "You promise to help?" she asked calmly. "Yes. Just remove the handcuffs," Alora answered freaking out. Terra snapped her fingers making the female cop remove Alora's cuffs. She walked up to her glaring. "Don't make me regret it," she said. Alora smiled in response. "I won't," she walked over to Ally and Night hugging them. "Thank you," she said crying. "You're welcome," Ally said awkwardly trying to get her breath as she let go. Night did the same. "Didn't know you were that strong," she sounded out of breath herself. "Are we going?" Terra sounded impatient again. Everyone ran over getting in the SUV. "Finally," Terra drove fast as she could it seemed.

Amunet laid on the floor thinking about her life before and the fact she couldn't remember it. She only remembered faces and voices, but that was it. One of the lines she could remember was: **You're mine now**. She remembered the person sounding like an 16 year old teenager. A knock on the door made get up to answer. "Hello," she said not surprised a H.I.P agent at the door. "Follow me," he said leading the way, "And leave any weapon behind please." Amunet begrudgingly gave up her knife. "How did you get this?" he asked. "A friend," she answered bluntly.

Alora glared across the table at Terra. "What do you want to know?" she asked. "Everything," Terra answered. "Fine," Alora took a big breathe. "The leader is Bastet Caro," She sounded determined. Terra looked at her confused at the name. "Emperor Blaine's advisor?" she raised an eyebrow. "What advisor? She's controlling him," Alora's tone became angry, "She killed I don't know how many to get where she's at. In fact she is classified by her more sane minions as a psychopath. The worst crime she got away with was killing his parents. Why do you think Damon left?" "Did she take someone from you?" Eva gave her a concerned look.

Alora looked down ready to cry. "My dad," Alora wiped a tear, "They used the Durand war as an excuse to kill him. You see we were as respected as the Argyis family." "How do you know this?" Eva was curious now. "Bastet wanted the perfect army. In other words, an army that would listen without question," Alora pointed out, "There are a few who question, like me. Most are like Reaper. They never think for themselves. Plus you have the genetically altered, forcibly." "My guess is she's hunting you down. So in all of this, what was your job?" Eva asked. "I was in charge of training the kids. Though I never used her propaganda. I used my own subliminal messaging," she answered. "What do you know about Reaper?" Terra looked at her concerned. "He's ruthless and he only does what his 'mother' says," Alora's grey eyes became piercing, more piercing than Alice's.

"You mean Bastet?" Eva gave her a befuddled look. "Yes," Alora stood up, "Can I go now?" "Of course," Eva said deep in thought, "Just one more question. Did you train Amunet?" Alora sat back down quietly. "No, but I know who did. Amethyst, I can't tell you her real name," she answered. Terra watched as Alora grabbed her leather jacket. "How about your tattoo?" she asked. "I thought there was one question left," Alora pointed out as she turned to her annoyed, "All Black Lotus members have them and they're always on the left arm." Terra watched her leave in shock. "She'll be fine. Now you should take them to the train station," Eva turned to Terra. "Understood," she said getting up. The door reopened revealing someone. "We don't need Amunet," Terra said. "Got it," he said leaving.

Amethyst drove up to the parking lot. She got out as a slightly warm breeze blew by. She fixed her green blouse and dusted of her black slacks. "Come on," she said grabbing her luggage. Jinx exited the car his jade green eyes full of anxiety. "Come on," Lyric said walking by in her black trench coat and gothic Lolita outfit, "this is going to be an interesting trip." Jinx stared at her black suitcase as he grabbed his own. "Calm down Jinx," Lyric smiled slyly as she walked up ahead. "I am calm," he protested angrily. Lyric giggled. "If you say so," she said smiling mischievously. "Always pack light," Amethyst thought, "That's what Bastet taught us.

Ally put her bag down gently staring at the presidential car. The black leather couch and burgundy walls made an odd combination. "Not bad," Nico said smiling gently while putting his bag down. "Yeah," Ally turned to him blushing. Nico fixed his short sleeved red t-shirt overlapping a long sleeved black shirt barely hiding his lean muscle. "Something wrong?" he asked curious. "No," she sat on the couch staring at the glass table as the train started. He sat next to her staring at her lovingly. "You shouldn't worry," he said kissing her cheek, "We'll be fine."

"I'm worried about my dad," she retorted. "I'm sure he's fine," he sighed, "I think so at least." She gave him the big eyes. A knock on the door interrupted them. "What now?" Nico complained as he went to the door. "Hello," Alice said cheerfully, "Is Ally in?" "Yes," Nico answered. "What's up?" Ally asked. "Not much. Just thought we could spend some time together," she smiled as she spoke. "Sure," Ally answered excited. "Great," Alice grabbed Ally's hand, "Come on." Ally looked worried as she followed.

Alora sat at the table poking her steak. "Are you that bored?" Amunet asked raising her eyebrow. "Yes," she answered blandly. Suddenly she felt a chill run down her spine. Alora turned to see a familiar red head staring at her with vicious eyes. "Amethyst," she thought scared. Amethyst smiled sadistically back as Alora ate the last bite in a hurry. "Come on, let's go," she said standing up. Amunet stared at the table in horror. "Alright," she stood up following Alora, "I'll go." "We'll need to talk to Damon and Night," Alora pointed out. "Why Night?" Amunet gave her a confused look. "She's going to find out anyway," Alora said in a serious tone. "Whatever you say," she thought worried.

Alice smiled mischievously as she sat next to Ally. "He's nice," she said looking at her. "Who?" Ally asked. "Nico," Alice said nonchalantly. Ally glared. "Your point?" she asked confused. "You two have been really close lately," Alice grinned. Ally felt her eye twitch a little. "I consider him a friend," she said blushing. "So you let your friends kiss you?" Alice asked confused. Alora came to Ally's mind. "Yes," she lied. "Worst lie ever," she laughed, "You love him." Ally stood up insulted. "I'm only pointing out the obvious," she said calming down. Ally sat down ignoring her. "You make it sound...," she was cut off by Alice. "I think it's good," Alice sighed, "You two make a cute couple." Ally blushed embarrassed. "Everyone else can see it too," Alice said. "Really," she said in shock. "Of course, you two have gotten close," Alice smiled at the thought. Ally smiled shyly in response. "She is right," she thought.

Damon and Night sat in their seats not even worried. "These people are dangerous," Alora said explaining everything to her audience. Night raised an eyebrow. "Her name is Amethyst," she said worried, "She is a ruthless killer." "I don't see the problem," Night said leaning against her seat. "She is dangerous," Alora turned to Damon, "She has no remorse, no guilt." Damon looked at her scared. "Was anyone with her?" Night asked confused. "Just a Gothic Lolita and random guy," Amunet said blandly. "Yeah," Alora said anxiously.

The old man's prediction came to mind. "I'll keep an eye out," she said leaving the room. She bumped into someone as she left. "Ally," she said helping her up. "Yes," Ally said rubbing her head. Night's eye glimmered making the scene change. A four year old lay in bed as Catherine told her a bedtime story. Slowly Ally's eyes closed as the scene faded away. "You okay?" Night asked concerned. "Yeah," Ally said walking down the hallway. Night turned around to see Carmen. "Yes," she said. "Where's Amunet?" Carmen asked curious. "In there. Give her a minute," Night said turning around. "Okay," Carmen said smiling.

Amethyst walked out of the conductor's car with a huge grin. She wiped the blood of her cheek. "Let the games begin," she said walking away. She walked down the hallway stopping at her comrades. "You know what you have to do," she ordered. Jinx and Lyric nodded walking away. "This is getting interesting," Alexandria thought watching them as she held an empty box off dynamite.

Chapter 20

Ally stared at the night sky amazed. "Wow," The word escaped from her mouth. "We'll be in Durand in two days," Nico said yawning. "So the twenty-second," Ally raised an eyebrow. "Yes," Nico stood up staring at the door. "What is it?" Ally asked concerned. "It's too quiet," he answered concerned. Ally listened attempting to listen for any noise, even a cricket. Nothing made a noise, especially the cricket. That's when she felt it, an unnatural sudden stillness. "Someone just died," she suddenly said. "How do you know?" Nico asked. "When my last bodyguard , George, passed away something in the Air fell unnaturally still," She explained, "That's how I know." He opened the door warily as he walked down the hallway followed by Ally.

Suddenly Ally saw two figures laying in the distance. "Are you okay?" she ran through the hallway until she got to the two strangers. Two women laid in a pool of blood. "How sad?" Night said solemnly. Carmen held back a scream. "What happened?" she squeaked. "They were hit," Night turned to Ally, "We should be careful." "Agreed," Ally walked past the bodies carefully. "Did you see who did it?" she asked. "It was too dark," Night answered, "Anyways we should head to safety." "Agreed," Ally followed.

Huey opened his door not surprised by the dead body in front of him. "This isn't good," he thought looking both ways, He walked in the direction of conductor's car. As he walked down to see what happened he noticed an empty box in the corner. "What is it?" he was about to look closer when he heard Alice scream. "I'm coming," he said running as fast as she could.

Alice walked down the hallway until looking for survivors until a clicking got her attention. "Who's there?" she demanded. Lyric walked out, her steel grey eyes fixed on her. "Alice Coupe I presume," she said holding a bloody dagger. "Who are you?" Alice asked giving her a death glare. "Lyric Raptis, your executioner," she smiled sadistically. Alice glared at her intensely. "Traitor," she thought hurt. Alice ran up swiftly, ready to attack. Suddenly a knife was thrown at her leaving a cut on her face. "I'd be careful," Lyric said mischievously. "Fine," she got into fighting position. She ran at her almost hitting in the stomach. Lyric smiled excited at the prospect of a good challenge. "Bring it," she said. "Oh I'll bring it," Alice punched the air almost hitting her face. "Traitor," the thought stayed in Alice's mind.

Alora walked down the hallway looking for any signs of life. "Hello Alora," a familiar voice said. She turned around to see Amethyst standing behind her. "Long time, no see," she said, her jade eyes glowed with excitement. Alora grabbed a kunai preparing herself. "Still using small weapons like that," Amethyst took out a small and thin cylinder with a button on it. Alora threw the kunai only to have it deflected by a metal rod. "Like it?" Amethyst laughed, "It's perfect. In fact it was used quite recently." Alora glared at her angrily. "Bring it," Amethyst said tauntingly. Alora grabbed a chair attacking her head on. She defended herself only to hit Alora in the stomach with her weapon. Alora quickly took a acupuncture needle throwing at her only to have it deflected as well.

"How desperate," Amethyst walked over as Alora keeled over in pain, "You're weaker than I remember, Maybe I should whip you into shape like I do my students." "Those aren't students...they are mindless zombies," Alora answered, "All except Amunet." "Oh, you mean 'Project Feline'. We have a friend for her too," Amethyst pointed out. Suddenly a gunshot made Amethyst move like lightening. "Found her," Night said holding a pistol. Damon ran in picking up Alora. "I'll take it from here," Night stood in front of Damon and Alora defensively staring at Amethyst. "Night Fiore I'm guessing," she said getting excited. "Who are you?" Night's eye glimmered. "Amethyst," she ran up almost hitting Night. "She'll pay," Night thought as she watched Catherine's death in front of her.

Ally ran down the hallway stopping at two new bodies. "Carmen! Sam!" she yelled running over. She felt for a pulse on both of them sighing in relief as she found one. "Are they alright?" Nico asked concerned. "Yeah," Ally stood up picking up Carmen, "Can you help me bring them in that room over there?" "Sure," Nico picked up Sam placing him on the couch. Ally's eyes glowed gold as she put her hands on their heads healing their wounds. "I'm going to look around," Nico turned to Ally concerned, "Will you be okay?" "Yeah, I'll be fine," Ally answered as Nico walked out looking around carefully. "I hope you will too," she thought.

Amunet walked through the train cars looking for her friends. "Huey! Damon! Alora!" she yelled, "Where is everyone?" A low growling caught her attention. "Hello Project Feline," Alexandria said sitting in a seat. "How did you...?" She stared in shock at her adversary, "I killed you." Alexandria turned around revealing no scar. She smiled revealing her fangs. "Let me see your fangs," she said. "No," Amunet answered.

"Just give me a smile," Alexandria stood up holding a dagger, "You were a born hunter just like me." "I'm a born predator, but not by choice. After all I am human," Amunet pointed out poetically. "You are half and half like me. Accept it or die. After all we were supposed to be a duo," Alexandria pointed out. She was now pointing the dagger at Amunet. "Bye," Amunet threw smoke bombs running away as the smoke cleared. "Amunet!" Alexandria yelled.

Alice hit the wall hard. "You monster," she said angrily turning to Lyric. Lyric smiled mischievously, her steel grey eyes locked on Alice. "That's the best you can say," she pinned her against the wall putting a dagger to her throat. "No, I can do better," Alice smiled mischievously, "Huey!!" The scream echoed off the wall. "Huey, You mean your younger sibling. HA!" Lyric laughed as she dropped her dagger. Alice kicked her in response hitting her chin with her high heel.

"Not bad," Lyric said feeling her jaw for a loose tooth, "Now how about we aim for better." "Fine by me," Alice hit her gut, grabbing her arm and pulling her down, "How's that?" Lyric glared at her intensely. "It was good," she sounded mad. She punched back missing by an inch. Alice went low almost kicking her again. "I won't fall for the same thing twice," Lyric almost laughed as she jumped back. Alice smiled as she hit a window by accident. "Not funny," Lyric responded, "at all."

Ally stared at her friends worried as silently she left the room. Soft footsteps caught her attention. "Nico?" she asked confused. She turned around to see Jinx holding his naginata. "Jesse," she thought terrified. "Let's get this over with," he said attacking her head on. Ally jumped out of the way missing the blade by mere inches. "Wait," Ally said dodging every attack. A sudden explosion caused Ally to fall causing pain to shoot up her leg. Jinx picked her up pinning her against the wall. "Any last words?" he asked her, his eyes showing his reluctances. "Your such a jinx," her words surprised Jinx making him drop Ally with fear in his eyes as he ran away. "What just happened?" Ally thought confused, "Why did he attempt fight me?"

Catherine stood by the army bed checking the patient's vital signs. "You'll be fine. I'm quite sure you'll make home safe and sound," she spoke cheerfully. Suddenly she heard gunfire outside the tent. One woman's voice stood out. "Everyone stay out here, I get the prize," she said. Catherine kept her hand on the gun being the only Doctor in the hospital tent. "Amethyst," she wasn't scared of the attacker as she entered the tent. "Oh, so you know about me," Amethyst gloated. "Who doesn't? You're a paid mercenary, not a soldier," Catherine pointed out. "So I got kicked out of the Crimson Knights for bad behavior," she retorted, "A girl has to make a living." Catherine pointed her gun at her. "You can't be serious," Amethyst shot her in cold blood, "But you were."

Amethyst laughed manically as Night shot her with a small pistol. "You think that's going to stop me?" she said tauntingly as she dodged each bullet, "Last person who believed that didn't survive." Night remembered the scene with Kitty getting shot in the head by Amethyst. "Was her name Catherine Bellerose?" Night asked unusually calm. "Yeah, She was an idiot," she said about to laugh, "She took out a gun, but couldn't shoot it." Night's violet eye turned black. "She couldn't cause you didn't give her time. Plus, her name was Kitty," she said shooting the pistol as an explosion went off interrupting them.

Amethyst fell staring at the wound in her leg. "No," she said as it bled heavily. "Not very pleasant is it, the sight of your own blood?" Night walked over as she scooted herself into a corner, "I would and should shoot you on the spot, but I won't for Kitty. Instead I'll let you go with the train; you took her from me, so you don't deserve a quick way out." She turned around walking out of the car.

"Wait," Amethyst yelled scared, "Don't leave me." She accidently threw her weapon out the window as the door closed losing all hope. "She left," she thought scared, "She outsmarted me. In the end I lost, all because of that psycho Bastet. She's all about self-gain. She never cared." Suddenly she felt the heat knowing what was about to happen. "Get her Alexandria," she thought as the heat started to warm up.

Alice fell as the train shook. "Keep your eye on your opponent," Lyric said attacking head on. The knife disappeared flying out of nowhere stopping her. "Picking on my sister again," Huey said pinning her against the wall. Suddenly he was pulled off. "Come on," Jinx said turning to Lyric making her follow him. "What was that about?" Alice asked dusting herself off. "I don't know, but we have to get off. The bridge is out," Huey grabbed Alice's wrist guiding her. "The bridge is out?" Alice asked. "Yes my parrot," Huey led the way annoyed.

"Was that that great big shaking?" she asked. "Of course," her brother answered as he opened up the door. "You first," he ordered. Alice jumped without question. Huey jumped as well landing nearby. Alice saw Night watching the train fall into the flames as if in a trance. "Night," she called knocking her out of it. "Yes," Night turned around unfazed. She looked around as if seeing no one. "Come on," Sam called. Night followed making the twins follow as well worried.

Nico ran over as Ally rubbed her leg in pain crying in agony. "Come on," he said opening the door. Sam rubbed his head as Night picked up Carmen. "We got to get going, the bridge is out," she left the room followed by Sam. Nico walked over picking up Ally. "Follow me," Amunet ordered nearby. Nico turned around to see her near a door. "Okay," he said as Ally locked her hands around his neck.

Amunet walked over to the nearest door opening it. "You first," she said turning to Nico and Ally. Nico jumped out staring at the inferno that used to be the bridge. Amunet landed next to him staring at Ally concerned. "We should find a place to hide," she said getting up. She entered the wilderness looking unprepared. "Come on," Nico said picking up Ally as she whimpered in pain. "What if I sing?" he asked. "Please don't," Amunet answered.

Alice walked on the trail annoyed. "We got hijacked," she angrily said looking at the buds on the trees. "Spring is coming," Huey said trying to change the subject. "Yeah, so what? How are we going to contact mom? We lost the O-Pals," She leaned against a tree angrily. "You're safe," Sam said running up and hugging Alice and Huey. "Don't choke them," Night said followed by Carmen. Alice looked around confused stopping at Night.

"Where is everyone else?" she asked. "Calm down," Night said, "I'm sure everyone is safe." Alice sighed in relief. "That's good," she said hugging Sam back. In a nearby tree Alexandria watched. "Five made it, none of them Amethyst," she whispered into a headset. "Please check the area closely. Especially the river," Reaper ordered. "I'll check the river first," she answered. She walked away unnoticed.

Amunet pushed the branch out of the way. "Come on," she said holding it. "Thank you," Nico said holding a sleeping Ally. Amunet stared at her swollen ankle. "We need somewhere safe to stay and fast," she said concerned. Ally whimpered in pain as Nico changed her position. "Nico," she said waking up, her eyes golden. Amunet walked into a clearing smiling. "I found shelter," she said turning to Ally and Nico. Nico ran up to see an abandoned farmhouse. "Great," he said excited. "Let's hurry," she said running.

Alora held her stomach leaning against the tree. "She hit you pretty hard," Damon said picking her up concerned. "I was weak," Alora cringed in pain, "And she was my former boss." Damon glared at her. "You're not weak," he pointed out while walking on the trail, "And who cares who she was. We're going to get you help." "Admit it...I couldn't beat her," she smiled is an attempt to beat the pain.

He leaned in kissing her gently. "Doesn't mean anything," he said making her blush. "But," she was cut off by Damon. "End of conversation," he said holding her close. Alora stared at him surprised. "We need to continue," he said smiling. She held her stomach tightly as she cuddled up to him. "Okay," she finally agreed. Both walked down the trail carefully. "We...have...to hurry," she stuttered trying not to puke. "We will," he said attempting to comfort her.

Nico put Ally on the couch as Amunet reached into her pocket. "What are you doing?" he asked curious. She pulled out a roll of gauze handing it to him. Nico looked around the house sitting across from Ally. The wallpaper was decaying it seemed while the furniture was covered in dust. "What's your analysis?" he asked wrapping the gauze around Ally's ankle. "Durand war," Amunet's words made Nico cringe angrily. "Bad memories," she thought. Ally gave him a concerned look.

"I'm fine," he said taping down the gauze, "Here you go." He handed the gauze back to Amunet. "Thank you," she said worried. She walked over to the window watching the outside world as Nico grabbed a pillow to prep up Ally's foot. "You don't have to," she said. "I want to," he said sitting across from her. Ally smiled back. "Thank you," she said. "So what do we do now?" Nico asked. "We wait," she answered.

Alexandria stared at the rod with its button perfectly intact. She turned to the destroyed bridge knowing what happened. "Who did this?" she thought angrily. Suddenly she heard footsteps coming her way. "The D.P.A.," she said jumping in a bush. "What's this?" one officer asked. "I don't know, but I bet it has to do with the charred remains," another officer said. Alexandria snarled wolf like slightly. "Let's hurry before an animal attacks," the first officer sounded cautious. "We'll be fine," the other commented.

"She's gone sir," Alexandria whispered into her earpiece. "Well, she was nuts anyways," he commented, "Come back immediately." "Negative," she whispered as the officers walked away. "What? Don't you dare be like Project Feline…," she stepped on the earpiece jumping out of the bush running away. "Did you see that?" one officer asked. "Nope," the other answered.

Jinx cut at the tree angrily. "Calm down," Lyric demanded. "I couldn't do it," he said angrily. Lyric looked down worried. "Neither could I," she thought. "How disappointing," Reaper walked out from behind a tree as if he came from nowhere. Lyric and Jinx stared at him frightened. "Why couldn't you get the job done?" he asked nonchalantly. "She wouldn't fight back," he answered terrified. "I was interrupted," Lyric said worried. "What about Amethyst? I mean you were the only two who made it," he walked up glaring, "You could've chased them." Lyric and Jinx exchanged terrified looks. "Anyway, Bastet is giving you one more chance, with probation of course," he smiled slyly. "Who's the officer?" she asked. "Come on out," Reaper said turning around.

Dante jumped out from a tree dusting off his blue jeans. "Hello, I'm Dante Durand," he said apathetically. "Jinx Blanchette," Jinx glared at him. "Lyric Raptis," she said making sure he wasn't dangerous. "I'll leave you all to get acquainted," Reaper faded away. "Isn't Durand a rare surname?" Jinx asked glaring. "Yes," Dante said glaring back, "Though I've never made an excuse." Jinx's eye twitched annoyed. "How could you tell?" he wondered. "Anyway let's review what went wrong. I say it was the Crimson Knights as well as all of her allies. If we can separate them we can get the job done," He leaned against a tree, "I'll take care of her friends but you take care of her." Jinx's glare worsened. "Agreed," Lyric stepped on Jinx's foot. "Ditto," Jinx said reluctantly. "Good," Dante looked at them confused.

Alice walked down the trail finding an opening. She smiled mischievously at what she found. "Found shelter," she said staring at a cave. Carmen stared at it surprised. "Couldn't you find better?" Night asked blandly. "Yeah, I'll just look for the nearest hotel," Alice retorted sarcastically. Sam laughed as he left the woods and Night glared at him. "That's funny," he said calming down. "I'll check out that way," Night walked in the opposite direction. "Next time less sarcasm," Huey said turning to Alice.

Night walked on the trail ignoring the sunlight. She took her gun out staring at it for a moment remembering what she did. The unusual painfully numb calm returned as she realized her actions and the possibilities of what could happen to her. She felt no regret, but pain that her dearest friend was gone. She knew she needed psychological help. Suddenly a twig snapped causing her to turn around and point it at a target. Alora leaned against the tree half-smiling. "Hey Night," she said struggling to stand up. Damon walked over picking her up. "You're too proud," he said. "You okay?" Night asked concerned. "She's injured," Damon answered worriedly. "Follow me," she said leading the way. Damon followed quickly.

Chapter 21

Alice stared at Alora as she rested against Damon's shoulders. "She's going to be fine," Sam said calmly. "I don't know she was hit pretty hard," Night stared at Alora concerned. "We're not far from Paris, Durand. She can probably hold," Sam sat next to Huey anxious. "Yeah," Huey gave him a strange look. Alice stared outside suspiciously. "Something wrong?" Night's eye glimmered. "Yeah, I have to go," she said running out. Huey looked at her suspiciously. "To the bathroom?" he asked. "Yeah, to the bathroom," she answered. "Didn't need to know that," Night pointed out.

Amunet stared at the distant forest, her cat eyes scanning the trees. "Hey," Nico sat next to her staring out. "Is she asleep?" she asked curiously. "Yeah. I figured it would look suspicious if I stayed," he said staring at the forest. "We're close to Paris so she should be taken care of soon," Amunet sighed. Suddenly Amunet became alert jumping up to catch a hunting knife. "What the…?" Nico stared at the knife befuddled as Amunet threw it back at the bush. Lyric jumped out catching the knife by the handle. "Very good and what catlike reflexes," she said excitedly, "This will be interesting." Amunet glared at her recognizing her immediately. "Then again you are 'Project Feline'," Lyric's voice became taunting making Amunet growl.

"Behind you," Amunet pulled Nico aside as a naginata flew out of nowhere. Jinx ran out of the woods retrieving it from a nearby tree. "You are part cat," he mocked. Amunet's glare worsened as she didn't recognize him. "That aside….Where is she?" Lyric demanded. "Why would we tell you?" Amunet mocked back. Lyric took out a small dagger ready to throw. "Talk," her steel grey eyes locked on Amunet. "We're not talking," Nico said angrily. His eyes went to Jinx as he stared at him as a traitor. Jinx glared at him intensely ready to initiate a stand down. "Fine," he ran past Nico straight inside. Lyric threw her dagger missing Amunet by an inch. "This will be over soon," Lyric said as Amunet picked up the blade. "It will be," She smiled revealing small fangs. "Truly catlike," Lyric said mischievously.

Alice walked down the trail looking around suspiciously. She pulled out a gun pointing it at a tree. "Found you," she said shooting it almost instinctively. Dante fell off a branch dead. "That was easy," she thought walking away. "That hurt," He said surprising her. She turned around to see him completely healed. "You're a psychic," she said in shock, "And a new one at that." "You're right," he said with little emotion, "How smart?" Alice got into position attacking him head-on. Dante dodged every attack finally pulling out his revolver. Suddenly he got a flashback of a man with dark hair and crystal blue eyes glaring at him sadly. "Damon," the name slipped out as if he knew her. Alice watched as he dropped the revolver with remorse. "I'm sorry," he said to Alice. Huey jumped out of a tree making the revolver appear in his hand. "Leave her alone you lunatic," he yelled.

Dante turned around still in a flashback. "Ares," he backed up frightened. "Huey put the gun down," Alice ordered him. "No way. It was pointed at you," he said preparing to shoot. Alice ran up knocking him out with a branch. "Run," she said turning to Dante. "What's your name?" he asked confused. "Alice, now get out," she yelled. Dante ran away frightened as he hurried. She stared at her brother knowing the consequences of her actions. "I wonder who he was talking about," she said thinking out loud, "He looks like Ally's brother if she had one."

Amunet pulled out her hunting knife deflecting Lyric's dagger. Lyric laughed as she pulled out another hunting knife. "Hurry up Jinx," she said glaring, "Let's get back to Dante." "Got it," he said as he attacked head-on missing Nico by inches. Nico ran inside covering up Ally and hiding behind the couch. "That's obvious," Jinx said walking in. He looked around turning to the blanket. He pulled it off to reveal nothing. "Where are you hiding?" Jinx asked. Nico held Ally close behind the couch expecting the worst. "Found you,"

Jinx said showing up. Nico picked up Ally as Jinx put them in a corner. Ally glared as if she had her heart ripped out. "Do it Jinx," Lyric said fearlessly. Amunet watched something fall out of his pocket. "Yeah, Jinx," Ally's glare worsened noticing Lyric's jealousy. Jinx lowered his naginata as Ally's eyes turned gold.

"Let's go," Jinx ran out disorganized. Lyric glared at Jinx as she ran thinking of Ally. Nico stared at Ally confused as he put her down again. "At least you're safe," he said kissing her passionately. Amunet picked up the picture from the ground turning it around. "Jinx and Ally," she said muddled. She turned to Nico who was sitting next to Ally. "Did you know him?" she asked. Ally looked down. "He's a school friend," Nico looked at her concerned. "Can we talk about this later?" she turned to Nico. "No," he said worried. "He is an old childhood friend," She answered, "I used to write to him but he never wrote back. Now I see why." "We can see why," Nico pointed out. "This place isn't safe. Come on let's go," Amunet said leading the way.

Huey glared at Alice as they walked through the woods. "He was going to kill you," he said angrily. "He was unstable and besides he was wearing Ares's trench coat," Alice explained angrily. Sam stared at her worried about her judgment. "You're certain?" Huey asked concerned. "Yeah," she answered leading the way. "What does Ares's trench coat have to do with it?" Sam asked. "It was stolen by who knows. Mom won't tell us. We just know it was stolen," Alice explained as she stuttered.

"How?" he asked. "The room was burned along with Riley and Chloe Coupe. I saw the picture," she answered. "Who is Riley and Chloe Coupe?" Night asked curious. "Our grandfather and aunt," Huey answered, "So the fact that someone has Ares Dolan's trench coat means we might find who did it." "Don't tell Mom," Alice advised. "How do you know where Paris is again?" Damon asked carrying Alora as he tried to change the subject. "It's this way and I just know," Alice said. "We should be careful," Night sighed as Carmen walked next to her, "We'll probably meet them in Paris."

Ally stared at Nico as he walked attempting to make her feel more comfortable. "It will be fine," he said trying to calm her down. "Are you sure?" she asked, "You don't look it." Nico stayed silent. "The sun's coming up," Amunet pointed out. Nico sighed relieved as Ally stared at it amazed. "We should hurry," Amunet said walking faster. Nico ran to catch up with Ally still in his arms. "Be careful," Ally said as he followed Amunet. He slowed down a little bit. "Thank you," she thought.

Dante leaned against the tree scared. "We're dead," Jinx said nervously. "Not quite," Reaper appeared out of nowhere, "She is mad, but since you are all one of the best she'll give you another chance." Dante looked at Reaper scared. "Her instructions are relaxed while I spy on the targets," Reaper said maliciously. He turned to Dante. "And you keep an eye on them," he said disappearing. Jinx turned to Dante concerned. "You alright?" he asked. He glared as he became emotionless again. "Yes," he said angrily. Jinx turned to Lyric concerned. "We should follow his instructions," he said thinking about Alice. "Yes sir," Lyric said confused. Jinx stared at Lyric and Dante. "We should continue," Dante explained. Lyric smiled mischievously. "Yes sir," she answered. "He's starting to act his age, eighteen," she thought following him.

Amunet entered the clearing astounded. "Are you there?" Nico asked entering the clearing as well. He stared at the golden city as it glimmered. "Yes," she answered. "Ally," Sam walked over concerned, "What happened?" "I tripped during the hijacking," she said smiling faintly. "She'll be fine," Night said walking up. "I can walk," Alora said walking over slower than usual. "We still have to get you to the hospital," Damon said concerned. Amunet walked over. "She's safe sir," she said. "Good job," Damon sounded confused. He looked up concerned. "She tripped on the train," Nico explained. "Then we should hurry," Alice walked up with gauze on her face, "I'll explain later." "Fine," Amunet said glaring.

"Hello?" A man in a police uniform said walking up. He stared at Ally and Alora recognizing them immediately. "Hello, I'm Officer Green of the DPA. Are you alright?" He asked concerned. Alice stepped forward taking out her badge. "Alice Coupe of the Crimson Knights and no my friend Ally broke her ankle and Alora was hit in the stomach," she said professionally. "My car is this way," he pointed to a van. "How is this going to work out?" Sam asked looking around. "I'll call for help," Officer Green said grabbing an O-Pal, "I have friends nearby."

Ally stared out the window confused. "What is the DPA?" she asked. "Durand Protection Agency," Alora answered. "You heard of us?" Officer Green turned to her surprised. "In my former work," she answered. Ally sighed as she leaned against Nico. "I take it you're Nico Katsaros and Alette Bellerose?" he asked checking his rearview mirror. "Yeah," Ally answered surprised. "President Blanc said you were dead. He is sometimes such a drama king," he said smiling. "You're talking about the victory," Alora exclaimed. "It crashed in our territory," he said entering the city limits.

Ally stared at the golden buildings. "What's that?" she asked staring at a church. "Ah, Notre Dame de Paris," Officer Green drove up to a hospital nearby, "One of the few pre-war buildings to survive; we are truly blessed." "Come on," he said opening the door. Nico walked out picking up Ally while Alora walked out in pain. Damon held the door open for Alora. "Thank you," she said walking in. Officer Green walked up to the receptionist. "I would like to admit Alora Jones and Alette Bellerose," he said politely. "How about you?" she asked staring at the gauze on Alice's face. "I'm fine," she said. The receptionist smiled back. "I'll admit them right away," she grabbed a phone.

Ally laid in bed staring at the cast on her leg. "You're lucky it was a minor fracture," Alora said laying in the bed next to her. Alice sat at the table playing poker with Huey. "You're lucky yours was minor," Night said turning to Alora. "Yeah," she said embarrassed,

"All of that was just some minor stomach issues." Nico sat next to Ally holding her hand. "That's a better job than I did," he said staring at her cast. "What room is she in?" The demanding yet childish tone made Ally turn her head. "I wasn't the only one who heard that," Sam said in shock.

"Sir, She is probably asleep," a nurse said trying to calm him down. "Just tell me," The voice came again. "That one right there," the nurse said annoyed. A man walked in glaring at a young nurse walking by. His short copper hair and chestnut eyes complimented his suit. "Are you Alette?" he asked turning to Alice. "Alice, Alette is over there," she pointed to Night. "Very funny," Ally said sarcastically. "Yeah, right. I'm totally an eighteen-year-old Healer," Night joked. The man laughed at her joke heartily. He walked over to Ally almost immediately. "Justin Blanc," he said professionally. "Nice to meet you," Ally said politely. "You're President Blanc?" Alora asked confused. "Yes," Justin answered raising an eyebrow. Alice turned to Alora.

"Be nice," Sam said turning to Alice, "He went to a well-respected university." "Yes sir," she said. "Anyway...How about you introduce me to everybody," Justin suggested turning to Ally. "Of course," She snapped out of the shock, "That's Night, Sam, Huey Driscol and Alice Coupe, Carmen, Amunet, plus Damon and Alora," she said getting tired, "This is Nico and he's my fiancé." Justin smiled mischievously as he could tell she was joking. "She is joking, you know that, right? Anyway, how about you stay at my place? You'll have a comfortable bed, plenty of rooms, and much more," he said sitting next to Night, "Plus all the privacy you need." "Why not?" Night answered as her eye glimmered. "If Night thinks it's okay," Ally turned to Nico. "Sure," he said agreeing. "Great! I'll check you out immediately," he said leaving the room. "He's nice," Carmen said randomly.

Chapter 22

Alice stared at her room amazed. The violet walls and white carpet complimented the furniture and purple comforter. "He's kind, but a little off," she said sitting on the bed. "Who's insane?" Huey asked sitting next to her. "President Blanc," she answered. "What do you mean? He's letting us stay here. I think he's pretty cool," he sighed. Alice looked at the setting sun. "True," she said relaxing. "So I'm going to my room. Knock if you need anything," he said casually leaving the room. "I will," Alice smiled as she turned to the window. Suddenly Dante came to mind making her think. "He couldn't hurt a fly," she thought as the sun finally set, "So why did he attack?"

Dante stared at the sunset confused and deep in thought. Behind him, Lyric and Jinx were fighting. "Stop fighting you two," Lyric's high-pitched voice brought on a flashback. A short blonde woman with blue eyes glared at two men. "He started it," One said annoyed with black hair and crystal blue eyes. The other glared at him with his piercing cat eyes. "Ares," the woman said sadly. "He deserved it, Angie," he said embarrassed. He put his hands through his dark red hair.

"Damon didn't," she said defending him. Ares's glare worsened as everything returned to Dante. "You okay?" He turned around to see Lyric. "I'm fine," he said wiping away a tear. "Yeah. You like being alone a lot. We've noticed," she sat next to him concerned. "It makes me feel better," he said staring. "I see. Is there a reason?" she asked curiously. "Just because...I mean why are you here?" his sapphire eyes narrowed. "What do you mean?" Lyric asked confused. He glared at her trying to send a message. "Got to go," she stood up running away.

Ally stared at the red walls around her turning to her leg which was propped by a pillow. "Hey," Nico said closing the door behind him. He turned to Ally concerned. "Hi," she blushed lightly. He sat at the edge of the queen-sized bed pushing the hair out of her eyes. "You okay?" he felt her forehead. "I'm fine," she said smiling a little. "She's still shy," he thought pulling her closer. He heard a knocking on the door. "Come in," he said getting the door. Justin walked in as he closed the door behind him.

"Just seeing if you were comfortable," he said opening taking a seat, "Looks like you are." "Yeah, thank you so much," her voice showed her gratitude. "You welcome," He left closing the door behind him. "He's a bit off," Nico turned to Ally, "But nice." "Agreed," she sat up. Nico smiled faintly as he sat next to her. Another knock on the door grabbed his attention. Night opened the door with the same sly smile. "I'm spending the day with Carmen," she said closing the door, "Just letting you know." Her voice echoed off the wall. Nico turned to Ally. "Looks like we're stuck here for a while," he pointed out. She glared back. "You don't say. The leg wasn't an indicator," she pointed out.

Night walked down the sidewalk keeping Carmen close. Carmen looked around excitedly. "This place looks cool," she said turning to Night. "It is," she said in agreement, "Look it's the Eiffel Tower." Carmen stared at the people and in amazement. "Where are we going?" Carmen gave Night the big eyes. "It's not far," she answered. She stopped in front of a café. "After you," she said opening the door for Carmen. "Cool," Carmen stared at the light brown walls with a plant design. She stared at the wooden tables. "Why are we here?" she asked confused. "This is one of the oldest buildings in Paris," she pointed out, "And we're here for a snack." She walked up to the cash register.

"May I take your order?" the girl behind the counter asked. "Yeah. I'll take a mocha latte and one hot chocolate," she turned to Carmen. "Coming right up," The girl walked over to a machine.

"Thank you," Carmen said politely. "You're welcome," Night said taking the hot chocolate and latte. "Let's walk around some more," she said as an excited Carmen followed. "So is the vacation fun?" she asked. "Of course," Carmen answered, "Amunet makes it cooler." "Why?" Night asked curious now. "She's my age," She answered looking down, "I mean no one else is." "What about Ally and Huey?" she questioned. "They're eighteen," she answered, "And you left out Alice." "She doesn't count," Night answered, "She acts thirty." "In other words, she acts older than she should," Carmen laughed a little. "That's right," Night relaxed, "That's right."

Nico walked down the hallway deep in thought. Suddenly he heard someone fall down ahead. Running up he saw it was a teenage girl with long brown wavy hair and amber eyes. "Are you alright?" he asked. "I'm fine," she answered annoyed. She got up dusting off her blue jeans. "You must be Nico. I heard you survived," she said looking up. "Yeah...what's your name?" he asked trying to be polite. "Charlie," she answered blandly. Nico gave her a concerned look. "Nice to meet you, Charlie," he said shaking her hand. "Nice to meet you," she said politely, "Where's your fiancée?" "She's limited at the moment," he pointed out. "I guess I'll have to find her," she smiled mischievously. Nico glared. "Don't worry I'm not going to hurt her," she said walking away. Nico sighed in relief. "Who was that?" he wondered.

Ally sat against the couch staring at her cast. "Hey," Nico said sitting next to her. "Hello," she blushed embarrassed. "Does it hurt?" he asked concerned. She shook her head no. "Good," Nico stood up, "At least you're not in pain." Ally smiled faintly. "I guess," she said holding her choker. Nico gave her a concerned look. "Need anything?" he asked sitting down again. "Some air," Ally looked out the window. He picked her up with ease almost. "As you wish," he said leaving the room. Justin walked by anxiously. "Something wrong?" Ally stared at him nervously. "I'm fine," he lied, "You need a chair?" "No thank you," Ally answered.

"I will go grab one," he said walking away. "We don't need..," he was back before she finished. "Let's go," Nico put her down gently. "He'll be fine," Nico said walking down the hallway. "Hey guys," Alice ran up next to them, "What ya doing?" Her voice suddenly became childish. "Going outside," Nico answered as he pushed her through the hallway. "Can I come?" she asked curiously. "Sure," he turned to Ally. "That's fine," she said smiling faintly. "Great," Alice said happily, "and it's finally starting to get nice." "True," Nico smiled as he played with her hair. Ally sighed finally giving in. "Yeah, true," she said smiling, "So true."

Alexander stared at the picture in his hand. Catherine smiled back holding a four-year-old Ally making him happy. "Alex," Erica entered his room worried. "Yes," his voice sounded hollow. "You ok?" she asked walking over. She felt his forehead almost burning her hand. Alexander turned to the window. "Are you sure?" she asked. "I'm fine," he said returning to the picture. "You're obviously not," she fixed her suit, "You haven't made one design since Ally left. Plus you have a fever." He glared at her.

"Kitty would hate to see you like this," she sighed, "How about you visit her." "I did yesterday," Alexander stood up. "I mean Ally. She probably misses you too," Erica glared. "Ok," he gave her a childish look. "Now give it a try," she said leaving the room. Alexander turned to his O-Pal befuddled. He dialed Sam's number only to get his voicemail. "Erica, she's not there," he pointed out. "Then I'll call you a car," she answered, "So you can visit her."

Ally stared at the black and white roses amazed. "Beautiful," Alice said smelling a red rose. "Yeah," she smiled in response. Nico stared at a nearby Cupid statue. "Cute," he said laughing lightly at the toddler with wings. "Be careful, he might aim for you," Alice joked. "Too late," he said turning to Ally. She blushed lightly noticing his charming smile. "Yeah...too late," Alice pointed out. "Why am I blushing?" Ally thought confused, "I just consider him a friend, right?" "Charlie," Justin's voice broke through the silence. They watched an annoyed teenager walk by silently. "Charlie," Justin ran up scared.

He turned around embarrassed. "Sorry," he said sitting on the edge of the fountain. "She's your daughter I'm guessing," Alice pointed out. "Yeah and she ignores me," he said sighing. Ally glared at him. "Why?" she asked. "Cause her mother, she blames me that her mother moved out of Gaia," he explained. "That's horrible," she said insulted, "That's not your fault." "You're telling me," he got up, "Excuse me, I got work to do." Ally watched him walk away sadly. "That must've hit a nerve," Alice thought confused, "I mean your dad is dying and she can't...Nico, Ally?" She noticed they were gone. "Great," she said, "Just great."

Sam sat up yawning. A sudden beeping caught his attention. His O-Pal flashed as a missed call signal popped up. "Alex?" he said noticing the email. He pressed the button bringing up the message. "Hey Sam," Alex popped up looking like a nervous wreck, "Just calling to see if Ally was with you. I checked and no one was home. Alright bye." Sam stared as the screen went blank. "We've already been here one week," Amunet said outside his door. "I know. But she is still injured," Alora said blandly. "She should heal soon," Amunet walked away. "Wait for me," Alora said running to catch up to her.

Sam grabbed his clothes getting ready for the day. "Sam," Khepri said popping up on the screen. "Hey honey," Sam said putting his shirt on. "I was just calling to see how you and the kids are doing," she said rubbing her temple. "We're fine," Sam said sitting down. "How about Ally?" Khepri raised an eyebrow. "She broke her leg," he looked down. "How?" she nagged. "It was her ankle actually, and it was during the train hijacking," he explained calmly. Khepri glared. "She's fine, apart from that," he said sighing. "That's good," she said smiling in relief, "Keep an eye on her." "Yes," Sam said as the screen turned blank. Suddenly Alexander's message came to mind. "Poor Alexander. He's going crazy without Ally," he thought, "But then again, Ally is going crazy without him."

Alora yawned as she watched her movie. "Hey," Damon said trying to get her attention, "Hey!" Alora turned around with one eye twitching. "What?" she asked calming down. Damon took a minute to think about what she had to say. "I brought you something," he said trying to be romantic. Alora stared at him doe-eyed. "Really?" she said surprised. He sat next to her handing her a small box. She opened the to an engagement ring making her cry. "I figured Paris would be perfect for this," he said taking her hand. She put on the ring smiling. "Thank you!" she said kissing him.

Ally laid against her pillow bored. "Hey Ally," Alice said entering. "Hey," she smiled back excitedly. "I brought a guest along," she walked to the side revealing Charlie cautiously. "Hello Miss Bellerose," she said politely. "Hello," Ally sat up fixing her waistcoat and white t-shirt trying to be polite. "You look nice," she said sitting next to her. "Thank you," Ally glared at her lightly. "I'm sorry I couldn't visit you sooner, but I had school to deal with," she smiled politely as she spoke not noticing Ally's attitude. "What school do you go to?" Ally asked curious. "Durand Art Academy. I'm studying to be an architect," she said nonchalantly. Alice sat nearby confused.

"Sounds like fun," she said growling slightly. "You specialized in international law. So did Dad," Charlie sighed, "How about you?" "Weapons specialist," Ally smiled mischievously. "You don't look it," she pointed out. Ally glared insulted. "Why would you say that?" she asked. "You look like an artist, like me," Charlie answered, "His terms almost up. He only has two terms." Charlie smiled at the thought. "You should be happy, he's trying to make a difference," Ally pointed out. "Guess I should," Charlie stood up, "I should go." She left the room prancing.

"What a snob!" Alice said closing the door. Ally glared at her seat. "She is wishing the worst on her father," she said angrily, "She should be happy he is trying to spend time with her." Alice turned to her concerned. "Right, I'm sure Alexander is regretting it right now," she sighed as she sat down. "She will regret that too," Ally pointed out, "I wish I could tell her." Alice smiled mischievously. "I could find Durand Art Academy. Someone like that has to be placed on a pedestal," she said slyly, "Maybe even have D.P.A. protecting her. I'm sure we can work with them. I hear they are quite annoyed with her too." "Let's knock her down," Ally smiled slyly back, "Just a peg...or two."

Nico walked around the garden. "Hello," someone greeted him from behind. He turned around to see Justin. "Oh! President Blanc, sir!", he exclaimed. The distinguished politician waved his hand back and forth in a dismissing way. "There's no need to act so formally on my behalf, Nico. 'Justin' will be fine, thank you," Justin looked slightly embarrassed. "Alright," he said smiling back a little confused. "Have you seen Charlie?" Justin's question made Nico worry. "No, she's probably at school or something," he said. "It is nine...her friends probably picked her up," he said nervously, "But the D.P.A. is still here. Though she is good at annoying them."

"My worry would be Ally and Alice," Nico said staring at the black and white rose, "Ally doesn't like the way she treats you." "Really," he suddenly looked confused. "She and Alice can take things a little too far," Nico pointed out. "How?" he asked nervously. "Mainly embarrassing her. She wouldn't hurt her...physically," he said returning to the rose. "I see," Justin walked away deep in thought, "Maybe I should make a call." "I don't think she would do it," he pointed out only to be not heard, "Nico you Idiot, you're back on the couch."

Chapter 23

Charlie leaned against the wall lunch in hand. "Looks good," Sean said sitting next to her. "Yeah, just look at those clouds," Brie sat next to her smiling as well. "Whatever you say," Charlie said. "Hello Charlie," Ally greeted her surprising her. The trio turned to see Alice and Ally as her eyes turned gold. "How did you find my school?" she asked glaringly. "Phonebook and map," Alice giggled. "You know them?" Sean asked confused. "Yes, they're my house guests," she growled.

Ally walked up using a crutch for support. "You know what annoys me the most about you? How you treat your father," she pointed out, "So what did he ever do to you?" Everyone stared confused. "Can't even talk to your own dad. Why? Are you too good for him?" her voice was still calm. "You don't know…," Charlie was cut off by Alice. "Listen," she demanded. Ally continued. "I would do anything to get the attention from my dad that you get from yours. My dad worked all the time, and I was dropped off by his assistant, who was luckily my aunt, plus he is dying," Ally's eyes glowed bright, "And you can't talk to yours?" She leaned against Alice for support. "See you at home," she growled.

Charlie turned around to see everyone staring at her. "Was that true?" Sean gave her a concerned look. "No," Charlie lied, "Let's eat." She ignored the stares as she noticed Reaper disappearing.

Justin glared at Ally not sure what to do. "She was trying to help," Nico said trying to ease the tension. "By yelling at her," he turned to Nico. "I didn't mean to. My anger got the best of me," Ally said sitting up, "And it's true. She hasn't spoken to you once since I've been here." He sighed in defeat. "So you were trying to help," he said. "Yeah," Ally pointed out. "Dad," Charlie said surprising everyone as she walked in. Everyone turned around to see Charlie in her school uniform.

"Yes," he got an excited look on his face. "Can we speak in private?" she asked curiously. "Sure," he stood up following her. "What is it?" he asked. "I'm sorry," she said about to cry. "It's alright," he said sitting down on a bench. She sat down next to him uneasy. "Something else on your mind?" he asked confused. "Nothing. Just a weird event," she answered. "What happened?" he asked. "I was sitting at lunch and as Ally and Alice left this guy standing by a tree just disappeared," she said frightened. "Which way did he go?" Justin asked defensively. "Nowhere. He just disappeared," she explained. "We'll find him," he said worried.

Reaper stared at his notes. "She should get her cast removed in a week," he thought happily, "Now to get help." Dante and his group came to mind. "They will have to do," he thought. He faded away smiling evilly.

The night felt tired as she walked down the hallway. "This better be good," she demanded. She walked to an unfamiliar door. "Strange...," she said opening it. Inside was what seemed to be a party. "What's this for?" she asked. Everyone stayed silent. She saw a coffin nearby. "Kitty," she said holding back tears. She sighed as she walked up. Opening the coffin she saw herself.

Night woke up retching as she got up. She ran to the bathroom, but nothing came out. "That's a first," she said as the nausea went away, "What was that about?" Getting up she headed back to bed. Suddenly she felt someone nearby. Turning around she saw no one. Quietly she went back to sleep unsure of tomorrow.

Dante stared at the night sky through the ceiling of the old house they hiding in, thinking of Alice. "Drop the dagger," Jinx said annoyed. "You drop your naginata," Lyric demanded. Dante turned around curious. "Stop it you two," he said bored. Jinx stared at him shocked by his emotion. "Hello," Reaper entered the ruins of the old house smiling. "Hello," Dante said suddenly becoming emotionless. Lyric glared at Reaper. "I have a job for you," he said looking at everyone. Jinx stared at him anxious. "What's the job?" Dante asked curious.

"Same as before, only I'm in charge," Reaper answered. "I ob...," Lyric covered Jinx's mouth before he could speak. "We'll be happy to do it," she said rationally. "Good. Since you failed twice before you're going to be given the job of taking care of her friends," he smiled mischievously. "Agreed," Dante said deep in thought. "Good. The plan will take place in a week. See you then," he faded away. "I don't like this," Jinx thought frightened. "Why?" Lyric asked. "He likes Ally," Dante pointed out. Lyric glared at Jinx as if she already knew.

Ally smiled as she moved her leg. "Great," she said sighing in relief. "Feels good I'm guessing," Alice said. "You bet," she stood up. Nico walked in surprised. "You can walk again," he said smiling. "Yeah," Ally said excitedly. Nico sighed in relief. "What's the big deal?" Alice asked raising an eyebrow. "Nothing, she's just been in a cast for two weeks," he answered. "Okay," she left the room confused. "What do you have planned?" Ally asked puzzled as well. "How about a walk through the garden?" he asked curiously. "Sounds like fun," she answered. Nico took her hand leading the way.

Ally entered the garden amazed. She walked over to the black and white roses which were now in bloom. "Beautiful," she said in amazement. "Yeah," Nico looked at Ally. "May I help you?" Both turned around to see a maid. "We're fine," Nico said suspiciously. The maid smiled slyly as she faded away being replaced with Reaper. "Hello," He said glaring. Ally stared in fear as an acupuncture needle flew out of nowhere only to be caught by Reaper. "Is that the best you can do Alora?" he asked taunting her. Alora jumped out of a tree, mini crossbow in hand. "No," she said aiming for his head. Reaper smiled slyly as he disappeared. "You jackass," she looked around. An acupuncture needle flew out of nowhere almost hitting Ally. "Come out Reaper," she demanded as she caught it.

Alice patrolled the garden deep in thought. Suddenly she heard a twig crack. "Who's there?" she demanded. Dante walked out from behind a bush. "Dante," she said confused. "Hello Alice," he said pinning her against a tree. She looked at him concerned. "You couldn't hurt me for the world," her voice cracked. Dante glared. "You don't have it in you," she continued. Dante stepped back pulling out his revolver. Alice stood there rubbing her throat. Suddenly Dante's eyes widened. "I'm sorry," he dropped his gun freaking out. "Just leave before Huey gets here," Alice said worried.

A gunshot got their attention. Huey stood there holding Dante's revolver. "Leave her alone," he demanded. Dante stepped back terrified. Alice stood in front of Dante defensively. "Alice, step aside," Huey said. "No," she answered. She turned to Dante. "Get out," she demanded. He ran away as Huey shot him. "Why did you...?" he turned to Alice. "He was harmless," she answered. "Says you," Huey pointed out. He walked away angrily as she followed.

Night stared at the Purple rose deep in thought. She thought about her past and how it has affected her future. Suddenly she put her hand up catching a hunting knife by the handle. "Nice try," she smiled slyly as she turned around to see Lyric. Lyric smiled mischievously enticed by the challenge. "You're good," she said grabbing two daggers. "You're not planning on throwing those are you?" Night asked putting her hand in her trench coat. Lyric threw the daggers only to have them land on the ground.

She looked up to see Night holding an ancient pistol. Lyric quickly pulled out a dagger running towards her. Night shot her pistol as Lyric dodged. Lyric threw her dagger only to have Night dodge it shooting her in the arm. Suddenly Night walked away. "You're not going to finish?" she asked scared. "I won't finish a Crimson Knight," Night walked away solemnly.

Reaper pulled out his sword attacking Nico head-on. "You're an idiot," Nico said pushing him away. Suddenly Ally jumped out of nowhere, her eyes glowing gold. "You're going to defeat me," he said laughing. She kicked him hard causing him to hit the fountain. He got up angrily attacking him head-on. "Prepare to die," he said running at her at full speed. Jinx came out of nowhere defending her with his naginata. "What are you doing?" Reaper demanded stopping. "I don't know," Jinx answered apprehensive. Nico stood up dumbfounded by the event. "He can't kill her," he thought. "Step aside," Reaper demanded angrily. "No," Jinx said in shock. "They're over here," Justin said nearby.

"I'll deal with you later," Reaper threatened. Reaper disappeared while Jinx ran away giving Ally one last hopeful look. "What happened?" Nico asked concerned. "I don't know," she answered. Justin ran up hugging Ally. "You're safe," he said surprised. "Yeah," Ally said smiling. "That's good," Alice said gladly. She turned to the fountain. "Oh my," she said in shock. "So what happened?" he asked staring at the damaged fountain, "To the fountain I don't own and is an antique." "He was going to hurt Nico," Ally pointed out, "So I kicked him." "So we all were attacked," Night walked up scaring everyone, "But we can't find our attackers." Justin stared mesmerized by Night. "They'll show up. I have people looking everywhere," he said proudly. "We should head inside," Ally said turning to Nico. "Agreed," he said taking her hand. "Well I guess we should hurry," Night said staring at the fountain.

Chapter 24

Jinx sat in the chair scared. "You protected the target and rebelled against Reaper," a woman with short black hair and blue eyes glared at him. "I'm sorry Bastet. It won't happen again," he said frightened. "You're right. See I'm generous and you…you're a main character. You're on continued probation," she smiled slyly. "Thank you Bastet," he said scared still. "Good, now go. Lyric and Dante will be joining you on your new assignment," she said glaring intensely at him. Jinx ran away not knowing what to do. "Idiot," she thought. "What to do? After all, there are spies among us that overstayed their welcome," she thought.

Lyric stood in front of the computer typing. Quickly she removed the flash drive. "Almost done," she thought calmly. She left the room quietly closing the door. "What's she up to?" Reaper thought as he watched the surveillance cameras.

"It's getting bad," Alice said pacing Justin's office. "I agree. We should do something now," Huey stared at the screen. "Agreed. I want you to return to Psyche tomorrow!" Khepri demanded. She turned to Ally and Nico. "That includes you," she said angrily. "Yes," Nico said confused, "We're not from Psyche." "I'll go," Ally thought of Jinx, "We should hurry." "I'll help you get there," Justin said, "I have a specialized glider." "Great," Sam exclaimed, "I'll see my wife again." Alice stared into space thinking of Dante. "He couldn't hurt a fly," she thought. Nico turned to Huey concerned. "Don't worry. I'm sure she'll be fine," Ally said smiling. Huey wasn't sure.

Night stared out the window. "Hello," Amunet stood next to her. "Hey," Night said smiling. Amunet stared at her confused. "You okay?" Night asked concerned. "Yes, I'm just thinking how Night turns to day," she answered. She gave Amunet a confused look. "What does she mean?" she wondered.

<u>Part 3</u>

Alexander spun Catherine around in disbelief making her wedding dress float. "How lovely," Night walked over with a genuine smile. "You came!" Catherine ran over hugging her. "Wouldn't miss this for the world, Kitty," she answered, her violet eye glimmering, "I bought you a gift." She handed Catherine a small box. She opened the box to a locket marked A.D. "It's beautiful," she said surprised. "Allow me to put it on," Alexander put it on carefully, recognizing the necklace. "Thank you," Catherine gave Night a big grin. Night smiled as the scene turned back to normal. "If only," she thought sadly.

Chapter 26

Ally stared out the tinted window not at all surprised by Barcelona's beauty in the moonlight. "We're almost there," Alice said driving carefully so as not to be seen as. She parked at an abandoned office building. The first floor was still intact it seemed. "Ally, you're with me," Alice pointed out. Ally followed Alice out to an intact elevator. Both girls entered only to have Alice press ground. Slowly the elevator started, slowly going down stopping at a metallic-looking lobby. Ally walked out surprised to see all the people walk by and stare at her. "Wow," Ally looked around in shock. The others joined shortly stopping at Sam and Night. "So bright," Night thought.

"Welcome to the Crimson Knights," A woman said walking down the long staircase. Her long straight black hair was in a tight bun and her cat eyes pierced more than Alice's. She wore a black pantsuit to compliment it all. "I am...," she was interrupted by Sam. "Khepri," he said hugging her. "Khepri Coupe," she attempted to regain her composure as he let go. Out of the blue, she slapped him lightly. "What was that for?" he asked. "For being gone seventeen years," she answered. She almost looked angry at him. Sam sighed disappointed in himself. Khepri looked around stopping at Ally. "Something wrong?" she asked. "I imagined you taller," Ally answered honestly. Khepri glared ignoring her words. "Alice, Huey, Show our guests to their rooms," she ordered. Turning around she walked up the stairs. "Now if you follow us," Huey led the way as everyone followed them back onto the elevator.

Alice and Huey led the way down the long hallway full of doors. They stopped at one door marked reserved. "These are the guest rooms. This is one is Night and Carmen's. Ally and Nico, your room is across the hall," Alice pointed out. She turned to Damon and his trio. "Follow us," she said walking deeper into the sea of doors.

She stopped at another random door. "Here's yours and Alora. Amunet is right next door," she said. Amunet politely grabbed her key. She entered her room as Alorfacepalmeded. "Come on," Damon said gently taking her hand and guiding her. "Okay," Alora said grinning.

Ally stared at the purple walls surprised at the space. The queen-sized bed had a white blanket with red pillows while a table sat in the corner. A television showed the outside weather. "It looks nice," Nico said walking on the plush brown carpet. Ally sat at the table smiling as she watched him. "You're excited," she pointed out. "To be here with you, that's enough," he answered. Ally blushed as he kissed her. "How cute," Night said standing in the open doorway. Both stared at her in shock. "You should've closed the door," she closed the door as she left. Ally sighed as Nico stood up. "I'm going for a walk," he said taking the key. Ally smiled as he laid on the bed. "This will be safe," she thought, "Right?" "Why worry?" the thought popped into her head. "This is big," she pointed out. "You'll be safe, don't worry," the voice went away confusing her. "Must be a telepath nearby," she said smiling.

Khepri stared at the painting of Ares Dolan. "That is neat," Nico walked up to her. He turned to Khepri as she turned at him. "That's Ares Dolan," she answered. "Wow," he said in shock. "Yes, that's an appropriate response," Khepri said sarcastically. "Anyways, what happened between him and Damon Chaput?" Nico asked curious. "He was protecting Angeline when he scared Damon away. He didn't foresee her death from cancer," she answered. She smiled as she spoke again. "He made up for it by helping Damon and partially raising her kid," she pointed out.

Nico stared at her deep in thought. "To put it simply, he was a great help," she pointed out, "After all, it was his idea to start Gaia. In fact how about you tell me about Reaper." "He's an asshole," Nico answered. "Not that reaper! Benjamin Dempsey," she pointed out. "I've never met him," he answered. "Strange, you are his descendant," she said nonchalantly. "So are thousands of others," he retorted. "But only one bloodline is direct," Khepri smiled as Nico thought about it. "Direct?" he asked.

"Hey Nico," Night said walking up. "Hey Night," Nico ran over to her excitedly, "I've got to get back." Khepri watched him running not surprised. "Nice kid," she thought, "Why haven't you told him?" "Told him what?" Night asked pretending not to know. "That he is your son," She answered making Night mad. "He doesn't need the pressure. He is the first male in two generations and he is marrying his job," she pointed out, "He doesn't need to know he is a Dempsey." "He will find out if you don't tell him," Khepri was persistent. Night walked away ending the conversation.

Sam sat in his former work area waiting to be called in. Suddenly the door opened revealing his boss and father. "Dad!" he looked shocked and scared. "So you do remember me?" Sean asked glaring at him. "Yeah, whaarear...I thought Khepri was coming," Sam almost stammered. "She's on her way. I want to hear from you why they disappeared," Sean continued to stare. Sam sighed in preparation. "You remember the big boss set me to find Alette Bellerose...well I did. The problem was that she was one year old. I wasn't risking kidnapping," Sam abounded annoyed.

"So you stayed and adopted an orphan?" Sean demanded an answer. "Don't say that about Nico," he said defending his son. Sean looked down slowly. "Fine, just tell about Notte," he sighs. "She's a friend...a very good friend," he said blushing a little. Sean's glare got worse. He left the room silently and slammed the door closed behind him. Sam got up as a tear ran down his cheek.

Night walked down the hallway disappointed. "I have to use more power," she said out loud. "We aren't spying are Notte?" Khepri walked towards her. "No," she defended herself, "I'm sorry I didn't know Pre-Teachers couldn't use their ability." Khepri walked by almost looking sad. "Just be careful," she demanded. "She hates me," Night thought sadly.

Alora sat at the table eating her chicken alone. Night sat next to her staring at Ally and Nico nearby. "You heard our conversation," she said staring at Alora. "I heard nothing," Alora said with no sarcasm. "Does everyone know?" Night whispered. "Everyone who knows you except Nico," she answered. "It's that obvious," Night thought for a second. "You and Nico are a lot alike," Alora sighed, "Though I don't think anyone cares at this point. It's between you and Nico." A woman walked up smiling politely. "Miss Coupe wants to see you, Miss Fiore, Miss Jones," she said. Night shrugged as they followed her. "What's going on?" Alora thought confused as she got up.

Ally walked down the hallway staring at the metallic interior all around her. She looked ahead to see Amunet entering a random room. Following her she entered the same room. She was surprised by all the games, videos, and boxes. "Hello," Amunet said snapping her out of it. "Do you care?" she asked bluntly. Ally stared at her shocked and troubled. "Of course I do," she answered trying to help her. "Is that why you're here?" Amunet questioned. "Yes," Ally answered, "You've always been strange. But you are acting stranger." Amunet got a blank look on her face. "What do you mean?" she questioned. "You've been showing more emotion," she pointed out.

"Is...that bad?" Amunet looked insulted. "No," Ally sighed, "It's fine." "What about Huey?" Amunet asked curious, "Does he care?" "Yes, He cares about you too," she answered honestly. Amunet almost smiled. "That's why he's so nice," she said. "Yeah," Ally answered. "I've been trying to figure him out," Amunet spoke honestly. "May I ask why?" Ally asked now curious. "Because he's always nice to me," she answered. Ally sat down as Amunet did. "We are nice to you too," she pointed out, "But I see what you mean, he means it. You don't usually see that with him," she said. "Thanks," Amunet said almost smiling, "I always knew I was a rarity."

"So, Miss Jones and Miss Fiore," Khepri said sternly, "I called you here to talk about Bastet Caro." Alora glared at her as Night grinned. "What about Bastet?" Alora asked. "The basics you see," Khepri answered, "So what do I need to know?" "Bastet is a dangerous sociopath, that's all you need to know," Alora almost yelled. Night's scenery changed to Khepri fighting a young Bastet almost beating her. She fast-forwarded to Khepri crying at a funeral with two caskets. She then turned back time to her playing chess with what looked like an older Huey while a younger Alice played solitaire.

Returning to the present she could feel Khepri's pain. "Yes, Miss Fiore?" Khepri asked. "Nothing," Night answered. "Anyway," she returned her stare to Alora, "Tell me about Bastet Caro." "She is an illusionist who is bent on destruction," Alora answered. "A magician," Night said nonchalantly, "That's rare." "We should prepare," Khepri said hurriedly, "Renee! Stephanie!" Two young, identical twins, ran in. One had straight long blond hair in a ponytail while the other's hair was in a bun. One wore all pink while the other wore all blue. "Renee," Khepri ordered. "Yes," the one in pink answered. "Prepare for surveillance on Bastet," she ordered again. "Yes mam," Stephanie sounded more cheerful.

Night watched them walk away. "Who's the twins?" she asked. "My 'assistants'. Don't worry about them, you two should get prepared too," she turned to Alora and Night. "Permission to stay?" Night asked. "Permission granted," Khepri answered. "Okay," Alora left the room unsure. Night waited for everyone to leave and the door to close.

"Tell me what you know about Bastet Caro, Khepri Coupe," Night ordered. "You dare to order me around?" Khepri asked. "Out of concern," Night sounded sympathetic, "I feel your pain cause I lost two friends. One to war and one to Reaper." Khepri's eyes widened. "You've met Reaper?" she asked. "Yes, he left his mark on me," Night pointed to her eye patch. Khepri sat down shaking. "She's a monster, a creature of destruction and chaos. Where ever her lackeys go pain follows and lives end," she answered. Night gave her a frightened look. "You know this personally," she retorted. "Did you look into my past?" Khepri asked.

"Yes, but you look it too," she answered. "She killed my family. My father and sister," Khepri gave her a scary calm look, "Do you know why?" "No," Night answered. "Power!" she exclaimed calmly, "She was going insane and only I could see it. My father gave her chances because of her 'situation'. Her parents may not have been insane, but she was. Was her cause worth the life of the family that raised her?" "No," Night answered, "Did you consider her family?" "No, I had my own," she answered. "Thank you for listening. Now if you excuse me I would like to be alone," Khepri requested. The night left me unsure and concerned about her.

Nico walked down the hall staring at the intricate designs of the building. "Hey?" Alice said running up, "How are you doing?" "Hey," Nico said grinning, "Studying the architecture." "What's up, guys?" Huey ran up next. "What's wrong?" he asked, worried. "We never spend time together, Come on, the game hall is this way, " Alice said leading the way. "Okay," Nico was nervous as he spoke. "So do you like it here?" Huey asked curious.

"It's kind of like living in a Neo-Victorian armory," he answered. "And that's the look the remodeling crew was looking for," Huey's sarcasm was obvious. "No it's nice, it's just a little overwhelming to be surrounded by chrome," Nico answered. "I can see that," Alice defended Nico. "Okay, you win this one Nico. Besides we're here," he said. Nico entered curious. "How much fun," he thought, "And all I want to do is work."

Ally sat next to Amunet as she stared at her sandwich. "Hungry?" she asked. "Yes," Amunet answered, "It just doesn't look right." "That's...I don't know," she answered. "Hi," Carmen said sitting next to Amunet. Ally watched as Night sat across from her. "Hey

Ally, Hey Amunet," Alice sat next to Ally. Huey and Nico sat with Carmen. "So how is everyone?" Night asked curious. "Great, I beat Nico and Huey at the pool," Alice pointed out. Ally sighed. "We played poker," Amunet answered. "How much fun," Alora showed up. "Be nice," Damon said. Amunet looked around watching people talk. "I've got friends," she thought blissfully.

Chapter 27

Bastet stared at the computer screens in front of her being intensely involved. "Yes mother," Reaper said entering. "Tell me about Night," Bastet stared at the screens that showed Night Fiore's life. "Can't remember that name," Reaper answered annoyed. "You sure?" she showed a video of Night and Reaper fighting. "Oh yeah, that girl," he said smiling, "I thought her name was Notte."

"It's time for a rematch," Bastet grinned as she spoke. "Why?" he asked, "She'll find everything out. After all, she is a pre-teacher." "Yes, but if you put her out of commission then Khepri can't use her against me," she pointed out. Reaper thought for a second, grinning at the prospect of a rematch. "Yes mam," Reaper said leaving, "What a rematch it will be. After all, there won't be survivors on her end." "That's what I'm hoping for," Bastet thought.

Alexandria sat in the Barcelona coffee shop staring at the TV as the evening news played. "And it's only a few months into Blaine Bellamy's reign and he refuses to show his face. Not even his most trusted guards are allowed inside. He is being guarded personally by mercenaries hired by his royal advisor, the Black Lotus. Little is known about these mercenaries though, it has been speculated...," Alexandria got up paying her bill and leaving. "So that's how far the witch has gone," she thought, "Time to put her in her place."

Bastet left the surveillance room followed by Reaper. "Bastet!" came a familiar voice. She turned around to see Blaine Bellamy, Emperor of Psyche. His messy black hair and amber eyes complimented each other as he glared at her. He wore a black suit and leather shoes. "Hello your Majesty," her voice sounded almost sarcastic. "Where is she?" he demanded. "Noelle is here," she said. A young woman walked up with long brown straight hair and silver eyes. She wore a blue dress and low heels. "Hello," she said calmly.

Kat watched nearby annoyed at Bastet's antics. "He's blind," she thought, "Noelle would never act this way. What an idiot."

Night smiled as she stared at the ceiling. "Night," Carmen yawned. "Let's go to sleep," Night spoke tired herself. Both went to sleep as Night tried. "Poor Khepri," she thought. The memory came to her causing tears. *Night stared at the empty bassinet glaring. At eighteen she couldn't believe her son was taken away. "It was for your good," Sol pointed out. Night stayed silent. "Who has him?" she asked. "What?" Sol retorted. "Who has Nico!?" she demanded.* As a tear fell down her cheek she couldn't help but be happy she found him.

Ally stared at the pool table deep in thought. "Come on, it's a pool," Alice pointed out. "Let me do it my way," Ally said hitting the white ball. The white ball hit every ball knocking them all into a hole. "Why you...?" Alice's words were covered by the alarm. "Miss Coupe, there's an intruder," a guard opened the door. "Come on," Alice said running out. Ally followed shocked by the intruder. "Dad," she said surprised. "Ally," Alexander said in shock. "Miss Bellerose, This is...," Khepri whispered. "My father, Alexander Bellerose," Ally answered, "At least I think it's him." Khepri's eyes widened in fear. "Let him go," she ordered. One guard removed his handcuffs.

"Ally," he said hugging her. "It's him," she thought, "He looks like a mess." She looked at her father worried. His messy brown hair and his brown eyes made his messy clothes look horrible. "Hey Dad," she said worried. "How may we help you?" Khepri asked. "Just give me a room close to Ally," he answered. "And a shower," Ally suggested. "You heard the man and his daughter," Khepri ordered, "No offense sir." "Yes mam," Everyone went to work immediately.

"So she's Alexander's daughter," she thought, "I thought the name sounded familiar." "Where did you find him?" Ally asked curious. "In one of our warehouses," Khepri answered, "We thought he was a spy pretending to be homeless." "That's not good," Ally sounded worried, "What did he say?" "He wanted to see Catherine," she explained. Ally felt a tear fall down her cheek. "Look we have a Doctor that specializes in flames. We'll send him his way," she attempted to cheer her up, "Come on, we should hurry."

Ally sat in the chair in the doctor's office as they examined Alexander. "Sir how did you make it here?" the Doctor asked. "I took two trains and a taxi," he answered, "Your building stands out...plus I have the address." The Doctor raised an eyebrow. "Who is sitting in that chair?" he asked. Alexander looked at Ally smiling. "Kitty, My wife," he answered. "Dad?" Ally asked worried. "Miss Bellerose, please feel your husband's forehead," the Doctor ordered. Ally felt his forehead immediately pulling her hand away. "He's hotter than a bonfire," she answered. "Just as I feared, His temperature has settled. It's only a matter of time now," he pointed out. "What do you mean?" Ally demanded.

"Mr. Bellerose, please go with the nurse so I can talk with your wife," the Doctor suggested. Ally watched her dad leave painfully. "His body heat is boiling him alive. This happens to all flames eventually. After all, this is one of the most common side effects of the ability," he explained. Ally felt a tear fall down her cheek. "What can I do?" she asked. "Just make his remaining time the best you can," he suggested. Ally attempted to smile. "Thank you," she said wiping away the tears as she left the room. Alexander got up surprised to see her. "Come on Dad, I'll show you where your room is," Ally said leading the way. He followed her. "Thanks, Ally," he said making Ally sad. "No problem," she tried to act chipper.

Sam sat at the table trying to mix two chemicals. He felt everyone staring at him like he was a criminal. Finally, he did his job, even if it was quick. "So what are we making?" one of his coworkers asked. "Just a smoke bomb," the other coworker answered. Suddenly a woman ran in trying to catch her breath. "One of our vendors," she said trying to talk, "Is here." "Which one?" Sam asked.

"Alexander Bellerose," she answered. Sam suddenly felt a sense of hope. "That's great," he thought, "We can be lonely.

Reaper stood in the shadows watching the people walk by. Hidden in the dark He wondered how many people were psychics ready for a job with the Black Lotus. He felt his sword's sheath knowing what was about to happen. He was going to relish this battle.

Ally sat at the table staring at the rain outside. "Hey," Nico sat next to her, "I heard the news." "So you heard about Dad," she said with a sigh. "Yeah," Nico answered, "I can't believe he hunted you down." Ally put her head down ready to cry. "What's wrong?" Nico asked. "He's going away," she said wiping the tears. "Ally, I'm so sorry," Nico said holding her close. A knock on the door made Ally answer it. Alexander stood there looking scared. "Hey Dad," she said politely. "How about lunch?" he asked. "Sure," she answered. "By the way are you okay? You look like you've been crying," he said. "I'm fine," she answered.

She walked out following him. "So how have you been?" he asked. "Great," Ally answered. "Night kind of filled me in," he pointed out. "Great," she said sighing. "I'm just glad you're safe and sound," he said. "So, how have you been?" she asked changing the subject. "Great," he answered. "Liar," she thought, "I know better." "So, I know I've been busy," he said sorrowfully. "Dad," she was in shock at her father's words. "I'm sorry," he apologized. Ally looked at him a tear forming. "It's okay," she said wiping a tear away. "No, it isn't! I ignored you," he pointed out, "I will make it up to you." "Okay Dad," she sounded worried. "How are you planning on doing that?" she wondered.

Nico sat next to Night. "You look occupied," she pointed out. "I am," he answered. "Thinking about Ally?" Night asked. "Yes and no," he answered. "Well, you need to hold on to her," Night messed up his hair as she left. Ally walked out of nowhere making Nico stare.

He turned around to see Night gone as Ally walked towards him. "Were you waiting for me?" she asked. "Yes," Nico answered. "She was unusually motherly," she pointed out. "Agreed," He said, "So how are you holding?" "I'm holding the best I can right now," she answered.

"You know when I was fifteen, I hated the idea of being in an arranged marriage," he randomly said. Ally looked at him surprised. "I'm not kidding. Sam had to let me date to calm me down," he laughed at the memory, "But then one day Night and him sat me down and showed that picture in my workshop. It made me realize how fragile you were. How much I wanted to help you. Well, your father needs you now." Ally grinned as he caressed her face. "Besides I have a family the size of Haven. I think I'll get by," he said laughing. Ally laughed too. "True," she said getting up, "Thank you." Nico smiled as she left.

Night stared at Ally deep in wonder. The scene changed all of a sudden to a high school as Ally disappeared.

"Kitty, you really should be careful," an eighteen-year-old Night said worried. Her violet eyes shined bright as her short-length black hair radiated. Kitty grinned back, her sapphire eyes and dirty blonde hair complimented each other. Both wore green school uniforms. "We should head home," Night said heading for her car, Kitty followed being her happy self. "How was class? I know Mr. Grim can be well...grim," she pointed out. "Not always, sometimes he's not a mortician," Kitty disagreed half-jokingly. "So where do you want to go?" Night asked, "I think Dimitri or Elizabeth isn't at the park today," Night pointed out. "Sounds great," Kitty answered. "To the park, we go," she drove off the lot excitedly.

Night drove up to a park, sighing in relief. "He's not here," she said. Kitty stared nearby at a boy covering his face with a newspaper. Noticing, Night walked over glaring at him. "Who are you?" she demanded. "Alexander Bellerose," he answered. "Nice to meet you," Kitty introduced herself, "I'm Catherine." "Nice to meet you,"

Alexander said shaking her hand. "Bellerose?" Night asked. "Yes, Bellerose," he answered sarcastically. "Who's the Bellerose's? Are they important?" Kitty asked. "No, Just some weapons specialists," Night pointed out. "You don't know me?" he asked, "But you're an Alkeav." "What does that mean?" Night asked. "Nothing, Names mean nothing," he turned to Kitty. "Sir," A woman ran up to him, "We need to go." "Okay," Alexander said getting up, "See you around." "See you," Kitty said grinning. The scene ended with a gunshot before returning to normal.

The scene returned to normal making Night smile as a tear ran down her face. "If only," she thought. Alexander sat next to her. "So what were you remembering?" he asked. "Take a guess," she answered. "I see," he sighed, "You're always in such pain." "Yeah," she said walking away, "So are you." "What does that mean?" Alexander demanded. "You're lying to Ally. You know your fate, you even have your affairs in order, so why lie?" Night demanded. "Normality, she doesn't need to remember me as a fading remnant. I know she knows my time is up; But I've already ruined her childhood, I just want time with her," he said smiling. Night looked at him in horror. "You've accepted the fact that you'll be gone," she said in shock. "And what about you? Does Nico know?" he asked.

Night slapped him lightly. "Everyone else is playing kid gloves with you, but I won't. I don't know my fate, but I want Reaper's head on a platter," she got a dark tone in her voice. "What about Kitty's killer?" he asked. "She's taken care of," Night walked away. "How? What did you do?" Alexander asked. "Need to know basis," Night answered. "**Need to know**? I was her husband, I have the right to know!" he demanded. "She went down with my burning passion," Night answered. "You loved Kitty, didn't you?" he asked.

Night blushed a bright red. "Why did you let her marry me?" he was persistent "She found the right person...or so I thought. I mean you let her die," she calmed down. "I couldn't do anything. She was in Durand," he pointed out as he started to cry, "I loved her too." Night walked away ignoring him. "You have nothing to say for yourself," Alexander pointed out. "I don't," she walked away leaving him to grieve.

Nico laid in bed asleep as Ally laid next to him sleeping. A falling pin woke her up to Nico cuddling her. She cuddled back only to have him wake up. "Ally," he said surprised. "Don't be surprised," she said. "Are you awake?" he asked. "No," she answered. Nico held her close until a knock on the door woke her up. "Ally," Alexander said in a sad tone. "She's busy," Nico announced. Ally got up answering the door anyway. "Hello," she opened the door not surprised. "So you're okay," he said. "Ally, Khepri wants to see you," Renee walked up interrupting the conversation. "Coming," Ally followed her. "What's going on?" Alexander asked. No one answered.

Ally entered the room with Khepri and Night standing in front of a full screen. She stared at the screen as Bastet stared back. "Hello, I am sorry to say you are all unnecessary characters. So I'll send a message to you. Please just stay where you are," the screen turned off scaring Khepri. "Shut down the building," she ordered. "Yes mam," everyone said getting to work. "Don't worry," she said turning to Ally, "We won't let her in."

Night stared at the screen, a look of rage on her face. "Are you alright, Miss Fiore," Khepri asked. "I'm fine," she answered snapping out of it. "Maybe you should get some sleep," Ally suggested. "Yeah, I just need some sleep," she said leaving with an uneasy calm. Khepri stomped up to Night concerned. "Maybe you should get psychhe eval?" she asked. "I don't need that," Night sounded insulted as she left the room. "Night and Khepri have the same look," Ally thought, "What does that mean?"

Night sat on her bed staring at the stars projected on the ceiling. She thought about Reaper making her remember why she was in pain. Suddenly she got up as Carmen slept leaving the room. "It has to be done," she thought passing Ally and Nico's room. Her footsteps woke up Ally. "Where is she going?" she asked peeking through the door. "I don't know," Nico answered as he got out of bed. He snuck out followed by Ally. They followed her quietly to the lobby and watched her put in the code. Ally followed Nico watching him do the same thing after she got on the elevator. As she left the building they followed her closely not missing a step. Both watched her enter a nearby park looking determined. She was followed off the trail leading them to an opening where Reaper sat on a rock, a sly smirk on his face.

"Long time no see," Reaper spoke nonchalantly. "How about we lose the formalities?" Night threw a dagger at him only to have him catch it between his two fingers. "You kept it," he said surprised. "I should've, right?" she shot at him immediately with an old pistol finally missing him by a hair. "You're going to kill me with a puny century-old pistol?" he asked. "This is Benjamin Dempsey's pistol. Still in mint condition and shooting as you can see. Fascinating isn't it," Night pointed out. "That's the pistol that ended the Bellerose regime," he pointed out. He started laughing. "I imagined a shotgun," he taunted. "You're not getting the picture. The Fiore's descended from the 'original Reaper'," she pointed out, "The one that protected and not killed." She shot him point blank in the left arm as he stood in there in shock, immobilizing him. "I will enjoy this," she said putting the pistol to his head, "The assassin wants to be being brought down by his namesake's weapon."

Suddenly she felt a pain in her abdomen. Looking down, she saw Reaper pull out his sword making her fall against a tree. "By the way, he did kill. He just killed his clients. Why do you think they all disappeared?" he asked. Leaving he felt surprised. "Night," Ally screamed as she ran from behind a bush after Reaper disappeared.

She noticed a gold line disappearing into the woods. Nico ran over, holding Night close. She looked at him smiling. "You found me," she said. At that moment Nico realized why she had always treated him as her own. "Do something!" he demanded. Ally put her hand over Night's wound healing it. "That's all I can do," she said sadly. Nico felt heartbroken. "She's alive," he thought, "Mom is alive."

Chapter 28

Night laid in the hospital bed in a comatose state, Nico by her side. "You found me," The words resonated in his head. "She's his mom!" Alice pointed out in shock. "I knew that," Ally randomly said. "Why didn't you tell me?" Nico asked. "It was between you and her," her voice sounded sad. Nico looked down with melancholy. "She should wake up, thanks to Ally," a doctor walked up. "You think so?" Nico asked hopeful. "Yes, by the sound of it she had untreated PTSD," He said worried, "It was lucky no one died." Ally stared at Night scared and worried.

"How did you find out?" Alice asked curious. "Khepri asked me to do a psyche evaluation," he answered, "She showed all the signs." Lightly she touched her hand. Suddenly the room changed to Night's house and a sixteen-year-old Night was yelling at her parents, suitcase in hand. "You let her take Nico away from me," she yelled. "No we didn't," her father said. He turned to Sol. "You are disowned," he said angrily, "For giving away your nephew." The night left with Seth ending the memory. "Well Amethyst did disappear after fighting her, not to mention being defeated," Alora pointed out bringing Ally back.

"Really," Khepri said walking in. She walked over to Night. "It seems Notte Fiore, Night as she was called, was their main objective," she pointed out, "Carmen will be here soon." She turned to Alora and Ally. "I'll send someone to pick you up later. For now, I'll wait," she said walking out. "At least she is giving you time to absorb this a little," Alice tried looking on the bright side. Ally got up deep in thought leaving the room. "I have to use the restroom," she said calmly. She left without a word.

Sam stared at Night with only a sleeping Nico in the room. "Hey," he said attempting to wake him. Nico awoke as Sam sat down. "How about you head to bed? Remember Ally is also having a hard time," he pointed out. Nico got up leaving reluctantly. Sam waited for the door to close patently. When it closed his attention turned to Night. "I knew something was wrong," he thought sadly, "I should've done something about it." He hid as the door opened. When it closed he walked unseen. "Safe," he thought to himself.

Ally yawned as she got up. Getting out of bed she grabbed her brush. As she got ready for the day a knock on the door got her attention. Renee stood in the doorway. "Come with me," she ordered. "Why," she asked. "Khepri wants you," she answered. Alora walked by following the other twin. Her bubblegum pink hair rolled down her back, while she wore a red t-shirt and sweats. "Why?" she asked. Renee and her twin shrugged their shoulders. "Come on," Renee ordered.

Khepri sat at her desk looking through her virtual files. A knock caught her consideration. "Come in," she closed her file. Ally and Alora walked in a little more awake. "Presentation?" she asked staring at Alora. She ignored her guest being snarky.   "PTSD, how sad," Khepri said hiding her o-Pal, "I knew something was wrong." Ally and Alora were officially awake. "We didn't know either," she thought. "What happened to Amethyst?" Alora thought confused.

Ally sat across from Khepri's desk with Alora. "I'm going to take you to meet Emperor Blaine," she said bluntly, "I have finally got us access." Ally looked at her shocked while Alora laughed. "You're serious," she said surprised, "They have Black Lotus everywhere." "Yes, I'm serious," Khepri pointed out, "Be ready at nine am tomorrow." "Yes mam," Alora said leaving. Ally stayed deep in thought waiting for the door to close. "Something on your mind?" Khepri asked.

"You found something and you're not telling us," she pointed out. "Unfortunately yes, we found an unrecognizable skeleton at the bottom of the Rhone River at the train crash site," she answered, "All we know is it's a woman." Ally felt horrified realizing what Night might've done. "We're thinking it's Amethyst seeing as she hasn't popped up. We've tested the small amount of DNA we found that was left, but there were no results. All we found is this," She put down a well-preserved metal pole and pressed a button expanding it. "It was Amethyst," Alora thought in shock.

"We know it's her, we just can't prove it. Plus who killed her?" Khepri asked, "Anyways, This is a mystery." "Why do you say 'who killed her'?" Ally asked. "Bullet in the bone indicating she was shot in her leg. There were also bone shards around it as well. It looks like it belonged to a pistol from a century ago," Khepri explained. "Thank you," Ally left knowing the answer. She took out Night's pistol handing it to her. "Try comparing it," she offered. "Who did belong to?" Khepri asked as an uncomfortable Alora and Ally left. "Notte Bellissimo Fiore," she answered, "Aka 'Night'."

Nico sat next to Night thinking of ways to help. "You need to eat," Ally said hearing his stomach growl. He got up reluctantly following her to the cafeteria. His silence made her nervous. "Um...what do you want?" she asked grabbing a plate. He sat down not answering. All grabbed him his usual order as well as something for her. "So...," Nico stopped her. "You don't have to force yourself to talk," he said sadly. He sighed as he picked at his food. Ally sighed defeated. She was in the position he was in in October. "I'm just trying to help," she said. "Why? " he asked. "She is going to be fine. Isn't that good?" she pointed out. "Yeah," he answered raising an eyebrow, "besides I'm not allowed to worry?" "You are," Ally looked embarrassed. She got up finishing the last of her food. Nico stayed. "I'm sorry," she whispered as she left.

Khepri walked down the hall walking into the game room. Amunet stared at the bullet hole in her forehead. "Are you okay?" Khepri asked curious. "Yes," Amunet answered. "Now Alice you're in charge while I'm gone tomorrow," she told her daughter. "Yes mam," Alice said almost hitting Huey as she saluted her. "Good," Khepri said leaving. "One won't make it," Amunet said scaring Alice and Huey. "Who?" Huey asked. Amunet stayed silent.

Khepri drove up to the palace parking in front of the entrance. They opened their doors revealing Ally in a pink dress and flats while Alora wore a tan pantsuit and high heels. Walking in they were greeted by Bastet immediately. "Hello Khepri," she said. "Hello Bastet, we are here to see Emperor Blaine," Khepri retorted. Their eyes locked intensely as if they were battling. "He's busy," Bastet pointed out. "No I'm not," he walked up insulted. He looked at Ally surprised. "Come in," he said. "I'm Ally Bellerose," she introduced herself. "Sophia Turner," Alora answered. "Please come in," he said. They entered surprised by the difference in the air.

Ally spied a young girl following them. "Allow me to introduce you," Blaine said, "That is Kat Boucher, my bodyguard, and this is Bastet, my advisor." Ally looked at Kat carefully. Her short brown hair and silver eyes complimented her brown blouse and jeans with low heels. She turned to Bastet wondering about her laid-back demeanor. Her short black hair and blue eyes complimented her pale skin and black suit.

She looked eighteen, but she got the feeling she was older. "Wait till you meet my wife," Blaine continued talking as Ally ignored him and checked out the surroundings. Ally stared befuddled at the faint glow around Bastet that came and gone. "Alora," Bastet thought ignoring his talking, "Welcome back, traitor." Kat looked into Ally's mind seeing Night Fiore. "Poor woman," she thought, "She didn't deserve that."

Alice shook uncontrollably as she watched the romantic comedy with Huey and Amunet. "Wow, the pressure is getting to her," Amunet said. Huey looked at Alice worried. "It's okay, Mom will be back soon," he tried to comfort her. "Something doesn't feel right. Amunet's words and Mom's mission aren't going together right," she explained. "You think something is going to happen to mom? She's a pro," Huey pointed out. "She's also protective, Huey! Don't think for a second that she won't pull out plan C," Alice exclaimed. "She wouldn't," Huey started to look worried. "She will," Alice sounded serious, "Anything to do her job." Huey suddenly felt worried.

Alora stared at her dress in the mirror. "What was the point of bringing us here?" she asked. "Don't know," Ally answered dressed in blue, "Whatever it is it has to do with Bastet." "Are you done?" Khepri asked opening the door, "Come on then." Ally walked out gracefully while Alora followed. Khepri noticed the thoughtful look on Ally's face. "Just enjoy the party," she said. They entered a room full of people dancing. "Ally," Blaine ran up excited surprising her.

"Hello," she greeted as she had been taught. "Ally," Alora tilted her head to Reaper nearby. "That's why," she thought. She noticed a gold line around him. Khepri watched Bastet smile nearby. "Your time is coming," Khepri thought. "Ally, this is Noelle," Blaine held his wife's hand. "Nice to meet you," Noelle said politely. Ally noticed a gold line around her too and the distance she kept. "Would you like to dance?" Blaine asked Ally. "Sure," Ally answered. Blaine took her hand dancing with her. "So, how is Damon? I haven't seen him in months?" he asked. "He's fine. He's as wacky as ever," she answered.

"Of course, he's always had that strange...flare," Blaine pointed out. Nearby Alora and Khepri watched. "This is how I imagined Damon Chaput and Angeline Durand got along if they were cousins," Khepri said randomly. Alora gave her a weird look. "How much guilt does your family hold?" she asked. "More than you know," Khepri answered, "I plan to end it." The music stopped and Ally and Blaine stopped dancing. She noticed Alora motioning nearby. "Sorry, Could you point me to the bathroom?" she asked. "Just down the hall," he answered.

Ally followed her worried. She followed Alora out only to find out she was following Kat. They followed Kat into the library only to find her gone. "This way," Alora whispered leading the way to one bookcase. She pulled a book opening another bookcase. "How did you...?" Alora walked down the stairs ignoring Ally's question. Ally and Alora ran in following. "What's she up to?" Ally asked worried. "Don't know," Alora answered as they walked down the stairs. They walked to a room lit by torches.

"Hello," Kat said sitting in a chair. "What's going on?" Ally demanded. "I'm sure you saw it, the line around Reaper and Noelle," Kat pointed out. "What!?" Alora asked. "They are figments, well Reaper is here, But Noelle isn't," Kat pointed out plainly. "She isn't?" Alora sounded surprised. "Where is she?" Ally asked. "In a cell," Kat answered stalling, "Do me a favor. Show Blaine what's going on." "How?" Ally thought. "Just touch her," Kat explained. Ally walked out followed by Alora. "What are you planning?" she asked. "Don't know," she answered, "I'm winging it."

Ally reentered the room to Blaine talking to Noelle. She walked over smiling. "Hello," she reached out for a handshake only to have her move away. Ally thought for a second finally ending with a 'enough of this'. "I'm sorry," she said turning to Blaine as she touched the fake Noelle making her disappear. Blaine stared at the spot where she stood ready to cry. "Bastet!" he yelled. "Everyone out," Khepri said as everyone ran out. "You too," she said turning to Ally and Blaine. Ally grabbed Blaine's hand dragging him out.

"Alora," Khepri said handing her a dagger, "Give this to Alice. I'm initiating plan C." Alora shook her head, yes running. "Why?" Alora thought running. Ally ran to Alora and Kat. "I'm going back," she said turning back, "It's my only option." "Ally," Alora said worried. "Where are you going?" Reaper asked. "Run," Alora yelled. Kat took Blaine and ran. Alora threw a small smoke bomb disappearing as it cleared. "At least we have her," he thought.

Chapter 29

Alora rode the elevator down feeling melancholy. She got off to Damon running up. "Blaine," he said hugging his brother. Kat looked at Nico who glared back. "Where's Ally?" he asked. "Where's Khepri?" Sam demanded. Alora gave the dagger to Alice making Sam walk away in shock. "No," he whispered walking away. Alice stared at the dagger knowing the symbolism. "I'm gonna finish this," Alice said attempting to hold back her tears. She walked away as a tear fell down her face. Nico was still fuming.

She walked down entering Khepri's office. She turned to the pictures ..her favorite was always the one with her grandfather and aunt. The door opening made her turn. Huey closed the door behind him. "So...You have a plan?" Huey asked concerned and grieving. " Yes," Alice answered. Amunet showed up next to Huey. "And I know where they will take Ally...Zodiac Industries," Amunet announced. "What do you mean?" Alice asked. "It's where all of Bastet's prisoners go," she answered. "Make everyone involved show up the next morning. We will talk about then," she said assertively. "Fine," Amunet agreed.

Alora sat next to Damon about to cry. Sam was next to Huey and Alice with a box of tissues while Nico comforted Carmen. "Sam, I'm so sorry about Khepri," Damon wiped a tear away, "She was like a second mother." Sam burst into tears completely unable to speak. Alora noticed Alice leaving the room. She entered her mother's office about to cry. Alice stared at her mother's office feeling the weight of the world on her shoulders. The empty desk where she sat and gave orders seemed lifeless, while the family photos made her cry. She walked over to one picture, a full family photo of when they were born, which made her smile slightly. "What are you doing here?" she turned around to see Alora standing in the doorway. "I'm sorry, she told me to give you the dagger," Alora said feeling responsible. "It's not your fault. She knew Bastet would be her last battle," Alice said about to cry. "Can Amunet and I come by tomorrow at three?" Alora asked. "Sure," Alice answered. "Good, we'll be there," she said leaving her alone. "I need a plan," Alice thought, "to save Ally. What am I saying they probably have one."

Alice sat behind her desk surprised to see all the people in her office. It seems Amunet and Alora bought along with Nico and Huey. "What's going on?" she demanded feeling overwhelmed. "Amunet has a plan," Alora pointed out as gently as possible. "Great, I need one," Alice spoke trying not to be snide, "So what is it?" Amunet turned to her, ready to talk. "It started during the Durand war. My whole family was killed and I was taken because I was the youngest and because of our family name, Argyis," she explained, "We see people die before they die. I was experimented on, turned, and twisted into a weapon. When they discovered that I still had emotions. I was supposed to be terminated. My trainer Amethyst was set against my death, but Reaper overrode her order. As they walked me down to my execution, I stomped on the guard's foot as hard as I could. Even though I was chained I ran for my life aiming for a nearby window. Reaper came at me, but I used his sword to cut the chains. Freed, I jumped through the window from I don't know how many feet. When I reached the water, I was horrified by my appearance. I never even knew my family." She wiped a tear. "The plan is simple, We go in and leave with our friends. Now Nico messes with the server while I protect him. Huey and Amunet go after Ally and Noelle," Alora explained. "I'll make Amunet head of this mission. Now bring them back," Alice ordered.

Ally sat in her cell in a white shirt and pants sad. She looked around the completely white room in shock as plain as it was. "This was a horrible idea," she thought. "Hello," a voice said from the other side of the wall. Ally walked over cautiously. "Hello?" she asked unsure, "Who are you?" "I don't know who are you?" the voice asked back. "Miss, this is not the time," Ally whispered. "You're right," the woman stopped talking as she heard footsteps walking away and footsteps coming towards her cell. "Not now," she thought running for the bed, "What are they going to do with me?" The steps continued right outside her door. Opening automatically, the guard walked slowly to her. She stared in fear at his lion-like appearance. He grabbed her dragging her along. "Caveman," she thought.

Lyric entered the computer room putting in the USB port. Leaving the room quietly she took the USB port almost unnoticed. Reaper stood at the computer trying to figure her out. "What are you up to?" he asked himself. He turned to the past images trying to put her plan together. "She is crude and stealthy," he thought as a scientist entered. "We can't find anything wrong with the system," she thought. "More stealthy," he thought.

Jinx walked in circles staring at computer screens and going mad. "Security duty sucks," Lyric mentioned as she entered. Jinx stopped staring at one screen. Ally was asleep in her bed. "It kills me," he said as the memory from school hit him. *So you have a bully?" he asked Ally. "Of course, her name is Cassandra Favre, "Ally answered. "Just tell her off," he suggested. "She is too scared to," Sybil pointed out eating a candy bar, "Too bad this is considered contraband." "Our schools suck," Jesse said, "I'm always in trouble, but I do get good grades." "So you're a natural jinx," Ally pointed out. "Not funny. You know I hate it when you call me that," he sounded annoyed, "Besides you're my only real friends."* The moment on the train returned to him. "You're such a Jinx." The words hurt more than anything else. "I'll cover for you," Lyric said randomly. "Really?" he asked running for the door. "Of course," she answered as the door closed.

Jinx took his key out unlocking Ally's door. Ally woke falling off the bed. "Ow!" she stood up rubbing her head, "Jinx." "Hey Ally," he said sitting next to her. Ally suddenly felt uncomfortable as he put his arm around her. "What's wrong?" he asked. "You tried to kill me," she pointed out removing his arm, "And not very well." "I've missed you. I even joined H.I.P. to protect you. After I found out about Nico it was all I could do. I mean I love you, Ally," his words made Ally sputter. He kissed her lightly making her push away. "What's wrong with you?" she asked walking away, "You never responded to my letters even." "I was trying to keep you safe," he answered. It hit him like a ton of bricks. "You're in love with Nico," he sounded disappointed as Ally blushed, "See that proves it." "Jesse, you're right, I love Nico Katsaros. But you're still my friend," she pointed out hurting his feelings, "We are family." Jinx got up heading for the door. "Jesse?" Ally asked worried. "As long as you're happy," he said leaving. Ally sighed as the door slammed. "I'm an idiot," she thought about to cry.

Alora stared at the guards in front of the gated door. "How about now?" she whispered. "Now," Amunet ordered quietly. Alora threw two needles knocking out the guards. "Come on," she said running in. Everyone followed her. "This way," Alora whispered breaking away to the surveillance room. She entered the room to no one inside. "How strange? It's empty," she pointed out. Nico sat down looking for Ally. "Found her," he almost said immediately. "She looks sad, by the way. You ran fast," Alora pointed out. "I jog every morning," he retorted. Alora sighed. "Of course," she said, "Exercise for Ally."

"She's in cell 2B and Noelle Bellamy is in cell 2A," Alora said into her earpiece. Amunet smiled to herself. "Got it," she said. "So let's hurry," Huey led the way. A dagger flew out of nowhere almost hitting Amunet. "No way," Lyric grinned as she grabbed another. Huey fell holding his arm. "Huey!" Amunet carried him to safety. Lyric's grin disappeared… Amunet looked at him in shock as she grabbed the bandages. Bandaging him up immediately she quickly grabbed the gauze. "How bad?" he asked in pain. "It's minor," she lied, "Just leave it to me." She quietly made a sling. "I'll leave it to you," he whispered.

Lyric walked down the hallway annoyed. "They got away," she complained. Two guards walked up to her looking serious. "Miss Raptis, Bastet would like to see you," One said. Lyric followed befuddled and unsure. She entered Jinx sitting in a chair. "Take a seat," Bastet's words made her sit down. "I know who both of you are, especially you Jesse," she turned to Jinx, "But I have a job offer for each of you. Just join me." "Never," Lyric answered. "No way," Jesse glared at her. "Too bad...kill them," she turned to Reaper. Suddenly a red light went off alarming everyone. "What happened?" he asked. Lyric smiled as Jesse and she ran away. "No," Bastet yelled disappearing, "Get out or you will be locked in." Reaper shook his head in agreement before running.

"It won't open," Amunet complained, "And the shutdown sequence is engaged." "Let us try," Lyric ran up. Jesse walked up unlocking the door as Ally fell out shaking. Looking up she saw Nico causing her to be excited. Nico picked her up holding her carefully. Ally turned to Jesse noticing his melancholy. Jesse unlocked the other door allowing Noelle to exit calmly. "Let's get out," Amunet said running. "Agreed," Nico said holding Ally. Everyone ran out of the building only to see a metal shield go around the old building. "We'll help them," Noelle spoke as if it was a promise.

Chapter 30

Nico cuddled Ally as she slept. "It's great to have her back," he whispered to himself. Ally woke up looking up at him. "Hey," she said smiling. "Just sleep. You need it," he held her closer. "Okay," Ally fell back to sleep smiling.

Terra looked through the gigantic screen glaring at Jesse. "What happened?" she demanded loudly. " I couldn't communicate 'cause I was under surveillance," he answered. "What do you have to say for yourself?" Alice asked Lyric. "Nothing, I was doing my job," she answered. "I expect a report tomorrow," Terra signed off. "Me too," Alice ordered. "Yes mam," Jesse and Lyric said in union. The alarm went off surprising everyone. "What happened?" Alice asked. "We have an intruder," Renee sounded in shock. Alice stood up running immediately. She ran to the cell he was in confused.

"He's asking for you," Stephanie pointed out. Alice walked up to the cell to see Dante sitting inside. "Alice," he ran up hugging her. "Dante," she looked surprised. Huey stared at them in shock. "How did you get here?" she asked. "I followed your friends," he answered. Alice smiled understanding his situation. "Welcome," she said. Dante gave her a big smile. "Where is going to sleep? All the rooms are taken," Huey pointed out. Alice thought about it. "In your room," she answered, "He can sleep on the couch." Huey stared at her dumbfounded. She turned to Huey in realization. "Fine," he sighed...

Amunet entered the hospital floor looking for Huey. Finding his room she entered to see him asleep. "I know you are awake," she pointed out. "I almost got you," he said sitting up. She sat next to him smirking. "You are a mystery," she said blandly. "I know," he answered. "I thought this would make you feel better," she pointed out. She handed him a box. He opened it carefully to a picture of Khepri. "Thanks," he said about to cry. "It does help, right," she said smiling slightly. "I hope so," Amunet thought worried.

Nico sat next to Night as she lay in bed still in a coma. "How is she doing?" Alexander asked. "She's getting better," he answered, "slowly." "Ally healed her. She's going to be fine," Alexander pointed out. "I know," Nico spoke sadly, "I miss my mom though." A tear came to Ally's eye as she walked away from the room. "I want to be there for him," she thought, "Poor guy." A woman walked up to Ally, smiling pleasantly. "Please get Mr. Katsaros and meet Miss Coupe in her office," she ordered politely. "That might be a little hard," Ally pointed hard. "It's her words, not mine," the woman said walking away. "I have to do it," she thought hurt, "He is going to kill me.

Ally sat next to Nico comforting him. "I'm sorry if this is a bad time, but we need to talk," Alice pointed out. "Why?" Ally asked curious. "Bastet is now in power and we need to stop her," Alice said blunt and loud. "Say that again I don't think Bastet heard you," Nico said annoyed. "Anyways I have a plan," she continued. Nico stood up leaving the room. "What's wrong with him?" Alice asked. "Night is his mother and in a coma. Please have more compassion," Ally left the angry.

Ally walked down the hallway to Damon standing nearby. "Ally," he said excitedly, "It's time for your last lesson." Ally turned to see Nico walking away. "What is it?" she asked. "Suppressing another psychic's ability. All you have to do is...," he was cut off by Dante. "To put your hand on them and think of sealing off their ability. That's it," he explained. Ally and Damon stared at him shocked by his words. "It was meant for Damon Chaput," he answered. "There's the lesson," Damon pointed out as Ally walked away. "Interesting lesson and one I can't practice," she said. "You don't have to, it's instinct," Dante explained. "How do you know?" she asked curious now. "I just do," he answered.

Huey sat in his room typing on his O-Pal. He was trying to ignore his situation until the door finally opened. He glared at Dante as he walked in. "Hello," he greeted him. "Hi," Huey said with annoyance, "May I help you?" Dante sighed annoyed himself. "I'm just here to help," he retorted. "How?" Huey demanded. "I'm from the Black Lotus. Plus I can shed light on her illegal cloning experiment," he answered. "Illegal what?" Huey stared in surprise, "How do you know this?" "I'm one of them," Dante spoke with disgrace. Huey looked at him confounded. "How is that?" he was still asking questioning. "I was going to tell Alice," Dante pointed out. "I'll call her, but I have to be there," Huey said. "Agreed," he said.

Alice stared at the ceiling deep in thought as a knock on the door broke her train of thought. She opened it up to see Dante and Huey standing in front of her. "What's wrong?" she asked. "We have to come in," Huey sounded worried. Alice stood aside as they entered. "What's going on? How is it important?" she was curious. "It's.. it's a bit complicated," he answered. "I'll listen," Alice explained. "I'm what they continually refer to as a 'forced reincarnation' of Angeline Durand. They just reversed her abilities- and her gender, obviously," he answered.

Alice sat next to him befuddled. "That's cool...what is that?" she asked, "And where's the proof." "A clone with memories of the original," he answered, "I guess it's cool." "What?" Huey and Alice were shocked. "I think I had something in my ear...explain again please," Alice sounded like her father. "I'm a clone with the memories of Angeline Durand," Dante was getting annoyed, "Plus...How am I supposed to prove it?" Alice sighed still in shock. " A DNA test," she answered. He looked scared. "Don't worry, you're safe," she spoke softly. Dante sighed in relief. "I'll do it," he said. "Follow me," Alice said as they followed.

Dante sat down waiting for the test. "We just need some blood," A nurse said holding a small needle. Carefully she drew out as little as possible. She put it in a vial and was ready to put on the band-aid. "Where do I put? There is nothing there," she was confused now. "Please just test it. Everything is fine," he tried to cover up his emotions.

Alice stared at the band-aid thinking about why it happened. Suddenly she grabbed a scalpel cutting him only slightly. Everyone was in awe as it healed in two seconds. "You're kind of like a phoenix," she pointed out, "Are you the only one?" "No, Reaper is one and there's a lot more," he answered. "Test it," she turned to the nurse. "I already did... It's positive," she answered. "Sorry I didn't believe you," Alice turned to Huey and Dante, "I should've been nicer." "She's nice," he thought, "A lot better than them."

Chapter 31

Ally laid in bed taking a nap as Nico entered. He closed the door sitting on the bed tired. Turning to Ally he smiled. "At least I have you," he said. "Of course you do," she said in her sleep, "Femi." Nico sighed disappointed. "For the first time she is asleep," he thought. A knock on the door woke Ally up making her jump out of bed. "She hasn't changed," Nico pointed out. "Who hasn't changed?" Ally asked insulted. She walked up opening the door to Alexander. "Do you want to play cards?" he asked. "Sure," she answered. She turned to Nico. "I'll hang out with Carmen," he answered.

Ally left with Alexander. "So he's nice," he said. "You did pick him out," Ally pointed out. "I didn't foresee him staying the same," Alexander retorted. Ally sat down ready to change the subject. "So how is Femi?" she asked. "Happy to be home," he answered. "That's good," Ally's voice showed relief, "How is Erica?" "She's doing great!" Alexander answered. "Wonderful," she said. "Awkward," she thought. "I see Jesse is back," her father's words surprised her. "Yeah," she looked down. "Is something wrong?" he asked. "He's in love with me," she answered. "He thinks he is," Alexander pointed out, "He likes Lyric." Ally sighed relieved. "That's good," she thought.

Nico walked down the hospital hallway with Carmen by his side. "So how are you doing?" he asked. "Fine," Carmen lied entering Night's room. Carmen stared at Night holding a teddy bear, staring at her with a dead stare. "Hey, how about you tell me what's on your mind?" he asked. She shook her head no. "Did you guess?" he asked. She shook her yes. "No one tells me anything," he said. "It's between you and Night," she said solemnly. "Ally said that too," he looked down sad. "I hope she's okay," Carmen almost cried. "She will be, she will be," Nico said.

Ally sat at the table staring at the virtual sunset in the window as Nico walked in surprising her. "You get surprised easily now," Nico moved the hair out of Ally's eyes. Ally smiled in response. "Thanks, for helping Night, I mean Mom," he blushed as he spoke. "You're welcome," she said. Suddenly the alarm went off ruining the moment. "An intruder?" Ally asked. She ran out to Carmen running on the elevator. "She wasn't as sly as her mother," she pointed out. "True, but she is fast for a teenager even," he answered.

Nico and Ally followed as fast and quiet as they could. Both of them followed her to a park as she sat down on a park bench. "Carmen," she said, "Are you alright?" She stayed silent as a response. "Poor child," A familiar voice spoke sarcastically. Ally looked up to see Reaper in a tree. He jumped down drawing his sword. "So how is Night doing?" he asked. "Doing better than you think. After all, she'll recover and you won't," Carmen's eyes shined with rage scaring Reaper. "How do you know that?" he asked trying to regain his courage. "You are messing with me now," she answered, "Now put back your sword." Reaper put his sword back.

"Now then...," she was interrupted by a burning tree branch falling off the tree. Everyone turned to Alexander as another tree branch fell off near Reaper. "Don't draw your sword," Carmen ordered Reaper. Reaper glared at her intently. "Come on," Nico grabbed Ally and Carmen dragging them away from the fight. "You're gonna defend that siren brat?" Reaper asked. "Her and everyone else," He said as another branch fell, "Especially Ally though." "What are you going to do?" he asked. "Take you down with me," Alexander answered standing up to him face to face. Ally screamed as she saw all the flames block her.

The fire department put out the flames as fast as they could as Ally stared at the body bag in front of her, her eyes lifeless. "He did it to protect the one thing in his life that still mattered to him. After all, he cut himself off from family only to find it again," Nico's words brought a tear to Ally's eye. "What have I been doing?" she asked herself out loud. "What did you say?" Nico asked. "I've been fooling around. Something has to be done," she stood up a look of fire in her eyes, "Come on, let's head back." Both people followed unsure of her attitude.

The sunlight hit the room landing on Nico. He opened his eyes to Ally gone. "Ally," he sat up scared only to see Ally sitting at the table staring at a photo in her hand. Suddenly she got up ignored him and headed for the door. "Is she okay," Nico thought concerned as he stood up, "First her mom, then Night, Next is Khepri, and finally her dad." Walking over to the table he saw the picture she looked at. It was of everyone, not just herself. He felt sad as he thought about Ally's loss since she turned eighteen. Not knowing what to do he tried to think positively. "I must be her support if she wants me to," he said, "She seems to have lost more than me."

Alice sat at her desk neck deep into her paperwork. "You can't go in," Renee exclaimed as Ally entered. "Watch me," Ally sounded annoyed. "So, you finally came to a decision,?" Alice asked curious. "Of course," Ally answered. "What is your answer?" Alice already knew her answer. "I'll do it," Ally answered. "Good, I'll call in the team," Alice sounded excited.

Ally stared at the team Alice put together. Alora, Nico, Amunet, Huey, Lyric, Jesse, and Dante all sat in the room around the table. "Do we need this many people?" Ally wondered. "Good, now that we have our star we can initiate our plan. Ally and I will go after Bastet. Alora and Nico, you're on surveillance. Amunet and Huey, you get the guards. Lyric, Jesse, and Dante, you run interference," she ordered, "Am I clear?" Four people raised their hands. "Is that people who got it or not?" Alice asked. "Not," Nico answered. "I foresaw this," she handed out papers stating everyone's job, "We work tomorrow, so study." Everyone left happy with their jobs.

"So we're going to distract the guards?" Huey asked smiling at the prospect. "Yeah, the perfect job for a cat," Amunet pointed out.

"What does 'run interference' mean?" Dante asked. "It's the same job Reaper gave us," Lyric answered, "Only this time we are not going to fail." "Do I get a copy of the tape?" Amunet asked. "If you mean Bastet's defeat? No," Nico answered, "That is just cruel." Ally listened knowing she was the only one who could do her job. "It is what it is," she thought.

"You're sure about this?" Nico asked as Ally put her hair in a ponytail. She fixed her black tank top, camouflage pants, and combat boots. "I'm sure," she answered looking at herself in the Black Lotus uniform. "You don't have to do this," he pointed out. She turned to him looking determined and annoyed. "Let's go," she said leaving the room as she ignored his words. He followed her out unsure of her intentions. They finally found the elevator getting on it. "Let's go," Alice said unusually excited. "That's not good," Alora thought.

Chapter 32

Alora watched the guards intently waiting for her moment. Hiding in a nearby tree she threw two needles at once hitting and knocking out two guards at once. "Coast is clear," she whispered in her earpiece. "Roger, Everyone in as we planned," Alice ordered. Alora and Nico entered first looking for the surveillance room. "It's this way," she said leading him down the narrow hallway. Both stopped at a door marked surveillance room. "Ready?" Alora asked. "Oh yeah," Nico answered. Alora and Nico kicked down the surveillance room door shocking the staff. "Miss me, boys," she said throwing four acupuncture needles and knocking out all the security guards.

"Little harsh if you don't mind me saying," Nico said entering. He walked up to the computer hacking the system and traps. "Is that necessary?" Alora asked barring the door. "Yes it is," Nico answered, "We need control of all systems. By the way, how did you find this room so fast?" Alora thought for a second. "Because of Damon and Emperor Blaine," she answered. Nico looked at her confused. "I was sent to kill both of them so Bastet could have power," she didn't sound proud. He stared in shock. "That's how I met Damon. He gave me such a fight I wanted more because at that point I wanted to die," she spoke sadly, "We both ran away that night. Didn't want Bastet to find us. Anyways back to work." "Agreed," Nico thought.

Huey and Amunet snuck through the halls carefully, trying not to gather attention to themselves. "I see one," Amunet whispered as a guard walked by, "Ready?" "Ready," Huey answered. Amunet mewed like a Jaguar cub freaking out the guard. "What's that...a tiger cub?" one guard asked. "Sounds like it," the other one said, "Maybe Reaper got a new pet." Suddenly Amunet roared and growled at the name. "Get it, Gary," one guard pushed another, "I don't think that's Reaper's. I think something escaped the zoo." Gary walked over there only to be stabbed in the leg by a dagger and fall. "Gary," The guard ran over terrified. His eyes opened in fear as he saw Amunet. "I thought you were dead," he pointed out. "You wish," she said stabbing him in the leg as well. "Others are coming," Huey exclaimed. "Good," Amunet retorted calmly, "Let them."

Jesse pulled back his naginata with skill as Lyric grabbed her dagger. "Finally, we don't work with that conniving psychopath anymore. I hated faking people's death," Lyric exclaimed. "That was the fun," Jesse pointed out, "Especially the one in which we had to use ketchup." "Shut up and concentrate both of you," Dante ordered. "Yes sir," Both said knocking out an enemy together. "Great, we're all on the same page now," he said punching one guy.

Huey and Amunet prepared themselves as more guards arrived ready to fight. Amunet kicked one causing them to fall injured. Suddenly a cherry bomb went off causing smoke to hit everyone but Huey and Amunet. They stared in silent horror as they heard the screams of the guards as something attacked them. As the smoke cleared they saw the guards killed and Alexandria holding one of Amunet's daggers. "What just happened?" Huey asked. Alexandria turned around scaring only Huey. "Don't worry I'm on your side," she explained. Amunet grinned at the thought. "Finally," she said.

Ally and Alice walked through the palace not noticed in their disguises. "You two!" Reaper's voice was recognizable, "Over here." Ally and Alice walked over acting professionally. "It seems we have intruders. Why are you heading towards The throne room?" he asked. "Bastet needs protection too," Alice answered. Reaper laughed out loud. "Not really, who are you?" he demanded taking Alice's words as a joke. Ally punched him sending him across the room. "You're worst nightmare," she answered. She picked up Alice disappearing. "I want her caught," he ordered, "She is our worst fear." "A little busy," Two guards answered. "Great," Reaper thought running after them, "It's my job now."

"Is he still on our tail?" Alice asked holding in her breakfast. "Yeah," Ally answered, "How is everyone doing?" "We are in charge of their systems," Alora answered, "Plus we found their lunch." "Lucky," Ally thought. "We are good," Dante answered. "The panther has attacked," Huey answered on his end. "You know what that leaves," Alice pointed out. "Yeah," Ally answered, "The raven."

Ally and Alice stood in front of the throne room with the open door as Ally stopped. Both entered what looked like Ally's family home. "What is this?" Alice asked. "A joke," Ally answered angrily. "Ally," Catherine walked down the stairs with Malice in her eyes. "Is that your mom?" she asked. "No," Ally answered, "That's a fake image." "How perceiving of you," Catherine turned into Bastet insulting Ally. "My mother is kind, not cruel" she pointed out.

"Are you going to keep running? If I recall your mother did that. I mean at least Khepri went down fighting," Bastet's words made Ally's fist tighten. "You witch!" Alice yelled. "Three is a crowd," Reaper appeared out of nowhere grabbing Alice and dragging her out before the door closed. "Ally!" Alice exclaimed, "You're the worst." "Am I?" Reaper asked. "Yes, you are! You have killed and caused the death of so many people. One of them being my MOM!" she yelled. Reaper tried to punch Alice only to have her grabbing his fist.

"My turn," Alice punched him as hard as she could. "You little...," He ran at her only to her kick him as hard as she could in the leg, injuring it lightly. "That's all you can do?" he asked. "No, but how about you tell me why you look like a man when you are a woman?" Alice asked figuring out the lie. Reaper smiled as he turned into Regina Woods, Prince Adonis's former assistant. "Better?" she asked. "It evens the playing field," Alice stood there as Reaper ran at her ready to attack head-on. Alice attacked full force making Reaper unable to attack her. "Finally, a real opponent," she thought.

Ally dodged a bullet almost getting hit directly. "You're more like your father than you know," Bastet said holding Night's pistol. "You are crazy," Ally yelled creating a gun out of energy surprising her. "Am I crazy?" Bastet asked as the scene turned to a graveyard, "Or are you? After all, it must be sad to be an orphan. Especially in such a horrible way." A grave opened up marked Alette Bellerose allowing her to fall in almost causing her pain, but not before taking a shot. Bastet dragged her out ignoring her victim. "Now let's finish this," she said looking slightly taller.

Three screens appeared next to Ally showing her friends losing. "What do you think? They can't defeat me," Bastet mocked. Suddenly the scenes changed to the truth: to them winning. "What are you talking about?" she asked spying an open spot on her sleeve, "I'd be more worried about you." she grabbed the spot making Her and Bastet glow. Bastet felt her very soul twist as her power was being turned off, dropping Ally and breaking Ally's leg. "Why is it always my leg?" she thought. Ally looked up to see a fifty-year-old woman. Suddenly the door opened revealing Alice with backup. "Bastet Caro, You are under arrest for treason," Alice said putting handcuffs on her, "I thought you were thirty." Bastet spat, almost hitting her.

Bastet was brought to her cell while she was being threatened by the other prisoners. They passed Reaper's cell as Alice laughed to herself. "Don't worry, she has no abilities either," she pointed out. "So you're leaving us to fend for ourselves?" Reaper asked. "Not at all, Just don't leave your cell," she said locking Bastet's cell. She walked up to Alora who had a solemn look on her face. "They found her base of operation open," Alora explained. "You mean Zodiac Industries Inc.?" Alice asked. "Yes," Alora answered, "At least fifty children were being trained for my job." Alice gulped scared.

"That explains so much," Alice said getting into the car, "So what happened from there?" "Some fought, some didn't," Alora looked like she was about to cry. "Some were yours," Alice looked at the road feeling her pain, "How about the survivors?" "In the hospital. Some are clones of Bastet while others are 'natural'," she answered, "It was mainly the clones that fought." "I'm sorry, your students were probably stuck in the crossfire," Alice gave Alora her condolences. "To think if the Durand War never happened then we wouldn't be here," Alora shed a tear.

Nico sat next to Ally as she stared at her cast. "At least you're safe," he pointed out. "That's true," she answered. Alice ran in in a hurry. "Why are you here? Night's waking up," she exclaimed happily. Nico picked up Ally bolting out of the room excitedly, Nico to Night's side immediately. The night opened her eyes to Nico smiling. "I'm sorry, Dimitri," she said randomly. "It's me...," he was cut off by Night turning to Ally. "Hello kitty," she greeted. "I'm Ally," she pointed out. "Ally!" the shock woke her up. She turned to Nico. "Son," she gave him a big hug, "Son." "Hi, mom," he hugged her back.

"I'm so sorry I killed that woman," her words shocked everyone. "Who?" Alora asked. "Amethyst," she answered. Alice walked up. "I see, I'll leave this to President Blanc," she said, "It is in his area." Night looked down in shame. "We'll put in a good word for you," she said cheering her up. "What about Alex?" Night asked looking around. Everyone looked down. "Not everyone was as lucky as you Night," Ally pointed out. Night looked down smiling a little. "He was a good man and a hardworking man, and he gave his life to save others. I hope that's how he'll be remembered," her words cheered Ally up a little. "Thank you," she said crying.

<u>Epilogue</u>

October 1st , 2163

Ally sat at the table staring sadly at the wedding decorations. "What's wrong?" Nico asked. "I thought my dad would be here," she answered. "Don't worry," Nico sat next to her smiling as Sam walked up. "How about a father-daughter dance?" he asked. Ally smiled pleasantly surprised. "Sure," she answered. Ally got up dancing with Sam happily. Suddenly the music got upbeat sung by Huey and Nico took his place dancing with Ally. Alice put her head down embarrassed. "What's wrong?" Terra asked, "He's jamming out like Huey Lewis." "His name is Huey Lewis, Huey Lewis Driscol," Alice answered, "It was Dad's idea." Terra burst out laughing.

"I like it," They turned around to Amunet behind them smiling. "Take him to the closet deary," Empress Eva said walking by. "Not again," Alice thought sadly. Alice danced with Dante nearby, kissing him and making him blush. Carmen danced with Adonis making Terra and Eva watch carefully. "Don't be so picky," Night said nearby. Terra looked down at her ankle bracelet which kept her location on it, or so Night thought. Night looked away ignoring her. Amunet smiled big as Huey stood beside her while Ally kissed Nico passionately. "I love you," she sounded excited making Nico look at her in shock. "I love you too," he answered back.

Nico opened the Reaper's trunk door as Ally left the car to a cabin in the middle of nowhere. "Come on," He lead the way opening the front door for her. As she entered she saw the huge fireplace complimented by the paintings of landscapes. "The bedroom is over there and the bathroom is over there," he winked. "You think I packed something special?" she pointed out. Opening the suitcase she grabbed a black plastic bag with the name of a boutique. "Night did," she retorted entering the bathroom. Nico gulped scared at what his mother might buy. Ally screamed shocking him. "It's so hideous," she said making Nico worry. Suddenly the door opened revealing Ally in her new clothes. "Nice," Were his last words of any substance for quite some time.

October 3rd , 2163

Night read the newspaper bursting into laughter. "What is it?" Alora asked curious. "Listen to this: *Artemis Favre was arrested for embezzlement into Favre Explosion Co. funds.* I always knew she was crazy," Night closed the newspaper putting it on the sofa. "How do you think the honeymoon is going?" Alora tried to change the subject. "We don't need to know," she answered. "Aw, come on!"

October 5th, 2163

William Bruce walked off the plane entering his taxi. At age twenty he was just in Gaia learning of the Caro incident, an incident that seems to have caused some trouble in the Celtic Union(Formerly the UK). As he entered his taxi, Ethan Crimson the local lunatic, was sitting in the driver's seat. "How did you get here?" he asked curiously. "I paid off the driver," Ethan answered. "Why?" William asked now worried. "Just to hear the state of Gaia that you are keeping a secret," Ethan answered, "So we could do the easy way or the hard way." "Hard way," William answered, "I was visiting Empress Eva Chevalier. A 'insane' illusionist tried to take over."

"That's not all," Ethan knew he was holding back. "Vittoria is gone, Ethan. I met a teenager who looked like her, but I couldn't be sure," he gulped scared. The care screeched to a halt. "What was the teenager's name?" his voice changed to stern. "Carmen Crimson Bello," he answered. Ethan couldn't believe his ears. "My girlfriend is dead, but our child is alive... Who raised her?" he asked. "That's confidential," William smiled as if he would know who said it. Ethan smiled back getting the gist. "So who's the girl?" he asked curious. "She's taken anyway," William answered, "By Nico Katsaros." Ethan continued to drive unfazed. "Alette Bellerose, of course," he answered, "Why does everyone want her?" William stayed silent for a second. "No reason," he answered. Ethan looked away staying silent himself "Okay," he thought.

About the Author

Carolyn Anne Yunek is an aspiring author; *Simply Psychic* is her first novel to be published. She lives with her husband Ray and her cat Hakkai in Central Missouri.

www.ingramcontent.com/pod-product-compliance
Lightning Source LLC
Chambersburg PA
CBHW040859010826
48978CB00013BA/1084